JUL 2 0 2012

⁀UC LIBRARY

D0207653

LIBRA...

D ✓

F Wilks
Wilks, Eileen, 1952-
Blood magic

WITHDRAWN FROM
Dickinson Public Library

PRAISE FOR EILEEN ₩

MO

"Filled with drama and a
Lily is made even more special w
sess, and the unconditional supp
their time of
the World of ₁

"The latest Ag
refreshed by t
A strong entry

"This is a gr
and kept me
are intriguing, ___ __ _____ __ ___ _____ __ _____ and
thought-provoking . . . Even better, Ms. Wilks has a skill with
description and narrative that truly brings a world and its characters alive." —*Errant Dreams Reviews*

"Fabulous . . . The plot just sucked me in and didn't let me go
until the end . . . Another great addition to the World of Lupi
series." —*Literary Escapism*

"[Lily and Rule are] a crackling couple . . . [Wilks manages] to
translate that indefinable tension, that absolute and utter chem-
istry which happens between real couples . . . onto paper."
—*Romance Novel TV*

NIGHT SEASON

"A captivating world." —*The Romance Reader*

"Filled with action and plenty of twists."
—*Midwest Book Review*

continued . . .

BLOOD LINES

"Another winner from Eileen Wilks." —*Romance Reviews Today*

"The magic seems plausible, the demons real, and the return of enigmatic Cynna, along with the sorcerer, hook fans journeying the fantasy realm of Eileen Wilks." —*The Best Reviews*

"Intriguing . . . Surprises abound in *Blood Lines* . . . A masterful pen and sharp wit hone this third book in the Moon Children series into a work of art. Enjoy!" —*A Romance Review*

"Savor *Blood Lines* to the very last page." —*BookLoons*

"Quite enjoyable, and sure to entertain . . . a fast-paced story with plenty of danger and intrigue." —*The Green Man Review*

MORTAL DANGER

"I've been anticipating this book ever since I read *Tempting Danger*, and I was certainly not disappointed. *Mortal Danger* grabs you on the first page and never lets go. Strong characters, believable world-building, and terrific storytelling . . . I really, really loved this book." —Patricia Briggs,
#1 *New York Times* best-selling author of *Bone Crossed*

"*Mortal Danger* is as intense as it is sophisticated, a wonderful novel of strange magic, fantastic realms, and murderous vengeance that blend together to test the limits of fate-bound lovers." —Lynn Viehl, *USA Today* best-selling author of the Darkyn series

"[A] complex, intriguing, paranormal world . . . Fans of the paranormal genre will love this one!" —*Love Romances*

"Terrific . . . The cat and mouse story line is action-packed . . . A thrilling tale of combat on mystical realms." —*The Best Reviews*

FURTHER PRAISE FOR EILEEN WILKS AND HER NOVELS

"I remember Eileen Wilks's characters long after the last page is turned." —*New York Times* best-selling author Kay Hooper

"Eileen Wilks writes what I like to read." —*New York Times* best-selling author Linda Howard

"If you enjoy beautifully written, character-rich paranormals set in a satisfyingly intricate and imaginative world, then add your name to Eileen Wilks's growing fan list." —*BookLoons*

"Exciting, fascinating paranormal suspense that will have you on the edge of your seat. With a mesmerizing tale of an imaginative world and characters that will keep you spellbound as you read each page, Ms. Wilks proves once again what a wonderful writer she is with one great imagination for her characters and the world they live in." —*The Romance Readers Connection*

"Destined to become a big, big name in romance fiction." —*Romantic Times*

"Fantastic . . . fabulous pairing . . . Ms. Wilks takes a chance and readers are the winners." —*The Best Reviews*

"Fun [and] very entertaining!" —*The Romance Reader*

"Should appeal to fans of Nora Roberts." —*Booklist*

"Fast paced." —*All About Romance*

"Eileen Wilks [has] remarkable skill. With a deft touch she combines romance and danger." —*Midwest Book Review*

Books by Eileen Wilks

BLOOD
MAGIC

EILEEN WILKS

DICKINSON AREA PUBLIC
LIBRARY
139 Third Street West
Dickinson, North Dakota 58601

BERKLEY SENSATION, NEW YORK

THE BERKLEY PUBLISHING GROUP
Published by the Penguin Group
Penguin Group (USA) Inc.
375 Hudson Street, New York, New York 10014, USA
Penguin Group (Canada), 90 Eglinton Avenue East, Suite 700, Toronto, Ontario M4P 2Y3, Canada
(a division of Pearson Penguin Canada Inc.)
Penguin Books Ltd., 80 Strand, London WC2R 0RL, England
Penguin Group Ireland, 25 St. Stephen's Green, Dublin 2, Ireland (a division of Penguin Books Ltd.)
Penguin Group (Australia), 250 Camberwell Road, Camberwell, Victoria 3124, Australia
(a division of Pearson Australia Group Pty. Ltd.)
Penguin Books India Pvt. Ltd., 11 Community Centre, Panchsheel Park, New Delhi—110 017, India
Penguin Group (NZ), 67 Apollo Drive, Rosedale, North Shore 0632, New Zealand
(a division of Pearson New Zealand Ltd.)
Penguin Books (South Africa) (Pty.) Ltd., 24 Sturdee Avenue, Rosebank, Johannesburg 2196,
South Africa

Penguin Books Ltd., Registered Offices: 80 Strand, London WC2R 0RL, England

This is a work of fiction. Names, characters, places, and incidents either are the product of the author's imagination or are used fictitiously, and any resemblance to actual persons, living or dead, business establishments, events, or locales is entirely coincidental. The publisher does not have any control over and does not assume any responsibility for author or third-party websites or their content.

BLOOD MAGIC

A Berkley Sensation Book / published by arrangement with the author

PRINTING HISTORY
Berkley Sensation mass-market edition / February 2010

Copyright © 2010 by Eileen Wilks.
Cover design by George Long.
Interior text design by Kristin del Rosario.

All rights reserved.
No part of this book may be reproduced, scanned, or distributed in any printed or electronic form without permission. Please do not participate in or encourage piracy of copyrighted materials in violation of the author's rights. Purchase only authorized editions.
For information, address: The Berkley Publishing Group,
a division of Penguin Group (USA) Inc.,
375 Hudson Street, New York, New York 10014.

ISBN: 978-0-425-23305-4

BERKLEY® SENSATION
Berkley Sensation Books are published by The Berkley Publishing Group,
a division of Penguin Group (USA) Inc.,
375 Hudson Street, New York, New York 10014.
BERKLEY® SENSATION and the "B" design are trademarks of Penguin Group (USA) Inc.

PRINTED IN THE UNITED STATES OF AMERICA

10 9 8 7 6 5 4 3 2 1

If you purchased this book without a cover, you should be aware that this book is stolen property. It was reported as "unsold and destroyed" to the publisher, and neither the author nor the publisher has received any payment for this "stripped book."

ACKNOWLEDGMENTS

My thanks to Dr. Craig Nelson, Deputy Medical Examiner in San Diego, for patiently answering my questions and sending me that photo of his workplace. Any mistakes are purely my own . . . though I hope one thing, at least, is wrong, and that by the time you read this, he and the rest of the staff have been able to move into their new building.

Special thanks go to my editor, Cindy Hwang, for checking and re-checking the Chinese words and phrases I've used. Most of an editor's work is invisible to readers—and sometimes to writers, too—but books are very much a partnership. I've got a fantastic partner—and an able helper in her assistant, Leis Pederson.

I'd also like to apologize to residents of San Diego for the liberties I've taken with their city, such as rearranging the physical properties of one hospital to suit the needs of my story. Please overlook this and other discrepancies, bearing in mind that I don't write about your San Diego, but one in an alternate world where lupi have recently become U.S. citizens—as long as they're on two feet.

ONE

ON a blistering noon at the tag-end of July, Balboa Park in San Diego offered plenty of green to sun-weary eyes. The paths in the Palm Canyon section were some of the park's prettiest byways, though shade was scant now. With the sun directly overhead, it was reduced to furtive puddles at the feet of the palms' arcing trunks.

A tall man walked one of those paths alone, dressed head-to-toe in black.

His hair was dark, his skin lightly tanned. His eyes were hidden by expensive sunglasses. From a distance he looked like a clump of shadow visiting its more dappled cousins along the bone-colored path.

Rule Turner touched his sunglasses lightly. They didn't need adjusting. He just liked the tactile reminder. They'd been a gift, a surprise present from Lily when the two of them returned from North Carolina with his son yesterday. She'd even found a smaller, identical pair for Toby, which the boy wore constantly. So Rule touched the shades and thought of Toby, and of Lily, and why he was here.

Two men rounded a curve in the path, heading toward Rule.

Neither wore sunglasses. The older one looked like a black-smith or some primordial earth deity—bearded and burly and as if he might burst out of his slacks and shirt at any moment. His beard and hair were rusty brown shot with gray; his eyes were the color of roasted nuts. Tanned skin creased around craggy features in a way that suggested smiles came easily and often.

He wasn't smiling now.

The other man looked younger and more dangerous . . . which was true in a sense. Benedict could kill faster and more surely than anyone Rule knew. He shared his companion's muscular build, but fitted over an additional five inches of height. Benedict's features reflected his mother's heritage, the cheekbones flat and high, the mouth wide, and his black hair was long enough to club back in a short tail.

No smile lines around those dark eyes. He moved with the economy of an athlete or martial artist, which he was; he wore athletic shoes with jeans and an oversize, untucked khaki shirt.

The shirt did nothing for his build or the bronze of his skin, but Benedict wouldn't have thought of that. Clothes, like most things, were tactical tools to him. The shirt was appropriate for the setting and hid whatever weapons he'd deemed appropriate. Knives, certainly. Probably a handgun.

Neither of them looked like Rule. Nor did they much resemble each other. A stranger wouldn't have guessed the three of them were a father and his two living sons.

The older man stopped some fifteen feet away. Benedict dropped back a few feet, guarding his rear. Rule continued walking until he was only three feet away, then stopped, too. Waiting.

"Do you not kneel?" Rule's father demanded.

"I'm waiting to see who greets me."

Now there was a smile. A small one, but it reached the nut-brown eyes. "Your Rho."

Immediately Rule dropped to one knee, bending his head to bare his nape. He felt his father's fingers brush his nape, and in Rule's gut the portion of mantle that belonged to his birth clan—to Nokolai—leaped in response.

The other mantle—the complete one—remained quiet. Leidolf didn't answer to Nokolai.

"Rise."

Rule did. And still he waited. Isen Turner might be wolf in his other form, but his son thought of him as more like a fox—canny, tricky, highly maneuverable. Isen could trip Machiavelli on his assumptions, so Rule did his best not to possess any.

For once, Isen was blunt. "Why did you assume the Leidolf mantle?"

Rule had already told him how it happened, though over the phone. For some months he'd carried the heir's portion of the Leidolf clan's mantle, due to trickery of the man who had been Leidolf's Rho. Then Lily had been possessed by the wraith of one who, in life, had been Leidolf. Rule had needed the authority of the full mantle to command the wraith and save Lily. He'd taken it, killing the former Rho—and becoming leader of his clan's enemies.

But if anyone understood the difference between a chronology of events and a revelation of motive, it was Isen Turner. Rule kept his answer brief. "To save Lily."

"Was that the only reason?"

"No."

Isen hmphed. "Taught you too well, haven't I? Very well. You don't speak of your other reasons. Is that because they are Leidolf business?"

"In part. Mostly, however, I am bound by a promise I gave."

Isen's bushy eyebrows climbed in surprise that might have been real. "A promise! Obviously I can't ask what you promised, but who . . . That *is* my affair, as your Rho. Who did you promise?"

Rule had considered what to say on this score already. He'd hew to the words of his promise, but give his father some meat to chew on. Cullen wouldn't mind. "I can't in honor give you the name, but he's Nokolai, and you already possess the information he gave me, if not the conclusions he drew from that information."

"Do I, now?" The bushy eyebrows drew down, but in thought, not anger.

One of the tactics Rule had learned from his father was when to shift the subject. "Benedict is angry with me."

Isen brushed that aside. "That's a matter between brothers, not clan business. How can you be both Rho to Leidolf and Lu Nuncio to Nokolai?"

With great difficulty. "If we speak of status, I'd suggest some default settings. When I'm at Nokolai Clanhome, I'm your Lu Nuncio. When I'm away from it, I'm Leidolf Rho."

"You assume you will remain my Lu Nuncio?"

For the first time Rule smiled—small and wry, perhaps, but a genuine smile. "I assume only that your decision will not be based on anger or affection, but on what you think best for Nokolai. You asked how I could be both. That's what I answered."

"True, true—though that's a tiny dab of an answer, compared to the size of the problem. Do you see any advantage to Nokolai in having my heir be Rho to another clan?"

"Certainly. Leidolf won't be trying to kill you anymore."

Isen chuckled. "A refreshing change, yes, and one I'll appreciate. But I think that with you as Rho, Leidolf will stop its assassination attempts whether you remain my heir or not. What else?"

Rule stepped out on shaky ground then, but he stepped surely. Hesitation, doubt—both were reasonable, but revealing them was seldom useful. "No lupus has held two mantles in over three thousand years. Our oldest enemy has been stirring. Times are changing. I believe this is our Lady's will. That it's part of her plan to defeat the one we do not name."

This time Isen's surprise was unmistakably real. Both eyebrows shot up—then descended in a scowl. "You think you're privy to the Lady's plans now?"

"I'm guessing, of course. If the Lady has spoken to any of the Rhejes, they haven't told us. But it's a guess based on my gut, on . . ." Rule hesitated, then did his best to put words to what didn't fit into words. "The mantles I carry are pleased by the situation. They . . . help. They make it easy for me to separate my roles."

"Hmm." For a long moment Isen didn't say anything. Then he asked, "And can you carry both full mantles? If I dropped dead right now, could you assume Nokolai's complete mantle?"

"If I thought I couldn't, I'd ask you to remove the Nokolai portion from me immediately. I will not risk the clan."

"A good answer, but a simple 'yes' would have been even better."

"A simple 'yes' would mean I was confusing fact with opinion."

"Your opinion."

"Yes. It's based on unique experience, however. Assuming the full Leidolf mantle was . . ." He paused to fit words around what he meant as best as possible. "Simple. Not easy, no, but much simpler than when I was first forced to carry portions of two mantles. There's . . . room now. They're both already here. I've no reason to think assuming the full Nokolai mantle would be beyond me."

Isen nodded slowly. "Very well. I trust your judgment. I'll make no definite decision yet, but for the time being you will remain my Lu Nuncio. We will use the protocol you suggested, but the parameters must be different. On this side of the country, you are my Lu Nuncio. On Leidolf's side, you are their Rho."

"No."

This time only one eyebrow shot up. "No?"

"If you and I meet on the street and I submit to you, the other clans won't see your Lu Nuncio submitting. They'll see Leidolf's Rho submitting. I can't agree to that."

"Who am I speaking to now—my Lu Nuncio, or Leidolf's Rho?"

"Both. The other clans are uneasy about what they see as Nokolai's growing power. We don't want to feed that."

A grin broke out on Isen's face, folding up the creases in the way they were meant to go. "You're good," he said happily. "You're damned good. I've done well with you. Yes, I agree, with some stipulations to be worked out—but that discussion will take place between the Leidolf Rho and the Nokolai Rho." His eyes twinkled. "You can put me in touch with him later. Right now I want to embrace my son."

Isen was a world-class hugger. However much he held himself apart when he was being Rho to Rule's Lu Nuncio, when he dropped that role and was a father, he brimmed with love, support, and hugs.

When they broke apart Rule was grinning as widely as his father. He braced his feet—and sure enough, here came the clap on the back, hearty enough to stagger the unprepared. "Lily's good, right?" Isen said. "And Toby. I can't wait to see that boy. You'll bring him to Clanhome soon. Today."

Isen could have come to Toby, but Rule didn't suggest it. Today's meeting was very much the exception. His father seldom left Clanhome—though that might change, with Leidolf no longer a threat. "I will. He's eager to see you and his Uncle Benedict." Rule glanced at the silent man still standing guard behind their father. "Speaking of whom—"

Isen squeezed Rule's arm. "Leave him be. He's brooding. Always been a hell of a one for a good brood, my Benedict. Leave him be for now."

Rule looked at his brother's unrevealing face. "I didn't expect him to object so strongly to my becoming Leidolf Rho."

"No, no. He considers that good strategy. It's getting yourself engaged he has problems with. Now, when do I get to see my grandson? He'll stay at Clanhome for the rest of the summer," Isen announced. "Once school starts, well, we'll see how that works out. But it's summer still."

That was all he said about Rule's upcoming marriage. They walked and talked for another half hour as father and son, arranging for Toby to spend time at Clanhome, if not quite as much as Isen wanted. And Rule's father didn't again refer to Rule's intention to break one of the strongest taboos of his people. When Rule tried to raise the subject, Isen dodged it neatly.

It would have been nice, Rule thought as he headed for his car, if he could trust that silence meant support, or at least a lack of opposition. But this was Isen Turner. By definition, he was up to something.

TWO

Three Weeks Later

SAN Diego slid from July into August like a baker slides a fresh sheet of cookies into the oven—quick and smooth, with the new panful of days set to cook up crisp. The weather experts muttered among themselves about the inversion layer, but no one really knew why the city was experiencing such unprecedented heat. Sales of charcoal and grill supplies were down; alcohol sales were up. So were rapes, domestic violence, suicides, and auto accidents.

And homicides, of course. People were too hot to cook out, but they still killed one another. Lily Yu walked along the hot concrete, carrying her new patent-leather sandals instead of wearing them, and reflected on how odd it felt not to be investigating any of those shootings, stabbings, or beatings.

She stopped short of the sticky red scum baking on the street. Her bare soles weren't picking up a thing except heat and grit, and she'd crossed the street four times now.

One of the small gaggle of looky-loos cluttering the convenience store parking lot on the corner called out a disrespectful and unlikely suggestion. Lily sighed.

"Hot weather sure brings out the loonies," the officer standing next to the black-and-white said.

"That it does," Lily agreed, bending to slip one sandal back on, then the other. Her feet were filthy. She had some wipes in her purse, though, so she could clean them up in a few minutes. "Doesn't seem to be anything here for me."

The officer who'd spoken took off his dark blue cap, dragged his forearm across his forehead, and reseated the cap. "Sorry to drag you out in the heat, but we've been told to call you people."

"You did right. I wanted to check out one of these events right after it happened, anyway." She just hadn't wanted it to happen today, dammit.

Technically she hadn't had to respond. It was Saturday; it was after five o'clock—no one would have minded if she'd let this wait until tomorrow. No one but her. It was annoying sometimes, being so meticulous.

Lily looked at the twisted chassis of the little Honda. It had certainly lost the argument with the pickup. "I'll need to check her car, too. The steering wheel, the dash—all the areas the driver might have been in contact with."

"Have at it. Guess you have to be thorough." He shook his head. "Funny job you have, though."

"Yeah," she said dryly, and headed for the pleated Honda.

Officer Munoz was short and solid, with a round, cheerful face that his mustache struggled valiantly to dignify. He was also young. Terribly young, to Lily's eyes . . . which was almost as disconcerting as checking out wacko calls instead of homicides. She wasn't yet thirty, for God's sake. Not for another eight months.

No, seven months. Geez. That wasn't long. She frowned as she skirted the bright red transmission fluid drying on the cement. Then she reached the driver's door. "Well, shit."

They'd removed the driver on the other side, for obvious reasons. There was no way Lily would get the door open. She tried anyway.

"Guess you were headed somewhere," Officer Munoz observed. "With that pretty dress you're wearing and all." His face fell. "Shit, I'm not supposed to say that, am I?"

"That's okay. I'm on my way to a baby shower. I'm one of the hosts." She tugged harder, but the door wasn't budging.

"Really?" He brightened as he moved toward the passenger's side. "My wife is due in January."

This child had a wife? Lily told herself to get over it, but a new thought intruded. Did Rule ever look at her and think she looked painfully young? There was a lot more of an age difference between the two of them than between her and the earnest young officer. "Congratulations. Boy or girl?"

"She hasn't had a sonogram yet. I'm sort of hoping for a boy, but you know, as long as it's healthy . . ." He yanked open the passenger door. "This one works."

"Yeah. Thanks." Only she'd have to crawl across the front seat if she got in that way, and she had not dressed for this occasion. She glanced down at her cream-colored trapeze dress with pretty bronze bands at the neckline and hem. She'd bought it especially for today.

At least it was loose. Maybe she could climb across and still leave Officer Munoz uninformed about the color of her panties.

A black Mercedes was parked on the other side of the patrol car. Its door opened, and a tall man wearing jeans and a black dress shirt got out. "Need a hand?"

Her heart gave a happy little bump. Funny how just looking at him still did that for her. She shook her head. "Even you couldn't get this door open. I'll climb across."

He gave her a bland smile. "You'll get your pretty dress dirty." Of course he'd heard Munoz's comment. He started toward her. "Let's see what I can do."

"Hey!" Munoz said. "You're that lupus!"

Lily tensed, but Rule had a smile for him. "I'm *a* lupus, at least."

"No, you're the prince one! The one in all the magazines with . . . I mean . . ." Munoz took a breath. Lily suspected that if his complexion had been paler, she'd have seen an embarrassed flush. "Never mind."

He'd been about to comment on the plethora of lovely women Rule had been photographed with. Though not recently. Recently, all the articles were about him and Lily . . . way too many articles. She touched the little lump beneath her dress where her engagement ring hung on a chain, dangling next to the *toltoi* she'd been given to mark her status as Chosen.

Until they made an official announcement, she was keeping her ring out of sight.

"Uh . . . Turner, right?" Munoz smiled hopefully.

Lily took pity on the officer's embarrassment. He meant well, which a lot of cops didn't. Not with lupi. "Officer Munoz, this is Rule Turner. Rule, Officer Jesse Munoz." She looked at the young patrol officer. "Rule's right about my dress, though. I'd rather not get it dirty, plus there's some broken glass. Do you have anything I could put on the seat?"

Rule touched her arm. "Give me a moment. You know I enjoy flexing things for you."

She shook her head but stood back to let him have at it. "Just don't bleed. I hate it when you bleed."

Rule gave her a quick grin, stepped up to the door, braced himself, and pulled. Metal groaned, but nothing happened. He frowned. Then he put one foot up on the frame next to the door and heaved. With a loud shriek, the door opened. He didn't even fall over backward.

"Thanks. You know, most men open pickle jars."

"Fortunately, I can open them, too."

She grinned and glanced at the convenience store, where the looky-loos were getting excited. "Better watch out. I think someone in that crowd recognized you." And not everyone felt the same sort of excitement about lupi as Officer Munoz . . . who was forgetting his professional dignity again.

"Hey, that's cool! You just yanked on it and opened it. I'd always heard lupi were strong, but man." Munoz shook his head, all admiration. "That's cool."

Lily left Rule to his one-man fan club and went to do her job. Which, as Munoz had said, was sometimes pretty odd.

Until last November, Lily had been a homicide cop here in San Diego. Now she worked for Unit 12 of the Magical Crimes Division of the FBI. Usually that didn't mean running her hands over what was left of the driver's seat in a crumpled Honda, but the walking-around-barefoot part happened fairly often.

Lily was a touch sensitive. She experienced magic as a texture on her skin, but couldn't be affected by it. When local police thought magic or those of the Blood might be involved in a crime, they called MCD—who passed most of it on to the Unit.

Lately she'd been called out a lot. In the dog days of summer, some of the citizens of San Diego were seeing monsters. Big, hairy monsters with tyrannosaurus teeth. Grinning demons chittering at a window. Leprous undead charging a house.

Every time the nutcases called the cops, the cops called her. Every time, she had to check out the sighting. Because these days, there was always a chance the loonies were right.

THREE

~~~

CREATURES unseen on Earth in hundreds of years—creatures never seen here at all—had been swept here at the Turning, when the power winds blew open barriers between realms.

The power winds had been temporary, thank God, and the experts said it would be impossible for anything to wander here without them. They also said that any crossing would release a burst of nodal energy, and the D.C. coven, who kept watch over a sophisticated simulacra map, swore there'd been no significant node disturbances recently. And while there was now a gate between Earth and one other realm—Edge—it was on the other side of the country and was warded and guarded on both ends. Nothing was slipping through there.

But *unlikely* doesn't mean *impossible*, and Lily wasn't convinced the experts knew all that much, so when the cops called the Unit, she went to check out the scene.

First she ran her hands over every inch of the steering wheel, from which the deflated airbag hung like the world's biggest condom. The monster du jour had been a giant snake, one as big around as a cow, which the Honda's driver swore had suddenly reared up in front of her car, fangs dripping venom. Naturally she'd swerved—right in front of a pickup.

Luckily for that driver, it was a quiet, mostly residential street and the pickup's driver had kick-ass reflexes. The Honda's driver had been taken to the ER, but the EMTs didn't think she was hurt badly. The pickup's driver insisted he didn't have so much as a bruise.

And guess what? He hadn't seen a snake, giant or otherwise. Nor had Lily found any traces of magic on the street where the snake was supposed to have been.

Nothing here, either. She began checking out the dash.

It wasn't as if she didn't have anything else to do. She was finishing up a magical fraud case she'd worked with the local FBI office, and had just returned from the tiny town of Eagle's Nest. That case hadn't taken long, thank God. She'd handed off the supposed lupus attack to the locals. The victim, it turned out, had been drunk, and the assailant was a bear that had wandered into town to check out the trash cans.

The dash was devoid of magic, so she started on the oddments the woman had collected in her car—an empty soda can, a newspaper, a wad of crumpled receipts.

No doubt a social scientist would have a blast analyzing the current vogue in crazy calls, and who knows? Maybe they really were the result of a collision in the collective psyche between reason and magic. The Turning had spooked people, no doubt about that. But Lily preferred more concrete answers—like a new, undetectable drug. Or a new, undetectable spell.

If the latter, it was her job to detect it, dammit. And she wasn't.

She scooted out and crouched so she could run her hands over the driver's seat, and underneath it. She didn't expect to find anything, having checked out the driver before the EMTs took her away. If the woman had been hexed or enspelled, Lily should have felt it on her. She hadn't.

Nothing on the seat, either. She straightened, careful not to touch her dress with her dirty hands.

Rule handed her the bag of wipes from her purse. She took it and gave him a smile. "I knew there was a good reason to keep you around."

"Don't forget the pickle jars."

That turned her insides mushy. He'd proposed over pickles. Also blini, cheese, and a really lovely Dom Pérignon, but it was the pickles that got to her. She gave him a smile, but no words—couldn't say what she wanted with Munoz standing by—and finished wiping her hands. "Officer, there's nothing more I can do here. It's your case. Thanks for your cooperation."

Her skin prickled faintly, as if she'd picked up enough of a static charge to make the little hairs on her arms stand up. Automatically she looked up.

"What is it?"

"Nothing." The prickle had been from what Cullen called sorcéri—wispy threads of raw magic that drifted around until absorbed. They were cast by the ocean, nodes, and thunderstorms, and they were attracted to dragons. She'd checked to see if Sam was overhead—he often trailed sorcéri—but the sky was as blankly blue as a crashed computer.

But Sam often preferred to go unseen. Cullen insisted the dragon habit of winking out wasn't true invisibility; he said they just went out-of-phase the way demons could. Whatever that meant. "You'll send me a copy of your report, right?" She glanced at her watch. "Shit. Rule, we need to go."

The shower didn't start till seven, but it was being held at Clanhome, which lay twenty minutes outside the city. And she had a lot to do beforehand, because the shower was only part of the festivities.

Rule had been at Clanhome all day getting ready for the other half of the party. He'd come back into the city to pick her up, which was necessary because both her personal car and her government-issue vehicle were in the shop, dammit. Her six-year-old Toyota needed transmission work. The government's Ford was still in Eagle's Nest, which had a small body shop.

Turned out that bears do not like the way lupi smell. A four hundred-pound black bear can do an amazing amount of damage when he uses the roof of a car for a trampoline.

Lily was already checking messages on her iPhone as she slid into Rule's Mercedes. It hadn't seemed like a bad idea, combining the shower with a traditional lupus baby party.

Ignorance, she reflected, was bliss. Reality was a pain in the butt.

No urgent messages, so she tapped in some quick notes on the accident as they pulled away from the scene. She was getting pretty good at thumbing it. Not as fast as a preteen, but good enough to get the basics entered. "How are the ribs doing?" she asked Rule without looking up. "It didn't hurt them for us to be delayed, did it?"

"They're still in the pit. Isen is going to start the chicken for me, with a little help from Toby. He's looking forward to tonight."

"Good." She looked up. "Good about Toby, I mean, and about your father taking a hand in the cooking. Having the Rho in on the barbeque has to up the status thing, right?"

He drummed his fingers on the steering wheel. "I'm having trouble remembering why I explained the political implications of the baby party."

"Because I gave you no choice."

"Oh, yes, I remember now. To answer your question, no, Isen is known to be my father, so the fact that he helped grill the chicken has no special value. Fathers often help sons."

The desert dryness of his voice irritated her. "How am I supposed to know what does and doesn't affect status if I don't ask?" She put away her phone. "So you think you guessed right about the amount of brisket needed? And ribs. It's not too late to pick up some at Jonny's. They make good ribs."

"Mine are better, and we'll have enough."

"Party favors," she said suddenly, twisting around to look in the backseat, where a large, wrapped present rode beside a couple of packed totes. "I don't see them. Rule—"

"They're in the trunk, where you put them yesterday so you wouldn't forget."

"Right. That's right. I'd better check with Beth. She's bringing the cake." She punched in her sister's number. "I didn't have time to get the receipt to her, so I want to make sure they don't charge her a second time. It's such a pain not having my car. I . . . damn. Her line's busy." She switched to text.

"Lily, relax. It's a party. You're supposed to enjoy yourself."

"Hosts don't enjoy the party. Hosts give the party."

He laughed almost silently.

She sent the text to Beth and slid him a dirty look. "You're not laughing *with* me. I can tell because I'm not laughing."

He reached over and cupped her nape, rubbing gently. "That business about the hosts not enjoying the party—that has to be something your mother would say."

Shit. He was right. "All right. I'm supposed to enjoy myself, so I will. After it starts. I get to worry until then."

"Why do I think you just jotted 'enjoy myself' on a mental to-do list?"

"Because I'm too sneaky to write it on an actual list where you can see." Speaking of lists . . . She dived into her purse again and pulled out a little spiral, flipped it open, and looked at her Shower/Party list. "I feel better now."

"Good." He squeezed her shoulder and dropped his hand. "I want you to quit worrying about the political aspects. Those are for me to deal with."

"Yeah, that's going to happen." She contemplated her list. According to it, everything was done except the setting up, and she had a list for that. She flipped to it. "You know, I worry about forgetting the cake server or leaving the guest book someplace, but I gather information on the political shit and status and all that. I don't understand it, and I need to." She looked at him. "You don't get to shut me out here."

He reached for her hand. She gave it to him. He continued silent a moment, then said, "I don't mean to shut you out. It's reflex."

"I know. You're working to get over that, right?"

He smiled. "Right."

His touch, the contact, soothed her. It always did. That was a matter of magic, the mate bond, which enhanced both the need for physical connection and the benefit of it. His people believed the bond was a gift from their Lady, a belief reflected in their title for Lily: Chosen. Chosen by the Lady, they meant, for neither she nor Rule had done the choosing. Not at the start, anyway.

But the comfort of his touch also rose from an older, more universal magic. Most people, Lily thought, feel better when they hold hands with someone they love.

Some of her worries, she admitted, were her own fault. Cynna was a good friend, and she was pregnant, so naturally Lily had offered to give her a baby shower. No one had forced her to combine the shower with the baby party Rule and the Nokolai Rhej were giving the baby's father—Cullen Seabourne, sorcerer, former lone wolf, and the first married lupus on the planet. But it had seemed like a good idea. There were still gaps in Lily's knowledge of Nokolai and lupus ways in general, but she'd been to a couple of baby parties in the nine months since she met Rule. They hadn't seemed like a big deal.

Turned out this one was different. *Way* different.

Most of the people Cynna knew who could be hit up for a baby gift were part of the FBI unit she and Lily worked for. They didn't live nearby, so the number of shower guests had been small and easy to plan for.

Not so with the baby party. Take the ribs she'd asked Rule about. Getting the amount of food right wasn't just a matter of feeding whoever showed up. It had implications. You were supposed to have leftovers, Rule said, so your guests wouldn't feel they were straining your resources. But not too much. If too much food went uneaten, it looked bad, as if you might take offense because not enough people showed up. Or as if you thought you were more important than you really were—and that would be taken as weakness. The clan's Lu Nuncio could not appear weak.

The ribs were the big test. They were the most popular, so they'd go fast. The goal, Rule said, was to run out of ribs and maybe brisket, but have some chicken and sausage and sides left by the time everyone had filled their plates.

The problem was, lupi didn't believe in RSVPs. They didn't believe in invitations, either, at least not for baby parties. No, the entire clan just assumed they were welcome, and the only way to get an approximate head count was to subtract those who sent a gift ahead of time and take a wild guess about the rest.

That guessing had been pretty wild—and highly political, dammit. Lily hated politics. Grandmother said that was naïve, that hating politics was like hating the weather. Pointless, since both were inevitable.

But lupi politics were so damned . . . lupi.

The baby party gave Rule a chance to gauge the degree of opposition to his recent controversial actions—assuming another clan's mantle and getting engaged. At the same time he meant to use it to reduce opposition by creating the *appearance* of reduced opposition.

It was enough to make her head ache.

Attendance at a baby party was a matter of status and friendship. Cullen was new to Nokolai, having been adopted into the clan less than a year ago, so he wouldn't normally have had a big turn-out. Not many close friends, and his status was uncertain. But Rule was Lu Nuncio and Lily was his Chosen, so they were both high status. High-status hosts ought to mean lots of guests.

But Cullen had violated a huge taboo by marrying the woman who was having his child, and Rule was planning to marry. A lot of clan might stay away to express disapproval.

Only that wouldn't happen, according to Rule, because the baby party's third host was the Nokolai Rhej. A Rhej was similar to a priestess or bard. She held the clan's memories and, in rare cases, spoke for the Lady—who the lupi claimed was not a goddess, but sure seemed to bat in that league. The Rhej's status was equal to the Rho's . . . and Cynna had recently become her apprentice.

Very recently, Cynna had begun acquiring those memories. The process was slightly more secret than whatever codes were required to launch the nation's nuclear weapons. Whatever the process, though, the result was a drained, too-silent Cynna.

She needed this party, needed to put aside whatever trauma she'd lived through in the memories. It was almost always the bad stuff that got saved.

The clan would turn out, Rule said. Not everyone, for though the majority of Nokolai lived in California, California was a large state. But everyone who could attend would show up to honor the Rhej and Cynna, which would reflect well on Rule, making the clan's disapproval look less serious than it otherwise might.

And if they don't? Lily had asked. *What if they are so opposed to you marrying that they stay away in spite of everything?*

Then his father would have to choose a new heir. He wouldn't risk the clan's stability by forcing them to accept his choices.

Was it any wonder she was tense? Better, she decided, to think about monsters. "You didn't smell anything funny back there, did you?"

Rule shook his head. "Of course, in this form I don't detect scent as well, but snakes have a distinctive aroma—and generally speaking, the larger the animal, the more scent it leaves. You didn't ask me to Change."

"Maybe I should have, but it seemed pointless. No one else saw a snake, and I didn't pick up any traces of magic." She frowned. "Mass hallucination is not a satisfying answer. They're not all seeing the same kind of monster. They're not seeing the right kind of monsters, either."

"The zombies, you mean?"

"And the yeti. Sure, yeti exist—but not with big, jagged teeth, and for God's sake, not in southern California. And they're peaceable, not aggressive. And you remember that first one—the woman in Hillcrest who swore that a wolf man broke down her door and attacked her." That one had been easy to disprove, thank God. They did not need the public thinking that lupi could turn into the kind of ravening half man, half beast beloved by Hollywood. Both the woman and her front door had been undamaged.

"People are seeing movie monsters."

"Doesn't make sense, does it? Half a dozen apparently unconnected people have suffered sudden, temporary delusions. The cops are calling me every time it happens, on orders from the chief. Am I paranoid to think Chief Delgado issued those instructions because he's still pissed at me for leaving the force? Or conceited to think I matter that much?"

He lifted her hand to his mouth and kissed it. "You know what they say. Even paranoids can have real enemies."

"Hmm." She felt oddly better. "Or he might be playing CYA. The press hasn't gotten hold of this yet, but if it keeps up, they will. He wants to be able to say that the FBI's oh-so-important Unit hasn't discovered anything, either. I wonder . . ."

"Yes?"

"Delusions, hallucinations. Could be a new drug, but the cops aren't aware of anything new on the streets. Of course, some of the upper-end stuff circulates more at parties and clubs, so . . . Max," she said, referring to the owner of Club Hell.

"Max is about as antidrug as you can get."

"But he'd hear about it if there's something new. Something upper end," she repeated, thinking of the Hillcrest woman. Hillcrest was not a cheap neighborhood, and the woman was of an age to be hitting the clubs. None of that fell in Lily's jurisdiction, and yet . . . She pulled out her phone. "I'll give him a call later. I'll call the chief first."

"Want to see if he's persecuting you on purpose?"

She snorted as she thumbed through the directory. "As if he'd answer that question. No, the other possibility that occurs to me is some kind of toxin. Maybe these people ingested something in the water or on a tomato or whatever. I want to find out if he's notified the public health people. If not, I am." And she knew who to call. She knew this city. It was a comfort to her, after all the traveling she'd done lately.

"Officer Munoz looked really young," she said as she selected the number for the SDPD Chief of Police.

"Mmm-hmm."

"Do I sometimes look really young to you?"

"You always look exactly right to me."

"That's not an answer."

He smiled and kept looking straight ahead. "And I'm not an idiot."

Lily smiled, too, as the chief's secretary announced herself in her familiar smoker's growl. It was good to be home.

BEHIND the 7-Eleven, next to a full and fragrant Dumpster, a small man was doubled over, laughing. "Oh, did you see the woman's face?" he said in Chinese. "Did you see? *'Oh, help me, help me, the big snake wants to eat me up'*!" He added the last in a squeaky falsetto and slapped his thigh. "Crash she goes! Bam!"

He looked a bit like an Asian Hercule Poirot with his slicked-back hair, though he lacked the impressive mustache. Mostly, though, he looked ordinary—somewhere over forty with dark, merry eyes and a stubby nose. He wore athletic shoes with white socks, baggy khaki shorts, and a T-shirt that read, "San Diego Chargers."

The laughter faded to a grinning giggle. "You were brilliant, my dear, brilliant as always," he said to the air beside him. He spoke English now, with a decided British accent. He bent to pick up the black cap that had fallen off while he was carried away with laughter, revealing a bald spot on top of his head.

"Did she?" He frowned as he straightened, but the frown slipped away as if his face had been greased by good humor. "I didn't see. Ah, well, the blood is there, I suppose, or it could be coincidence. And she only looked. She couldn't see you."

"Oh, of course." He began walking in the idle way of a man with no special need to be one place rather than another, nodding now and again as if in response to his invisible friend. He passed the small group of bystanders in the parking lot, breaking up now that the show was mostly over. None of them noticed him.

"But I'll take care of *him* for you, my beautiful one," he said as he stepped into the street after looking carefully both ways. "You know I will. Soon now, eh?" He smiled. "Won't they be confused! I wish I could . . . No, no, I won't linger. I understand the difficulty for you. But," he added wistfully, "it would be great fun to stay and see their faces after I kill him."

FOUR

THE mountains east of San Diego were almost always hotter than the city. Their higher elevation didn't make up for losing the cooling power of the ocean. But the sun was down now, and in the small valley that held the village at the heart of Nokolai Clanhome, the temperature had dropped to a balmy seventy-eight.

The moon wasn't yet up, but Lily kept track of that sort of thing these days. She knew it would rise half full just after midnight. The clan's meeting field was alive with song, laughter, and people—far more people than actually lived there—and Lily was relieved bordering on smug.

The baby shower had gone off without a hitch. And the baby party was going splendidly.

Lily threaded her way through the crowded meeting ground. Most of the shower guests—the human guests—had left. The number of adult lupi actually living at Clanhome varied, but was usually around fifty. Most of the rest of the party guests lived fairly close to Clanhome, but she didn't know all of them.

They all knew who she was, though—a bit disconcerting, that, but she smiled and nodded when strangers greeted her.

There were also dogs and kids. Lots of kids. Both raced through the crowd in shoals like minnows swimming a living current. Toby was undoubtedly part of one of those shoals, though she hadn't seen him since he finished bolting his food and jumped up with the announcement that he and "the guys" were going to play tag.

Lupus tag was a complex game involving teams, age-adjusted rules, multiple targets, and elements of hide-and-seek. And running. Lots of running.

So far, becoming a parent to Rule's son was almost too easy. The only hard part was prying the boy loose from the rest of the clan. Lupi adored babies and children of all ages, and they saw no reason Toby shouldn't spend all his time at Clanhome.

One person wasn't at the party anymore. The Rhej, the party's third host, had eaten with Lily, Rule, Isen, and Toby, given Cullen his gift, then headed back to her house partway up the slope that bordered the west side of the little valley.

She liked people fine, she'd said. Just not so many all at once.

Most of the adults were male, and most of them weren't wearing much. Among adults, male clan outnumbered female about three to one, and lupi possessed no body modesty whatsoever. Every man in Lily's sight was bare-chested, bare-footed, and barely covered between the navel and the knees. Cutoffs were the most popular choice.

Lily enjoyed the view. What woman wouldn't? Even the chests with grizzled gray hair were worth a second glance. There was no such thing as a fat, sloppy, out-of-shape lupi. Everyone knew that. Just like everyone knew that the lupus ability to turn furry was inherited, not contagious. And that they were always male. And that they didn't marry. Ever.

Lily rubbed her thumb over the ring she'd slipped onto her finger for the party. Everyone could be wrong, it seemed. Including her. She'd never planned for this because she'd known it couldn't happen, yet here she was, engaged to marry a man who should never have contemplated asking her.

Some of their guests were still eating at the picnic tables set up around the perimeter of the field. Others ate standing up. Lily had been among the first to eat, and that bothered her. In her world, hosts didn't eat until all their guests were served. In the lupi world, hosts ate first—or almost first, since the Rhej, the Rho, and the Lu Nuncio ate ahead of everyone. Rule said this was because the meal was the hosts' "kill." To a wolf, providing food for the clan was good. Letting everyone enjoy your kill ahead of you was absurd.

Weird as it was, Lily understood him. Understanding hadn't made her comfortable with filling her plate first, so she'd skipped dessert. That's what she was going after now.

Underfoot, the grass was soft and giving. The meeting field was the one place the clan kept thoroughly watered, even during a drought—which was every summer in southern California. With no major wildfires near, the sky was spangled darkness, with about a zillion more stars than you ever saw in the city. Despite the lack of moonlight, there was plenty of illumination. Poles bearing lanterns added the glow of candlelight to the scattering of mage lights overhead.

The party was easy on the ears, too. Amid the chatter and laughter, music sprouted like mushrooms after a rain—a cluster of singers in one spot, someone tuning up a fiddle elsewhere. And wasn't that a flute off in the distance?

The smoky scent of barbeque hung in the air. When she reached the tables where the food was set out she saw that there was still some chicken and sausage left, but no ribs or brisket.

She breathed a sigh of relief and made a beeline for the desserts. Two brownies weren't excessive, she decided, considering how hard she'd worked.

A hand landed on her shoulder as she selected the second one. "Give me chocolate," a woman demanded.

Lily smiled over her shoulder at a tall woman with cropped blond hair. "How much?"

"Heaps of chocolate. Huge heaps." Cynna thrust an empty plate at her. "I can't drink, so chocolate has to do the trick."

Lily piled three brownies on Cynna's plate. "What's up?"

"Did you know I'm supposed to make the baby's food myself?"

At nearly seven months pregnant, Cynna could have stood in for a fertility goddess—if that goddess doubled as an Amazon and liked to cover her skin in arcane symbols. She had the sculpted arms and shoulders of a warrior accustomed to drawing a bow. No lopping off of a breast for this Amazon, though. Cynna's breasts were large and expanding along with her vanished waist, as was easy to see in the stretchy red top she wore with loose linen trousers.

"From the look of things, you could feed half a dozen babies," Lily said.

Cynna waved an impatient hand. "I'm not talking about milk. That will be easy—my body just does it." She crammed half a brownie into her mouth, closing her eyes as she chewed. "Ah. That helps. I mean the actual baby food."

"Oh, I see." Lily nodded. "You've been talking to my sister."

Lily had invited some of her own family to the baby shower so there would be more guests present; most of the gifts had been mailed in. Her mother had made some excuse, which Lily had expected; Grandmother had intended to come, but her companion, Li Qin, had gotten sick, so she wasn't here. But both Lily's sisters had come. To Lily's amazement, Cynna seemed to have hit it off with Susan.

"Well, she's a doctor, isn't she?" Cynna said. "She knows about this stuff. Only I can barely cook for me! Eggs. I can scramble eggs now. And make macaroni and cheese that isn't from the box, and Cullen's chili is great, and so's his pot roast, but a baby can't eat chili or pot roast, can it? I thought I'd have months and months to get up to speed on the cooking thing, but—"

"Susan is a dermatologist, not a pediatrician. She's also perfect. No one can live up to Susan's standards, not even Susan." Hard as it had been to grow up with a perfect big sister, Lily had finally realized it was even harder being the perfect big sister.

Cynna snorted. "Pot and kettle, Lily."

"Oh, come on. I'm nowhere near as bad as she is."

"Are you kidding? You wore a white dress to a barbeque, and—"

"Cream. It's cream, not white."

"—and didn't get a spot on it. You hang up your clothes by color and type. I've seen your closet," she added darkly. "You line up your jackets according to the spectrum—red to orange to yellow to—"

"That's anal, not perfect, and besides, I don't have any orange jackets. Orange makes me look sick. The point is, you've got to stop taking everything Susan says as gospel."

"I don't, but additives are evil, right? Organic is good. Fresh and organic is really good."

"This is California. You can buy organic baby food." Lily was pretty sure it was available in the rest of the country, too, but it had to be available here. You could buy organic rope in California, for God's sake.

"I can?" Relief warred with doubt on Cynna's face. Relief won. "I could buy a bunch of it. I could buy a blender, too. See, the Rhej gave me this steamer thingy. It's for vegetables, and all you do is dump them in and put water in the base and set the timer, and they cook. It's real easy. It probably wouldn't be a big deal to blenderize steamed veggies if I ran out of organic baby food or something."

"There you go." Lily patted her friend's arm. "Between blenderized veggies and organic baby food, it will work out."

"Yeah." Cynna turned to survey the crowd. For a moment they ate brownies in silence.

It was good to see Cynna like this—obsessing over silly stuff, more like her usual self. The acquisition of a couple of the early memories had been hard on her, but tonight she'd shaken that off.

Lily finished first—she'd ended up with a single brownie after all—and fingered the little object in her pocket. She needed to find Cullen and give it to him. And there was another way lupus parties were different. No one wrapped presents— lupi were such guys sometimes—nor was there any set time to hand over your gift.

The presents themselves were different, too. Lupi considered it tacky to buy a baby gift. They were either handmade, hand-me-down, or "for the baby jar"—which meant cash. Most gave cash. Lily could relate to that. Cash gifts were a Chinese custom, too, though not at baby showers, and the money was tucked into red envelopes, not a big glass jar.

But the close friends of the father-to-be were supposed to either make a gift or pass on something with a story attached. The story was part of the present, a tale of all those who had slept in the cradle, gnawed on the blocks, or been warmed by the quilt.

This was one lupus custom she hadn't needed explained. With their hand-me-downs and handmade presents, the clan claimed the child. The objects were made by clan, used by clan, woven into the history of the clan. They didn't come from the external, human world . . . which had made it hard for her to decide on a gift, because she *did* come from the external, human world. And she didn't know how to make anything except an arrest.

Cynna ate the last bite of brownie with a sigh of pleasure. "That was good, but now I need liquid. Not water and not milk—I'm ready to party."

"Dr. Pepper?" Lily smiled at Cynna's current definition of partying.

"Right. If there's anything left. Man, there must be a thousand people here. Come on."

Lily smiled as she followed. Cynna hadn't come to the FBI via conventional law enforcement the way Lily had, so she'd never learned to estimate crowd size. "Roughly half that, I think, counting the kids."

"Still, that's a lot. Lots of presents, which is good." Cynna patted her protruding belly. "Lots of work for you, though."

"Not really." They'd reached the tubs filled with melting ice and soft drinks. Lily dug out a can of Dr. Pepper for Cynna and took a Diet Coke for herself. "Rule and the Rhej handled almost all of the baby party stuff."

"Yeah, but you did the shower, too, and then there's all those weirdo calls you've been getting."

"At least those cases are easy to clear, and otherwise things are pretty quiet right now."

"You know you shouldn't say shit like that."

Lily snorted. "You're superstitious?"

"Of course not, but you're never supposed to say things are quiet. That's when you get hit with three urgent cases or a performance review or you get sick or—"

Lily held up a hand, laughing. "All right, already. I take it back. Things are hectic and my plate is full, and yes, the party was lots of trouble. And worth every bit of it."

"Oh, now you've done it. I tear up over commercials these days." Cynna sniffed, grinned, and added, "I guess all this organizing is good practice for your wedding. Have you set the date yet?"

"Not yet." She tipped her can and drank.

"You're avoiding the subject."

"No, I'm thirsty." Lily glanced around. "I need to find Cullen. I haven't given him my present yet."

"Now you're changing the subject." Cynna was downright gleeful. "You're scared."

"I'm not scared." She loved Rule. She not only wanted to spend the rest of her life with him; she had to. The mate bond gave them no options there, but she'd stopped resenting that, so getting married would just put a legal gloss over what was already true. There was no reason to be scared; the annoying lump in her throat wasn't fear. It was . . . aggravation.

"I'm not scared," she repeated. "But I'm contemplating Las Vegas. My mother is insane."

"What flavor of insane are we talking?"

Lily gestured with her Diet Coke. "Every flavor a wedding can come in. The dress. The date. Flowers. Attendants. Doves."

"Doves? Doves as in big gray birds?"

"White ones, actually. She wants to release dozens of white doves when Rule and I say our vows. Not exactly the right aesthetic message when the groom turns wolf on occasion, is it?"

Cynna snickered. "Oh, yeah, some of your guests might miss out on the aesthetic message. They might think the doves were a party game. Flying appetizers."

Lily pictured a bunch of well-dressed men taking one look at the doves, Changing, and racing off yipping after them. A smile tugged at her mouth. "Maybe I should let her have her way. It might be worth it to see her face if . . . But no." Reluctantly she abandoned the fantasy. "They wouldn't really do that. Besides, I don't know if we'll have any lupus guests."

Cynna squeezed her arm. "You'll have Cullen. And I bet there'll be more, once they get used to the idea."

"Maybe." She didn't like thinking about what marriage might do to Rule's standing with his people and veered back to the part she had some control over. "I do not want birds crapping on me at my wedding."

"That's a strong argument against. I guess you've pointed out the crap problem?"

"Yeah, and admittedly she let that notion go, but she'll just come up with something else." Something grand and showy and expensive. To think that only a couple weeks ago, Lily had worried that her mother wouldn't accept the marriage. She shook her head. "Never mind about my mother. Today is all about you."

"All about the little rider, really. But since he can't appreciate his presents yet, I get to help."

"Still haven't settled on a name?"

"Do you have any idea how hard it is to find a name neither of you has any strong associations for? Cullen likes the old-fashioned names. And magically, the older names are stronger, so—"

"Does that count?' Lily asked, startled. "I thought the idea that names have power over you was an old wives' tale."

"Oh, that part's bullshit—for us, anyway. It's true for anyone who has what Micah calls a true name, but humans mostly don't, or we don't know it. No, for us names don't so much have power as affect power. We don't understand how, but . . . well, look at your people." She waved a hand, accidentally slapping the bare back of a fair-haired man who was talking to two equally bare-chested men. "Whoops. Sorry," she said with a grin when he turned around, one sandy eyebrow raised.

Lily knew there were a lot of superstitions about names in Chinese culture. She hadn't really paid attention—it had seemed like one of those relics of the past the older people cling to. "Hi, Jason," she said to the fair-haired lupus, who was eyeing Cynna appreciatively; and, "Flirt later," she told Cynna, taking her elbow and getting her moving. "We really should get you back to Cullen. It must be nearly time for the dancing."

At a lupus party, you always eat first. Best if none of the wolves is hungry.

Her mind slid back to what Cynna had said. "You mean all that stuff about, ah . . ." Numbers. There was something about the way a name added up, wasn't there? Oh, yeah. "You mean that business about the number of strokes in the name matters?"

"Uh . . . you might say that some elements of the Chinese system are disputed by other practitioners. But every people in the world pays attention to names and how they're bestowed."

"I can see where that would make it hard to pick a name."

"No kidding." She heaved a sigh. "I suggested Isaac, but Isaac makes Cullen think of a little guy with glasses who shot him once. So he suggests Andrew, but then we'd call him Andy, and to me Andy is a guy with a hairy back and no sense of humor." She shook her head. "Didn't have much class in bed, either, so I'm thumbs down on that one. I'm leaning toward Micah. Both of us like him, so it's got good associations. What do you think?"

"Micah's a good name." If you wanted to name your kid after a dragon, that is. Which might strike Cullen and Cynna as exactly right.

"Hey! Hey, Lily!"

She turned and saw a woman exactly her height but younger, with a rounder face, shorter—and trendier—hair, and an abundance of earrings.

The earrings and the hair were new. Beth was always trying new things. Lily waited while her little sister plunged through the crowd toward her with all the frisky determination of a half-grown pup.

"Hi, Cynna," Beth said as she reached them. "Wow, you are so pregnant. You look tremendous. Makes me want to go get knocked up, but I'm not quite that shallow. When do you count the loot in that jar?"

Cynna beamed. "The baby jar comes last, after the dancing. It's really full, isn't it?"

"Sure is. Speaking of dancing, you don't mind if I dance with that mouthwatering husband of yours, do you?"

"Might as well. Everyone else will. Cullen's a fantastic dancer." Cynna grinned. "Even when he keeps his clothes on."

"You think he will, then?" Beth looked wistful. "I never got to see him dance at Club Hell, and Lily says he's not working there anymore. I'd sure like to see—"

"Beth," Lily said warningly.

"—him in a G-string. It's a purely innocent lust," she assured Cynna. "Coupled with a certain artistic curiosity."

Lily spoke dryly. "Except that you aren't an artist."

"It's okay," Cynna said, but she had a funny expression on her face. She tipped her head, looking at Lily. "Is this how you feel when I flirt with Rule? Sort of smug and embarrassed, only you have no idea why you'd be embarrassed?"

"Lily probably stops at smug," Beth said. "She doesn't do embarrassed. How come I haven't seen any teenage boys here? Babies, I've seen. Toddlers and kids of both sexes. Teenage girls, yes, but no teenage boys."

Lily exchanged a glance with Cynna. "After lupus boys reach puberty, they live separately until the age of seventeen or eighteen."

"Really? Wow. That's the most sensible system I've ever heard of."

Lily grinned because she knew what Beth meant, but the boys weren't sequestered because young male adolescents are obnoxious. They lived apart so they wouldn't eat anyone.

From the other side of the field she heard deep voices break into song. "Hey, listen! That's that Russian song. 'Kalinka.'"

"Yeah!" Cynna grabbed Beth's arm. "C'mon. You have got to see this."

"Okay, but—"

"They're going to dance," Cynna said. "Some of them, anyway. It's one of their training dances, so it's about half dance, half acrobatics. Cullen says the one tonight will be special."

"Okay," Beth said again, tugged into motion, "but I need to talk to Lily a minute."

Cynna's eyebrows shot up. "One of those kinds of talks? The kind I shouldn't stick around for?"

"It's about Grandmother."

"I'm going to go watch the dancers," Cynna said decisively. And left.

FIVE

LILY watched her friend disappear into the sea of bare backs and chests. "It's amazing. Cynna has body-tackled a demon, but she scurries away at the mention of Grandmother."

Beth didn't smile. "I'm worried about her."

"About Grandmother?" Lily sorted through a half dozen questions and settled on, "Why?"

"She didn't come to the shower or the baby party."

"Because Li Qin got sick."

"If it were just that," Beth said darkly, "I'd still be suspicious. When has Li Qin ever been sick?"

Now that Beth mentioned it, Lily couldn't remember ever seeing her grandmother's companion down with so much as the sniffles. But that didn't mean anything. Even people with sturdy constitutions got sick now and then—and when they did, they often got really sick.

Should she be worried about Li Qin? Lily frowned and tugged on her sister's arm. "Walk while you talk. I don't want to miss the dancers."

"You won't miss anything," Beth said. "Rule's probably saving you a spot. Where is he?"

"Over by the dancers," Lily admitted. She didn't have to guess. She knew. That was one of the neat things about the mate bond. She always knew roughly where he was.

"About Grandmother . . . you must have noticed how Chinese she's been lately."

"I haven't seen much of her since I got back from North Carolina."

"That's the other thing. No one's seeing much of her."

Lily shrugged. "We're talking about Grandmother."

"Yes, so strange is her normal, but she only turns über-Chinese when she's annoyed or upset or up to something. I think she's up to something, but if not, there's something wrong. And the thing that proves it is Freddie."

"Freddie?" Lily blinked. "Our cousin Freddie?"

"Of course our cousin. Who else could get him to come here? Aside from his mother, I mean, but she wouldn't. So that leaves Grandmother. Why would she send him here instead of coming herself?"

"Ah . . . Beth, Freddie's not here."

"He *is*. I saw him not ten minutes ago. I tried to catch him, but he ducked into the crowd when he saw me coming."

If Lily hadn't known for a fact that there was no alcohol at the party, she'd have suspected her sister of being drunk. "Maybe you saw Paul."

Beth's lip curled. "You've got to be kidding."

The scorn was possibly justified. Aside from the fact that they were both Chinese, Susan's husband looked nothing like Freddie. But at least Paul was here, unlike Freddie. Lily figured he'd attended to protect Susan from attack by ravening werewolves. Or from being hit on, which would probably happen anyway, though very politely. "Beth, it couldn't have been Freddie you saw. He wasn't invited, and there's no way Freddie would crash a party. Especially this one. Lupi scare him."

"I know that. It proves Grandmother is involved. He's more scared of her than he is of lupi."

Lily had to grin. "It's a good thing you didn't decide to be a cop. You've got a seriously loose notion of what constitutes proof."

"Okay, don't believe me, but check on Grandmother anyway. She likes you best, so maybe you can find out what's up."

It was usually easiest to just agree with Beth. Besides, she might be right. Beth's intuitive understanding of people owed nothing to magic, but she was often right about them. "Okay, I'll go see her."

"When?"

"Soon, okay? I want to see the dancing now."

The singers had stopped, but a number of people had migrated to that end of the field and Lily wasn't sure they'd be able to see. One of them turned around as they approached—Jason, the blond hunk Cynna hadn't had a chance to flirt with earlier.

Lily liked Jason—she really did. He was impossible to dislike. But he was certain he owed her for something that had just been her job, and took every opportunity he could find to pay her back. She didn't know how to make him quit, and Rule thought it was funny.

"Have they started?" she asked Jason.

"No, Michael and Sean decided they wanted their fiddles, but they're back now. I hear them tuning up. You'd better get up front. You'll never see from back here."

She couldn't argue with that, but his methods were embarrassing—and never mind what Beth had said. She damned well could be embarrassed. He grabbed her hand and called out cheerfully, "The Chosen's back here. She needs to be up there."

Sure enough, the crowd parted, people turning with a smile, shifting to let her pass. Jason pulled her forward.

"My sister," Lily said. "I'd like her to see—"

"Your . . . oh, my." Jason paused, his eyes traveling over Beth as a smile spread. "I can't believe I overlooked this one. Yum."

Beth dimpled at him. "My name's Beth. I'm the nice sister."

"Very nice," he assured her, his eyes making it clear which elements he considered especially worthy. "And yet I can't help hoping . . . not *too* nice?"

Lily resisted the urge to roll her eyes, settling for retrieving her hand from Jason's grip. She didn't think he noticed. "Jason, this is Beth. Beth, Jason Chance. Can you hit on each other later? I really don't want to miss this."

Beth didn't resist. She rolled her eyes. "Well, I'm nicer than *that*."

"No doubt. I'm going to find Rule. You coming?"

Beth slid a sideways smile at Jason. "I'll catch up with you."

Lily suspected her sister was going to miss the training dance. Oh, well. Jason wouldn't show Beth any more of a good time than she wanted to have, and at twenty-three, Beth was technically a grown-up. Lily went to find Rule.

The violins had started by the time she reached the front of the crowd, passed there by people she knew and those she didn't. Someone had brought a drum, which he was beating slowly. The dancers had assembled into a circle of about a dozen half-naked men, arms locked together. None of them moved. They seemed hardly to breathe.

Rule wasn't watching the dancers. He was with them.

Lily's breath caught in surprise. Like the others, he wore only ragged cutoffs that hung low on his hips. He was magnificently male, achingly human . . . yet in that moment she almost glimpsed his wolf hidden in the human architecture—a powerful, intense presence illumining the taut muscles and hooded eyes of the man. Friendly, perhaps, that wolf, but not tame. Not at all tame.

Someone had started a small bonfire in the center of the circle. The ruddy dance of the firelight turned the blades of Rule's cheekbones hard, gathering shadows to make mysteries of his eyes. Then he looked up, caught her gaze on him, and grinned.

In delight, she grinned back. After a moment, she thought to look at the others in the circle—and was startled to see Rule's brother, Benedict. He looked like the statue of some Aztec god turned flesh, his expression as calm and unrevealing as stone, his skin gleaming in the firelight.

She'd never seen Benedict join the dance before. He probably taught it—he trained young Nokolai in fighting—but she'd never seen him dance it. Why was he in the circle tonight?

Opposite Rule stood Cullen. He was the most overtly beautiful of them all, his face almost too perfect in its coined symmetry. His eyes glittered with excitement—a merry Pan or Loki about to launch some cosmic mischief.

Benedict gave a short nod to the drummer, who suddenly kicked up his tempo. The fiddles joined in with a wild opening flourish, the singers launched into the old Russian song—and the dancers erupted from stillness to fury.

The steps were simple enough. The speed and vigor of those steps flung the men into a rapid clockwise swirl that spun itself from fast to faster before snapping out into a line—and the line dipped in a wave as each man sank to his heels, kicked out with each leg, and rose again.

After three undulations of the line, those on the ends spun forward. First two men, then four, then more, flung themselves into the air as if they could take flight—and they nearly did, over-leaping one another in a dizzy pattern.

Then they began hurling one another into the air—a pair of lupi using their hands as a catapult to send a third flying, somersaulting through space, landing with a bounce to leap again or join hands with another to send someone else up. There was a pattern to it, but they moved too fast for her to pick it out. Faster than human, certainly, but also faster than she'd seen them dance before.

In a heartbeat they clicked into a new pattern—not bouncing as they landed, but catching one another to build two pyramids of five lupi each, three on the ground, two on their shoulders. The pyramids kept one man aloft like a living projectile, tossing him between them. Cullen.

He'd land on one set of shoulders, crouch, and be hurled to the other side, his body tucked up like a ball, righting himself at the last second to land on the opposite pyramid, still crouched—and be flung back.

Two times. Three. Four—and then both pyramids dissolved while he was in the air, those who'd formed them melting away into the crowd.

One man stood where five had been. Benedict. He watched, unmoving, as Cullen shot at him like a cannonball. Benedict dipped his knees slightly as he stretched up one hand.

It couldn't have happened the way it looked. Because it looked like he *dribbled* Cullen—as if the curled-up ball of the man smacked into Benedict's hand and bounced to the ground, then up into the air again, unfurling into a man only then to land lightly beside Benedict—sweaty, panting, grinning like a madman.

"And that, younglings," Benedict said lazily, "is how the dance is supposed to be done."

The crowd exploded—applauding, yelling. Lily heard someone call out, "Piers—for Lady's sake!" and someone behind her was saying over and over, "Get back, get back. Give him some space."

It was the name—Piers—that got her attention. Wasn't that the young lupus Rule had mentioned who'd just been allowed to leave *terra tradis*, where young lupi were sequestered? If so, he was only eighteen, not an official adult yet. She turned, trying to see over or through people.

What she saw was Rule slipping through the crowd. She followed. He stopped and held out his arm. She stepped into that welcoming circle. He was warm and sweaty from the dance.

Another circle had formed, she realized—a circle of men around a panting, excited wolf with a brindle coat. One man was laughing. Another grinned and shook his head. Another sighed.

Lily was the only female in the circle. The only human. There were no children nearby, either. The wolf was surrounded only by other lupi . . . and her.

Piers must have gotten so excited that he lost control and Changed. For an adolescent, that was a huge no-no—because he might lose control in other ways, too. Lily was contemplating the wisdom of stepping back when Isen strode up to the wolf. He stopped, hands on hips, and shook his head. "Piers," he said. Just that, but with such disappointment.

The wolf's ears went flat. His tail drooped. His head sagged in sudden dejection.

"You know what you must do now."

The wolf cocked his head, gave a hopeful wag of his tail. Isen said nothing.

The wolf sighed and nodded.

"Straight back," Isen said. "No interesting detours. You'll Change as soon as you're able and explain to Mason what happened."

Mason was the lupus in charge of the *terra tradis*. Lily hadn't met him, but she'd heard stories. He sounded like a combination drill instructor and headmaster with a sprinkling of priest.

"Isen?" one of the older men said. "Do you want me to . . . ?" He made a little circular gesture.

"Thank you for the offer. However . . ." Isen gave the abject wolf another look. "I trust Piers to take himself back."

That perked the wolf up. He gave another, firmer nod.

"What just happened?" someone behind Lily asked.

She turned to see Susan's husband frowning at the wolf trotting out of the circle. Paul was a tall, gangly man with rimless glasses and shiny black hair that he had cut every week so there was no chance of a single hair falling out of place. He was as serious as a rain cloud and rather shy.

"Hi, Paul. Uh—Piers was sent back to the *terra tradis*."

"The what?" He shook his head. "Never mind. Is he dangerous?"

They all are, Lily wanted to say. But that was both too much information and too little. She kept her mouth closed.

Rule answered in the same relaxed way he fielded questions from reporters. "Simply overexcited, but he wasn't supposed to Change, so he had to be disciplined. We're firm with our youngsters about the circumstances in which they're allowed to Change."

"I wondered because Susan and I were moved away when he . . . when he did that. Changed. We were moved away *physically*."

"I apologize for any rudeness."

"No, no, I wasn't offended. I simply . . ." Paul was still watching the place in the crowd where the wolf had vanished, an odd expression on his face. "I've never seen anything like that."

"Not many have, outside the clans." Rule's tone was perfectly matter-of-fact, yet somehow suggested that Paul was both privileged and too wise to make a fuss about that privilege. "Paul, I was hoping for a chance to chat with you tonight. I won't keep you from Susan long—I think the regular dancing will start soon—but I'd like your opinion of a stock I'm considering, a medical technology company. You'll have an insider's knowledge of their products."

Paul perked up much as the wolf had, if not quite so obviously. He had an important position in hospital administration—Lily could never remember the exact title, but he made a lot of purchasing decisions and loved to talk about the technology of medicine.

She hid a smile and let Rule do his thing. His flattery worked because it was sincere. He probably was considering that stock—he maintained a diverse portfolio for Nokolai—and he did appreciate hearing Paul's opinion of the company. And before Paul left Clanhome tonight, he would be convinced Rule Turner was an unusually astute and sensible man. One with an odd ability, maybe, but his occasional furriness would no longer seem important.

The drumming had started up again. After a moment the fiddles joined in. The regular dancing would begin soon. Lily let her attention drift away, looking for Benedict or Cullen. She wanted a word with the former, and she needed to give Cullen the . . . Wait. Was that who Beth had seen earlier?

The man she'd seen moving through the crowd was certainly Asian, but he didn't look like Freddie. He was shorter, for one thing, and his face was rounder than Freddie's. She thought he was older, too. She'd gotten only a quick glimpse, but he'd looked older. Plus he'd been wearing a T-shirt and baseball cap. Stuffy Freddie didn't own a baseball cap. She wasn't sure he owned a T-shirt.

She touched Rule's arm. "I need to find Cullen and give him his present."

He gave her the kind of smile he ought to reserve for when they were alone, brought her hand to his lips, and kissed it. "You'll save me a dance."

"Maybe two." One dance here. One when they were alone. Lily smiled at that thought and left him to his business talk.

Ten minutes later she gave up on finding the Asian man.

She couldn't even find anyone who'd seen him. In this sea of Caucasian faces and bare chests, he ought to stand out, dammit. Any human male ought to stand out here, but the few who'd noticed an Asian man apparently meant Paul, based on what they remembered about height and clothing. No one remembered seeing anyone in a baseball cap.

Of course, that proved nothing. Lily had interviewed too many witnesses to have much confidence in human memory and attention to detail, and she had no reason to think lupi did any better.

But some of them did. Some, she realized, would have been paying attention. She nodded and started looking for a man no one would overlook.

Sure enough, Benedict was easy to find.

The fiddlers had launched into a lively song and people were making room for dancing—square dancing, she thought, from the sound of the music. Or maybe it would be Western swing. That was another thing about lupus gatherings—there was always music and almost always dancing, but you never knew what kind. It depended on who showed up and what they wanted to play.

Lily knew one of the men fiddling for them tonight. In his other life, he was first violinist at the San Diego Symphony—and no one he worked with knew he was lupus. Which was reason enough to track down Benedict. Nokolai might have gone public, but some of its members hadn't. With the Species Citizenship Bill still bogged down in committee, some couldn't afford to. It was legal to fire a lupus for being a lupus, and plenty of places would do just that.

Benedict was at the north end of the field near the tubs of drinks, talking to a man she didn't know. Lily raised her voice slightly. "Benedict."

He turned and waited, giving her a nod when she reached him. Benedict was in charge of Clanhome's security. Now that the dance was over, he'd added some of his usual accessories to his cutoffs—a large sword sheathed on his back, a holstered .357 at his hip, and an earbud. His phone was fastened to his belt opposite the .357.

The combination of low-tech and high-tech weaponry, bare

skin, and impressive musculature gave him the look of an animated gaming character, with a whiff of Secret Service from the earbud. She smiled. "No machine gun?"

"No. I'm not expecting trouble."

He was serious. At least she thought he was—with Benedict it was hard to tell. "That dance was really something. I've never seen anything like it."

He nodded, agreeing. Maybe pleased.

"Does it mean—"

"I won't discuss my relationship with my brother with you."

Her eyebrows climbed. Good guess, even if he was wrong about the outcome. Sooner or later, they would discuss it. "I'll table that for now. I have a security concern."

He didn't move. His expression didn't change. Yet everything about him sharpened. "Yes?"

"I've seen an Asian man here I can't account for. Not Paul—you've seen Paul Liu, my brother-in-law? This man is shorter than Paul and possibly older. I only got one glimpse, so I can't give much of a description, but he was wearing a dark baseball cap and a pale T-shirt with short sleeves."

"I haven't seen him or received a report of him, and my people are tracking all the *ospi* currently at Clanhome."

Lily blinked. *Ospi* meant out-clan friend or guest. "My sisters? You're tracking my sisters?"

He smiled slightly. "I keep track of any out-clan who enter Clanhome."

Had she been mistaken? Lily drummed her fingers on her thigh. No, she decided. "There aren't any Asian Nokolai, are there?"

"Two," Benedict said promptly. "Half-Asian, of course. One has a Korean mother and lives with her in Los Angeles. He's ten years old. The other is an adult whose mother was Japanese. John Ino is fifty-seven and lives in Seattle, and I doubt he's here today. But it's possible."

"Find out. I saw an Asian man in a baseball cap. He's not a guest, and it sounds like he isn't Nokolai." Maybe he'd worn the cap for only a short time. Maybe he'd seen her looking for

him and faded away from the crowd. Maybe he'd left altogether, in which case they were too late, but it was worth finding out. "This party would be one hell of an opportunity for
paparazzi, and they make cameras really small these days."

Benedict considered her for a moment, then nodded. "All
right. Whoever he is, this man didn't come in either of the
gates. It's possible to enter elsewhere, but only on foot. Which
means he's left a scent trail." He pulled out his phone and hit a
number. "Saul. I need you. I'm by the soft drinks."

He put up the phone. "Saul's got the best nose of any of my
people. He'll Change and you'll show him where you saw the
man. With so many trampling over the ground, he may not be
able to pick up the scent there, but it's a place to start."

"Good. Why did you participate in the dance tonight?"

"To impress the youngsters so they'll try harder."

"That's not the only reason. Rule danced, too, and neither
of you usually does."

His mouth curved up a fraction. "You're perceptive. It's
annoying at times. Very well. I also sent a message. I'm not
speaking to my brother, but I fully support my Lu Nuncio. It
was best everyone understood that."

So his problem with Rule was personal, not a "good of
the clan" thing. "You think they'll get that message from the
dance?"

His eyebrows lifted about a millimeter. "Of course."

Hmm. "Well, it made for a fantastic show. But how in the
world did you end it that way? Even if you're strong enough
to just stop Cullen one-handed, it seems like you'd break a few
bones—his, yours, both."

"For someone who isn't combat-trained, Seabourne's a—"

Half the mage lights bobbing overhead went out.

Benedict's head whipped up. Without a gesture or word or
a single damned clue what was wrong, he took off running.

When Benedict moved, people got out of his way. Fast. She
couldn't come close to keeping up, but by putting everything
she had into her sprint she managed to catch the openings in
the crowd he created.

People called out. The music died. She lost the Benedict-driven opening and was faced with a wall of bare backs. She resorted to shoving. This crowd wouldn't care about her badge, and she had to get through.

Rule was ahead. She felt him. Something had happened, something had gone wrong—

"Nokolai!" Isen's deep voice bellowed. "If you are not a guard, sit down! Now!"

All over the field, they dropped. Men and women alike—even children—they all sat on the grass as their Rho had commanded. No questions, no hesitation.

Except Lily. She was Nokolai and technically not a guard, but it didn't occur to her to sit. Not when the way was suddenly clear. Not when she could see over the heads of those in front of her.

Several hadn't dropped to the ground. Guards. Benedict, of course, wasn't sitting. He stood beside Isen, his eyes busy and his Glock in his hand. But he had nothing to shoot.

And Rule. He wasn't standing, but kneeling, kneeling next to a man stretched out in the grass. At first all she saw of that man were the legs, bare like most legs tonight. The rest of him was hidden by Cynna's crimson-clad back, bent over him, and by the woman kneeling beside her, whom Lily recognized by the hair—long, dusty gray mixed with brown, a frizzy, flyaway mane trailing to her waist.

Nettie, the clan's healer.

Lily's feet carried her two more steps at an angle, and she saw the rest. Saw Cullen Seabourne's body lying peacefully in the grass, his still, empty face staring up at the starry sky.

SIX

"YOU are not dead," Cynna was saying fiercely, her hands digging into Cullen's shoulders. "You are not. You are not dead. Dammit, Cullen, you—"

"I've got him," Nettie said crisply. She'd flattened her hands on Cullen's chest. "Cynna, get back. You're leaking. It interferes."

Lily couldn't feel her feet. She was standing, so they must still be there at the end of her legs, but she couldn't feel them. Her last breath had pulled something bad inside her, unreality spreading like poison through her body, paralyzing her. *No,* she wanted to say along with Cynna. *No, he can't be dead. Cullen can't be—*

Cullen's chest quivered. It lifted, ever so slightly, then fell. His eyelids drifted closed.

Lily sucked in a breath, too. This one dispelled the poison and she hurried to Cynna. "Come on, Cynna. Move back. Let Nettie work. You're right. You're right, he isn't dead, but you have to move back."

He wasn't dead *now*. Seconds ago, he had been. Or at least he hadn't been breathing. An atavistic shiver threw goose bumps along Lily's arms. She pulled on Cynna, who allowed it, lurching to her feet with Lily's arm around her waist.

"He's not dead." Cynna's face was dry but oddly slack, as if shock had cut the muscles.

"No, he isn't. Look at his chest. Look at his eyes, Cynna. He closed them. Nettie did her thing and Cullen's breathing."

A shudder traveled through Cynna like a minor earthquake. Lily tightened her arm as the woman's knees went soft, bracing her legs so they didn't both tumble to the ground.

A second later Cynna stiffened, taking most of her weight again. "I'm fine," she said. "I'm good. Cullen—"

"Nettie's got him. She isn't letting him go."

As if agreeing, Nettie spoke. "Helicopter." Her head was upright, her eyes closed, the frizzy waves of her hair hanging down on either side of her face like half-drawn drapes. "Medevac."

"Nettie—" Isen began.

"Now." There was no give in her voice. Iron couldn't be harder or more certain. "Stabbed in the heart. There's poison. It's interfering."

"I sent for the Rhej," Benedict said.

"Good." With that, Nettie shut the rest of them out, beginning a low chant.

Poison? Lily twitched, wanting to check for herself. To see if the poison had a magical component, because there were precious damned few things that poisoned a lupus.

But Cynna was leaning on her, and she didn't want to interfere with Nettie. Who was keeping Cullen alive.

Rule already had his phone out and was speaking into it. ". . . need a medevac helicopter at Nokolai Clanhome. Stabbing victim, a heart wound, and there's some sort of poison involved." A pause. "That's not acceptable. We have a doctor on scene, and she says she needs a helicopter."

Lily glanced around. "Here," she said to one of the men still on his feet. Shannon was a freckled, redheaded guard who looked about twenty. He was probably twice that. "Keep her on her feet."

Cynna scowled. "I don't need to be passed around like—"

"Yes, you do." Lily waited until Shannon slid an arm

around Cynna, then hurried to Rule, who was speaking with controlled fury to the person at the other end. She held out her hand. "Let me."

He broke off in midsentence and put his phone in her hand. His pupils had swollen, black overtaking color in his eyes but not swallowing the whites. Yet. The edges of that black quivered as he fought back the need to Change.

He wanted to hunt and catch and kill. She understood.

Lily took his hand so the mate bond could help him hold on to his control and spoke into the phone. "This is FBI Special Unit Agent Lily Yu. I need a medevac helicopter at this location. Immediately."

The 911 operator told her all the copters were out on other calls, but she'd send an ambulance. Lily had to let go of Rule's hand to retrieve her own phone from her pocket . . . not the pocket that held Cullen's present.

And she was not going to think about that. "I need a copter. You can divert one of yours, or you can call the Navy." Naval Base San Diego was the largest in the country. They kept fully equipped medevac copters standing by. "Priority authorization for that—be *quiet*. This is an order, not a request. Call this number"—she read it off her own phone's directory—"with authorization code Elder, Elder, M as in Mary, S as in Susan, six-one-one-five. Got that?" She listened. "Right. I'll stand by while you confirm."

While the operator made the call, Lily took in the scene.

Nettie chanted. Her expression was serene, but beneath the natural coppery pigment of her skin she looked strained. How long could she keep pouring energy into Cullen? He was pale. Shock? Could a lupus go into shock? She didn't see any blood, not a mark on him anywhere.

Stabbed from behind, then. No sign of the weapon. Did the perp still have it, whoever he was?

An assumption there, but the odds favored a male assailant. It took strength and a great deal of skill to hit the heart with a single strike.

Was Cullen still breathing? He must be. Nettie hadn't given up. Lily took a breath herself, as if that would help. Her palms were damp. She wiped one absently on her dress, switching hands with the phone so she could wipe the other one, too.

One of the faces in the seated crowd snagged her attention. Her sister sat beside Jason, holding his hand, about twenty feet away. Beth looked shocky, her gaze jumping all over as if she expected the next knife to come straight at her.

Lily took a single step, then stopped. Beth would have to wait.

Benedict was speaking urgently to Isen. Rule had moved away when she released his hand, and now he replaced Shannon, folding Cynna up in his arms. Several men had formed a perimeter around them, facing out—the guards, watching for another attack.

What the hell had happened?

Finally the operator came back on the line. "A naval medevac copter is taking off now. ETA ten minutes. Please stay on the line while I—"

"No," Lily said. She disconnected and went to Rule.

"You've called out the Navy," he said, raised eyebrows making a question of it.

"A naval helicopter." For the first time, she'd used the code Unit agents were allowed to use in an emergency, one that let them call on federal forces, including the military. There might be trouble over that later. "They'll be here in about ten minutes. We need to clear the field, make a place for them to land. When we do, I want to separate my witnesses."

"*Your* witnesses?"

"For now." She had no reason to think she had jurisdiction, but . . . but dammit to hell, that was Cullen lying on the ground. Someone had nearly killed him. "The nine-one-one operator will have notified the sheriff's department, of course, but I can get things started." Movement at the end of the field snagged her attention.

A burly man with brown hair was running flat-out toward them carrying roughly two hundred pounds of little old lady. She wore an unfitted cotton dress with an embroidered yoke and yards and yards of crinkly apple green that would have reached her ankles if she'd been standing. Lily knew how long the dress was because she'd seen the woman standing earlier.

Her hair was short and white as milk. Her eyes were milky, too.

The Nokolai Rhej was entirely blind. It didn't slow her down much, but her age did. Enough, at least, that she put up with what had to be a bumpy ride.

"Damn, boy," the Rhej said when he stopped, his chest heaving, his body shiny with sweat. Even a lupus could tire after a three-mile run while carrying so many lumpy extra pounds. "One of us is out of shape, huh?" She chuckled as he put her down. Her face turned toward Cynna, those blind eyes seeming to pick her out easily. "You're not crying. Good. Don't, not yet."

She waddled forward. The Rhej couldn't see, no—but she didn't have to. She was the strongest physical empath Lily had ever met. She *knew* her surroundings in a way most people couldn't.

Cynna met her and put a hand on her shoulder, bending to say something Lily couldn't catch. The Rhej shook her head, spoke quietly, then patted Cynna and moved up to stand behind Nettie. Cynna circled Cullen. As she started to lower herself to the ground, Benedict moved quickly to help her.

"Hannah," Isen said.

That was the Rhej's name, but normally no one used it. Even if you'd been given permission, you didn't use a Rhej's name in public. Apparently the Rho could, though. Lily felt a familiar frustration. No matter how much she learned about Rule's people, there always seemed to be more she didn't know.

"Isen." The Rhej gave him a nod. "How much?"

"I want him alive, and we're not in combat."

"Good. Nettie's going to need it." With that the old woman put her hands on Nettie's shoulders and closed her eyes.

Lily moved closer to Rule to ask quietly, "What's she doing?"

"Feeding Nettie power. From the clan. She . . ." He stopped. Swallowed. "They've done this before. The Rhej can't heal—it isn't her Gift—but she can shape the power so Nettie can use it."

Lily dragged in another breath, let it out slowly. "What the hell happened?"

"I wasn't close enough to see. I heard Cynna cry out, so

I came running. Cullen was down. I smelled blood. I didn't see any, but I knew he'd been injured. I gave the alert for an attack."

A middle-aged woman seated on the ground nearby spoke, her face incredulous. "But you were there, Rule. I saw you. You were standing right behind Cullen."

"No, he wasn't," the man on her right said. "I was beside you, Sandra, and I didn't see Rule until he came running up."

"He was there," she insisted.

Sandra was not going to make a good witness, but maybe someone with Rule's height and coloring . . . ? Lily glanced at her watch. "We have to get the field cleared."

"I'll do that," Isen said from behind her.

She turned and met his eyes.

Isen Turner wasn't a short man, but neither was he as annoyingly tall as his sons. His eyes were the color of wet bark, topped by bushy brows that lacked the elegance of Rule's. Those eyes blazed now in a face gone still.

He was furious. In complete control, but beneath that, the beast raged. Startled, she spoke formally. "Thank you. I need possible witnesses separated from the rest. Also from each other, as much as possible. I don't want them discussing what they saw or thought they saw. I need to be sure no one leaves, too."

"They won't leave. They won't discuss it if I tell them not to."

She wondered at his cooperation. Lupi were not known for welcoming the authorities into their affairs, and Isen would see this as a Nokolai matter. "You're accepting my authority in this?"

"I accept necessity. You're Nokolai. You will handle this."

"Uh . . . for now. The dispatcher will have notified the sheriff's department."

"So Benedict told me. He's notified the guards at the gate to admit whoever they send, but you'll be in charge."

"I don't know if this falls within my jurisdiction. By law, magical crimes are those—"

He made a chopping motion with one hand. "You'll find a way to work it. I don't care how. I haven't asked for obedience from you because you weren't raised to understand the need, but you are Nokolai. You'll find a way."

Prickles traveled up her arms. She wanted to agree. She was immune to whatever pull his mantle gave him, yet she wanted to agree. "And if I don't?"

A glint of humor passed through his eyes. "Oh, I'm not fool enough to threaten you. No, you'll find a way to make this your case because that's best for Nokolai—as you'll understand when you've thought on it. And you are Nokolai."

He turned abruptly and raised his voice to that full-throated bellow. "Nokolai! This is an offense against the clan." He paused, letting them absorb that. Calling a clan-offense was serious. "Our Chosen will act for me in this, along with my Lu Nuncio. Anyone with information that might help, come forward. Anyone who was close to Seabourne just before the attack—even if you don't think you can help—come forward. You will *not* speak of it to each other. Come forward and wait. Children and tenders, go to the Center. Everyone else, go to the south end of the field. Quickly. We need room for the helicopter."

He turned to Benedict, who'd come up as he was speaking. "Make sure our elders are comfortable."

Benedict gave a single nod and moved away.

"Does he magically know when you need him?" Lily shook her head. "Never mind. Did you see what happened?"

"No. I was at least twenty yards away, talking with Sybil and Toby."

Toby. God, she hadn't thought—"Where is he?"

"With Sybil, of course. She was a tender for thirty years. She'll take him to the Center with the other kids."

Guilt washed through her. She shoved it back. No time for that now—but it was just as well she had plenty of help with this parenting business. She wasn't very good at it yet.

The crowd was moving, most heading for the south end of the field, as instructed, while a few swam against the current to come forward, also as instructed. Isen directed them to wait about twenty feet away.

They were all so orderly—no panic, no one complaining or assuming that Isen couldn't possibly have meant him. Or her.

They scarcely spoke. She felt Rule move up beside her. "It's kind of eerie."

"What?"

"Them." She gestured. "Everyone's just . . . They're so calm. Earlier one of them got so excited from watching a dance that he Changed. No one's Changing now."

"Isen is drawing heavily on the mantle." He paused, then added, "They don't smell calm. They trust him to deal with the situation, but they aren't calm."

"Hmm." *Scent-blind*, lupi called humans. They had a point. She turned to Rule. "I need to talk to the wits. You can help with that."

As Lu Nuncio, he'd smell it if they lied—the lupus ones, anyway. According to Rule, lupi couldn't lie to someone carrying a portion of their clan's mantle without reeking of guilt.

Rule didn't respond. He was looking at Cullen, his face blank. Shut down.

Lily realized she was staring, too, watching Cullen's chest as if her eyes could keep it lifting, ever so slightly, with his breath. She closed her eyes, took a deep breath, and touched Rule's arm once. Then moved away.

Keeping Cullen alive wasn't her job. Nettie and the Rhej were in charge there, and thank God for that. She'd do what she knew. She moved closer and crouched down beside Cynna. "Can you answer a couple questions?"

Cynna nodded without taking her eyes off Cullen.

"You were with Cullen when it happened."

"Yeah, I—I was standing beside him. Someone came up to congratulate us. I didn't know him, but Cullen called him Mike. They were talking when he . . . Cullen jerked, then he fell. He just collapsed. I don't know who was behind us. It was crowded. I didn't notice."

Suddenly Cynna gripped Lily's arm, her fingers digging in. The bones of her face stood out starkly. "You'll find him. Or her. Whoever did this, you'll find them."

In the face of that need, Lily didn't speak of jurisdictions. "I will. Cullen's going to make it, Cynna. He's got too much holding him here. The Rhej and Nettie will hold on to him in their way, but you and the baby—you'll keep him here, too."

Cynna jerked out a single nod and looked at Cullen again. One hand went to her belly, rubbing gently. Her lips moved. Lily caught the words, just barely . . . "Hail Mary, full of grace . . ."

Among her other improbabilities, Cynna was Catholic. Maybe that helped right now. Lily hoped so. She stood.

Twenty or thirty people had collected where Isen told them to. They didn't talk to one another. They were waiting, as they'd been told.

Lily shook her head, more aware than usual that lupi might look human—but they weren't. She headed for her witnesses, and had a small shock. One of those waiting so quietly was her sister Beth. Jason the hunk had his arm around her. Lily paused, absorbed that surprise, and asked, "Who's Mike?"

"Me." The man who spoke was the skinniest lupus she'd ever seen. Not emaciated, but stringy, and well over six feet tall. His hair was a dusty black, straight and shaggy, his skin a pale caramel. He looked sick.

"Last name?"

"Hemmings."

"Okay. I need you to come with me, Mike." But she didn't move right away, instead glancing behind her.

Rule was coming. "You okay?" she whispered when he reached her.

He made a single brushing-away gesture. "You're doing your job. In this case it's my job, too. I'll need to Change. I can probably tell even in this form if anyone lies, but we need better than 'probably.'" He glanced around. "The food tables. If you want to question people separately, we'll need some distance so the others won't overhear."

"Okay. Good idea. I need one of the guards to do the things I'd have a uniform do—fetch witnesses, mostly. Can you—"

"Of course." He gestured to the nearest guard, who happened to be Shannon, the youthful-looking redhead, and told him he was needed to help Lily with the witnesses.

Then he pulled off his watch and tucked it in his jeans pocket. Then he Changed.

Lily had watched the Change often enough. She still couldn't say precisely what she saw. Every time, she thought maybe this time she'd be able to really *see* the process, but she never did. Not quite.

It wasn't like the way the movies depicted it, though—an arm sprouting fur and elongating into a leg, a face stretching into a muzzle. Nothing so clear and linear. Nor did she see the same thing a camera recorded. Rule had been caught on TV once when he Changed, and the space his body occupied had simply frizzed into visual static until he was wolf.

It didn't help that Rule was extremely fast about the business, but her eyes couldn't track it when she watched other lupi Change, either.

This time she tried watching out of the corner of her eye instead of head-on. Didn't help. Reality folded itself up, space and flesh bending into places her brain couldn't follow. Then it snapped back, and a wolf stood beside her. A really large wolf with black and silver fur.

Lily glanced at Cullen—then forced herself to think, dammit, think about what she could do, not what lay outside her scope and skills. She bent to pick up the cutoffs that had fallen from Rule when he put reality on hold, then nodded at Mike and Shannon.

"Let's go over to the food tables. Shannon, I need my purse." Her notebook was in it, for one thing. Also her weapon. "It's in the kitchen at the Center, in the cupboard by the rear door. Can you get that pretty quick, then join us?"

He nodded and took her at her word. He ran. Since he went at lupus speed while they simply walked, he was on his way back before they reached the tables.

Potato salad. Coleslaw. An opened pack of buns. A spill of plastic forks. For some stupid reason the sight of all that made her eyes burn. She swallowed. Swallowed again. This shouldn't have happened. Shouldn't have happened at all, but especially not here, where Cullen was safe. Happy. He'd been so blasted happy, without his usual guards of cynicism and humor.

He couldn't die. She hadn't given him his baby present yet.

That thought nearly tipped her over, but Shannon arrived before she lost it. She got herself under control, took her bag, and dug out her notebook and a pen. She turned to face the gangly lupus.

Jittery, she decided. She didn't have to smell him to know he was strung tight. "Mike, you okay? You look pretty tense."

"Never mind making nice. Let's get this over with."

His hostility puzzled her. Sure, sometimes wits took out their anger on the cop questioning them, but this felt personal. "All right. First, I'd like to shake your hand." No point in hiding what she intended. Everyone here knew she was a touch sensitive.

Mike's palm was damp. No magic other than the familiar wash of lupus magic—cool, furry, with something that reminded her of the scent of pine needles, rendered tactilely.

She dropped his hand. "Thanks. Did you see who stabbed Cullen?"

His gaze darted to Rule, standing four-legged beside Lily. He nodded once.

"Tell me what you saw."

He looked at the ground, his mouth tight. "I'll tell my Rho."

Rule didn't move. He didn't growl or snarl, yet all at once he was *more*. Not more of any one thing—just twice as present as before. He stared at Mike out of yellow eyes, hackles raised.

Mike's head came up. He twitched as if fighting the need to abase himself, his gaze darting toward Rule, then dropping. "All right. All right, since you'll have it this way, I'll tell what I saw. I saw *you*, Rule. I saw you come up behind Cullen and slap him on the back. Then he fell, and I smelled his blood."

SEVEN

LILY looked at Rule. It was automatic, unthinking. He'd been accused of an impossible and horrific act, of trying to kill his best friend. Of course she looked at him.

He dipped his head slowly in a nod.

It took a second for her brain to work past the confusion. He meant *Yes, Mike's telling the truth*—but the truth as Mike knew it. Not the actual, factual truth, but what Mike believed.

Shit.

In the silence, Lily realized she'd been hearing the approaching *whomp-whomp* of a helicopter without it registering. She looked up and saw the copter's running lights moving against the inky sky. It was close.

"Okay. Mike, you say you saw Rule. Did you smell him, too?"

He shook his head. "I didn't notice his scent, but I wasn't standing all that close."

"Who was standing near you? Who did you see close to Cullen other than Rule?"

He named seven people, including Cynna and the woman

who'd spoken earlier—Sandra, last name Metlock. She jotted them down, then turned the page. "Give me a picture of where they were. Here's Cullen." She drew a small circle. "Where were you? Cynna?" She led him through the placement of seven circles, then wrote his name at the top of the page. "One more question. Have you seen an Asian man here tonight?"

Mike blinked. "Sure. Your brother-in-law. Uh, sorry, but I don't remember his name."

"You're sure he's the only Asian man you've seen?"

"Pretty sure. He's got a distinctive scent. No offense intended."

"None taken." Though she'd love to know what Paul smelled like to a lupus. She closed her pad. "Okay. That's it for now."

"Wait a minute. Aren't you going to—"

"I'm going to ask a lot of people questions. Shannon, escort Mike back. I want him to stay near Isen." That should reinforce the order not to talk. "Bring back . . . No, wait. I'm heading back there, too. Rule, I need you two-footed."

His hackles lifted. He shook his head.

"Don't pull that mantle crap on me." But dammit, he'd guessed what she meant. Or part of it. She went to one knee in front of him, putting them eye to eye, and gripped his ruff. "I know better," she said fiercely. "You can't think I suspect you, even for a second. But you can't help me question witnesses, either. Not when you're implicated. It would taint the investigation and I'd be pulled, and then I wouldn't be any help."

He shook his head again.

Damned stubborn wolf. "You need to go with Cullen, anyway." The sound of the copter was loud now. "Or not with him—the copter won't have room for you or Cynna. But you can drive her to whatever hospital they're taking him. She's going to need you, Rule."

He didn't shake his head this time, but he didn't Change, either.

"I'll get Isen to question wits with me. He's got most of the mantle, right? If you can scent a lie, so can he."

Rule made a huffing noise. It might have been a lupine laugh, or sheer disbelief.

"He'll do it," she told him. "I'll see to it. Now, get yourself two-footed so I can ask you a couple questions, and so you can drive at your best bat-out-of-hell speed to the hospital."

"A Rho does not act as Lu Nuncio." Isen's face, usually so mobile, was stone. "I do not interrogate my people."

The *whomp-whomp* of helicopter blades was distant once more. They'd loaded Cullen aboard—still breathing—and found room for Nettie. Cynna was heading with Rule to his car. Someone had loaned him a T-shirt to wear with his cutoffs.

"A Rho does what his people need him to do," Lily said, and bent to slip off her shoes. She'd check out the area where the perp must have stood to strike Cullen from behind.

It was much darker now, with only a thin scattering of mage lights overhead. Most of the cheery little balls had come from Cynna and Cullen. Still, a few remained. Lupi, with the exception of Cullen, didn't perform magic; they *were* magic. But their female children were sometimes Gifted, and a handful had learned the new spell that produced mage lights.

At Lily's request, most of those bobbing lights were concentrated where she stood now, facing Rule's father. She straightened with her shoes in one hand. "You won't question them. I will. You'll tell me if they're lying."

"You misunderstand. The clan is accustomed to their Rho acting as judge, not as a policeman. You might be asking the questions, but if I'm present, they'll believe they are being judged."

"I'd say that it's up to you to handle that."

"I am. I'll send Shannon to retrieve my Lu Nuncio—who knows better than to leave at this time."

"Fine. I won't be needing Rule, however, nor will he be allowed to question anyone on his own, since I'm being forced to hand this case over to the local cops."

"Almost," he said thoughtfully, "I could believe you are threatening me."

"I'm giving you facts. You want me to conduct the investigation. Rule can't participate in questioning witnesses when he's been implicated by one of the witnesses. If I let him do that, any information I get will be tainted, and I'll be pulled off the investigation."

"Your superior is Ruben Brooks. He has confidence in you, and he's shorthanded. Very few could take over the investigation."

"Which is why the case will land with the locals if I don't claim it. At this point, there's a vague suggestion that magic could be involved. There's no compelling evidence of it."

"Compelling." Isen repeated that one word, then said nothing more, his expression revealing little more than a certain intensity of interest.

Lily recognized the tactic, having used it often enough herself. If you leave a large, blank space in an interview or a negotiation, most people will rush to fill it. Especially if you watch them while you wait.

Lily watched him back.

Finally Isen's mouth crooked up. "Tried that on you once before and it didn't work. All right." He raised his voice slightly. "Benedict." He continued in his normal voice. "I'll sniff for you, but not in this form, so I won't be able to speak. I need to give Benedict some instructions first."

Benedict was at the other end of the field. Could he really pick out Isen's voice from so far away?

Apparently so. He started toward them at a trot. "When I look at you," Lily said, "one nod means the witness is telling the truth. Shake your head if they lie."

"They won't. Did you know those are the signals a Lu Nuncio gives?"

She hadn't, but it made sense. They were what Rule had suggested. "Do you act as judge when you're in wolf form?"

"Ah. Now you ask a better question. No, I do not."

In other words, his people weren't going to react as if he were judging them because he'd be in wolf form, so what he'd said earlier was misdirection. "Then what's your real objection?"

He sighed, a teacher unimpressed by his student's progress. "You should be able to figure that out by now."

She huffed out an impatient breath. "You're going to make me guess, aren't you? Fine. My first guess is that it's a status thing. You don't think a Rho should do the work of a Lu Nuncio."

"Not status."

"Authority, then. But you have the mantle. Nokolai lupi *know* you for their Rho in a way I can barely imagine."

"Ah, but Rule now has a Rho's mantle, too."

"Not the Nokolai mantle, and Rule would not dispute your authority over Nokolai. Not for a second."

He nodded. "True. But he and I do not convince Nokolai of that by announcing it. Our actions must make it clear to them. My assuming his responsibility will not reassure them."

"Why didn't you just say that?"

He smiled and patted her on the cheek. "Ask your grandmother."

THE mountains cradling Nokolai Clanhome were scarcely mountains at all compared to their larger brethren to the north or south, but they were every bit as rugged as those higher ranges. Dirt and rock crumpled by some giant's petulant fist was mounded in ridges, hills, crags, and gullies—a rough, broken land, hardened by heat and drought.

In spite of the dryness, there were trees—oak and sycamore, manzanita, juniper and pine. The ridge where a single man paced, however, was bare. Perhaps the top of this ridge was too often scoured by wind for seeds to linger and root. This, too, was Clanhome land, but another ridge lay between him and the lights of the interrupted party. That ridge was lost to sight now, invisible in the night.

It was quiet, but not silent; wind fingered the branches of trees and tickled weeds, raising vegetative whispers all up and down the slope. The man's athletic shoes kicked up little scuffs of dust.

He stopped, peering out at empty air. Riding the darkness was a new sound, the measured beat of wings shushing the wind. His eyes tracked that beat, but there was nothing to see—no blurring of the darkness, no occlusion of stars. Still he watched, his feet shifting restlessly. Eagerly.

Nothing landed on the ridge's crest—yet dust swirled as if thrown up by unseen wings. He rushed forward, exclaiming in Chinese, "Well? He's dead, yes? He must be!"

The air shivered. Where there had been nothing, there now stood a woman.

She was tall and thin and nude. Her skin was white—truly white, not some version of beige, however pale. White like the white of an eye. Even the fluffy cap on her head was white, but it was a cap of down, not hair. There was no matching fluff on her pubis, which was as bare as a child's.

She was no child, though. Her breasts were high and full, set on a prominent rib cage and tipped by nipples that looked pink only because they were set against such a purity of white. Her arms and legs were thin and oddly elongated, her torso brief in comparison.

Her face was beautiful. Asian in cast, perfectly symmetrical, vaguely childlike with the features set low beneath a high, curving forehead. Her eyes startled. They were black, as truly black as her skin was white.

"He lives."

Her voice was barely above a whisper, yet so clear and lovely the words seemed more a stroking of the air than sound shaped for speech. Those words had a profound effect on the man, who cried out. He threw himself in the dirt, prostrating himself at her feet. "I have failed you! Oh, my beauty, my love, punish me. Hurt me. He is a danger to you, and I failed."

She bent and stroked his back. "Ah, my little man, do not fret yourself. You did not fail. Your knife was true, and he may yet die. Yet these wolf demons have more magic than we knew."

Slowly the man rolled over and sat, then stood. He clutched her hand. "You are gracious to forgive, but I do not forgive myself. I will not fail again. The sorcerer will die, but I know what pain it is for you to delay your revenge when—"

She struck out casually. One hand smacked his cheek, sending him tumbling. Her voice was calm, her expression soft and fond. "You do not know. In another hundred years or two you may begin to understand, but not now. Such a thin word, *revenge*. A human word, as weak as human bodies. You do not know what I mean by revenge, no more than I understand your laughter when things break."

At that he giggled. "No, you do not understand humor. So wise in so much, but laughter wasn't given you, was it?" He stood again, brushing at his clothes. "Even if I do not understand fully, I know revenge is like blood for you. Necessary. The delay—"

"I do not delay."

"But the sorcerer—"

"May die, and if not . . ." She shrugged. "He will be occupied with his healing for some time. You will try again to kill him, but only when it is safe. You will not endanger yourself with haste."

"Ah, but thanks to you, I am very hard to kill or even to injure."

"It is not a chance I am willing to take. You say you worry for me. I think you do not like the competition."

He smiled, placating. "If I worry for myself, well, I am human. But that worry is a dash, a tiny pinch, compared to my feelings for you. If you will not countenance an immediate attack on the sorcerer, what of the sensitive? She is a lesser threat, but still—"

"You know my plans."

"But if you could alter some small part of them . . ." He came to her then and clasped one of her hands in both of his. "My beauty, my beloved, you will do as you must, but if you could hasten that one aspect of your revenge . . . ?"

She gave a little sigh, a very human-sounding sigh, and wrapped her long, thin arms around him. She was taller by several inches, so she rested her cheek on top of his head. He began stroking her back, and her eyes slitted, almost closing, like a cat's when it purrs.

"I worry," he murmured, his voice soft. "I worry for you."

"How can they harm me? You will kill the sorcerer when it is safe to do so, and I will consider some slight alteration in my plans, to please you. But nothing major, not unless you can give me some reason other than these vague fears. This is a rich place, so much to feed on, and the kine so unwary. I will eat my enemy's fear, and not rush my meal. And you, beloved . . ." She smiled down at him, both hands moving to cup his face. "You will have your city. Just as I promised."

EIGHT

BY the time the deputies arrived, Lily had checked out the trampled grass near the spot where Cullen had fallen. She'd also done preliminary interviews with seven witnesses and was about to start on number eight.

Working with Isen was different from working with Rule. Efficient as hell, but different. For one thing, Lily had never seen Isen in wolf form until today—an omission that surprised her once she noticed it. Was that a courtesy on his part, to always meet her in the form she best understood? Or did he just not Change all that often? If so, was that a matter of age or personal inclination, or connected to his position as Rho?

She banked those questions for now.

Isen made a gorgeous wolf. Smaller than Rule, though still larger than a normal wolf, and very strong through the chest and shoulders. His coat was a reddish brown, almost foxy, which struck her as appropriate. But he was very much a wolf.

When Rule was wolf, Lily was so conscious of who he was that what he was seemed secondary. With Isen, she was aware every second that a large, strong wolf stood beside her. She wasn't frightened. Just really aware.

The witnesses were uniformly courteous and responsive. And—as Isen had said they would—they told the truth.

The truth as they knew it.

Lily had two witnesses—Mike Hemmings and Sandra Metlock—who had seen Rule stab his best friend with a poisoned blade. She had a witness who'd seen Cynna do it. Three others had seen three different attackers—Mike Hemmings, Piers, and "some stranger. Never saw the guy before." And yet another wit was convinced the knife had been thrown because no one had been standing behind Cullen when he collapsed. He was sure of that.

No one had seen an Asian man anywhere near Cullen.

The knife itself was still missing.

The grass and ground where the perp must have stood gave off the kind of furry tingles she associated with lupi. Normally lupi didn't leave traces of magic on objects, not unless they Changed, but strong emotion sometimes made them leak a bit, maybe because they pushed the lupus toward Change. There was a very faint trace of the dancing tickle she associated with sorcery, but that wasn't surprising. Cullen was a sorcerer.

Shannon brought the next witness to her. This one didn't come solo, but hand in hand with another wit. Lily sighed. "Jason, I'll speak with you separately."

"I'd like him to stay with me," Beth said. Her chin had a defiant tilt.

"Sorry, that's not possible—not unless he has a law degree and you're wanting a lawyer present."

"Maybe I do want a lawyer."

Lily looked at her sister for a long moment, then gestured at Jason. "Go back and wait. Shannon, escort him, please."

Jason started to protest. The big, reddish wolf standing beside Lily gave him a single glance. He left, Shannon trailing him.

Lily moved close to Beth and spoke quietly, though Isen would hear every word anyway. "All right. What's going on?"

"I just . . . I don't want to say, that's all."

"Did you see what happened?"

Beth didn't answer out loud, but the wincing around her eyes said "yes" pretty clearly.

Lily took her arm, running her hand up and down in a light, soothing way. "Beth. You know you have to tell me."

Beth swallowed and looked away. "It was Freddie," she whispered. "I told you he was here. F-Freddie stabbed Cullen. I saw him. I know it doesn't make sense, because why . . . But he did."

"Never mind about that now. You're sure? Where were you standing?" Lily took Beth through the same questions she'd used with the other wits, getting her sister to place everyone she remembered in a diagram. "Okay. Okay, that's good. Listen, Beth." She gripped her sister's shoulder. "You've helped. You've helped a lot. Don't worry about Freddie. He wasn't here."

"But I saw—"

"I know, but trust me, okay?" She glanced at her watch. "Shit. I need to call Ruben."

Benedict came up. "You wanted to know when the sheriff's department showed up. They just passed the gate."

Thirty-eight minutes. Thirty-eight damned minutes it had taken them to respond to an attempted homicide. Never mind that their absence made things smoother for her. "Thanks. Ah—Isen, I'll need to talk to the deputies before I question anyone else, so if you want to . . ." She made the little circular motion she'd seen lupi use to refer to the Change.

He did. By the time she'd pulled her phone out of her bag, a two-legged and entirely naked Isen Turner stood beside her. He was less hairy in this form, but not by a lot.

Lily pretended she was fine with people standing around naked. She pressed seven on her speed dial.

Cynna picked up right away. "We're not there yet. We're about six blocks away."

"I hear a siren."

"We've got an escort. Police escort. I called Ida before we left Clanhome and she arranged it. They caught up with us on the highway and Rule wasn't crazy about it because he had to slow down some—either their cars aren't as fast as his or they just won't drive that fast—but it helped once we got off the highway."

"You're holding up. You're okay."

"He's not dead. I made Nettie promise to call if he—if he got worse. She hasn't called, so I know he's not dead." Lily heard Rule speaking in the background, then Cynna added with a thread of humor in her voice, "Rule says Cullen would almost have to try to die for him to kick off at this point."

If a lupus lived through the first thirty minutes after an injury, he usually made it—especially if he had Nettie watching over him. The problem was, Cullen's healing was being affected by an unknown poison. The thirty-minute deal might not apply.

Lily forced a smile so Cynna would hear it in her voice. "I'm not going to worry. Cullen's too ornery to die."

A single sheriff's car pulled into the parking area along the east side of the field. She told Cynna to hold on a sec, then asked Benedict to have one of his people bring the officers to her. Normally she'd have met them halfway—but not when it had taken them nearly forty minutes to show up. And they'd sent a single car?

She bit back her anger. For now. "Listen, the locals have finally arrived, so I don't have time to explain, but there's reason to suspect the perp is capable of changing his or her appearance radically. I know illusion isn't supposed to be possible—"

"Not in this century. Not unless we've got a killer elf hanging around. One with a grudge against Cullen—which, admittedly, is possible. The grudge part, I mean."

"I don't know what we've got. It isn't making sense yet. But for now, I want you to be paranoid. Stay with Cullen and . . . is there some way you can check out everyone who comes in contact with him? Use those spell patterns of yours somehow to make sure they're who they seem to be?"

Cynna was the best Finder in North America. Her Gift allowed her to track what she sought, but for most things she first had to create a pattern. She did that with a spell.

"Hmm. Maybe. It would help if I knew something about

the perp—his age, whether or not he's human. Something specific to check for."

"I don't have anything for you. I can't even say 'he' for certain. But . . ." Lily hesitated, then tossed the dice. "The perp may be an Asian male. Does that help?"

"Asian?" Cynna's surprise was supplanted by haste. "I didn't see—okay," she said, possibly to Rule. "Listen, we're there. I've got to go. I'll stick with Cullen—well, except for surgery. I don't think they'll let me in there. But I've got to go."

The line went dead. Lily put up her phone, frowning. Had she helped, or added a ridiculous complication?

Why had Cullen been attacked in the first place? He had enemies, sure. But why this enemy, at this time and place? Why come after him in the middle of a few hundred lupi?

The deputies were headed across the field toward her. She frowned. She needed to interview the people Rule said he'd been speaking with when Cynna cried out. She knew he was telling the truth, but she had to confirm it.

Not yet, though. She had to go be diplomatic with the uniformed assholes headed her way.

"Lily," Isen said.

"What?" she snapped.

"Don't bite the nice officers." Someone had brought him a pair of jeans, which he'd pulled on while she was talking to Cynna. He zipped them now. "We haven't encouraged the sheriff's department to come calling."

"You have some kind of understanding with them so they won't rush out to investigate?"

"Of course not." He was bland. "That would be wrong."

She snorted and returned her attention to the two men crossing the field.

She couldn't see faces. There wasn't enough light. But she could see that both deputies were male; one was white, the other black. Both looked fit. The white guy was tall, maybe six-two, and slim; the black guy was shorter and wider. Not fat, not a bit of it, but built husky, like a smaller version of Benedict. He moved like a big cat, smooth and effortless.

Lily's body caught on before her mind did. She was still

wondering why the black guy looked familiar when her breath hitched. A second later, she knew.

From ten feet away she could see that the taller deputy had sandy hair, a rookie's spit and polish, and the stiff expression of someone who hopes he looks tough. The other man had a wide nose, deep-set eyes, no hat, and hair buzzed close to the skull. He didn't have to try to look tough. He was the real deal . . . even if he did have a butterfly tattooed on his left cheek.

Not the cheek on his face. The one currently covered by his crisp khakis.

Lily waited until they stopped in front of her. She didn't bother wishing Isen away, but she did wish—fleetingly but fervently—that her sister wasn't here. "Hello, Cody. It's been a while."

NINE

HOSPITALS were tricky places for a lupus. The smells of blood and sickness are exciting to a wolf on a fundamental level; the injured and ill are the easiest kills. Not that Rule's wolf would wrench free to wreak havoc. His control was excellent, and besides, his wolf was no crazed adolescent, too easily excited to understand the risks or forget that humans are not prey.

But the scents kept Rule's wolf edgy in spite of three of the most god-awful tuna sandwiches he'd ever eaten. And the man . . . the man did not like waiting. It gave him too much time to think. To remember.

The first time Rule set foot in a hospital, he'd been only a little older than his son was now. Before First Change, a lupus was almost human. With his wolf still sleeping, the smells hadn't been as acute, or affected him the same way. He'd waited in a room much like this one, waited with his father and brother and a few other clan while Benedict's Chosen struggled for life.

She hadn't made it.

Some memories were better than that one, yet not restful.

He thought of a time he and Cullen had gone for a hunt, just the two of them, below the border, and had gotten into a bit of trouble. That memory made him smile, but pricked his heart. He thought of the time—much more recent—when Cullen had literally gone to hell for him. To hell and back . . .

He also remembered a time or two when Cullen, still a lone wolf, had damn near spun out of control—yet hadn't. He'd endured so much for so long, and now . . . now he had everything he'd ever wanted. A clan. A son on the way. A woman who loved him wholly . . . and wasn't that odd? Rule hadn't known Cullen wanted that. He didn't think Cullen had, either.

Rule glanced at the messy blond head of his friend's love, currently pillowed on his thigh.

The chairs made Cynna's back ache, so about thirty minutes ago they'd moved to the floor. This had garnered them a few odd looks from the room's other occupants, a small Pakistani family. Pregnancy exhausted the body; stress made it worse. Rule had encouraged her drowsiness with a back rub, and eventually she'd dozed off.

Problem was, with her asleep, he no longer had the distraction of focusing on someone else's needs. He was alone with his thoughts and memories.

He'd seen Cynna's head on his pillow a few times, many years ago. But it wasn't those moments he remembered now. It was the first time he saw Cynna, standing straight and strong and pissed when a man she'd been involved with at the time insulted her publicly.

Rule had taken pleasure in making it clear that a real man appreciated a strong woman. Later, he'd taken even more pleasure in tossing the man and two of his friends up against the side of a building when they decided to teach Cynna a lesson for "talking back."

He'd been attracted from the first, of course. She had a beautiful body, and she smelled good. But more, he'd just plain liked her. He still did. How strange that two of the people he cared for most had found each other.

Had *married* each other.

Rule's muscles tightened. His hands clenched. Cynna

stirred without quite waking. He swallowed and forced ease on a body that wanted to move—or to hit something. Someone.

Cullen's surgery had gone on so long. Too long.

Most lupi never went into surgery, which was problematic for them. Set a bone, sure. Cut into them with a knife? Not such a good idea. Anesthesia didn't work on lupi—and a conscious but badly wounded lupus might try to kill someone who cut him open.

Nokolai, however, had Nettie—shaman, doctor, healer. The combination of her healing Gift with her shamanic training let her put a lupus patient in sleep so they could be operated on. She'd done so to Rule twice—once after a spectacular motorcycle crash when he was young and foolish. Once when a demon gutted him during his sojourn in hell.

Neither of his surgeries had lasted much more than an hour.

Rule checked his watch. Four hours and twenty-one minutes. He and Cynna had been waiting almost four and a half bloody hours. What was taking so long?

Nettie's a fighter, he reminded himself. *She hasn't given up.*

Why did people think of medicine as a gentle profession, anyway? Doctors were vicious, bloody warriors, and their battleground was the patient's body. They brought terrible weapons onto that field. They cut people open and poisoned them.

Not that they called their drugs poisons, but what else were they? Mild poisons usually, poisons administered in small enough doses that the body could endure their assault while they killed bacteria or cancer cells or rendered the patient comatose so the surgeon could cut him open.

Drugs didn't work on lupi, but something had worked on Cullen, hadn't it? Whoever stabbed Cullen had known enough to find one of the few poisons that affected a lupus. Wolfsbane? Gado?

Whoever stabbed Cullen . . .

Deliberately, he turned his mind away from that thought. He couldn't afford to speculate, not if he was to stay in control throughout this bloody, bedamned, interminable wait.

Cynna made a small sound and jolted. Her eyes popped open.

He touched her shoulder. "Bad dreams?"

"Uh-huh." She sat up. "I keep seeing him fall. He just went down, you know? No warning. I wish I had your trick of know-ing. You and Lily always know that the other one's okay."

No, they didn't—but they knew the other one wasn't dead. That's what she meant, and right now Rule would define okay as "not dead," too. He studied Cynna's face. She talked strong—she *was* strong—but she had a bruised look around the eyes that worried him. He kneaded her shoulder lightly. "Maybe you should eat."

She gave him a wry glance. "Cullen's always trying to feed me, too. I promise you, it won't help right now."

"Hmm." Humans did benefit from regular meals, if not as dramatically as lupi, but Rule didn't argue. "I don't know if it will help you, but I remind myself frequently that we would have already heard if he'd died. The waiting is hard, but bad news would arrive quickly."

"True. And he's going to be okay. I know that in my gut. It's just that my head knows other stuff—like that it shouldn't take this long. I don't know a whole lot about healing, but I know it doesn't take this long, so whatever Nettie's doing isn't working right."

Hard to argue with her when she was right. He did his best. "Her healing may not be working normally against this poi-son, but he isn't dead, so it *is* working."

"Right." She gave a firm nod, grimaced, and said, "Give me a hand up, okay? I'm stiff."

He stood and helped her rise. He wasn't sure how much she really needed the help—her center of balance was disrupted, but she was extremely fit.

Once on her feet she ran both hands through her hair, glanced at the room's other occupants, and said quietly, "Guilt always makes the other feelings worse, doesn't it?"

Startled, he blurted, "You don't have anything to feel guilty about."

"Of course I do. I didn't say the guilt was accurate, just that I feel that way. This wouldn't have happened if we hadn't gotten married. My choices led to him being attacked. His choices, too," she added, "not to mention the bastard with the knife. But that doesn't eliminate my guilt-o-meter."

Now he truly didn't know what to say.

She nodded as if he'd spoken. "Yeah, I hate it, too, but who could attack him at Nokolai Clanhome except clan? And why would they? Cullen makes people mad all the time, but mad enough to stick a knife in him at his baby party . . ." She shook her head. "It's the marriage thing. It sent someone round the bend."

"We don't know that for fact, but if it was someone in Nokolai, my father will find him. He declared the attack an offense against the clan."

Her brow wrinkled. "He did? Oh, yeah, I sort of heard that, I just wasn't paying attention at the time. That's . . . shit, could that mean clan war? I mean, if it wasn't a Nokolai who did it."

He'd meant to reassure her. It sure as hell reassured *him*, since it meant his father hadn't been involved in the attack, however indirectly. "No. You're thinking of the clan wars of the 1600s." Cynna was learning clan history from the Rhej, he knew. "This isn't the same situation. Ah—put roughly, back then, several of the dominant clans were too even in power, which encouraged excesses. The only clan that is equal in power to Nokolai today is Leidolf." Several others were strong enough to be a problem if they acted together, but he decided not to go into that possibility.

"Obviously it wasn't anything Leidolf did officially, because you're their Rho. But is there any chance someone from that clan acted . . . you know, unsanctioned?"

"If they did . . ." One of the mantles in Rule's gut stirred, and a chill place opened inside him. His voice dropped. "If someone took that upon himself, Leidolf will deliver a full apology to Nokolai."

"You're worrying the Parwanis."

"The what?"

"Them." She waved at the other end of the room. The Pakistani family—matriarch, youngish couple, and toddler—were staring at him. The toddler giggled. The others, as Cynna said, did look anxious. "I'm not hungry," he growled, annoyed. "Do I look hungry?"

"You look pissed. You look like you meant you'd deliver a body, not an apology."

That was precisely what he meant, but in an effort to do better with the reassuring, he didn't say so. "In some ways it would be convenient if the attacker were an unsanctioned Leidolf assassin, but I can't imagine one penetrating Clanhome at such a time. Even if he got past Benedict's guards and no one recognized his face in that crowd, he would still smell of Leidolf."

She frowned. "Lily said something about it maybe being an Asian guy. I don't . . . What is it?"

He'd turned away from her to face the door. Footsteps in the hall . . . soft-soled footsteps like dozens of others that had passed, almost inaudible even to him with so many other noises masking them. He didn't know why these particular footsteps had brought him to alert, but—

A tall woman in green scrubs paused in the doorway. Smiling.

"He's good," Cynna said, bouncing on her toes. She took two quick steps toward Nettie, stopped, and grinned back at Rule. "Didn't I tell you? I told you he'd be okay. My gut knew it."

"You did." He came to her and put an arm around her, right where her waist used to be. "You're crying."

She dashed a hand across her face, her grin shining through the dampness. "Of course I'm crying. It makes sense to cry *now*. Can I go see him? Lily said I need to watch out for him. The perp could try again. I need to . . ."

She wobbled suddenly. Rule tightened his arm. "You need to sit."

"Weird. I'm not going to . . . I don't faint."

"Of course not, but you will sit down now." Rule half carried her to the nearest chair—which was a couple seats from a young teen, who'd been texting the whole time she'd been here. The girl looked up, amazed. Perhaps she'd just now noticed there were others in the room. He lowered Cynna carefully and knelt in front of her. "Head down."

"I don't faint," she repeated, but didn't resist when he gently pushed her head as far toward her knees as it would go with her expanded tummy in the way.

Nettie sat in the chair beside Cynna and rubbed her bent back.

"I'm fine," Cynna informed her feet.

"Of course you are," Nettie agreed, "but keep your head down a moment or two. It will make the rest of us feel better."

The barest intake of breath alerted Rule. Lily stood in the doorway with Jason directly behind her. She stared at Cynna, stricken.

TEN

"CULLEN'S okay," Rule said quickly, rising and going to her. "Cynna turned dizzy from relief, that's all."

"Okay." She nodded firmly. "That's okay, then."

He asked very low, "Did you find him?"

She shook her head.

"I didn't expect you to leave the scene this soon unless you'd identified the attacker."

"Turns out I know one of the deputies they sent. He's a good cop. He'll do the job."

He understood what she hadn't said: she'd wanted to be here, with him, in case the news was bad. Rule took her hand and squeezed, then glanced at Jason, lifting his eyebrows in question.

Lily answered the unspoken question. "Cullen will need a nurse. Ah, Rule, who gave you that T-shirt?"

"Modean Webster. She's a large woman, so she thought it would fit, which. . . . ah," he said, looking where she was. "I hadn't noticed that." The T-shirt read in small letters, "Well-behaved women rarely make history."

"It needs a postscript," he said. "Something like, 'I'm Rule Turner, and I approved this message.' "

That made her grin.

"Approved what?" Cynna said. "Oh, never mind. I'm fine, Nettie. Really." She stood to prove it. "See? No one listens to me, even though I was right. Wasn't I right, Rule? I said he'd be okay."

He turned, his smile coming easily now. "You were right. You get unlimited I-told-you-sos."

"Oh, you're gonna regret that." Cynna's grin spread. She stretched. "I'm glad that's over. When can I go see him?"

"Soon," Nettie said, standing. "But—"

Lily spoke. "One of us has to be with him. He needs to be guarded."

"Shit. Yes." Cynna frowned. "You said something about that earlier."

"Cynna." Nettie stood and took Cynna's hands. "You can go see him very soon, but I need to tell you something first. The surgery was a success, but Cullen's recovery may be . . . difficult."

Worry flashed through Cynna's eyes. "What do you mean?"

"I called it poison initially. It isn't. I could have eliminated a poison. I think it's a spell, but I can't identify it and wasn't able to rid him of it. This is difficult to put in words, but I more or less forced the intruding agent, whatever it is, to expend itself until it reached a level his healing can cope with. At this point, though, the intrusion is still there and active."

Cynna's throat worked as she swallowed. "But he's okay. He's going to be okay."

"He's okay now. Long term, of course, we want to find a way to get that intrusion out of him."

"I need to see him. I need to be there." She glanced at Lily. "I want to know what you've learned, too, but—"

"Later," Lily told her. "I'll fill you in later, when I relieve you."

"Relieve me? But you'll be . . . You've got to find him. Or her. Whoever did this. You can't just stand guard."

"Right now I don't have anyone else who's qualified to act

as guard. Ah . . ." She glanced at Nettie. "I've already contacted the hospital's administration. Cullen will receive no visitors, and regular hospital personnel will not be allowed in his room, except for you."

Nettie frowned. "Cullen needs ongoing care. Professional care. That's why we're in a hospital rather than at Clanhome."

"That's why I brought Jason. He's not on staff here, but he's qualified. We'll need more than one nurse, I suppose, but he can handle it for now."

A rare spark of temper lingered in Nettie's eyes. "I suppose that will work temporarily. Jason doesn't have his RN yet, but he's an experienced LVN. He can handle both nursing and orderly duties for now."

"Good. Where's Cullen? Cynna needs to be with him."

"He's in post-op. Visitors aren't allowed there. Have you made arrangements to change that as well?"

Nettie had spoken sarcastically. Lily answered straightforwardly. "Cynna's officially part of security, so yes, that's taken care of. Jason, you know where post-op is?" When he nodded she went on to Cynna. "Take Jason's and Nettie's patterns so you can confirm who they are. Mine, too, and Rule's, if you don't have them."

"I'll take Jason's, but I don't need to with the rest. When it's someone I know well I don't have to take a pattern."

"Good. Allow no one in the room with Cullen unless you can confirm who it is. Do you have your weapon?"

Cynna nodded grimly.

"Okay. Go. I'll join you as soon as possible."

Cynna and Jason left. Lily turned to Nettie. "I didn't want Cullen carried in the records under his name, so when you look for your patient, look for Adrian Fisher, a patient who's been here since Tuesday."

"You're thorough."

"And you're pissed. I've trespassed in your territory."

After a moment, Nettie sighed. "Never let it be said that lupi are the only territorial critters around. Yes, you have, and I reacted poorly."

Rule went to Nettie. Up close, she gave off the faint, acrid scent of exhaustion. He dropped a hand on the back of her neck, using his fingers to unknot some of the tension. "Maybe because you're exhausted, drained, and scared. Cullen's not in good shape, is he?"

Nettie leaned her head back, her eyes closing. "Do that for another hour or so. No, he isn't. He's been through open heart surgery, and that—that intrusion is still there, still affecting him. Not as strongly as it was, thank the Mother, or he'd be dead, but I have no idea what his prognosis is."

Lily spoke with quiet urgency. "Could this be like that demon poison that kept Rule's leg from healing? Is it like that?"

God, he hoped not. Rule kept rubbing Nettie's neck, but tension overtook his own muscles. His body hadn't been able to throw that off, and if such a poison was in Cullen's heart . . .

"I don't think so." Nettie frowned, opening her eyes. "I didn't examine Rule when he was infected with that, so I can't truly compare the two. That was localized at first, though, wasn't it? This is, too, but it isn't completely preventing healing." She hesitated. "It reminds me of a Vodun curse."

"How so?"

Nettie lifted a hand vaguely. "The feel of it. A Vodun curse uses something from the victim's body—nail clippings, hair, or blood—to focus an ill-wishing. This has the same feel. Not identical, but similar. The spell or intrusion has Cullen's body fighting his healing magic." She sighed. "I nearly killed him before I figured that out. I kept trying to heal his body, but giving his body energy fed the ill magic, too. I had to switch to feeding his natural magic."

Rule squeezed Nettie's nape gently. "You've emptied yourself. You need rest."

"I won't argue with that. I plan to kick one of the residents out of the bunk they use."

"Do you want to use my apartment instead? Or a hotel? There's a Sheraton nearby."

She shook her head. "I can't be that far from him. At the moment, Cullen's magic is winning the fight, but the balance is . . . iffy. "

"Before you go," Lily said, "could you take a minute to describe the wound? I need to know what the dimensions of the blade were, where it entered, the angle."

"Thin blade," Nettie said promptly. "Maybe half an inch wide and extremely thin. It was inserted between the fifth and sixth ribs and angled up to enter the left ventricle—"

"Wait, wait. Show me." Lily grabbed Rule and turned him so his back was to Nettie. "Show me where it went in, what kind of angle we're talking about."

His eyebrows rose, but he complied. With his back to the women, he had a good view of the Parwanis, who watched in silent alarm as Nettie probed his back slightly to the left of his spine.

"Here," she said. "The blade entered between these ribs. The angle was about like this."

He looked over his shoulder to see her miming a thrust.

"That looked awkward," Lily said. "Maybe our perp was shorter than you are, relative to Rule." She moved directly behind Rule and made the same thrusting motion with her fist. "Not this much shorter, though. I can't get the right angle. Rule, crouch down a bit."

Obediently he bent his knees. The Parwanis were perturbed. The young husband said something to the matriarch. Rule heard it, but couldn't translate—Urdu wasn't one of his languages. "I can tell you that the attacker was shorter than Cullen," he said. "Nettie, are you sure the blade was only a half inch wide?"

"It might be less. It's not more."

Lily said, "Nettie, see if you can achieve the same angle and entry point."

Again Nettie mimed a blow to his back.

"Still doesn't look smooth," Lily observed. "Crouch a bit more, Rule, and let's try it again."

He did. Nettie tapped his back again.

"That looks right," Lily said.

The Parwanis had had enough. The matriarch issued instructions, and the lot of them gathered their things and scurried from the room.

"What's wrong with them?" Lily asked.

"I believe they misunderstood." He wondered if they would summon security. "Lily, an assassin who's as tall or taller than his target would have used a different strike, coming down from about here . . ." He used Nettie to demonstrate. "He'd drive into the heart from above in an attempt to sever the artery as well as pierce the heart. It's a quick kill."

"Hmm." Lily tapped her fingers on her thigh. "Nettie, you're five-eight or -nine?"

"Five-nine in my stocking feet."

"So you're five inches under Rule, who's two inches taller than Cullen." Lily nodded. "A six-inch difference between attacker and target would make the perp five-seven. I'm guessing the difference was a bit more than that."

"I may not have indicated the angle perfectly," Nettie cautioned.

"Still, we've got a range. Call it five-two to five-eight. That helps. That fits. When will Cullen be awake?"

"Soon, probably, though I won't leave him awake long. You want to talk to him."

"If I can. It's important. I need to touch him, too."

Nettie's smile was wry. "*Now* you're asking permission? Oh, never mind. I'll get over it. Before I can sleep, I need to check on him again. I'll do that now—assuming Cynna lets me in the room—and call you once I see how he's doing."

"Okay. Thanks."

Rule spoke. "Should I be there when he wakes?"

"It would be easier on me if you were. I'll call." With that, Nettie left.

They were alone in the room. Questions pushed at him, but before he could settle on one Lily voiced her own. "Why did Nettie want you there when Cullen wakes up?"

"He may be agitated. She can calm him, but she's drained. I'm his Lu Nuncio. Even if he's confused, if I tell him he's not in danger and to be still, he'll accept that. Lily, I don't understand how you're handling security. I assume my father cleared Jason of any complicity, but there must be others who've been cleared as well who could act as guards."

Lily looked at him strangely. "Neither Jason nor any of the

others would be able to tell if someone isn't what he or she appears to be."

"Scent," he said impatiently. "Regardless of how he's disguised his appearance, a lupus can't change his scent."

"Two problems with that. First, you're assuming the perp is a lupus. Second—"

"It happened on Clanhome." The pain and offense of that nearly closed Rule's throat. "It happened there, surrounded by Nokolai. No human could have gone unnoticed. No human would have tried."

"Ah, Rule." She ran her hands down his arms to his hands, clasping them. "You think it was one of yours. One of Nokolai. When I arrived, you were afraid I'd tell you I'd arrested one of your clan."

"It wasn't arrest I feared."

"If you thought I'd let your father commit murder—"

"Lily." He squeezed her hands. "Isen can pull any of the clan into Change, if he wishes." And killing a lupus who was in wolf-form wasn't murder in the eyes of the law.

"Is that why you left? Why you didn't argue," she corrected herself, "when I told you to go? You expected your father to find the perp, make him Change, then kill him."

"It's unlikely he would do it himself—but no, that isn't exactly the reason. I left so *I* wouldn't kill him." Not without his father's orders, at least, and he hadn't been sure he could wait on another's word. Not even his Rho's.

"I did consider the possibility the perp was Nokolai, but it's unlikely."

"If you're thinking about what Nettie calls an intrusion, that makes it less likely. But not impossible. Someone could have acquired a spelled blade."

She nodded. "Benedict, for example. If anyone from Nokolai other than Cullen would know how to get something like that, he would. But he wouldn't be able to magically alter his appearance. He isn't between five-two and five-eight. Besides, he wouldn't act without your father's approval, and Isen is royally pissed."

"Which lets Benedict off the hook. But there are short Nokolai."

"Who use magic? I suppose it's possible Cullen isn't the only one, but how likely is it you wouldn't know about him? Besides, I think I saw the perp."

He went still.

"I saw an Asian man at the party who no one else seems to have seen. That makes me think he had some kind of magic deal going to confuse his appearance—which, of course, didn't work on me. Somehow I don't think there were two people at Clanhome who didn't belong but were magically disguised, so the Asian guy's probably the perp."

"You think he magically disguised himself as me?"

"Not exactly. Two witnesses saw you strike Cullen, but the rest saw someone else—several someone elses—except for one person who swears Cullen fell down all on his own. The perp seems to be able to baffle the senses, and I do mean *senses*, plural. Most of my wits are lupi. They didn't just see different attackers. They each smelled someone different."

That was emphatically not a lupus ability. It wasn't a known ability of anyone or anything else, either. "You must have checked for magic in the area."

"Found plenty, but it was all lupus magic except for a smidge that was probably from Cullen. This may mean we've got a human perp with a Gift we've never seen before, some kind of illusion Gift. Or it may mean we've got another Cullen. That's where my money's going at the moment, because it supplies motive."

"What do you mean, another Cullen?"

"A sorcerer. One who wanted the competition out of the way, maybe." Her phone buzzed. She took it out of her purse. "Yes?"

Rule listened with half an ear while Lily spoke with Nettie. Mostly he absorbed what she'd told him. She was convinced Cullen's attacker wasn't lupus. Not Nokolai, then, and that was a huge relief. Too, the apparent use of magic made this very much her case, which would help.

He should have felt better, but . . . if the killer wasn't lupus, what was he?

Someone who could fool the eyes and noses of a few hundred lupi. Someone who could fashion a killing spell and deliver it on the point of a knife while surrounded by witnesses. Someone who far outstripped any of the practitioners Rule knew, including Cullen.

Rule scrubbed both hands over his face, trying to force himself to be alert, to think. He didn't like where his thoughts were headed.

Lily disconnected. "Nettie wants us to head for—"

"I heard." He took her hand and started for the doorway. "Do you know where Cullen's room is?"

"Fourth floor. Rule, I need my arm free. I don't expect I'll need to draw on anyone here, but I need my arm free."

"Of course." He dropped her hand. Usually he was careful not to take her gun hand in public. He was distracted. It wasn't safe to be this distracted.

Lily moved quickly toward the red EXIT sign at the end of the hall—to the stairs, in other words, not the elevator. Rule decided to allow that. Normally he'd force himself into the damned tiny box so as not to feed his fear by conceding it a victory.

Just for tonight, he decided, he could cut himself this much slack: no elevators.

He moved slightly ahead so he reached the door to the stairwell first and paused briefly, listening. Smelling. No one on the other side. He opened it. "Can we know for certain that this hypothetical illusionist or sorcerer can't confuse Cynna's patterns?"

"I don't know anything for certain." Clearly that frustrated her. "It seems like he's using some kind of mind-magic—he's getting people to see and smell someone else, but they aren't all seeing the same someone. Who knows whether he could fool Cynna into thinking her pattern checked out? That's why I stopped at Grandmother's on the way here."

Relief bloomed. Of course. It might seem odd to enlist a tiny old woman as bodyguard, but Lily's grandmother was . . . Well, he wasn't sure the language held a word for her, but Madame Li Lei Yu had formidable defenses against magic. Formidable defenses, period. And she was fond of Cullen. She'd agree. "When is she coming?"

"One problem," Lily said.

Rule's eyebrows flew up in surprise. "She won't do it?"

"She isn't there. Neither is Li Qin."

ELEVEN

THE stairwell was well lit, utilitarian, and not entirely deserted. Lily heard feet moving somewhere above.

So it made her a little twitchy when Rule stopped her, turning her to face him so he could press a kiss on her forehead. "You're worried about your grandmother."

"No. Yes. Yes, I guess I am, though it seems pointless. I mean, we're talking about Grandmother. She left a note," Lily added abruptly. "Not Grandmother. Li Qin. It was taped to the wall facing the front door."

"I didn't realize you had a key to their house."

"Grandmother gave it to me years ago. I've never used it." She'd hesitated a long time before using it tonight, but finally decided she had to be sure no one was lying in a pool of blood. "The note was addressed to me. It said she and Grandmother had to be gone for a while, and that it would be foolish to tell me not to worry because words don't amend the anxiety caused by mystery, but they were both well and would return when they could."

Rule frowned. "When they could?"

"Yeah." And that was a big part of Lily's worry. Grandmother was not given to taking off this way. The only other time she'd done it, there'd been a nutty telepath, a hellgate, and a couple of Old Ones involved. But she hadn't taken Li Qin with her that time. "Grandmother's old Buick is gone, too," she added.

"She needed Li Qin to drive her, then."

Lily nodded. Grandmother either couldn't drive or refused to—Lily had never been sure which. "I'm pretty sure Grandmother wouldn't take Li Qin into a dangerous situation, so whatever she's up to, it probably isn't too dire."

The footsteps above them ended with the sound of a door opening and closing. Lily still felt twitchy. She started up the stairs. "I couldn't tell how much stuff they'd packed, but they definitely took some clothes. That suggests they don't expect to be back right away."

Rule kept pace beside her. "I know Madame Yu speaks English, but does she write it as well?"

"Sure. She claims to prefer *hanzi*, but she claims to prefer everything Chinese when she's in a mood. Why?"

"I wondered why Li Qin left the note rather than your grandmother."

"Good question. Grandmother may not even know she did it." Lily considered that a moment. "Li Qin wouldn't give anything away if Grandmother wanted secrecy, but she wouldn't make things up."

"You're sure it's Li Qin's handwriting."

"Unless someone's an expert forger. No one writes like Li Qin. Pure copperplate. Besides, it sounds like her. The note opened with her hope that I was well and her regret that their sudden absence might distress me." Lily frowned. "Though maybe Grandmother's decision to disappear wasn't as sudden as it seems. Beth said Grandmother has been acting funny lately. She wanted me to go see her, find out what was wrong."

"Ah, I see why you're upset. If only you'd gone to see her last week. No doubt she would have unburdened herself to you instead of indulging in all this secrecy."

She had to smile. "If you mean that she wouldn't have told me anything, you're probably right, but—"

"Probably?"

"Okay, okay, you're right. If she'd wanted me to know what was going on, she would have told me." And no one and nothing could force, persuade, trick, or cajole Grandmother into revealing one iota more than she wanted to. "But I should have noticed something was up. Beth did."

"So the problem is that you aren't your sister."

Lily grimaced. "I can be illogical if I want."

"You know, if you feel it necessary, you can always ask Cynna to Find Madame Yu."

"I guess I could." That made her feel slightly better, though she didn't want to do it. Not with what Cynna had on her plate already. "What do you think? Grandmother takes off on some secret business. A few hours later, Cullen gets attacked by a mysterious assassin who's able to do impossible things, magically speaking. Those events don't seem connected by anything but the timing, and yet . . . Am I trying to tie them together just because I know both people?"

"If so," he said grimly, "I'm making the same connection, and not liking it."

They'd reached the fourth floor. She hesitated, then faced Rule without opening the door. "You're afraid *she's* involved somehow. The one we don't name."

"Aren't you?"

Yeah. She was. "I don't want to blame everything I don't understand on *her*. That's not helpful. But . . . well, we'll talk about it, but not in the stairwell. Maybe Cullen will be able to fill in some blanks—such as why someone wanted him dead so badly they tried for him in such a freaky public way."

CULLEN'S room was interior, so no windows, which Lily liked. Admittedly, they were on the fourth floor and the killer was unlikely to do a Spider-Man up the outside wall, but this killer did unlikely things. Windows meant vulnerability.

One other thing she liked about it: it was in infectious diseases, not cardiology or critical care or any of the obvious places. According to the hospital records, "Adrian Fisher" suffered from a rare tropical disease and had enough money to pay for private nursing in his quarantine room. For now, making Cullen hard to find was their best defense.

Lily considered that a temporary ploy, though. They should be okay tonight and probably tomorrow. After that, she'd better come up with a way to guard Cullen against someone who might be able to look like anyone.

Or no one. That's what one of the witnesses had seen. No one at all.

Lily knocked on the door of number 418, then pushed it open. And was pleased to see Jason standing at the ready a few feet away—and Cynna standing by Cullen's bed, weapon drawn, her other hand outflung.

"Okay," Cynna said after a second. "You're you." She put her weapon on the table by the bed. "I've figured out what to do to check people out," she added. "If it's anyone but you two, I'll check for magic. That's quick and easy, and whoever is hiding behind other faces is using magic to do it. He won't be able to hide that."

"That's good." Lily's eyebrows shot up. "That's very good. I should have thought of that."

"You've been busy. I've been waiting. It gave me time to think. I'm going to set a ward on the door, too—a visual one. That way, if I get drowsy, Jason will be able to tell that someone with magic is trying to come in. He can stop them."

"Can you hold a ward when you aren't here? I'll be relieving you, so—"

"No, you'll be going home to get some sleep once you've talked to Cullen. I'm not going anywhere tonight, and there's no point in both of us standing guard. And you're the investigator. I want you focused and rested so you can catch the rat bastard."

Lily's eyebrows went up. After a moment she nodded. Tonight was probably the safest period, anyway. "Okay. I will relieve you in the morning, though, at least until we can figure out how to properly guard Cullen."

"I've a suggestion about that," Rule said, moving ahead of Lily so he could hug Cynna lightly.

He did that sort of thing easily, naturally. Lily wished it had occurred to her to hug Cynna. "Go ahead."

"Max."

Relief bloomed. "Of course. He claims he's immune to mind-magic, so . . . you'll call him?" Max was surly, lecherous, and train-wreck ugly, though the last was probably because his standard of beauty was wildly different from hers, since he was a gnome. A rather oversize one who for some reason didn't live underground like his fellows—gnomes were said to be very clever with stone—but a gnome nonetheless.

"He'll come. He'll bitch about it endlessly, but he'll come." Rule smiled at Cynna, his arm around her vanished waist. "You're doing okay."

"Sure." She glanced at the bed and its sleeping occupant. "Sleeping Beauty doesn't look so hot right now, but Nettie says he's hanging in there."

Nettie was on the other side of the hospital bed. She'd barely glanced up when they came in. "He'll wake in less than ten minutes. When he does, you can talk to him briefly, then I'll put him under again."

Lily nodded and moved to the foot of the bed.

The man occupying that bed was hooked up to an IV and a heart rate monitor, which beeped quietly. He was deeply asleep or unconscious. And much too pale.

Cullen Seabourne was the opposite of Max—as breathtakingly gorgeous as the gnome was ugly. Rule was sexier, in Lily's opinion, and possessed more sheer presence. But Cullen was the kind of gorgeous that makes strangers on the street stop and stare. At the moment, the perfect architecture of Cullen's bone structure was all too clear. He was pallid, the skin drawn and tight, and naked at least to the waist. A lightweight blanket covered him from there down.

His chest was a ghastly orange-yellow where they'd splashed it with Betadine. The incision to the left of his sternum had been left unbandaged. It was long and punctuated by staples. It looked fresh. She glanced at Nettie. "He hasn't healed the incision."

"The intrusion is localized around his heart, but it's like wolfsbane in one way. It keeps his healing magic tied up fighting it. I can help some with the incision after I've rested." Nettie's voice was lower and hoarser than normal. She needed sleep almost as much as her patient did.

Lily nodded and made a decision. "Cynna, I should talk to the Rhej about this, but you're here, so . . . Rule and I were wondering if the one we don't name could be involved." The Old One who was the lupi's most ancient enemy had a name, or maybe several . . . but lupi folklore said *she* could hear it when *her* name was spoken.

"Oh. Oh!" Cynna frowned, then shook her head. "I see why you're wondering. We've got an assassin with weird-ass abilities. But whoever he is, he's not *her* agent. It's possible *she* gave him some help in a roundabout way. We don't know how much she's able to do along those lines, but it's safe to assume she does have some agents here on Earth again. But the rat bastard assassin wasn't one of them. An agent of hers couldn't get into Clanhome secretly. The Rhej would know if one tried." She considered a moment, then added, "The Rho would, too, but he might not recognize what was wrong."

Rule's eyebrows lifted. "I wasn't aware of that."

"Sure," Cynna said. "Clanhome is claimed by the mantle holder, so the mantle knows it. The mantle is from the Lady, and the Lady recognizes her enemy. So the mantle would be aware if one of *her* agents was in Clanhome. I don't know how that would feel to Isen, but he would feel something. You might, too."

This time Lily's eyebrows lifted. "You know a lot about mantles all of a sudden."

She shrugged. "It's stuff from the memories."

The memories were literally that: incredibly vivid memories of various long-dead Nokolai that had been passed down from Rhej to apprentice for thousands of years. Since many of the memories involved battle and other calamities, there was a lot of pain and fear involved. A lot of stress for a pregnant lady, in other words. "I don't get why the Rhej changed her mind. She was going to wait on that part of your training until you had the baby."

"There was a reason not to wait any longer."

"You're sounding like a Rhej now. Cryptic."

Cynna offered a vague, apologetic smile and an equally vague gesture. "I'm not supposed to talk about some stuff."

Great. Lily dragged herself back on topic. "When you say 'agent,' you mean something specific, but I'm not sure what."

"Someone touched by the enemy. Someone using an object or spell touched or created by her. Uh . . . by touch, I don't mean physically, but contacted or acted upon."

"So if *she's* involved, it's indirectly."

"Real indirectly. Someone like the Great Bitch leaves traces. Take the incognito spell the assassin seems to have used—it couldn't have come from *her*. Even if it passed through others before the assassin got it, it would retain something of her energy. The Rhej and the Rho would have reacted to those traces because the Lady would feel them."

Lily cocked her head. Cynna was sure sounding cozy with the lupi's Lady. "Are you—"

"He's waking," Nettie said crisply. "Rule—?"

Quickly Rule moved beside Nettie and placed one hand on Cullen's upper shoulder. Nothing happened. Cullen looked as deeply asleep as before—right up until the second his eyes flew open, bright and burning blue.

"Be still," Rule said firmly. "You're safe. Cynna's safe. She's fine. The baby's fine. You've been hurt."

Cullen blinked. "No shit," he said, his voice faint. "Cynna . . ."

She'd taken Cullen's right hand. "Right here, not a mark on me," she announced cheerfully. Lily could see the strain in her eyes, but it didn't show in her voice. "And the little rider seems to like staying up late. He's frisking around like crazy."

Cullen's smile was small, but the relief behind it looked large.

"Cullen," Nettie said, "I know you're in a great deal of pain, but I need to know if your wound feels odd in any way."

Even his scowl looked weak. "Feels like I've been stabbed, stomped on, and cut open."

"Accurate," Rule said, "except for the stomping." He swallowed. "Cullen. I didn't like thinking you were dead."

The scowl eased to a thoughtful frown. "I came close?"

"You did. There was a magical component of some sort on the blade. It would have killed you if Nettie hadn't been close, and if the Rhej hadn't been able to channel power to Nettie. It's still interfering with your healing. That's why Nettie asked how your wound felt."

"Shit." He paused and lifted his head slightly. "Ow. Shit." His head fell back. "Can't see."

Lily knew why he'd been trying to see the wound. She felt magic. He saw it. That, according to him, was what made someone a sorcerer—the ability to see the energies he worked with. "Are you up to answering a few questions?"

"Gods. You here, too?"

She had to smile. That was such a Cullen thing to say. "Do you have any idea who stabbed you, or why?"

"No. Cynna, lift my head up. Can't see my chest."

Nettie shook her head. "Cullen, you've had your ribs cracked open and your heart stitched up. You aren't healing at your normal rate. You'll stay still and prone, and in a few minutes I'll put you back in sleep."

"Need to look," he insisted. "Find out what's wrong."

"Let me see what I can learn." Lily glanced at Nettie. "If that's okay?"

She nodded. "But we're not moving him one jot more than we have to, so no turning him to check the entrance wound. Scrub first. We don't know what's going on, and I don't want to take any chances."

Lily's eyebrows rose. Normally lupi didn't worry about infection, but with something messing with Cullen's healing . . . better safe than sorry, she supposed. She went to the small sink in the corner and squirted stuff on her hands. "Cullen, who was close to you when it happened?"

"Cynna. Mike. I was talking to him. Uh . . . Sandra, I think. Gods. Hurts like hell."

Nettie's voice was soft now. "I can put you back in sleep."

"No." He was quiet a moment. "Behind me . . . I heard Phil behind me. Uh . . ." His voice sank so much Lily couldn't hear the rest, not over the sound of the tap. She looked at Rule.

"He said that your sister was near, and Jason, and Teresa. I believe he means Teresa Blankenship."

"Okay. Didn't have her on my witness list, so that's something." Lily rinsed and used her elbow to shut off the tap. Jason handed her a towel. She dried her hands and moved up beside Cynna. "What about Rule? Was he near?"

"No."

"Did you smell anyone or anything that didn't belong?"

"No." His voice was blurry.

"An Asian man, maybe? One who didn't look like my brother-in-law."

"Don't know your damned brother-in-law. Can't . . ." He frowned, his eyes closing. "Can't remember anyone like that."

"That's okay. Did you see anything funny with your other vision?"

"Nothing funny. Some sorcéri."

"Okay. I'm going to touch your shoulder first, then your incision. Lightly. I'll do my best not to hurt you."

He grunted.

She took that as permission and laid her hand on his shoulder. The skin was warm, but she barely noticed.

Cullen's magic didn't feel like anyone else's. There was what she called fur-and-fir magic—the lupus magic that felt like fur yet reminded her subtly of evergreens. But mixed with it was a dancing tickle of heat. The heat meant a Fire Gift. The dance, though, that was how she read the sorcerous part of his power. As motion.

She drew her hand toward his chest.

There. Weird. She felt a little bump or ridge. On one side of the ridge, everything felt normal—fur and tickly heat. On the other, warm skin with just the faintest overlay of magic . . . and something else. Something smooth.

She tried coming toward the incision from another angle. Another. Soon she'd mapped out the edges of . . . whatever it was. And whatever it was, it was remarkably uniform.

Lily straightened. "There's an area five inches in diameter where your magic is thin, as if it's only skin-deep. I can feel the . . . Call it a barrier. It feels smooth, uniform. Shaped. I can't tell what kind of magic is involved, not with your skin between it and my hand."

"Need to look." Cullen spoke more strongly, but his eyes didn't open.

"We should let him," Cynna said. "He needs to know. It might help."

Nettie hesitated, then said, "All right. You can hold his head up."

Cynna slid her hand beneath his head and lifted. His eyes never opened. Lily knew he didn't need them to, not for his other vision. He'd still "seen" that way after his eyes had been gouged out.

But it looked pretty odd, the way he studied his chest with his eyes closed. Finally he spoke. "Hell." He took a careful breath, winced. "Nettie . . ."

"I'm here." She took his hand. "You're going back in sleep now."

"Yeah. Lily."

"Yes?"

"You're right. Shaped. It's shaped. Someone stuck a god-damned spell in my heart along with their knife." He took a slow, careful breath. "I can tell you one thing about it. It's blood magic. And the sorry bastard's using *my* blood to power it."

TWELVE

~

The city of Luan; Shanxi Province, China;
sixteenth day of the eleventh month of the
forty-fourth year of the Ching Dynasty

THE winter wind was like death—importunate and intrusive,
poking its cold, bony fingers through Li Lei's layered rags to
find flesh. She did not disdain the contact. She disliked being
cold, but death was a powerful acquaintance.

She could have been warm. Had she been in the midst of a
blizzard rather than squatting on the cold cobbles of the street,
Li Lei could have been warm. That was one of the more useful
tricks she'd learned from the one she called Sam in the past
year and seven months—how to craft a second skin out of will
and magic, one that warmed her precisely as she wished.

She didn't dare. Not in Luan. Sam had told her to assume
the sorcerer could track any use of power in his city. They did
not know that he could do this, or that he did so constantly, but
the caution made sense. In the eight days since her return to
Luan, Li Lei had confirmed that those who had actively practiced magic had been among the first to die.

Many others had died since. Some were killed outright
when they opposed the sorcerer. Some were killed more cru-
elly as they—or those they loved and trusted—fell through the
open door of madness.

A door opened by a demon. The sorcerer's lover. The Chimei.

Li Lei stared at the silent house in front of her. Had it been her father who went mad first and killed the rest, slicing or bludgeoning those he loved more than life? Had it been his wife, Li Lei's pretty, ambitious, and stupid stepmother, who'd first fallen through the cracks the Chimei opened in her mind? Or had it been one of the children who caught the nightmare and somehow infected the rest?

She had heard various tales. She could not, of course, ask directly, but she'd managed to steer the talk in the marketplace now and then to the story of the deaths in Wu An's house. The gossips had only a mishmash of tales, unhelpful save for the way they kept the wound open. No one knew. No one save, perhaps, the Chimei, who had caused it all.

The Chimei, who could not be killed.

Li Lei watched the house where everyone who mattered had died. And waited.

It was a finely crafted structure with beautiful carving on the lintels, built from the best materials, but it was not pretentious. The doors were red lacquer, centered amid the four columns upholding the roof, yet that roof possessed but a single tier. Li Lei's father had scoffed at merchants who aped the nobility. Wu An had been a commoner, only a few generations removed from pure peasant, and proud of it. How did you honor your ancestors, he said, by pretending to be other than they had been?

Used to say, Li Lei corrected herself. He said nothing now. Nothing she could hear, at any rate.

She did hear the giggles and stumbling feet approaching. Before their owners rounded the corner she reached for a small stick she'd selected earlier. She didn't look up. Her ears told her enough—a small group of young men, drunk enough to be foolish.

Few other than the drunk, the mad, or the desperate were out at night in Luan these days. Li Lei began drawing in the dust that covered the cobbles with her stick, pausing to grunt like a satisfied sow and move a few pebbles around, then "writing" with the stick once more.

One of the drunks called out, "Hey, you! What's your stinking carcass doing here, eh?"

"Leave him," another voice muttered. "Leave him 'lone, Zhi."

"Gonna get him outa here. Don't need stinking beggars hanging around—"

"He's no beggar." This voice was hard, the words less slurred than the others' had been. "He's one of the eaten, you fool."

"Still stinks." That young man was sullen now. He'd moved close enough that Li Lei saw his feet out of the corner of her eye. "Don't need this smell on my street."

Li Lei continued her meaningless writing as if she had no idea the others were there, but she wanted to look up, to see who claimed this street. She didn't know the voice, but that meant little. For all her father's leniency when they were in the country, in the city he'd followed custom. She'd seen her male neighbors from time to time; she had never spoken with them.

Her focus didn't let her avoid the kick he aimed at her side, but it allowed her to roll with it—roll like a log oddly determined to stand upright, for she ended up on her feet, staring blankly at the air directly in front of her. *Not* seeing the three young men so close.

She began writing in the air with her stick.

"Come on, Zhi," the tallest young man said to his friend, taking his arm. "Leave the poor bastard alone. You need more wine, eh?"

"Not enough wine in the whole cursed city," said the third one—the one whose speech wasn't slurred. "Not enough." But he, too, allowed himself to be chivvied onward.

Li Lei continued painting the air as they left, but her heart was pounding. She'd recognized Zhi. He was the youngest son of the merchant Jiao, who trafficked in salt and spices. Her father had invested with Jiao sometimes. She wondered if he was still alive. And his wife, the sharp-tongued Yi Mé—had she survived?

Most had, actually. Death and madness might stalk the city, but the sorcerer was canny enough to leave most of the population alive. He needed the people of Luan to continue in their usual paths, or what was his power for?

His lover needed them for other reasons.

Li Lei sank down onto the street once more, sitting cross-legged. *Thank you*, Li Lei told her father silently, wiggling her toes. Had it not been for his disdain for commoners who aped the nobility, she might be teetering around now on tiny lumps of flesh, their bones liquefied after years of binding. No one would mistake her for a youth then, no matter how clever her disguise.

Or perhaps not. Her mother had not believed in foot binding, and her mother had been . . . fierce, she thought with a smile, for that loss had faded enough for smiles. Qian Ya Bai had been fierce indeed.

Of course, she added with fair-minded practicality, had her feet been bound, she would not have been able to run off in the first place. Perhaps her father had regretted his decision to leave her feet whole. She'd hurt him, she knew. Surely he had understood why she left . . . She had told herself he would, once he traveled past his anger. Understanding did not always wipe away pain, but it helped, surely?

Her own hurt had been keen when he remarried so swiftly after her mother's death, but she had grown into understanding. He had needed a wife, and grief had led him to choose one very different from the fierce and beautiful Ya Bai. In time, Li Lei had understood that, and if understanding did not eliminate troubles, it eased the sense of betrayal.

Li Lei had never grown close to her stepmother, but she had adored the babies—Ji Wun, the boy whose arrival thrilled her father so, and the girls, little An Wei and An Mei . . .

Pain struck like talons ripping her gut. She folded over that grief, bending up like an old man passing a stone. But this stone wouldn't pass. She rocked herself as she could not rock An Wei, who had been only a baby when Li Lei left. *Ai*, little An Wei, who had always laughed for her big sister, reaching up pudgy arms . . . Ji Wun, who had strutted around so imperiously in his new finery on his birthday . . . An Mei, whose shy smile had surely charmed the flowers into early bloom. Each so different from Li Lei, and so precious . . .

Time passed. She did not know how much. Eventually she was able to straighten and resume her wait.

She owed them this much. It wasn't her gift, the ability to speak with the dead. But if any of those dear ghosts lingered—if they could reach her and wished to scream their anger or cry or simply be close—why, she could give them this.

Such an easy gift, when she herself wanted it so much! Wanted it in spite of her fears. She couldn't help but wonder if her father blamed her for what had befallen his family . . . but she did not think he would. Surely madness didn't accompany the dead into their land, and in life Wu An had never been one to make a sauce of blame to serve others while leaving his own plate unsauced.

But she had thought so herself, when she first heard. When Sam told her what had befallen Luan, and that her family was dead, she had feared the sorcerer had struck them down because he sought her.

Li Lei's mother had been beautiful and fierce, yes. And if she'd passed all that ferocity and very little of the beauty to her daughter, that was just as well, for great beauty could be a trap. But along with her nature, she'd passed a more rare gift to her daughter. Magic.

Ya Bai had grown up in the tiny mountain village near the mine that produced much of Wu An's wealth. Many there had some trace of demon blood; it was not unusual. Ya Bai had had more than a trace. No one was sure the type of demon, or else they would not say; nor did they know how far back the mating had occurred. But Li Lei's mother had carried strong magic in her veins.

The sorcerer would surely have killed Li Lei with the others who possessed magic, but she hadn't been here. Anyone could have told him she'd been gone for some time. His own vision would have told him that. He hadn't set the Chimei to destroy her family in an effort to kill Li Lei.

She was almost sure of that.

One year and seven months ago, Li Lei's stepmother had brought to their house the man she meant for Li Lei to marry—a merchant's son, bashful and dull. A man she could easily have ruled. That was her stepmother's thinking, and it was kind in its way, for Li Lei would infuriate most men.

DICKINSON AREA
PUBLIC LIBRARY

But he lived in Beijing. So far away! Yet even that she might have forced herself to accept, were it not for the other gift from her mother, one which was bound up in the magic. Li Lei had seen the man and known she could not blend her bloodline with his. Not *would* not. *Could* not.

Perhaps her stepmother could not have been expected to believe her. Her father should have. She'd told him she would never bear children to that man. Just as her mother had known she would bear Wu An's daughter, and only the one daughter, Li Lei had known she would never have babies if she married as she was bid.

She had to have babies—at least one baby. Her mother's blood demanded it. As did her own heart.

And bah, how tedious that she circled back through that stale story now. She'd learned better than to let her thoughts run her, hadn't she? Li Lei settled herself, body and mind, to the moment. However bitter and hard, she had this moment.

Her left knee ached. She'd banged it yesterday while avoiding the blow of a carter who had at least given up beating his beast to aim a fist her way. Her middle hurt, tight with grief. Her mind slowed.

After a time, the acrid scent of smoke tickled her nose. Smoke was a common scent, with so many cook fires in the city, but along with the smell came another sensation. One she knew well, but had no name for.

Several streets to the east, the darkness glowed red. Another fire had bloomed, this one in a good quarter of town. It was still small, but it would grow, for neighbors would not act together to extinguish the blaze. They didn't dare. What if the sorcerer himself had caused it? Instead they would bundle up what they could of their belongings and flee, hoping the fire was dealt with before their own houses burned.

They were right in one way—the fire would be dealt with. The sorcerer did not want his city to burn down. He did not object to a chance to strut his power, either, Li Lei thought. She'd been among the crowd who gathered to watch him attend the other fire, which was huge and roaring by then, having engulfed several houses.

He'd made a show of it, arriving in a litter carried by six

slaves, his silk robe so heavily embroidered with gold thread one might have mistaken him for the emperor. Li Lei had asked herself: why did he not ride on a showy stallion or fly through the air, as sorcerers were said to do?

She had answered the second question by adding her own extrapolation to what Sun Mzao had told her. The sorcerer could fly, but not through his own arts. That skill belonged to his demon lover, and while she could carry him, she would be unlikely to make the effort in such a cause.

The answer to the first question was even easier. The sorcerer did not know how to ride. He was known to be a commoner. She believed he was actually a peasant.

Now, Li Lei believed commoners were no more stupid than the nobility, and were perhaps a shade smarter, on the whole. But much of the peasantry existed in such profound ignorance and need that they were forever warped in their thinking. Whatever the sorcerer's innate intelligence might be, his thoughts, plans, and goals were distorted. He behaved as a child—shrewd in his way, but always grabbing for whatever shiny object caught his attention, lashing out when it broke, then moving on to the next bit of glitter.

At the fire he'd made himself impressive, raising his arms and commanding the flames in a loud voice—and fire answered him, yes, but sluggishly. He had triumphed over the blaze, but he had used a great deal of power to do so.

Fire was not his by nature. So Sam had said, and so her own observation confirmed. Li Lei smiled at the dark house where she had once lived, where so many she loved had died so horribly.

No, fire was not his. But it was hers.

THIRTEEN

NETTIE put Cullen back in sleep, left Jason some instructions, and went to get some regular sleep. Rule had a word with Jason, too, then called Max. Lily called her boss, Ruben Brooks, though at this hour she used his office line, not his mobile. He'd get her message in the morning. Cynna patted her tummy and went to use the bathroom. Jason left.

When Cynna came out, Lily had a question for her. "Blood magic, Cullen said. Could it be Vodun? Nettie said the spell reminded her of a Vodun curse."

"Vodun uses a lot of blood magic, but they aren't the only ones with blood spells. Some traditions consider blood magic just plain bad, like Wicca—though some Wiccans argue that it's okay if you use your own blood. Wicca isn't uniform like Catholicism. The Catholic Church ties itself up in knots on the subject, but that's par for their course." She lowered herself into the chair by the bed and heaved a sigh. "You think a single cup of coffee would hurt the little rider?"

"I think you don't like coffee, so you must be getting desperate."

"I'm not going to sleep," Cynna said.

Rule put away his phone. "You'll lie down, though, while we wait for Max to get here. Jason's gone to arrange for a bed. That chair isn't comfortable."

"Well." After a moment she grinned tiredly. "Guess I won't argue. Max is coming?"

"He'll be here in half an hour or less." Rule glanced at Lily. "I asked him to sneak in. He's rather distinctive. I don't want him associated with this room."

"Good thinking." And it hadn't occurred to her, which meant she probably needed either coffee or sleep, too. "Cynna, what can you tell me about blood magic? Anything might help."

"It's pretty much what it sounds like—magic that's sourced in part or whole on blood. Blood is highly magically active. Doesn't matter if it's from a null or a big, bad werewolf—it's got juice."

"I don't get that. Lupus blood carries some of their magic. Blood from a Gifted person might, too, I guess. But blood from a normal human? How is that magic?"

"Magic's everywhere. Or potential magic, maybe. Thing is, mostly it's sort of transmuted into being instead of acting. That's what spells are for. They take a bit of that being and make it acting."

"I know you think that makes sense."

Cynna ran a hand over her hair, making the spikes stand up straight. "Cullen's better at explaining than I am. Say you use a rose in a spell—and it's a good spell, and you know what you're doing, because if it's a poorly crafted spell, nothing happens. But this is a workable spell cast by someone with a bit of magic to feed into it. Some bit of that rose stops being rose and acts as rose. It's like the difference between a noun and a verb."

"And blood has lots of potential magic?"

"You could put it that way." Cynna yawned hugely. "Sorry. One reason blood spells have a bad rep is that a person's blood can be used to power a spell against them. A hex or curse, in other words. That's what someone's done to Cullen, though it isn't like any hex or curse I've ever heard of."

"He said the spell was powered from his blood. That's what any blood curse does, isn't it?"

"Not exactly. The way he said it . . . I'm guessing, but it sounded like it's drawing power from him *now*. Not like it was initially powered by blood someone stole from him somehow, but like it's powered from his blood while it's in him. That's real tricky. I never heard of a spell that could do that." She shook her head, sighed. "He's going to want to figure it out, and not just the way a sane person would, so he can get rid of it. No, he'll want to understand it."

She sounded gloomy, but not for the reason Lily's anxiety spiked. A spell like Cynna described would be hard to defeat. It wouldn't run out of power as long as Cullen was alive. "Nettie said the spell made Cullen's body fight against his magic."

"That fits. Healing—ordinary healing—is delivered through the blood. The spell either interferes with that or makes the blood actively toxic. Cullen's magic keeps fixing things, but it can't get rid of the spell, and the spell keeps messing up his blood again."

Lily's phone sounded. It was the chime that meant the call had been forwarded from her official number, so she answered it. "Yu here."

"Hey, babe."

The gravelly voice was immediately familiar. Funny. She'd thought she didn't remember Cody's voice that clearly. Lily felt a smile tug at her mouth. "I never did break you of that habit. What's up?"

"Not a damned thing." He sounded tired. "We're winding up here. Thought I'd let you know. Oh, and the big boss wolf said to tell you one of his people picked up a scent, but it petered out. He wants to know how the vic's doing. I'd like to know, too."

"He's alive. He's also still reacting to a nasty spell that damn near killed him, which makes this case mine."

Cody was silent for a long moment. "Guess I can't argue with that. Never thought I'd see you on the fed side of the fence, though."

"It feels weird sometimes." All at once she had a dozen questions to ask him. Questions that had nothing to do with the case. Nothing to do with the present at all. With an effort she shoved them away and asked the ones that mattered.

Still no sign of the weapon. No physical evidence at all, basically. They were talking about what role the sheriff's department would have in the investigation when someone knocked on the door. "Got to go," she said quickly, drawing her weapon and sliding her phone back in her pocket.

Rule opened the door. It was Jason. At her nod, he wheeled in a folded-up rollaway bed with one hand. Under his other arm he carried a large bundle of blankets.

The blankets spoke. "Can't goddamn breathe in here."

"Hang on a sec." Jason set the bundle down, unwrapped the top blanket, and revealed four and a half feet of scowling gnome.

Max had beady little eyes sunk beneath hairy, salt-and-pepper eyebrows. His nose dripped toward his chin like a blob of melted wax. His mouth lacked much in the way of lips, and his skin was the color of mushrooms. His shoulders were wide, his neck barely there, and his suit could have come from the 1920s. The black fedora covering his bald head went with the suit. The neon pink socks, not so much.

He straightened his suit jacket, muttering under his breath about idiots and assholes.

"Love the socks," Lily said.

He regarded his feet with satisfaction. "Gan gave 'em to me. Stupid female has the worst taste in the thirteen realms, but she sure can fuck. Say, you want to—"

"No," Lily said firmly.

"Guess not, you being Chosen." His gaze went to Cynna, still sitting in the room's only chair. Instead of asking if she wanted to fuck—his usual greeting, if he was feeling friendly—he looked from her to Cullen, lying motionless in the bed. He walked up to the bed.

"Crazy bastard," he muttered. "Got you good, didn't they? Good thing Rule had the sense to call me. You say the assassin changes his appearance?"

It took Lily a second to realize he was asking her, not Cullen. "It may be that he fuzzes people's minds." Briefly she described what the various witnesses had seen. "If it was a real illusion, he'd look the same to everyone, wouldn't he?"

Max turned to her. "Not dumb all the time, are you? Not

exactly right, but not entirely dumb. Yeah, a true illusion would look the same to everyone. This guy's doing something a lot simpler. Sounds like he told everyone to see someone they expected to see, and everyone's brains filled in whatever appearance fit the bill."

"Why didn't he just tell everyone not to see him at all?"

"Because he's not a goddamned idiot. In a crowd like that, he needed to be seen so people wouldn't bump into him." The eyebrows clenched in what might have been a thoughtful frown. "That's some powerful mind-magic the bastard's got. Big range. Real damned big."

Worry bumped at Lily. "Can that kind of mind-magic work on you?"

Max snorted. "Not hardly. That's close to compulsion, see—telling me to see something other than what's there. I don't like being told what to do."

"Neither does my father," Rule said dryly, "but the mind-magic seems to have worked on him."

"Poor bastard lacks my genetic advantages." He turned to Cynna with the oddest expression on his face. After a moment Lily recognized it. He was smiling.

Not at Cynna, Lily realized. At her belly.

Max marched up to Cynna and put both hands flat on her stomach.

"Hey," Cynna said. "You're supposed to ask before you touch."

"Didn't give you a baby present yet," Max announced. "I'll do that now." He stared hard at her belly. After a moment his eyebrows flew up. "Son of a bitch."

"He's my son," Cynna said, "so that means you're calling me a bitch."

"Don't be so touchy. Also shut up. I need to pay attention." He began muttering again, but not in English. Or any other language Lily had ever heard. It sounded kind of like someone with the hiccups speaking a mix of Russian and German, and it went on for several moments.

"There." Max sounded deeply satisfied as he pulled his hands away from Cynna's belly. His forehead was sweaty. "Gave him a birthing name."

"You don't get to name my baby!"

Max rolled his eyes. "I said birthing name, not call name. You've already given him one of those."

"No, we haven't. We're still deciding. What's a birthing name?"

"Well, *he* thinks he's got a name already, so take it up with him if you don't agree."

Cynna's eyes were wide. "You can talk to him?'

"Of course not. He's not even born yet. The birthing name will help with that. Bend down."

"What? Why?"

Another eye roll. "How's the birthing name going to help if you don't know it? Bend down so I can give it to you."

Looking mystified and slightly cross, Cynna did. Max moved to her side and whispered something in her ear, and her expression changed. "Oh . . ."

Faintly a voice came from the bed. "You gave my son a birth name."

Cullen was awake. He'd turned his head on the pillow and was watching Max.

Max scowled. "I should've asked. Was going to, but you went and got yourself damn near dead."

"Thank you, my friend. *K'recti afhar kaken.*" Cullen's hand moved slightly, reaching.

Max took it. Did he flush? Hard to say with that pasty skin. He said something back in the hiccupy not-quite-Russian tongue, adding in English, "Thought I'd better. Poor little tyke will be as puny as a human at first."

Cullen smiled faintly. His gaze shifted to Cynna. "The birthing name . . . If the little rider gets in trouble—sick or badly hurt— you use it. Lets him draw on Max's strength. Wears off after . . ." His gaze shifted back to Max, his eyebrows lifting slightly.

Max shrugged. "Don't know, with a lupus babe. A year, anyway. Maybe more."

"Wow." Cynna heaved herself up, grabbed Max's face with her two hands, bent, and kissed him on the mouth. "Thank you, Max."

He definitely blushed this time. "You are most welcome. Say, you want to—"

"No." Cynna grinned. "But thanks, anyway."

Cullen's gaze switched back to Cynna. He smiled—just before his eyes rolled back in his head.

Jason bent over him. "He's okay. Back in sleep. I don't know how he managed to wake from it in the first place."

"The ward, I guess." Cynna rubbed her stomach idly. "He and I put one up around the little rider last week."

Max's eyebrows climbed. "I didn't think that was possible, not in living flesh."

"Hey, I use my flesh for magic all the time. Seems to have worked. You triggered it when you did your naming thing, and the ward woke him."

"Hmph. Well," Max said, pulling a deck of cards from his pocket, "who's up for a few hands of poker?"

"We're leaving and Cynna's going to lie down as soon as Jason gets her bed ready," Rule said. He looked at Jason. "Don't play for money. Max cheats."

FOURTEEN

꩜

At 2:38, Rule pulled to a stop in the parking garage beneath the ten-story high-rise he called home.

Or maybe he didn't. Maybe he thought of this as the place he stayed. Lily decided to ask him about that some time when she wasn't half asleep but still wired, her brain buzzing on caffeine and nerves.

A few months ago, the lease on Lily's tiny apartment had come due. She'd allowed it to lapse. That was only sensible; she didn't have room for Rule at her place, and he had plenty of space at his—two bedrooms, two baths, a small office, and an open living area with a killer view. Besides, his place was about twenty times nicer. It was like HGTV exploded there and left it ready for a photo shoot. And if the mate bond dictated that they cohabit, well, that was okay. She wanted to.

However sensible the decision, the results had been bumpy, but she figured that was normal. One of the bumps was the cat that came with her. Dirty Harry did not like being confined to an apartment. He'd been a stray when she found him—or when he found her—and was used to being outside. He also didn't much like Rule. What cat would feel warm and cuddly with someone who smelled wolfish?

The second bump, of course, was money. Rule had oodles of it. She didn't.

Some of that was his own money. Rule managed his clan's investments and paid himself a percentage of the profits. He'd roughly tripled Nokolai's wealth since assuming those duties and had managed to hang on to the wealth in the current downturn, so there had been plenty of profit to draw from. But Lily couldn't discount the clan's wealth because the line between personal property and the clan's property wasn't hard and fast in Rule's mind.

This building belonged to Nokolai. Rule didn't pay rent. He didn't make a condo payment. And he'd been seriously insulted when she wanted to pay him for her share of the space. After prolonged discussion, they'd agreed she would pay half the utilities.

To Rule's way of thinking, there was nothing wrong with the clan providing Lily's living space as well as his. She was clan. She was Chosen. For Lily, a place she didn't pay for wasn't hers, wasn't home.

But if the apartment didn't feel like hers, it was still a great place. She was looking forward to getting there as she rode up in the elevator. She let her eyes half close and took Rule's hand to help him with the claustrophobia he rarely admitted to—but which was one reason he lived in a high-rise. He rode in the elevator every day, and hated it each time. And proved to himself over and over that he could handle the fear.

Stupid, obsessive, determined man.

"Who was it you spoke to at the hospital?" the obsessive man asked. "The deputy."

"Hmm? Oh, that was Cody. Deputy Beck, I ought to say. Why?"

"There was something in your voice when you spoke to him."

There shouldn't have been. She'd thought she kept it businesslike. Lily frowned, her eyes opening fully. "Discomfort, maybe. We, uh, we had a thing several years back, when he was with the SDPD. It didn't end well."

He didn't say anything.

"That's some really loud silence," she observed, wide-awake now.

"There was something in your voice," he repeated. "Something I haven't heard when you speak to other men."

Could he possibly be jealous? No, she decided. She was making a human assumption. He had some sort of curiosity or concern, but it wasn't jealousy. That had been trained out of him, or else lupi lacked the jealousy gene.

And yet, stupid as the question might be, she was about to ask it when the elevator doors opened.

Then she couldn't say anything. They weren't alone.

There were eight apartments on this floor—five small ones east of the elevator, three larger units to the west of it. Rule had the corner unit on the north side. Two men flanked that door. One was five-eight, white, blue and brown, built slim. The other was six-three and two-ten with the dark eyes and creamy caramel complexion of a mixed heritage.

"Eric," Rule said, giving a nod. "LeBron. All quiet?"

Eric and LeBron were Rule's bodyguards. Two of them, anyway. The Leidolf Lu Nuncio had more or less forced them on Rule when he and Lily returned to San Diego—these two and four others. Each pair worked an eight-hour shift so that Rule could be covered 24/7 with a few exceptions . . . actually, a lot of exceptions. Rule said he preferred them to guard his home rather than his person most of the time.

Rule had sighed and accepted the necessity. "A Rho must have guards," he'd said. "It's as much a matter of status as safety, but Leidolf needs to know I am protected."

The bodyguards were the most recent cohabiting bump, and the biggest for Lily. She had not adjusted to the loss of privacy.

"Except for the cat," Eric said. "We checked it out when he started yowling, but he was just bored and pissy."

"Did he get you?" Lily asked, digging in her purse for the key.

LeBron shrugged. "It wasn't deep. Nearly healed now."

"I need to advise you of a situation," Rule said, and, as she'd expected, began briefing them of the attack on Cullen.

It was only reasonable, unlike her spurt of resentment. Which she really wished she'd get over.

Lily let herself into the apartment. The thudding feet of a large beast greeted her. She closed the door quickly—and the ginger tabby streaking toward her stopped dead, glaring.

"Sorry, Harry," she said, moving close to scoop him up. "No nocturnal escapes for you tonight." She rubbed him along his jaw.

He immediately turned on his motor. Lily was the only one Harry allowed this particular intimacy. Others might pet him upon invitation, but only she was permitted to pick him up. It made her feel absurdly honored. She continued stroking, giving attention to the place behind his ears he especially liked. One of those ears was missing a chunk. He'd been pretty torn up when she found him.

Or he found her. "Anything to report?" she asked the cat. "No? Okay, let me put my purse up, then you get your pay." She headed for the bedroom at the other end of the apartment.

They'd left a single lamp on, but even without it there would have been enough light to find her way. The outside wall of the great room was glass and the air was clear tonight. City lights twinkled at her from that vast open expanse—Rule's reward, she thought, for having endured the closed-in space of the elevator to get here. There were drapes, but Rule never closed them, and she'd learned to live with the openness, even at night. They were high enough for privacy.

She'd checked.

Harry grabbed her hand in his teeth when she passed the kitchen. Not biting. Getting her attention. "You know the drill," she informed him. Even Harry didn't get his way every time. Her weapon was in her purse. Guards or no guards, she wanted to have it close when she went to bed.

Besides, she liked having things in their place.

With her purse in its designated spot in the bedroom and her weapon next to the bed, she headed for the kitchen, still holding twenty pounds of battle-scarred tomcat. "Guess Rule and I wouldn't be alone even without those guards, anyway," she said as she deposited Harry on the kitchen's shiny slate floor. "You're always here. At least the lupus guards don't scratch, bite, or swear at me."

Compromise. Living together was all about compromise. She came with a cat; Rule came with guards.

Plenty of compromising there, too, though not between her and Rule. She opened the refrigerator and took out a baggie with scraps of deli ham. Harry plunked his rear down next to his bowl and watched intently.

Rule's brother, Benedict, had long wanted Rule to have bodyguards. Once Rule accepted the necessity for Leidolf's guards, Benedict had promptly sent an equal number of Nokolai guards. They'd negotiated. The Nokolai guards had weekend duty while Leidolf handled weekdays.

Rule suspected that was what Benedict had wanted all along. Lily suspected he was right.

She tore up a half slice of ham and put it in Harry's dish, and he fell upon it like the starving beast he wasn't. Harry approved of ham.

So now the Leidolf guards lived in two of the smaller apartments in this building. More compromising had been needed there due to the question of who would pay for their living quarters. Nokolai was wealthy and could afford to subsidize them, but initially Isen insisted that Leidolf pay rent. Rule, wearing his Leidolf Rho hat, had refused. Nokolai benefited from having its Lu Nuncio guarded.

Of course, Rule could have done what he wanted about the rent, since he controlled Nokolai's investments. But that would have been a clear—to him—violation of his duty to Nokolai, so he'd brought the matter to his father for negotiation. Only Isen could deal officially with another clan—even when that clan was represented by Isen's heir.

It was sure as hell complicated. Lily couldn't recall the exact details, but she thought Leidolf ended up paying utilities for the two apartments plus a token rent.

Kind of like her. She sighed and shut the refrigerator. Then for a moment just leaned against it, so tired she hardly knew what to do next. She let her eyes close . . . and saw once more Cullen's motionless body stretched out on the ground, his eyes blank and staring.

Lily shivered. The sound of the front door got her moving.

Rule was in the little entry foyer, emptying his pockets. Unlike her, he had no problem dumping things the moment he stepped inside, which was why she'd put a small bowl on the console table for his keys and change.

His hair was messy. It so seldom looked mussed. His eyes were tired, distracted. And he was wearing that silly T-shirt.

Her heart turned over. "Hey," she said, walking up to him and sliding her arms around his waist.

"Hey, yourself." He ran his hands down her arms, then rested them at her waist. "Why aren't you in bed?"

"Harry," she explained. The warmth of him settled her, and if she was a bit warmer some places than others, that, too, was pleasant. "Then I got to thinking . . . Rule, was Cullen dead? Before Nettie got to him, I mean."

"It depends on how you define death."

"Define it for me."

He sighed and straightened. "His heart had stopped, but our magic sustains us for a time without a heartbeat." He paused. "It was close, though. Too damned close."

"I'm told close counts in horseshoes. When it comes to staying alive, it's pretty much yes or no. We got a yes tonight."

"So we did." He nuzzled her hair. Sighed. She felt some of the tension drain out of him.

"I've got a question."

"Why am I not surprised?"

"How long can you go without a heartbeat?"

"If you mean me, personally, I'm pleased to say that I haven't checked," he said dryly. "It varies from one lupus to another, and also with the amount of damage involved."

"Give me a rough average."

"This is very rough, but perhaps double the time a human could survive. Ten minutes or so. I know of one lupus who went substantially longer, but he's unusual."

"Who's that?"

"My father."

"Oh. Yeah. Your ability to last without a heartbeat isn't a deep, dark secret, but it isn't exactly common knowledge, either, is it?"

She considered that, frowned. "Yet this perp didn't expect a thrust to the heart to be enough. He reinforced it with a spell."

"Or she."

"I'm tired of saying he or she. I don't mean it. The perp's male. I saw him."

He brushed her hair back from her face. "You're just plain tired."

True. "I'm thinking the perp knew about the party. Seems like a pro would have, and I'm leaning that way. He's got the moves of a professional. If the timing was intentional, why? What advantage would there be to killing Cullen with everyone around?"

"He—or whoever hired him, if this was a paid hit—wanted to make a public statement."

"Maybe." Was Rule still fixated on the marriage-as-motive deal? "Or maybe he likes having a crowd. Some pros like to take out a target on the street, at a game, someplace where they can blend with a crowd to get close. This killer wouldn't have trouble blending, would he?"

"Not if he can make people think he's someone else." He fell silent a moment. "Cullen would have seen the killer's Gift if he hadn't been struck from behind."

"Yeah." Lily straightened. "Yeah, I should have thought of that. I should have asked Cullen . . . Maybe Cynna will know. Is it more likely a spell or a Gift that lets him hide in plain sight? Gifts work better. That's what everyone tells me, and Max said this took some real juice to pull off. So if it's a Gift, is it one of the mind Gifts, like telepathy or charisma? Max thought it was, in which case—"

"Cullen's shields would have blocked it. Yes, I think you're right. The perp had to strike from behind."

"If he knows about Cullen's shields, he did. Maybe the backstab is his standard MO. I need to find out if—"

His mouth came down on hers. Soft, not hard, with a lover's certainty and a taste of tongue. Heat curled low in her belly. Her fingers curled, too, holding on a little harder. "What was that for?"

"You." He pressed another kiss to her lips, then deserted them for her neck. "You need to go to bed."

"Probably, but not to . . . ah." He'd done that thing with his fingers at her nape that made her shiver. "Sleep," she said, trying to mean it. "Not sex. I need sleep."

"You need to shut your mind off." He painted a rune along her collarbone with his tongue. "Or you won't sleep." Now his hands reached for one of their favorite spots . . . her rump. "I can help."

A chuckle slipped out. "Always thinking of others."

"Certainly. For example, I think you're too warm." His hands deserted their post to find the zipper in the back of her dress. He pulled it down slowly, drowning her in another kiss, this one deeper, richer.

Seconds later, her dress crumpled to the floor, and his hands found new places to touch while his mouth tended to a spot on her neck he liked.

"Hey." The stirring was sweet, familiar, new. Always new. "I have a question. Something I've been wondering all night." Her hands slid to his denim-clad butt. "Commando?"

"Mmm. I can't remember. Perhaps you should check."

She did. She slid the shorts down to discover that, indeed, there was nothing beneath them but Rule.

He clasped her hand and her waist, leaving several inches between them, and murmured, "We missed our dance." And he began humming.

So she danced in bra and panties with her beautiful, naked Rule, with the lights of the city twinkling at them from the window wall. He danced her into the living area, humming a 1930s torch song, one that had been old-fashioned even back when he was born.

Lily didn't dance with him because he was right, though he was. She did need to shut off her mind. But a quick, hot bout between the sheets—or on top of them, or in the foyer, wherever—would have taken care of that. She didn't need to spin around the floor at nearly 3 A.M.

He did. He needed surcease, comfort, sex, and sleep.

The sex was easy. Sleep? She couldn't guarantee that, but sex would surely help it along. She had a good shot at comfort, too, thanks to the mate bond. As for surcease . . . that's what this dance was for, wasn't it? *Surcease* means to bring to an end, and he meant to bring this long, difficult day to an end his way, with the stubborn insistence that blood and violence might be part of their lives, but only part.

Play was just as real. What was romance but a lovely bit of play between man and woman?

Absurd, stubborn, impossibly romantic man. He kept touching her, but nothing they couldn't have done on any dance floor.

Not yet.

He paused their motion to bend and switch off the one lamp they'd left on. She laughed softly at the sudden darkness, the city lights, and herself.

His hands settled on her hips as he continued to move to his own music, but the tune changed to one with a hard, definite beat. "Something's funny?"

"Me." She looped her arms around his neck, swaying with him, humming along this time. So selfless she was, willing to give up a little sleep for a man who was clearly determined to make sure it would be no sacrifice. How did a woman give to a man who was so determined to give to her?

She tried harder. Lily smiled into the dimness and eased closer. Now she brushed against him with every motion.

He liked that. He rumbled low in his throat in a way she wouldn't dream of calling a purr—even if it did remind her of Dirty Harry. His hands tightened on her hips. One of them began wandering . . . brushing her lightly here and there, but never in the place that had begun to ache for him. She pressed closer.

"Uh-uh." The hand at her hip tightened, keeping a hint of space between them. Suddenly he whirled her around—once, then again—making her laugh in spite of her frustration, ending with them at the dark tunnel of the hall. Once more he slowed.

Two slow, humming turns into the hall, her bra fell to the floor.

Her panties slid down her legs at the entrance to the bedroom.

His fingers slid between her legs just as they reached the bed. An easy caress, a gentle rub, one quick stroke—and she went over.

The climax whited out her brain. She forgot about legs and standing. Fortunately, he scooped her up and tossed her on the bed before she collapsed. He followed her down and, with the aftershocks still pinging through her, he slid inside.

He'd dawdled all he wanted, it seemed, for he finished with quick, hard strokes that overloaded her sensitized flesh, bringing her a second pop.

The next she knew, he'd collapsed on top of her, his breath coming heavy and fast on the side of her head. She lifted one limp hand, stroked his chin. "Mmm. Tangy," she murmured.

"Tangy?" He was amused, sleepy.

She nodded, eyes closed. "Like a whole-body SweeTART. The second one, I mean, not the first. The first was . . ." Her drowsy brain couldn't find a sufficiently explosive food to compare it to. She settled for, "Wow."

"Ah." He lifted off. "Wow here, too. Scoot. I'll get the cover."

She scooted, tugged with him, and wiggled herself under the covers. There was a wet spot on the comforter—the only disadvantage of sex with a lupus. They couldn't get or give STDs, so no condoms were needed. No condoms meant wet spots, unless you took precautions. Which they'd forgotten to do . . . again.

But no matter. She'd wash the comforter in the morning.

Rule draped one arm over her. Lily snuggled close, closing her eyes, savoring the comfort of the bed and the contact, enjoying her limp body, the drugging pull of sleep.

A thought wiggled up from somewhere.

Rule hadn't made love like a jealous man, had he? There'd been no possessiveness, no claiming, in either part of their dance. Was she relieved or disappointed?

She couldn't tell. It didn't matter. Lily sighed and let go.

FIFTEEN

IT was still full dark when Rule stood in front of the window wall in the living area the next morning, sipping coffee. His view faced west, out toward the ocean. The moon hung near the horizon, her face half shadow, half light. Lily still slept. He'd reset the alarm to make sure of that. She wasn't always realistic about how much sleep she needed.

He watched the darkness and listened to the song of the partly veiled moon and remembered jealousy.

He'd experienced it, of course. Lupi weren't immune to the urge to hoard, whether it be toys, attention, love, or sex. Young lupi in particular—those who hadn't yet been received into the mantle—were subject to the flashy emotional noise of jealousy.

Sometimes adult lupi were, too.

A familiar sadness stole over Rule as he remembered his brother Mick. Mick had been ten years older than Rule, nine years younger than Benedict. Unlike Rule and Benedict, though, he'd been raised away from Clanhome until puberty rendered that impossible. His mother had refused to let Isen have custody until almost too late.

Rule often wondered how much that had shaped him.

Others had seen a simple dominance struggle between Mick and Rule—normal and even healthy. Rule knew it had gone deeper, been more twisted. Mick had been jealous of Rule. Jealous when Rule was young because of the time Rule had with their father. Jealous when they were both adults because Isen had named Rule Lu Nuncio. Mick's thinking had been so deformed by the bitter emotion he could see that only as a father's preference, not a Rho's choice. A theft of love.

Lupi had a name for that particular form of jealousy: *fratriodi*, or brother hatred. It was a grave sin. The poison of Mick's jealousy had left him open to the manipulations of a woman named Helen, who'd used it—and an ancient staff—to control him.

Yet in the end Mick had chosen to save Rule instead of killing him. He'd died, but he'd died clean of *fratriodi*.

Sexual jealousy was as poisonous as any other type. Rule had no intention of indulging in it. But this wasn't jealousy, he decided as he turned away from the window. He crossed to the breakfast bar, where his laptop waited. An illicit curiosity, perhaps.

The program had long since finished running the calculations he needed. He'd begun dabbling in currency trading, needing a way to bring Leidolf's disastrous finances into better shape. It was risky, no doubt about that, especially with the shaky state of the world economy.

But that very instability left room for traders to make—or lose—large amounts of money with a relatively small initial stake.

He checked his input figures one last time, then put in his buy order. Then he opened his browser and logged on to the site he used for background information on those he did business with. Google was handy, but this site, operated by a detective agency, offered a bit more. For his monthly fee he could obtain a records check on almost anyone. If that raised questions for him, he could contact the agency for a deeper look.

Beck, Cody, he typed in the first field. In one of the other fields he entered *San Diego County Sheriff's Department*. Then he hit SEARCH.

Short of death, it was impossible for him to lose Lily. She'd agreed to marry him, and would have been faithful even without the conventional human bond. She loved him. He knew that.

But he wanted very much to learn what he could of the man she'd spoken of with such smothered regret.

"You changed the alarm setting."

Rule smiled. Lily looked so disgruntled and tidy standing there in her pressed dress slacks, sleeveless white shirt, and bare feet. Her hair was still damp from her shower. She held the bunched-up comforter under one arm. "Only by forty-five minutes," he said.

"Which isn't enough to help. Just means I'll be running late all day." She came into the kitchen, where Rule was getting his second cup of coffee, took down a mug, and held it out. "Harry didn't wake me, either."

"I bribed him with ham." Rule filled Lily's mug and took the comforter from her. "I'll wash it."

She slid him a grin, took a sip, closed her eyes, and took another one.

He loved to watch her enjoy coffee. His coffee. She drank the stuff regurgitated by cop shop coffeemakers, but she didn't enjoy it.

He opened the sliders that concealed the washer and dryer in their nook off the kitchen. "Nettie's still asleep, as she should be. She expended a great deal on Cullen yesterday. Max won a hundred dollars from Jason at poker. Either he didn't cheat or Jason is smarter than I realized. Cynna and Cullen are asleep, or were an hour ago. Toby's with my father. When I spoke with him, he was worried about Cullen, but, ah, unaware of the spell. I decided to allow him that ignorance."

"He's not too upset?"

Rule shook his head. "He thinks Cullen is healing normally. He wanted to go see Cullen, but when told he couldn't, fell back on wheedling for permission to hike up into the mountains with some of the other children."

"Hmm." Lily followed, coffee cup in hand. "You've been busy. Up awhile?" She glanced at the breakfast bar, where his laptop was up and humming, though with a screensaver at the moment. She didn't say a word, but she didn't have to.

"I'm fine, Lily. You know I don't need much sleep."

"You need some, though, and the way things have been going lately—"

"Is temporary. I may have found someone to help with Leidolf's investments. Your father recommended him."

Her eyebrows lifted. "A human?"

"Unfortunately, Leidolf hasn't invested in its members' education sufficiently. I don't have anyone within the clan who can handle the sort of transactions I'm interested in." He wouldn't mention just whom Lily's father had recommended. More fun to surprise her, if things worked out. "Will you be going to the hospital right away?"

She grimaced. "I need two of me. Maybe three. I'll get to the hospital, but not yet. I had an idea while I was showering. A way to guard Cullen pretty damned effectively that doesn't involve me or Cynna, and it just might help with something else, too. Uh . . . I wondered if you wanted to go along. If you drove, I could get some work done on the way."

Amused, he tugged her hair. "You wouldn't be trying to guard me, would you?"

"Maybe a little. I don't really think *she's* involved. According to what Cynna told us it's unlikely, and besides, *she* would have tried for you or your father. Or that's what I think, but maybe I don't know how an Old One with a really big grudge lays her plans, so . . ." She shrugged. "Either way, I can use the drive time to read some stuff I requested. Research is getting me a list of suspected professional hits that might match this perp's MO."

"All right." Since he'd already planned to find a way to intrude himself into her day so he could guard her, that worked for him. "Where are we going?"

"Well." She sipped, smiled . . . but it was a complex smile, woven of many strands of emotion. "I dreamed of dragons last night."

SIXTEEN

HAD it been up to Washington, San Diego would not have received a dragon. True, it was home to a major naval base, and there was an Air Force base just north of the city. But after the Turning hit and ambient magic levels began rising, lots of cities wanted a dragon. Dragons were immense magic sponges—they soaked up all the free-floating magic that interfered with technology. The government had, not unreasonably, wanted a dragon sopping up excess magic in L.A., not the smaller city.

It hadn't been up to the government. The Dragon Accords that Grandmother had negotiated awarded each dragon a permanent base, but made an exception for one of them: the black dragon, the eldest of them, known to Lily and Rule as Sam and to others as Sun Mzao. Officially, Sam's territory was wherever he happened to be.

In practice—and in the eyes of the dragons—Sam's territory included much of the West Coast, down into Mexico. He'd agreed to overfly Los Angeles frequently, and Sacramento occasionally, but he laired just outside of San Diego.

At slightly under half a mile high, San Miguel Mountain

wasn't the largest peak around, but it was close to the city and highly visible. To the consternation of environmentalists, that was where Sam had dug his lair—in the west side of the mountain, facing the Sweetwater Reservoir. An unusually large dragon needed a great deal of fresh water, after all.

That's where Lily and Rule headed shortly before eight A.M. that morning, taking Highway 54 out to Reservoir Road. There was no guarantee that Sam would be home, but he usually flew at night, so they had a good chance of catching him.

Or he might know they were coming and either wait for them or leave to avoid them. Lily didn't know what the limits were on his ability to touch other minds or read thoughts outright. Distance mattered, but she didn't know what his range was. Earth and stone mattered, too, which was one reason most dragons liked a rocky lair. It cut out the ambient mind-noise.

On the way, Lily made a couple calls, then took out her laptop. She pulled up the list of suspected professional hits that headquarters had sent her, skimmed it . . . and thought about dragons.

In the Western world, dragons had been considered a myth for centuries. Lily had certainly believed that—right up until one seized her in his talons and carried her off. That happened in Dis, otherwise known as the hell region, where the dragons had emigrated more than three hundred years ago when Earth's magic grew too thin for them.

And now they were back.

At least some of them were—twenty-three, to be precise. Lily had the idea there might be more dragons in some distant realm. Sam wouldn't say, but they must have a home realm. She was pretty sure dragons weren't native to Earth.

Sam's bunch had lived here a very long time, though, before temporarily relocating to Dis when Earth's magic grew too thin for them. How long? No one knew except the dragons, and they weren't saying.

Lily did know a few things about dragons, at least about the ones living here. They were compulsively curious, hoarders of knowledge more than gold—but they liked gold, too. Part of their fee for overflying their assigned territories, soaking up excess magic, was a measure of gold dust. No one knew why they wanted it.

She knew that dragons were mostly solitary, but they got together at times that fit some internal rhythm rather than the calendar . . . and sang. They sang to fulfill needs she couldn't guess. They also sang to work magic.

That's how Sam brought them all back from hell. The dragons couldn't open a gate themselves—which did not make sense, because they'd left Earth once, so why couldn't they make a gate? But dragons weren't big on explaining, so that question resided in Lily's find-out-one-day mental file. Sam had either taken advantage of the arrival of Lily and Rule in Dis, or he'd in some obscure way been counting on it so he could use their gate.

Only their gate had been far too small for dragons, and they hadn't been able to open it for reasons that had to do with there being two of Lily at the time. Lily had taken care of the latter problem the only way she could. Sam had handled the first problem, singing the gate large, singing it open long enough to bring his people home . . . and with them, Max and Cullen and Cynna and Rule. And Lily, of course.

One of her. Most of her. She tried not to think about that too much.

She also knew why Sam had chosen San Diego for his lair. Li Lei Yu lived here. Therefore, so did the black dragon.

Lily wanted badly to know what her tiny, indomitable grandmother had shared with the enormous black dragon back in China so long ago. But Grandmother was impervious to questions—a trait she might have learned from Sam more than three centuries before Lily was born. Until this year, Lily had known Grandmother was older than she appeared; she hadn't known how much older. She assumed Grandmother's longevity had something to do with her interlude with Sam, but she didn't know what.

Lily supposed to she had no real right to ask for details. but dammit, she wasn't *good* at not asking questions.

Is there a verb for that? she wondered as she closed her laptop. They'd left the highway for Reservoir Road, and she knew from experience coverage was spotty here. Maybe she should call it minding her own . . .

Her phone sang out the first bar of "The Star Spangled Banner." She answered. The caller turned out to be Ida, Ruben's secretary, rather than Ruben himself. Her news was not welcome.

"She's going to what?" she exclaimed. "That's crazy. I can't be sued for performing my duty." She listened a moment. "That's crazy, too. Jesus. Okay, sure, thanks for letting me know."

"You're being sued?" Rule said.

"It's that Blanco case." Lily dragged a hand over her hair. Earlier this year, she'd stopped a killer with a strong Earth Gift. When Lily tackled the woman, Adele Blanco had used her Gift to try to bring down the mountain on both of them. "She still blames me for the way she burned out her Gift. Claims I sucked it out of her." Which wasn't possible, of course, but making the earth shake so you could kill your enemy along with yourself was not the act of a sane and balanced person. "She's suing from her jail cell, and get this—Humans First is financing the lawsuit."

"That's peculiar of them, considering their views on the Gifted."

"It's a win-win for them," Lily said bitterly. "The lawsuit will probably be thrown out, but in the meantime they can milk it for publicity. We'd managed to keep the earthquake thing quiet, but it will come out now."

"The experts were unable to say for certain that Adele caused the quake."

"People don't need proof to be afraid."

"True." He paused a moment. "I'm going to be seeing your mother tomorrow."

The change of subject gave her mental whiplash. "My mother? Why?"

"She asked me to go over a list of possible sites for the wedding. Apparently she's asked you already, with what she considered insufficient results."

"I don't have time for this. You don't have time for this." Lily wanted to grab her hair and yank. "I've got a case. It's a little more important to find this weird-ass killer than it is to chat about . . . You want me to call her and explain why we can't do this right now?"

"We aren't doing it. I am."

They weren't holding the wedding at Clanhome. That would have been easier—no reservation required—but Rule felt it would rub the clan's nose in his decision. He wanted his wedding free of that sort of tension.

Was that even possible? His business, Lily reminded herself. Hers was . . . Well, surely the bride was supposed to consult with her own mother, not the groom. "I'm pretty sure I'm supposed to do the sit-down with my mother about these details."

"Do you want to?"

"No, but—"

"Many places are booked a year in advance. We need to make this decision. I have some time; you don't. So I'll take care of it."

"You're already overloaded."

"Amazingly enough, I can tell when I've taken on too much."

She snorted. "You're an overachiever, just like me. You think you can do everything and still add one more chore to the list."

In the silence that followed Lily realized what she'd just said. And winced. "Ah . . ."

"I won't mention the possibility that you're projecting. I'll just ask which of us you think is more likely to get what we want from your mother."

Lily sighed and caved. "You're in charge of venue, then."

"Any preferences? Anything you absolutely don't want?"

"I don't want a big church wedding. Maybe someplace outside. I liked that about Cynna and Cullen's wedding, that they held it out of doors."

"You realize this means we have to set a date."

"I'm okay with whatever you pick. Though I guess it had better not be in the summer, not if we do it outside. Uh—do you want to do it outside?"

"Frequently. Oh, you meant the wedding. That, too."

She grinned. As some of the tension eased from her neck and shoulders, she realized she'd been wound way too tight. With reason, maybe, but it wasn't helpful. Impulsively she reached out and squeezed his hand. "You're good for me."

It delighted her to see surprise, then pleasure, spread over his face. "Good," he said. "That's good. I love you."

Happiness had a kick sometimes. She smiled. For once he was a bit tongue-tied. "Before I get back to work—which I really, really need to do—I'll just add that you matter. It still scares me sometimes, how much you matter, but I've decided . . . Well, sunshine matters, too, but I don't go around worrying about the sun, do I? So mostly I'm not worrying. Except about the wedding, and I'm trying to cut back there, too."

"You might let me be in charge of worrying along with venue."

She shook her head. "You're not good at it. Me, I'm a champion worrier. You remember what Grandmother said about how to get a dragon to do something?"

He followed her jump in topics without trouble. "There are only two ways—strike a bargain, or go to war. We're not interested in the second option, I assume."

"Good assumption. She also said never owe a dragon a favor, as they tend to expect a really healthy repayment. But it isn't a favor if they offer something without you asking."

Lily's dream last night had been the cobwebby sort—gossamer yet sticky. Its residue had clung to her as she stood under the shower's stream, sticky strands of event and emotion clogging her thoughts. While she was rinsing out the shampoo, she'd realized why she'd dreamt of dragons.

There was one place Cullen should be entirely safe from a sorcerer or Gifted assassin who could disguise himself magically: a dragon's lair. Like sorcerers, dragons saw magic. Like Lily, they were almost impossible to enspell. They were highly territorial. They were also telepathic.

It was damned hard to sneak up on someone who "heard" your mind buzzing if you got near.

There remained one problem: how would they get Sam to agree? Grandmother might have done it, had she been around. But she wasn't.

Lily rubbed her breastbone, where worry had lodged like a tumor, hard and bothersome. That was the other reason she wanted to see Sam. If anyone knew where Grandmother was, he did.

The reservoir spread along their left to the east, vast and still, smiling up at the sky in placid blue. Lily looked at the unruffled water and tried to absorb some of its stillness.

"Are you hoping you can get Sam to offer Cullen asylum without asking for it?" Rule asked.

"I'm hoping to appeal to his curiosity. Somehow."

"Hmm. I have some ideas. It might not be too difficult to persuade Sam. Cullen got along with Micah well enough back in D.C."

Micah was Washington, D.C.'s dragon. "Micah's a lot younger than Sam. I'm not sure Sam will find him inherently interesting in the same . . . Shit, there's the sign. I'd better come up with something."

The sign she referred to marked the entrance to a gravel road. "WARNING: THIS AREA IS RESTRICTED" it read in large letters. Fifty yards down the road was a gate and another sign: "DRAGON LAIR AHEAD. U.S. AND STATE LAW SUSPENDED BEYOND BARRIER."

That suspension of law had been one of the trickiest parts of the negotiation that ended in the Dragon Accords. Dragons considered human laws absurd and obviously not applicable to *them*. Unsurprisingly, the government disagreed. In the end, the dragons had agreed to abide by a few basics: Respect for private property. No eating pets. No killing at all, apart from their allotted livestock, save in self-defense—not even when some human was particularly annoying.

With one exception. A dragon cannot conceive of his lair being subject to any authority but his own. According to Grandmother, it wasn't that they insisted on absolute sovereignty there; they literally could not imagine anything else.

Technology had been faltering near the largest nodes, and it would only get worse. The country needed dragons, so tiny pockets were created where dragons' whims prevailed, rather than human law. States—or countries, since just over half of the dragons went to other nations—that refused to create the necessary pockets around lairs simply didn't get a dragon.

Every state except Utah and North Dakota had complied. So had Great Britain, Japan, China, Italy, Mexico, Germany, Brazil, New Zealand, and Canada, as well as twenty nations who had little hope of getting a dragon, but tried anyway. France refused, as did Russia and Australia.

In the U.S., the area around a lair was fenced and posted. Some of the dragons set magical booby traps or other defenses. The younger ones lacked their elders' magical expertise, but they did set crude wards. If someone entered in spite of fence, wards, and warnings, the dragon could do whatever he wanted with the intruder—chat, maim, ensorcell, kill.

People being people, there had been incidents. None here, but then, Sam had ways of discouraging pests. Even the paparazzi had quit hanging out near the fence pretty fast. Their cameras kept suffering mysterious breakdowns—when they didn't just explode.

Elsewhere, though, there had been problems. A photojournalist had tried to sneak past the fence in Seattle, snap some pictures, then run really fast back to safe territory. He hadn't been fast enough. Four gangbangers in Chicago had thought an area ungoverned by law would be a great place for drug deals, and saw no reason they couldn't do the deal quickly just inside the fence, then vault back over. Curiosity seekers in London and Houston had made the attempt, as had an unaffiliated witch in Toronto who wanted a dragon's scale.

All of them ended up injured, a couple of them badly. One of the gangbangers seemed to be permanently ensorcelled. He could speak only in nursery rhymes.

The Chicago incident had delighted some people. Jay Leno had told jokes about it for a week. That city's dragon—he called himself Alec—had thoughtfully deposited the injured gang members on the roof of Cook County Hospital. While he'd declined to give a statement, he had offered one comment to the chief of police.

Turned out the one who now spoke in nursery rhymes had had his iPod turned up especially loud when he entered the lair. And Alec didn't like rap music.

They were fortunate, Lily supposed, that no intruders had been killed. . . . as far as anyone knew. Since a dragon might decide to eat the evidence, that wasn't certain. What part of "can't sneak up on a telepath" did people not understand?

The narrow gravel road began climbing. Lily felt her heart rate climb, too.

Not because Sam would attack. He had informed them months ago that they would be allowed to visit occasionally, and Rule had done so. The first time had been an official welcome from Nokolai, in which Rule opened a discussion with the dragon about territory. He'd gone back officially twice and had made a purely personal visit recently, too.

Lily hadn't.

"You okay?" Rule asked as he stopped the Mercedes in front of the gate.

"Sure." Aside from cold, damp palms and an overly excited heartbeat. "I'm not scared of Sam."

"Hmm." He got out of the car, announced out loud that he and Lily were there to speak with Sam, and expressed the hope that their visit was not an intrusion. That was a courtesy, since Sam listened to minds, not voices—but he insisted that humans thought in such a cluttered way it was easier to "hear" what they meant if they spoke it aloud.

Lily took a slow breath, trying to settle herself. Rule hadn't argued when she said she wasn't afraid of Sam. He might have, though she'd spoken truly: she didn't fear the dragon. It was the stuff in her own mind that made her palms sweaty.

Memory could be a bitch sometimes. Even the memories she couldn't quite recall. Especially them.

It was a manual gate. Once Rule opened it, Lily scooted over to the driver's seat so she could drive the car through, then wiggled back to the passenger seat to wait while Rule closed the gate again.

"I believe," Rule said as he shut the door, "you might leave the bargaining to me."

"You do, huh?" Her heartbeat was calming down. *See there*, she told her inner fearmonger, *that wasn't so bad*.

"Cullen is clan as well as friend, so he's mine to protect. If anything must be offered to gain that protection, that's mine to give. And I can offer what you can't—limited hunting rights in Clanhome."

"Sam gets all the steers and pigs he wants."

"He doesn't get to hunt. Grabbing the animals released in this enclosure isn't the same. I'm already negotiating with him on this."

She looked at him, surprised. "You are?" She'd known he was negotiating something. He hadn't talked about the terms . . . and she hadn't asked, had she?

She'd been letting her fear control her. And hadn't even noticed.

The road was climbing sharply now. Gravel crunched pleasantly beneath the tires. "We'd already have reached an agreement," Rule said, "if he didn't enjoy the bargaining itself so much." He glanced at her, smiled. "Madame Yu advised me to bargain vigorously. Sam wouldn't trust a deal too easily struck."

Unconsciously Lily rubbed her breastbone again. Grandmother had survived wars, famine, and who-knew-what-all in China. In this country, she'd dealt with a minor god, negotiated with the president, and battled a really large demon. And those were just the things Lily knew about. Grandmother would survive whatever this adventure was, too. "What will Nokolai get in return?"

"A favor."

She lifted her eyebrows. "Just one?"

"That was our initial request. I'm allowing him to bargain me down."

"Down? Asking for more than one favor is being bargained down?"

"A debt that accumulates over many years could end up as a very large favor. He doesn't want that, so we're discussing how often Nokolai has to clear its tab. He wants it done frequently, so he can pay the debt with small favors. Naturally, I want the opposite."

"Hmm." The road curved up and around, a pale scar on a sere brown slope surrounded by ruffled land. It looked a lot like parts of Clanhome, and if you went by air—the way Sam would—the distance between the two wasn't great. By road it was much longer. "I wonder what Sam considers a very large favor."

Rule snorted. "Anything that seriously inconveniences him, I suspect."

"You like him."

"I do. The wolf understands him better than the man does, but I . . ." Rule's voice trailed off. He braked to a gentle halt.

They'd rounded a tall, knobby earth-shoulder. Ahead the gravel road petered out into a broad, flat expanse of bare dirt.

Lily had expected that. Rule had told her about Sam's architectural efforts. He'd used the rock and dirt excavated from his lair to build a large landing pad or front porch—first the rocks to make it stable, then enormous amounts of dirt, tamped down and leveled off.

She hadn't expected the brightly colored canopy over the bit of carpet set on this end of that long landing pad. Or the middle-aged woman in loose white pants and a blue, short-sleeved shirt standing in that small pavilion, smiling at them.

"Well," Lily said after a moment, "it looks like we've found Li Qin."

SEVENTEEN

RULE and Lily left the car where it was. Li Qin stepped out from under the striped canopy and offered a small bow as they drew near. She was a solidly built woman of uncertain age, her face square and plain, her voice inexpressibly pure and lovely.

"I am pleased to see you both," she said in her precise, softly accented English. "I was about to have tea when Sam told me you would be arriving shortly. Will you do me the honor of joining me?"

"Of course," Lily said, because it was impossible to be other than polite to Li Qin. She could see the tea things set out on the low table and cursed inwardly. Li Qin meant to prepare the tea properly, in the Gongfu style.

In other words, slowly. "Thank you. You honor us. Li Qin, is Grandmother here, too?"

"Ah." Regret touched the placid features. "I did not think. Of course you might hope to find her here. I am sorry, but she is not. Rule, I believe you like your tea in the English style, but I'm afraid I do not have sugar or milk."

"Your voice will sweeten it for me."

She smiled. "You are kind."

Li Qin's smiles didn't transform her face—it was still plain—and yet one smile always made Lily want to see another one. Which made it hard to speak bluntly. "Li Qin—"

"You have many questions. I understand. I will tell you some things while I prepare the tea. Sam will . . ." She glanced at the arched entrance to Sam's lair, which was about fifty feet away horizontally and ten feet up. A hint of mischief lit her eyes. "I have won a bet with Sam. He thought you would not be here for several more days. He is sulking, but will be down later."

Lily followed her gaze. The arch was high and broad, clearly shaped rather than natural. Shadows deepened to darkness immediately inside. She wondered how far back it went. Sam's lair in Dis had been flush with the entrance, not set ten feet up like this one. It had been part of an extensive cave system. She remembered the way Rule-wolf had forced himself to explore it in spite of . . .

A sudden shiver shook off the memory.

Rule caught her eye, his brows lifting in a silent question. Lily settled for a small shrug. It hadn't been her memory. Not precisely.

"Please be seated," Li Qin said. She moved to a bright blue cushion on the far side of the table.

That table was square and black, highly lacquered—and familiar. Lily recognized it, as well as the items laid out precisely on its gleaming surface—the rimless cups set in the tray, the small clay teapot and *cha pan*, the wooden teaspoon, the kettle. The rug was new, an inexpensive sisal. The rest were from Grandmother's store of treasures.

Why were they here? Why was Li Qin here, and not Grandmother?

For that matter, how was Li Qin going to make tea? Lily sat on a soft pink cushion; Rule lowered himself to the green one beside her. There was a kettle, yes, but no fire or heating element that Lily could see.

"I hope you will excuse me," Li Qin said as she began measuring tea into the pot with the wooden spoon, "if I begin the story immediately rather than engaging in more traditional conversation while I prepare the tea. I feel you are somewhat pressed for time, yes?"

"Yes," Lily murmured, relieved. To sticklers like Grandmother and Li Qin, this period would normally be spent in gentle inquiries into everyone's health and other such gripping topics. Innocuous conversation, in other words, that was supposed to relax people.

Not that Li Qin needed help relaxing. Her voice and expression were entirely calm as she began. "Two days ago, your grandmother asked me to stay with Sam for my safety while she dealt with the arrival in this city of an old enemy." She set the teapot in the *cha pan*—a large bowl—and lifted the kettle. "If you would, please, Sam?" She smiled at Lily, then at Rule. "I act as hostess, but you are Sam's guests. He takes part in the preparation of the tea, also. Ah, is it ready? Thank you."

Apparently Sam was the heating element. The water steamed as Li Qin poured it into the teapot, allowing it to overflow slightly. That's what the bowl was for—to contain water and tea intentionally spilled. Deftly she scooped out a few bits of debris and foam, then placed the lid on top and quickly poured the water into the cups. "This enemy is a Chimei. Do you know the word?"

Lily shook her head.

Having filled the cups, Li Qin emptied them. The first brewing was considered inferior and was used to warm and prepare the cups. "In China it is believed that many types of spirit creatures exist." She picked up the kettle, waiting for Sam to heat the water again. "Some are considered to be *gui*, which is that part of the soul that is separated from the higher soul upon death. Whether this is true of spirit beings I do not know, but it is not true of the Chimei. I am told the English word for such a being is *demon*, but it is a poor translation."

"*Demon* is what everything gets called," Lily agreed. "But it is misleading, as you say. As far as we can tell, demons as we know them in the West—the ones from Dis—never hung out in China. Grandmother told me that a lot of the Chinese folktales about demons are based on out-realm beings of different sorts, not spirits."

"That is so." Again she filled the teapot. This time, after

replacing the lid, she continued to pour boiling water over the outside of the pot. "Dis does not connect well with China. Other realms do, however. Or used to. The Chimei is not from our realm."

Lily shifted, not liking the direction this was going. "And this Chimei is Grandmother's enemy. Why?"

"Many years ago, back in China, your grandmother killed the Chimei's lover." Li Qin held up a single finger, an expression of concentration on her face. Very swiftly she poured the tea.

"She—" Lily took a calm-me-down breath. The tea was poured. She had to *appreciate* it, not ask about unimportant things involving murder or survival. To do otherwise would be a terrible insult, and she could not insult Li Qin.

She gave Rule a look intended to convey this. He either caught her glance out of the corner of his eye, or he remembered her coaching from the time Grandmother invited him to take tea. He waited, as apparently unhurried as Li Qin.

Must have been the corner-of-the-eye thing. The moment Lily reached for her cup, he reached for his. Lily forced herself to hold the gently steaming cup near her face and at least look like she was appreciating the aroma—which was pleasant, of course, but did Li Qin really think Lily could pay attention to a scent rather than the fact that some unknown demon enemy was threatening Grandmother?

Apparently Rule could. "Entrancing," he murmured, his eyes half closed as if he were immersed in the experience. "How is it a scent can both stimulate and relax?"

Li Qin's smile held pleasure and a hint of surprise. "That is what the tea ceremony is for. We surrender urgency and clamor and find ourselves awake, calm, and able to focus. Do you have such a practice, also?"

"I am aided in this by my wolf." His gaze slid to Lily, amusement crinkling the corners of his eyes. "Lily lacks such an aid."

"Lily is very like her grandmother." Li Qin took a sip of tea.

That was obviously false. Oh, she had some things in common with Grandmother, but in this they were totally different. Lily had never found sniffing and sipping tea interesting or transformative, but Grandmother clearly did. She immersed herself in the experience. She practically rolled around in all that calm, awake focus.

Obedient to the situation, though, Lily didn't argue. She sipped tea.

Rule seemed to be enjoying his. "I have wondered sometimes if Madame Yu was even more like Lily when she was younger."

Li Qin nodded. "I think she must have been, though I did not know Li Lei when she was Lily's age, of course. She is more mellow now."

Lily did not—quite—choke.

Rule quirked a brow. "Is she?"

"Oh, yes. She was very intense as a young woman. Much like Lily." She gave Lily a gentle smile. "More autocratic, I believe, but this is because she was born into a society that did not value females. She could not attach that lack of value to herself, and so concluded that she was exceptional. Circumstances have never detached her from this belief."

"Understandable," Rule said, while Lily sat dumbstruck at having Grandmother summed up with such tidy accuracy. "Since she is, in fact, exceptional." He smiled at Lily. "Much like her granddaughter."

Lily found herself smiling at him, because he meant it. Grandmother truly was exceptional. She wasn't, but Rule saw her that way.

"Li Qin," Rule said, gently setting down his empty cup, "I regret my need to bring up another subject, but we aren't here only in search of Lily's grandmother. We also need a safe haven for—"

Granted.

Memory shivered through Lily like sleet, tiny, stinging bits that melted when she tried to catch them. The voice that had spoken that single word was as cold and clear as the space between stars. And it was all in Lily's head. Literally.

Sam's voice.

EIGHTEEN

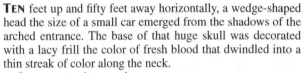

TEN feet up and fifty feet away horizontally, a wedge-shaped head the size of a small car emerged from the shadows of the arched entrance. The base of that huge skull was decorated with a lacy frill the color of fresh blood that dwindled into a thin streak of color along the neck.

It was a very long neck.

Bring Cullen Seabourne here, Sam told them. *He will be safe nowhere else, and we may need him. Think about his wound for a moment so I may see . . . Think clearly, if you are at all able.* No mistaking the acerbity in that command. *Ah. Blood magic, and it is sustained by his own blood. That may be tricky to unknot. I will assist. I expect I will dislike having him underfoot, but I concede the necessity.*

"Mr. Seabourne is injured?" Li Qin said, distressed.

Rule spoke to her softly. Lily couldn't pay attention to his explanation, caught as she was by the sight of the black dragon leaving his lair.

Sam was a very large dragon, sleek as a serpent if wider in girth, his length upheld by four short, powerful legs ending in talons. The cop in Lily tried to guess his weight. Three elephants' worth? Four? How much did an elephant weigh, anyway? Were Sam's bones heavy like an elephant's, or light like a bird's?

She had no idea.

Black and steel, sleek and huge, with the origami folds of the great wings riding along his back, Sam flowed down that ten-foot "step" onto his landing pad like molten midnight.

This midnight, however, was the black composed of all colors, not their absence. He sparkled. In the morning sunlight his scales cast a rainbow iridescence—fugitive gleams of blue, purple, red, gold, and green.

Lily found herself on her feet. Impossible to meet such huge and deadly beauty while sitting on the ground. Rule, too, had stood. He took her hand. Even Li Qin rose, though somehow with her it seemed more a courtesy than an instinctive response.

Sam's landing pad was as wide as a football field and about twice as long. He settled himself into a comfortable coil that occupied some thirty feet of it. His head remained raised about twenty feet in the air as he looked at the two of them.

I greet you, Rule Turner. I greet you, Lily Yu.

For a second, Lily forgot to breathe. For a second she forgot all the safeguards and looked directly into eyes that were all black and silver, with no white at all . . .

Falling. She was falling and falling, air whistling past like the cold shriek of hell—then someone said, *Remember!*—and then she—

"Lily." Rule's arm was around her waist. Holding her up. "Are you all right?"

"Dizzy." She shook her head, throwing off the lingering sensations. "It's passed now. I . . . It was the dream." He knew what she meant. The dream returned occasionally, though it wasn't really a dream at all, but a memory.

The memory of her other self. The one who had thrown herself off a cliff and fallen and fallen so the gate could be opened and the rest could return home from hell.

So Rule could come home. So he would live.

That self was part of her, part of her soul—but a largely

voiceless part. Now and then, she touched those memories. They'd never made her dizzy before. Lily straightened and frowned at Sam. "How is it I can hear you, anyway? Shouldn't my Gift block mindspeech?"

Your essential nature is unchanged, I see, regardless of what you remember or do not remember. A faint whiff of amusement flavored the near-painful clarity of Sam's mental voice. *You still acquaint yourself with the world through questions. Direct your questing to more urgent matters. Li Qin, you will continue with the story of the Chimei's history with Li Lei, as you understand it.*

"Of course." Sedately Li Qin reseated herself and looked up at Lily and Rule. "Please sit. This will take a little while."

She waited while they did, then said, "Lily, your grandmother takes much pleasure in retaining the mystery of her past, even with her family. But it is not only for pleasure that she does so. Many places in her past cause her great pain, even today. The occasion of her enmity with the Chimei is one such time.

"She was a headstrong young woman, as I have said, and was raised by a mother who had . . . They called it demon blood in those days. Some in China still do. We would say she had a Gift, a strong Gift."

"What kind of Gift?" Lily asked, leaning forward slightly. "Grandmother didn't . . . Ah, I've always thought she wasn't born being able to turn tiger. Was I wrong?"

"No." Li Qin smiled faintly. "Nor was her mother able to. Li Lei's Gift was Fire, though there were other, less common aspects to her inheritance. She was an only child. Perhaps because of this, her father was indulgent. He allowed her many liberties which were uncommon for women at that time in China. Many in her family believed this unwise, but few withstood Li Lei, even then, when she was set upon a course. And her mother was, from what I can tell, a most unusual woman, and she wished Li Lei to understand her full nature.

"Sadly, Li Lei's mother died when she was thirteen. Her father remarried very soon. Li Lei blamed her family for this haste, believing they pushed the marriage on him. I suspect they did, for he was a prosperous merchant with no son. Her new stepmother gave him that son, as well as two more daughters, and attempted to steer Li Lei toward more conventional ways. Instead, Li Lei grew even more difficult to handle."

That, Lily thought, sounded inevitable.

Li Qin paused to sip at her cooled tea. "I am guessing at some of this, for she has not said these things exactly as I say them. I like the English expression: *I read between the lines*. But this much is true. One day when she was fifteen she was wandering alone on the mountain near her father's mine, which no well-brought-up young woman would do. And she met Sam.

"Perhaps it was this meeting which decided her course. I believe so. She says she would not have, later on, disobeyed her father had her stepmother not chosen so poor a husband for her. And truly, she was aware of what she owed her family, as any Chinese girl of that time must have been. But I believe she would not have accepted any marriage. She had been offered another choice, which was so very rare then for women. From that moment, she was set on becoming a scholar of magic."

Hmph. The mental snort was accompanied by a physical one, a gentle pulsation of warm, cinnamon-and-metal-scented air that startled Lily. Her head swiveled.

Sam's head rested in the dirt some ten feet away. He'd lain down fully and she hadn't even noticed, so riveted was she by the story Li Qin told of Grandmother's early life.

A scholar, indeed. For once the chill, precise voice was neither cool nor impenetrable. Emotions seemed to echo up from the depths of the mind behind the voice. . . fondness, amusement, joy, loss. *Li Lei was not born to be a scholar. She was born to meddle.*

"You would know." There was rebuke in Li Qin's voice.

Lily looked back at her, surprised more by the tone of Li Qin's voice than the content of her words. "Sam meddles?"

"Oh, yes." Li Qin looked as placid as always. "His meddling may be in service of a worthy goal. I believe he considered his goal with Li Lei worthy. He knew the Chimei would come to Li Lei's city, you see, and that great suffering and destruction would result. When he accepted her as apprentice, he did so with the hope that, when the time came, she would destroy the Chimei's grip on this realm."

Grandmother had been Sam's apprentice? Lily could not resist asking, "Was she, um . . . was she a human apprentice? Or is that when . . ."

"Oh, yes, she was human, and quite young to our way of thinking—only seventeen—when she ran off to Sam. I gather it was not unheard of for a dragon to accept a human apprentice, but it was most unusual."

Rule spoke. "I'm curious about why Sam would leave it to hope and chance and a young human woman to defeat this Chimei. It seems he could have dealt with her himself."

This time the puff of air smelled more of metal and ash than cinnamon. *You know very little, man who is wolf.*

"Then tell me more. Tell us."

Silence, both physical and mental. Then . . . *You have stories, Rule Turner, that speak of the Great War. My people, too, fought in that war—and in its aftermath. The Chimei are like lupi in that they were created by an Old One involved in that conflict. Unlike lupi, they were not originally intended to be warriors. What do you know of the reasons for the Great War?*

"Very little," Rule admitted. "I know many players and peoples were involved. I don't know most of their names, natures, or goals. I do know why my Lady fought. She fought for the right of the younger races to determine their own destinies."

You refer to the younger races as "they." Lupi are a very young race.

Rule shrugged. "Lupi belong to the Lady. We were created to fight for her goals, and our destiny lies in her hands and ours, jointly. I suppose I see us as different from other races that way."

Lily looked at Rule, taken aback. Didn't he think lupi deserved to determine their own fate?

Sam, too, seemed to find his statement curious. *You do not find a contradiction in this? Did not the nature of your creation rob you of the very choice your Lady cherishes?*

"The human part of me understands your question. The wolf considers it silly. The contradiction you see exists only in words. I could hunt more words in an attempt to explain, but they would be imprecise and, I suspect, unhelpful. Dragons are by nature supreme individualists. A dragon might have difficulty perceiving the truth of a race founded in both individuality and mutuality."

Humans are such a race, also.

"Humans are more conflicted about it."

Lily tried to grasp what Rule meant. The conflict between the needs of the many and the needs of the one—that, she knew about. People had been searching for the right balance there since they came out of caves, and maybe before. But she sensed there was more to what he said.

I am intrigued, Sam said after a brief pause. *If you survive, I would speak more with you about this, but current troubles require the tabling of such digressions.*

Your Lady has conveyed to you the essence of the conflict. The Great War was fought by many peoples for many reasons, but it was the deep dispute among some Old Ones which sparked it and made it so terrible. They disagreed over . . . We might say, over the amount of meddling they would allow themselves. Some attempted to hasten the maturation of the younger races through judicious meddling. Some opposed any interference. And some vigorously strove to shape the younger races.

The Chimei are the product of such reasoning. They were made by conjoining the patterns of multiple species, both sentient and nonsentient, physical and nonphysical. Their creator made them largely nonphysical so that if their physical portion was destroyed, they would not die, and could eventually reconstitute their physicality. He considered fear of death an evil force.

Had he stopped there, his children might have persisted more or less as he intended them, but he went on to remove fear from them entirely, believing it lies at the root of warped and dangerous choices.

He erred. Perhaps fear is an essential component of sentience, for the Chimei, unable to experience it themselves, crave fear. In the vast carnage of the Great War they mutated, becoming a species that actively feeds on fear. In the War's aftermath, they developed another skill. They already had mindspeech; they learned how to touch other minds to cause them to create waking nightmares.

"Like giant snakes," Lily burst out. "Or murderous yeti, or whatever someone fears. It's the Chimei who's doing that. She's making people see what they fear."

Yes.

She shoved to her feet, furious. "Why didn't you tell us? Warn us, let us know what we were up against. This Chimei had something to do with the attack on Cullen, didn't she? If you'd told us instead of making bets about when we'd show up—"

Quiet.

The single word arrived with such force that, involuntarily, Lily took a step back.

I balance the fate of your world in what I say to you, when I say it, what I imply, what I leave for you to learn elsewhere or not at all.

Lily sucked in a breath. He meant it. He'd spoken as he always did, with inhuman precision—no rhetorical flourishes, no dramatic exaggeration. "The world. The entire world."

I said that my people battled in the War's aftermath. We are uniquely suited to fighting the Chimei, and there were many Chimei in realms outside their own, so the fighting continued for some time. The cost to us was great. It was decided there was need for a treaty to stop the killing. Almost all Chimei agreed to return to their home realm, where certain alterations rendered them less dangerous. They are not allowed to leave. Some Chimei, such as this one, refused to return. The treaty binds such Chimei in other ways—and, unlike treaties made by humans, it binds in an absolute sense. Chimei and dragons are unable to kill each other—unable to act directly against each other.

"Directly," Lily repeated. She knew a loophole when she heard one. "You can't just pounce on this Chimei, but indirectly you can do something?"

Operating against her indirectly is possible, but difficult. Small actions, intent, words—all may have cumulative power. Applied at the wrong time, in the wrong way, this power could break the treaty. If dragons break the treaty, two things may happen. Any Chimei still outside their own realm would be free to travel here. And any Chimei here would be able to breed.

"This treaty prevents their breeding?"

It does. This Chimei is still in attenuated form. She is extremely powerful, but without physicality to anchor her, she is unable to use her power effectively. If she succeeds in manifesting herself fully, San Diego and much of this coast will be lost. If she breeds, or if other Chimei travel here and manifest themselves physically, they will send your world spiraling into chaos and madness.

"Chaos and madness. The world. You're speaking literally."

Sam didn't deign to answer. Probably he figured he'd said it once, and that should be enough.

Lily's heart was pounding. Possible disasters spun through her head—or was it all one enormous tragedy, on a scale she couldn't conceive? And couldn't stop trying to imagine.

She looked at Rule. She wasn't sure what she wanted from him. He couldn't have any answers, either. He met her gaze, his eyes dark and troubled. And reached for her hand.

Oh, yeah. That's what she'd wanted. The reminder that they were in this together . . . whatever the hell "this" was. She turned back to Sam. "Can't the Old Ones who drew up this treaty—I'm guessing that's who was behind it—do something?"

They have bound themselves to not interfere. It is an imperfect situation.

Imperfect. Yeah, that was one way of looking at it. Lily had an ancient, not-quite-physical demon who couldn't be killed disrupting the minds in her city. Eating the fear her nightmares caused. What was she supposed to do? How did she fight such a creature?

Lily took a slow breath. *Start where you are.* That's what Grandmother always said. For Lily, that meant treating this like a cop. "Okay. I saw an Asian guy at Clanhome last night shortly before Cullen was attacked. No one else saw him. How does he fit in? He does fit somehow, doesn't he?"

I will not answer that at this time. I suspect you will be free to confer with the others about it, however.

Well, duh. Of course she was. That didn't—

Lily Yu. A tinge of exasperation lent the faintest warmth to Sam's words. *There is no "of course" to this. Do you not see? It is likely you will be bound, to a greater or lesser extent, by the treaty.*

That did not make sense. "The treaty was between dragons and Chimei. I'm human."

Your grandmother chose to return to her original form, but she has been dragon. It is impossible for one who has been dragon to ever be fully not-dragon. The treaty binds her, and you are of her blood.

Lily went blank. She wasn't—couldn't be—

Did you not ask earlier why I can mindspeak you despite your Gift?

She had, but he couldn't be right. That couldn't be the reason.

Rule squeezed her hand. His eyes were dark, concerned. "This troubles you? I remember Fagin saying something along those lines. That he'd heard a suggestion that sensitives were born of dragon magic, or something like that. You weren't upset by the idea then."

Because she hadn't believed it. Besides . . . "That's not the same. Being touched by their magic isn't the same as being, well . . ." She couldn't say it. It sounded stupid. Presumptuous.

She received what felt like the mental equivalent of . . . a chuckle? *In this, you are not like your grandmother. I do not believe Li Lei is capable of applying "presumptuous" to herself. In this, she was dragon before she was dragon.*

No, you are not a dragon, Lily Yu, but you partake of a portion of dragon nature. You sense magic directly, as we do, although you are blind to it and unable to shape it. You have already begun to manifest one ability common to dragons, though you seem determined to overlook it.

What was he talking about?

You are capable of acquiring mindspeech and possibly other skills common to dragons, though I have seen no suggestion that you know this or wish to spend the necessary years of study to do so. Most notably, you possess an immunity to worked magic that is equal to that of an adult dragon.

Her Gift. He was talking about her Gift, which he claimed wasn't a human thing at all. It was a dragon thing. All these years she'd insisted that being a sensitive didn't make her anything other than fully human, and now . . .

Your mind is unpleasantly noisy.

It was pretty noisy from her perspective, too. "You think this treaty enacted however many thousands of years ago will affect me?"

Affect you, yes, and be affected by you. I do not know to what extent. Neither does the Chimei, for the situation is unprecedented. For now, she goes warily. She does not strike directly at Li Lei or at those of Li Lei's blood.

"Strike at Grandmother." Who was missing. "And us. Me and my sisters. She wants to strike at us. You mean the Chimei intends to hurt my family."

She craves revenge as a human drunkard craves alcohol. More. I believe she remained here chiefly so she could seek revenge.

"For over three hundred years?" Lily asked, incredulous. "If this Chimei has been seeking revenge all that time, she isn't very good at it."

She has been largely unable to act. The Turning changed this.

"More magic around, you mean." With sudden urgency, Lily asked, "Where is Grandmother?"

Unhurt. And hidden.

"And my mother. God, my mother isn't of Grandmother's

blood. If this Chimei wants revenge and doesn't dare go after those of us who might—who partake of dragon nature—"

Two things protect your mother. Li Lei gave her a charm carved from one of my scales. It may not be necessary. Your mother is mated with your father and has borne him children. This comprises a bond which the treaty will recognize, though again I cannot say the precise degree of restraint it will impose on the Chimei. In essence, all residents of San Diego are at risk. Your mother's risk may be higher than most. It may be lower.

"But if mating with someone creates a bond that the treaty recognizes . . ." Lily couldn't figure out how to arrive gracefully at the end of that sentence. She glanced back at Li Qin.

Who rose gracefully, smiling, and came to her. "You are kind to be concerned, and to offer respect for my privacy. Clearly, I have not borne your grandmother's children, Lily. She concluded this was a critical factor, and that I would not be safe from the Chimei. That is why I am here. The Chimei will not attack those directly under Sam's protection, for in such a case he would be allowed to strike back."

"Okay." Lily nodded. "Okay." She had long wondered about Grandmother and this woman, whom she'd been raised to think was a distant cousin. A few months ago she'd decided their relationship went beyond that—if, indeed, Li Qin was any sort of blood relation at all. But it was weird to have Li Qin confirm it. Weirder than she'd expected.

Not really because of the same-sex thing. Grandmother was precisely as conventional as it suited her to be—she especially approved of conventions involving respect for your elders—and profoundly disinterested in any rules or norms she didn't agree with.

No, it was knowing for certain that her grandmother had a lover of any sort. Not in the past. In the present. That was just . . . weird. "Rule wouldn't be protected, then."

"We do not think so, no." Li Qin put a gentle arm around Lily's waist. "This is a great deal to hear all at once. I have been able to absorb pieces of this tale a little at a time over the years. You are trying to arrange it inside you all at once. This is difficult."

For no reason, Lily's eyes teared up. It infuriated her. She blinked frantically. "I'm . . . sort of topsy-turvy."

"Will you indulge me by taking tea once more? It is not your practice, I know, but I do not have a garden here to offer you. Perhaps a few quiet moments will allow your insides to settle."

"That . . ." Lily hesitated. "Okay. Yes. Tea would be fine." For maybe the first time in her life, she actually meant it. If nothing else, the ritual would give her something to do where she knew the rules. Speaking of which . . . As Li Qin released her and moved away, Lily looked at Rule.

He held her hand still, but was watching Sam, who'd risen from his curled posture. His wings were slowly unfolding as if he were about to depart for the sky. "One question before you go. No, two questions."

Sam didn't respond, but he paused.

"Was this Chimei behind the attack on Cullen?"

Certainly. Sorcerers are dangerous to Chimei.

"How?"

I will not explain. Was that your other question?

Rule grimaced. "No. You spoke of the consequences of your indirect actions breaking the treaty. I assume the Chimei can act indirectly, also."

She can.

"What happens if the Chimei's actions cause the treaty to break?"

There was distinct amusement in Sam's "voice" this time. *Lily Yu is not the only one to joust with questions. If this Chimei causes the treaty to break, I kill her.*

"But you said—"

I said the creator of the Chimei intended them to be fearless and impossible to kill. He achieved the first goal, however disastrously. He nearly achieved the second goal. Nearly, but not quite.

He did not allow for dragons.

Sun Mzao gathered a body whose nose-to-tail length might have stretched out over the entire twice-a-football-field span of his landing pad. He crouched, then sprang for the sky. The great wings unfurled fully and beat once, twice, again . . .

And he disappeared.

"Ah, good," Li Qin said. "Sam heated the water for us before he left."

NINETEEN

~~~

The city of Luan; Shanxi Province, China;
nineteenth day of the eleventh month of the
forty-fourth year of the Ching Dynasty

FOUR people waited outside the home of Chen Wu Yin, the
man who held the license for collecting night soil in the dis-
trict where the sorcerer had taken up residence—two hungry,
desperate women, a middle-aged man, and Li Lei.

She had planned to arrive after the women, who came every
day. She had not planned on the man.

He had long hairs growing out of his nose. Li Lei regarded
those hairs with disgust. How had he heard that the collector
would have a job available today? After all Li Lei had gone
through to make that possible, it was patently unfair for the
man to be here.

She'd needed to find a young employee, one without a family of his own who would be left behind to starve. Whatever
bribe or blackmail the sorcerer had used to procure his place,
it had been effective. The sorcerer controlled the city and its
gates. It was not too difficult to slip a single person through
the gate, but smuggling out an entire family without the proper
papers would have been impossible.

Then she'd had to persuade the young servant man to leave.
She had plenty of coin, which is a fine persuader, but by then

she hadn't been able to speak to him . . . or to anyone. In the end, she'd had to use one of the three stones Sam had given her as part of her training.

If he thought she was foolish to have used his gift on such a paltry target when she could simply have killed him, well, he could laugh at her later. If she had a later. If not, he might still laugh. But she hoped he would also burn things. A great many things.

Oh, she had considered killing the man. She was not squeamish, whatever Sam said. She could have told herself that the man died in service to the city or even the whole of China. Sam believed the sorcerer would not be satisfied with a single city, that his power would only grow . . . as would that of his leman, whose hunger was never sated. Eventually the sorcerer might turn his eyes on that shiniest of baubles, the emperor's court.

He could do great damage there. His lover could do even more.

But Li Lei was not here to save China, the emperor, or even the city. Nor was she here to further Sam's plans and manipulations. Her eyes had been open from the first. He had said he would have a use for her, and had bound her to fulfill it when the time came.

She called him Sam. That was a little joke between them, born of a punning game he enjoyed. To others he was Sun Mzao, much-storied and seldom seen. According to the peasants, he had lived in the mountains near Luan for one thousand years. According to the scholars, he had been killed many years ago at the Battle of Shanhaiguan, where he had fought against the Mongol invaders.

Sometimes the scholars were silly and the peasants wise.

Sun Mzao had known that the sorcerer and the Chimei would come long before they did. He had first called to Li Lei when she was fifteen, knowing she would one day run to him—and that she was the tool he would need to act against the Chimei when the time came. He had told her none of this until he considered the time right.

But he had not known Li Lei's family would be killed. She did not blame him for it. He was what he was.

Still, she was not here for him, or because of the word she'd given him when he took her as apprentice. She was here because the sorcerer and his lover had taken those who were *hers*.

"Lad, you might as well look elsewhere," said the man with the hairs in his nose. "You know I'll be chosen instead of you or those two poor women."

He was right, but Li Lei did not wish to agree. She ducked her head to hide her scowl—she had difficulty at times appearing properly subservient—and shook it in a firm negative.

"You were told to come here, eh? I guess you can't disobey, but you waste your time."

Li Lei wondered why a healthy man of thirty or so would seek a job hauling feces. He wasn't starving or coughing or marked by the pox, but there must be something wrong with him. Well, he did not wear the queue, which was stupid, but there were still those who resisted the Manchu emperor's edict for his Han subjects. Personally, Li Lei found it convenient. With her head partially shaved and the rest of her hair drawn back in a braid, people looked at her and saw a boy of fourteen or so. It never occurred to them she might be female.

The man shrugged and turned away. "Don't be sensible, then."

Perhaps she was not the only one who'd thought that working such a lowly job might gain her entry into the sorcerer's residence. It was a disconcerting thought. He might be a thief.

Was he with a tong? Surely he would have threatened her, if so . . . but no, he thought she was no threat to his getting the job. How would she get rid of him? She did not want to kill the man, even if he did have disgusting nose hairs.

The battered door of Chen Wu Yin's house opened. His wife stood there, eyeing the four of them. Chen Wu Yin's wife was very fat, very shrewd, but Li Lei had learned that she was prone to stealthy acts of kindness.

"So, you want a job, eh?" She studied the peasant man out of eyes reduced to new-moon slits by the greater moons of her cheeks. "Oh, quiet, quiet," she told the two women, who had begun bleating of their need for a job. "You know I do not send women with Wu Yin. My honorable husband has no sense with women. I do not know why you still come."

Li Lei knew why they came. Chen Wu Yin was a lecherous old goat, which was why his wife would not hire women. But when others were not around to take note, she often found an errand for these two women, and paid them with a bowl of rice. Li Lei thought she was wise not to let her kindness be known. Too many would show up at her door, looking for handouts or small jobs. She couldn't feed all the city's poor.

As for how Li Lei knew of it—why, it was winter, and Li Lei had learned much as apprentice to Sun Mzao. Chen Wu Yin's wife liked to be warm. She kept a small fire burning most of the time; Li Lei had listened through the fire. It was a use of magic, yes, and so a risk, but the sorcerer could not purge the city entirely of magic. Fire-listening took very little power for one of the fire-kin like her, and could easily be mistaken for some charm the woman had bought, if it were noticed at all.

"Mistress," the peasant man said, his voice soft, his gaze appropriately downcast, "I have hopes you might have a job for me. I am a good worker—strong and healthy—and I have a wife and two small sons. I need to work."

"Hmm."

Li Lei had a sudden inspiration. From behind the man's back, she pointed at him and made the sign for *tong*. The woman might not recognize it, but if she did—

"You look strong enough," she said grudgingly, "but I have promised to speak with my cousin's wife's sister's son today and see if he can do the work. It is a matter of family, you understand? If he does not work hard, I will speak with you again." For the first time she looked directly at Li Lei. "Well, boy? Are you going to keep me waiting forever? Come in, come in."

The house where the night soil collector lived with his wife was nowhere near as fine as the house where Li Lei had lived, of course. The small public room she entered was crowded and none too clean. But a fire burned cheerily in the hearth on the far wall. Its warmth was welcome.

"So the man was part of the tong, was he?" Chen Wu Yin's wife demanded.

Li Lei hesitated, then shrugged, tapped her head, and nodded. *I think so.*

"What, are you mute?"

Li Lei opened her mouth and showed the fat woman why she did not speak. She then dug out the soiled and much-folded piece of paper she'd prepared, which described her supposed antecedents. For who would hire a mute boy who had no people to speak for him?

A surreptitiously softhearted woman who lived off the collection of shit, it seemed. For the woman could not read, that was clear, yet she exclaimed at the sight of Li Lei's mouth, then muttered about fools and folly—it was not her husband who required mute servants, no, and why were people such idiots? And while she muttered, she retrieved for Li Lei a small bowl of bean curd, then lectured her about where she would sleep and how hard she would work.

To her disgust, Li Lei felt her eyes fill. She ate the bean curd and bowed her thanks, and her silly eyes stayed moist. At that moment she knew what she would do with the coin sewed into a sash beneath her clothes. It could stay here, with this woman who'd helped a dirty, mute young boy when she did not have to. She wouldn't be needing it herself, would she?

After that she did indeed work very hard, and when she curled up in the straw in the little shed where she'd been told to sleep, her muscles ached and she could hardly stand to smell herself. But she knew now that the first part of her plan would work.

The one flaw with Li Lei's disguise had been her voice. Try as she might, she could not sound like anything other than a young woman. So it was necessary that she not speak—and there was a good way to explain that. The night soil collector did not require mute servants, but the sorcerer did. A few impoverished but enterprising families had, early on, tried to place their surplus sons or daughters in his service by rendering them unable to speak. Chen's wife assumed Li Lei was one of them.

For now, Li Lei would collect night soil—which meant entering the grounds of the sorcerer's compound. Once she understood something of the workings of the place, she could change her disguise slightly. She did not need to pass for a servant there for long, after all.

Li Lei lay awake in the darkness, curled in the smelly straw, for a long time. She pined for sleep like a lover, but it would not come.

Just as the ghosts had not come. Not last night, or the night before, or the night before that. Or else they had, but Li Lei had been unable to see or hear them.

Her silly, fecund stepmother was dead. Her aunts were dead—her mother's younger sister, her father's older sister, and their aunt. So were the servants, even harmless little Shosu who used to giggle with Li Lei when she was supposed to be working, and fussy old Zi Jeng, who had worked for her father's father.

Her father was dead. The babies . . . and oh, would not Jing be incensed that she thought of him as one of the babies? But he would not know, for he and the little girls were dead. She would never see or speak to any of them again. She did not even know where their bodies lay, to take them offerings.

Sun Mzao claimed such offerings could not reach them in the land of the dead, but while he knew a great deal about death, he admitted he had no contact with the dead. Neither did Li Lei. Her knowledge of death lay entirely on this side of the curtain . . . but aside from that limitation, it was abundant.

The Chimei had killed her entire family, using one of her loved one's hands to deal the deaths. The demon could not herself be killed, much as Li Lei longed to send her across that dark curtain . . . but she could be hurt, diminished, stopped.

And the sorcerer *could* be killed.

He would be. Li Lei had vowed that on her true name—just before she'd cut off her tongue.

TWENTY

RULE sat quietly through a second making and pouring of tea. Alarm still pinged through his system, scattered after-quakes set off by Sam's revelations. His thoughts were jumbled; he made no attempt to gather them. Not yet. There was a time to bear down and think through a problem, and a time when thinking was mere froth on the surface of deeper processes moving forward, unseen, in their own way.

Mostly he watched Lily.

She was upset, and not just by the threat posed by the Chimei. *Topsy-turvy*, she'd said. He didn't understand. He tried not to feel affronted. He knew she'd always under-stood herself to be fully human, and it was rough to be forced to change one's view of self. But was her notion of humanity so rigid it couldn't flex to include a whiff or two of dragon?

Once the tea was poured, he inhaled deeply, allowing the scent to fill him. A question floated up into the froth of his thoughts. How would he react if he were told he wasn't purely lupus?

Badly, he decided, and sipped.

More questions, more insistent: What would they do about this Chimei? How would they stop her?

A year ago he would have pounced on those questions, wrestled with them, stuck doggedly to their trail. The balance between wolf and man had shifted since then . . . a forced shift, perhaps, and acceptance had not come easily. But the new balance worked. His wolf was more present these days. If that made some situations—like hospitals—harder to navigate, it steadied him in others.

Like now. His wolf understood waiting. They didn't know enough. Some shapes were emerging, but the murk was too thick to guess what those shapes portended. It wasn't yet time to act, or even to choose an action.

He glanced at Lily. There was a small crease between her brows, and though she seemed to look at the cup she held, he doubted she noticed it at all. He would leave the first action to her, he decided. Soon she would begin to ask questions. The shapes would grow clearer.

For now, Rule relaxed into the moment. The air was almost painfully dry, which muted the scents it carried, but those scents were delightful—creosote, cypress and sumac, wild mustard and cholla, all overlaid with the lush moistness of the reservoir. San Miguel Mountain smelled like home to him, only without much wolf-scent. And with a good deal of dragon.

Most wolves wouldn't care for that, and not because the smell was unpleasant. Sam's scent was as compelling as his sinewy form, but it bore the meaty whiff of predator among its notes of metal and spice and mystery. The smell awoke the crouched beast in the back-brain, stirring the hackles, making feet twitch with the need to escape something much larger and more dangerous than any wolf could be.

Rule's beast was calm. He knew this scent, this dragon.

The air was growing warm, perhaps unpleasantly so for humans. Rule asked Li Qin if she were comfortable here, if she required anything. She assured him it was much cooler inside Sam's lair. He'd dug her a small "room" inside and enchanted it to remain cool. Something to do with moving the heat elsewhere, she said, through the rocks.

Rule smiled. Even the black dragon was not immune to Li Qin.

Lily asked what she could bring Li Qin. Food? An air mattress? Books? Rule's thoughts drifted back to wolves and dragons.

Wolves prefer to run away if faced with an impossible battle—a more helpful attitude than human machismo, in his view. But Rule's wolf knew this particular dragon. Knowledge did not make him unwary, but it settled his hackles. They weren't friends, he and Sam, but there was respect and honor between them. Sam was deeply honorable, by his lights.

Deeply tricky, too. Rule contemplated that as he sipped.

This time, the consumption of tea seemed to settle Lily, though she hadn't quite emptied her cup when the first question emerged, shaped as a statement. "I wish I knew where Sam went. What he's up to."

Li Qin spread one hand gracefully. "Perhaps he is up to something, as you say, at this moment. Perhaps he left simply so he would not be tempted to steer our conversation."

"He did advise us to confer among ourselves. He thinks we can stir up enough answers to get started that way." Lily frowned at her almost empty cup. "Do you know where Grandmother is? What she's up to?"

"I do not. Sam said she is hidden."

"That doesn't mean she isn't up to something." Lily took a final sip of tea and put down her cup. "Maybe we could start the conferring by you telling us the rest of the story about Grandmother and the Chimei. You said that Sam—Sun Mzao—hoped she would stop the demon somehow. How?"

"The Chimei had taken as lover a young sorcerer, who had in turn taken control of the city. While Li Lei was in the mountains, studying with Sam, this sorcerer caused the deaths of her entire family."

"Bloody—" Rule stopped himself from finishing the oath. "Excuse me. But . . . she was only seventeen, you said."

"Seventeen when she went to Sam. Nineteen when her family was slain."

"She killed the sorcerer?" Rule asked.

Li Qin nodded. "Though I do not know the details, I know Li Lei returned to Luan with that intention, and she succeeded." She put her own cup down. "I have heard pieces of this story over many years. The questions I now wish to ask were not what seemed most important in earlier days. Li Lei never spoke easily of that time, so I did not press her."

Lily's fingers tapped once on the table. "She didn't explain when she asked you to take refuge with Sam?"

"She said she was unable to. She was clearly frustrated by this."

"This treaty Sam talked about stopped her from talking about it now, but it didn't stop her before."

"So I assume. I do not know."

Rule said, "Sam spoke of intent as a factor."

Lily's gaze flicked to him. "He did, didn't he?"

"I cannot claim to know another's full intent," Li Qin said placidly. "However, I do not think she told me anything so I would be able to act against the Chimei, should the need arise. I would say her motives were quite personal."

"Hmm." Lily's fingers drummed on the table again. "But Grandmother did kill the sorcerer who killed her family. You're sure of that."

"Li Lei is certain of it."

"The thing is, it looks like the Chimei . . . Does she have a name?"

Li Qin turned her palms up. "I do not know it. Could any being not possess a name?"

"I don't know. Dammit, I left my notebook in the car. Never mind," she said to Rule when he started to rise. "I'll take notes later. What I mean to say, Li Qin, is that it looks like our Chimei has hooked up with a sorcerer again. That's not definite, but it's a strong possibility."

"Ah. No, I do not believe this could be the same sorcerer. However, many folktales speak of men who unknowingly take a demon or spirit as wife or concubine. This is a common theme. I mentioned this to Li Lei recently, thinking it was funny to assume a spirit would wish for a human wife. She said she didn't know about spirits, but for a demon, mating with a human was the only way to be in flesh."

"In flesh?"

Li Qin tilted her head, considering that. "No, I believe 'in body' would be closer. Her words were *zài shen ti*. It's an odd phrase, which is why it stayed with me. At the time, I thought she made a naughty play on words—to be in a body, to be in a woman. Now I wonder if she meant this physicality Sam spoke of."

Lily glanced at Rule. "Shen ti is like *body* or *health*. Zài sort of means *in*, but not exactly. You'd use it to say you were in a location, or in the middle of doing something. Or if you use it a different way, it just means to be, to exist. So that fits. It works."

He nodded. "You think the Chimei's bond with her lover is necessary for her to . . . How did Sam put it? To reconstitute her physical portion."

"Sure sounds possible. Sex magic is an old tradition, and if she always picks a sorcerer for a mate, it may be she needs him to do a ritual or something. We can ask Cullen what he thinks later." She looked at Li Qin again. "Do you know if, when Grandmother killed the . . . Shit." Her phone had chimed. "I'm surprised I've got reception out here."

Li Qin smiled. "Oh, Sam arranged for me to have bars here. He did not want me to feel isolated. I think, too, he is curious about technology and wished to see if he could do this."

Lily flung her a startled glance, but whatever number she saw on the phone's display had her answering crisply, "Lily Yu."

"Sam is able to boost coverage for a cell phone?" Rule asked Li Qin. He didn't precisely listen to Lily's conversation while he spoke to Li Qin, but he didn't precisely not listen, either. He felt a frisson of displeasure when her caller turned out to be Deputy Cody Beck—and felt annoyed with himself for the annoyance.

"I do not know how it works—but then, I do not know how

cell phones work, either." She smiled. "I believe Sam understands it better than I."

"There would be a huge commercial potential, if what he does could be duplicated."

"I do not think Sam approves of money. Not for dragons, at least. He says he does not want his promises scattered all over, nor does he accept promises promiscuously."

Money as a collective promise? It was an interesting take on the subject. "Still, if he's found a way to make magic and technology coexist, or even work together . . . hmm." It gave him something to consider for the favor Nokolai would eventually claim, once they finished negotiating.

Lily disconnected. "We've got to go."

"What's up?"

"Cody's found a body for me."

THE body, it turned out, was already at the Medical Examiner's.

"So this victim was killed by a single thrust to the heart." Rule started the car, put it in reverse, and twisted around. He needed to get the vehicle turned around here, where Sam's landing pad gave him room to maneuver.

Lily clicked her seat belt into place. "Looks like. The responding officers didn't spot it, but no shame to them. The body was found yesterday, but the victim had been dead awhile. In this heat . . ." She shrugged.

Rule's nose twitched in sympathy. "They know anything about the victim yet?"

"If so, Cody didn't have it. Just that the man had been stabbed from behind by a thin blade that penetrated the heart. No suggestion magic was involved, but there wouldn't be. Um . . . you don't have to go in with me."

"I'm perfectly capable of controlling myself."

"Sure, but you hate that place."

Rule disliked morgues with both of his natures, but it was the wolf who truly hated them. Rule wasn't sure why. Wolves weren't upset by the deaths of strangers, but for some reason, the presence of all those bodies made his wolf anxious. Cemeteries didn't affect him that way. Just morgues. "I'm not fond of waiting in the car, either."

"Okay. What about your bodyguards? Going to have them meet us there?"

"They won't be much help against a killer who could make them think no one was around. Or that you were attacking me."

"True." She pulled out her phone. "I'm going to call my mother."

His eyebrows rose. "Voluntarily?"

"I just want to make sure . . . rats. It went to voice mail. Ah—Mother, this is Lily. I need to talk to you about something important. Give me a call, okay?"

"You want to make sure she's okay," Rule said as she disconnected.

"I want to make sure she actually wears that charm. Mother tends to discount what Grandmother says, which I guess I can understand, because Grandmother doesn't ask—she commands. And she seldom explains. But telling Mother to wear a dragon scale charm doesn't mean she'll do it."

True. "Madame Yu must be aware of that."

"She ought to be, but there's this dynamic in our family where Mother usually agrees with Grandmother, then does things the way she wants. So she might have nodded and agreed to wear the charm, but—" Her phone interrupted with the opening bars of "The Star Spangled Banner."

That particular ring tone meant her boss, Ruben Brooks. She answered right away. "Hi, Ruben. You must be psychic or something. I was just going to call."

Since Brooks was, indeed, psychic—his Gift was precognition, or awareness of events before they occurred—that was meant as a joke. But Brooks didn't laugh. Rule had no trouble hearing his response. His hearing might not be as acute in this form as in his other one, but with Lily's phone so close it would be hard to not overhear.

"Lily, I had a disturbing dream last night. Or a series of dreams, rather, centered on San Diego."

"I didn't think you did dreams."

"Normally my Gift doesn't manifest that way, no. On the rare occasions that it does, it generally means there's the possibility of a massive loss of life. I have a feeling it would be unwise to bring in troops at this point, but I'm unsure what steps I should take."

TWENTY-ONE

RULE saw Lily jolt. He felt the same shock in himself, a nasty, crawling certainty that things were about to go spinning out of control.

"Troops?" Lily repeated. "Like the Army? You're thinking of calling in the Army?"

"No, I've decided I'd better not. I'll explain. I dreamed of a series of possible scenarios. Many of them involved widespread arson, rioting, violent mobs—the complete breakdown of civil authority in San Diego. However, in some of the dream sequences, this breakdown wasn't limited to San Diego. I don't wish to alarm you, but there is a possibility the upcoming crisis could infect the entire nation. Maybe several nations."

"We just got warned about something like that," Lily said slowly. "Really bad shit that could happen all over the world."

Ruben's faint sigh suggested relief rather than increased tension. "Then I called the right person. Good. For some reason I doubted . . . Never mind."

"Do you have any feel for how close the crisis is?"

"Hmm. I can't answer that precisely. I'll try to frame this

better. That I dreamed of so many sequences suggests there are many decision points that could lead to what I saw. Some of those decision points may be fairly immediate. I believe my first impulse—which was to ask the president to put the National Guard on standby alert—was one such decision point. I decided that bringing in the military would increase rather than ameliorate the potential disaster. Do you know why that might be?"

"Shit. Shit. Maybe. Let me pull my thoughts together. We've just been to see Sam—Rule's with me—and what we learned has to explain those dreams. He said . . ." Her voice trailed off. A strange look spread over her face, as if she'd bitten into a steak only to have her teeth grind against steel. "He told us about this being, this . . . He said that I . . . There's . . . Oh, hell."

Lily thrust her phone at Rule. "I can't. I can't say any of it."

He took the phone, thinking fast. Lily had been able to discuss the Chimei with Li Qin, so why . . . but Li Qin already knew about the Chimei. Ruben didn't. That must be the difference. "Ruben, this is Rule. I'll have to brief you. Lily has just discovered she's unable to speak to you about this. There's a geas—an inherited binding—that's tied to Lily's Gift rather than being repelled by it. This geas prevents her from saying more."

"Hello, Rule." Ruben's voice was polite with a hint of wary. "What in the world is going on out there?"

Lily watched him, intent and furious. He wished he could take her hand, but both of his were occupied. "I need to ask you something. It's after noon, your time. Clearly you waited several hours to call Lily. Earlier, you said you had doubts, but didn't explain. Were you uneasy about speaking with Lily?"

"Yes, I thought our conversation might be or might precipitate one of the decision points."

"Do you have that feeling about speaking with me?"

Ruben was silent a moment. "Actually, it's stronger than before."

"All right. Let me think a moment."

Lily spoke very low. "Rule, you have to tell Ruben."

"Do I? It seems that the treaty considers Ruben pivotal,

or it wouldn't have stopped you. Ruben has an uneasy feeling about talking with me. This—my revealing information—could be one of those indirect actions Sam spoke of which can break the treaty."

"Or it could be exactly why Sam brought you in—so you could pass on information I can't!"

That was what had his mind spinning, trying to guess at ramifications that were essentially unguessable. Sam had included Rule in his briefing. That had been choice, not necessity, so it meant something, but what? "He made me part of this, though the treaty's geas can't act on me, and the treaty didn't stop him. Therefore it must be possible, even probable, for me to act in ways that don't break the treaty."

"I'm finding my end of this conversation interesting, yet frustrating," Ruben said.

"Sorry. I was speaking to Lily. I should have put you on mute. There are ramifications to your learning too much right now."

"There are also ramifications from my knowing too little, which is where I am right now."

"I'm sorry," Rule repeated, "but I have to put you on mute for a moment." He touched the screen.

Lily was ready to erupt. "Dammit, Rule, we can't just sit on this!"

"Before we act, we have to figure out why Sam brought me into this—and why the treaty let him."

"He did it so you could speak of all the things I am so damned not able to!"

"That's one possibility." Rule trusted Ruben as much as he did any non-clan human, but telling the man about the Chimei and the treaty would hugely increase the variables. "Here's another one. What if Ruben decides he can't rely on you, since you're being affected by an outside agency?"

"He wouldn't pull me. Someone else wouldn't have the geas getting in the way, but the Chimei or her lover could affect them." Her voice was crisp. She was thinking again, not just reacting.

"But Ruben might not accept my word for that. And it

would be my word, not yours, since you can't speak to him about this."

"Shit."

"Yes." And that was only one of a half dozen ways this could go wrong. A half dozen he could glimpse—how many more was he missing?

He couldn't afford to bring Ruben in. He couldn't control the decisions Ruben or those he informed might make. Maybe Ruben wouldn't bring in troops, but the president could overrule him. Adding Ruben to the mix meant adding a spiraling number of decision points.

No, that wasn't quite accurate . . . Withholding information didn't mean Ruben wouldn't act. He'd simply do so in the dark. "Bloody blast it all. Does Sam expect me to figure out what he thinks I'd do, then do it? How do I know what a dragon thinks I would do?"

Grudgingly, Lily said, "Sam knows you best as a wolf. He'd predict your actions based on the wolf, not the man."

Yes. Yes, that made sense. He flashed her a smile, then fell silent, letting himself slip partway into wolf . . . and gradually, many of the difficulties dropped away. His choices were fewer and clearer.

He took the phone off mute and spoke crisply. "Ruben."

"Still here." There was an uncharacteristic edge to the man's voice.

"Your hunch was correct. Do not call in the Army or the National Guard. We're dealing with a being who can affect minds en masse—up to about five hundred at a time that we know of, based on the number of people who failed to see, smell, or hear this being's agent last night. Lily was the only exception. Her Gift blocked the illusion."

"Yet it allows her to be silenced by this geas."

"As I said, the geas is inherent in her Gift, though it wasn't triggered until now. But the geas doesn't delude Lily's senses, which this being can do to almost everyone else."

"Including you?"

"Yes. It's not mind control, but sensory control. People see and smell what she tells them to. We don't know her range, either. She may be able to affect even more people than she did last night. Since she thrives on the fear of others, calling in the Guard could precipitate the very crisis we need to avert. The Guard might begin shooting at what they thought were monsters, and instead kill innocents."

"You said 'she.' What being is this?"

"I won't speak of that at this time."

"Won't or can't?"

"Lily can't. I won't. Nor, I'm afraid, will I explain that decision."

Ruben was silent for a long moment. "This has something to do with the treaty you spoke of before muting the phone. Treaties are the purview of the government, not your clan."

"The treaty I spoke of predates the U.S. government." He paused, considered options. "I believe that's all I will say about it."

"Does this have something to do with the one you lupi don't name? The one who tried to open a hellgate last year, and whom Lily and you ran up against in Dis?"

Ruben was amazingly bright—and was reaching for precisely the conclusion Rule intended. A stupid man would not have arrived at the wrong answer so quickly. "I'm not going to answer that question."

"That's not satisfactory."

"We aren't in a satisfactory position at the moment. I have to gather more information before I know what's safe to tell you—or anyone else."

"*You* have to gather information. Not Lily?"

"We'll both be doing so, of course. But since she's involuntarily mute on the subject, it falls to me to decide what to tell, who to tell, and when. We'll stop this enemy, Ruben," he added quietly. "But I'm not sure how yet. The situation is extremely fragile."

Ruben spoke very dryly. "That much I already knew. Let me speak to Lily."

"Very well." Though he wasn't at all sure Lily would back him on this, he handed her phone to her.

"Lily," Ruben said, "are you able to tell me anything at all?"

She scowled. "Not really."

"Can you tell me if what Rule has said—what little he's said—is accurate?"

"Yes." Surprise wiped away the scowl. "Apparently I can. He hasn't told you enough, but what he's said is true."

"You disagree with his decision to withhold information."

"I do, but . . ." She glanced at Rule. "But I understand his reasons, and they're valid. He's doing this his way, which pisses me off, but he's got the right goal in mind. I can see where the scenarios you dreamed about could happen. I can see that all too easily."

"What do you need?"

Rule almost closed his eyes in relief. Ruben was keeping Lily in charge of the investigation.

"I don't know yet. No, wait. A car. I need a car. Mine's still being fixed."

"With the fate of San Diego and possibly the world hanging in the balance," Ruben said dryly, "I think that can be arranged. What will you be doing?"

"Looking for the perp. The, ah, one Rule mentioned, whom apparently I can't mention—no, wait; I can say that he tried to kill Cullen. That perp. He's . . . Shit, it's closing me down again."

"This is frustrating for both of us. Ida will arrange for your car. Where do you want it delivered?"

"The Medical Examiner's office. That's where I'm headed."

"Very well. It may be there before you are. I'll see you tomorrow."

"What? You'll see me?"

"I'm flying out there," he said serenely. "I've a strong feeling I'm needed. Goodbye for now."

Lily took the phone away from her ear, staring at it blankly. "He's coming out here."

"Good."

"You want him here? When you won't trust him with the truth?"

"He's a strong precog who interprets his Gift with rare accuracy. I can't think of anyone better able to help us navigate this maze."

"But you won't tell him what maze we're navigating!"

He glanced at her. She was still deeply angry. Some of that was directed at him, but he wasn't the cause. "It's difficult to put my reasoning in words, since it's largely nonverbal. The wolf wanted . . . No, *I* wanted Ruben to have enough information so he wouldn't act blindly, but there was a good chance he would tell others what I told him. That feels extremely dangerous. Those others might react in too many different ways, ways that Sam couldn't have foreseen and accounted for."

"But now Ruben just has guesses and speculation to pass on. How is that better?"

"That's why I led him to believe we're dealing with the one we don't name."

"You what?"

"I didn't lie, but I encouraged that conclusion. You and I wondered the same thing last night, before we knew about the Chimei. It wasn't hard to steer him in that direction."

"You deliberately deceived him."

"Ruben will be more likely to trust us to deal with this if he believes it has to do with *her.* Lupi are the world's only experts on *her.*"

"That only makes sense if I accept your starting point— that it's better not to tell him the truth."

His decision was so obvious to him now it was hard to understand why she didn't see the same thing he did. "Sam needs the number of decision points kept as low as possible. Otherwise he loses control of the possible ways the treaty could be broken."

"You're letting Sam call the shots? You pulled a Rho on Ruben, but you let—"

"I did what?"

"Pulled a Rho on Ruben. You weren't making suggestions— you were telling him how things were and what he needed to do, then manipulating him like your father would. If he hadn't been on the other side of the continent, he'd have felt your mantle pushing at him."

"Humans don't feel the mantles."

She snorted. "Go right on believing that. I've seen you pull the mantle on a former Marine, and I saw him back down. Never mind—we can argue about that later. The point is, you're dancing to Sam's tune. We need to call Ruben back, fill him in."

"Sam knows the tune. We don't, not yet."

"So you'll just cede him the right to call the shots? That's not like you."

"I've ceded nothing," he snapped. Clearly his *nadia* partook of dragon nature in more ways than one—which gave him new insight into how difficult it had been for her to accept the mate bond, but he'd consider that another day. When she wasn't driving him crazy. "Sam and I are allies in this. You're overreacting."

"I'm damned well not! I'm not going to be shut out, shut down, by this—this—"

"At the moment, the treaty is controlling more of you than your speech. You're like an animal trying to chew off its leg to escape a trap. You're reacting, not thinking."

"I'm thinking just fine. I think I hate misleading Ruben."

"Ruben is a good man, but he acts for *the government*. If Sam's actions indirectly cause a separate power—a governing body—to move against the Chimei, that's likely to break the treaty. "

"I act for the damned government, too."

"And you weren't allowed to speak to Ruben. To bring that government in on this." He let that sink in a moment. "You can't tolerate having something imposed on you. I understand that. Sam understands even better, I'm sure, but he's had time to adjust. He doesn't allow his rage to dominate his thinking."

"His what?" She shook her head. "Sam was fine. Cool and collected as always."

"He doesn't allow his emotions to impinge on his mind-speech. That doesn't mean they don't exist. This treaty binds him even more tightly than it does you. How do you suppose the most sovereign race in existence feels about being constrained?"

Her fingers tapped on her thigh. She frowned off into space.

They were well back into town and traffic now. He gave her the silence to think through what he'd said for a few more blocks, then said, "This body you need to see. Why did the tip come from a deputy? Is it a county case?"

"Hmm? Oh. No, but Cody heard about it. He used to be city, plus he's second generation on the job. He's got a lot of friends in the PD still." She grimaced. "More than I do, apparently, since it was him—"

Her phone sounded. He recognized this ringtone, too—the theme from *Alien versus Predator*—and knew whom it belonged to.

Lily frowned at her lap, where the phone still rested. Sighed. And picked it up. "Hello, Mother. Thanks for calling me back."

"Of course I called you back. You said it was important. He hasn't backed out, has he? Changed his mind?"

The blank look on Lily's face made Rule grin in spite of everything. "Who?"

"Rule, of course! Who else would I mean? Is he getting cold feet? Did you have a fight? If so, well, you leave it to me. He and I are supposed to meet tomorrow to discuss the location for the ceremony. I'll make it clear your family expects him to—"

"No. No, Mother, this isn't about Rule, who is firmly committed to getting married. No cold feet. I understand Grandmother gave you a charm."

"You called about that? Eh! It's an odd little thing, a little black dangle on a chain. Very shimmery, like an opal, and pretty, but odd. Have you seen it? I never had, not until she gave it to me. Though she didn't precisely give it to me. She told me it was rare and valuable and I was to wear it at all times. Of course she couldn't just give it to me—she had to issue instructions. I'm not sure she considers it mine. You know how your grandmother is. She may think of it as a loan. You are sure Rule isn't going to back out?"

"I'm sure. When did she give it to you? Or tell you to wear it," Lily added hastily. "When was that?"

"The day before yesterday, I think. Yes, that's it, because I was about to go to see your Aunt Mequi, but of course your grandmother just dropped by without calling first, so I had to call Mequi and tell her I would be late."

"Are you wearing the charm now?"

"Now? I'm wearing my rose dress. You know the one I mean, with the white trim. That necklace would look very odd with this dress."

"You aren't wearing it."

"The charm is black, Lily. An odd sort of black, because it has other colors in it, but still, black would not go with my rose dress. Don't worry, though. I've put it up safely. I wouldn't allow anything to happen to one of Grandmother's treasures."

Lily took a breath, let it out. "It's vital that you wear the charm all the time. There's some—some bad magic stuff going on. Grandmother gave you the charm to protect you. Father and me and the girls are protected because we're related by blood to Grandmother. You aren't."

"That does not make sense. Your grandmother must be pulling your leg, telling you stories. She tried to tell me something of that sort, too—something about the charm having great magic. But if so, why have I never seen her wear it? If it were a powerful talisman, she would wear it. You are too credulous, Lily. You know how she is."

"Mother, please, I need you to believe me. Just this once, and even though I can't prove it, I need you to believe that your life could depend on wearing that charm."

There was a brief silence, then: "You're very serious about this."

"Completely."

"Oh, very well. You will have lunch with me on Monday so we can decide about your wedding dress, and I will wear the silly charm. I suppose it will go with something in my wardrobe. I'll have to change clothes, but I'm willing to do that."

Lily exhaled in relief. "Thank you, Mother. I know this seems odd, but it's extremely important. But, uh, about Monday—"

"We must make some decisions about your gown, Lily. You

can't buy something off the rack. It will have to be ordered, and there will be alterations. All this takes time."

"Maybe I could do it a week from Monday. I think I could do it then."

"Then I will begin wearing the charm a week from now."

"You can't! You can't put your life at risk just to blackmail me into doing—"

"Then I will see you on Monday. This Monday. We will meet at your Uncle Chen's place at noon. I know you like his orange chicken."

"But—"

"Monday, Lily."

Lily's eyes squeezed closed. Her voice sounded tight, too. "Monday. Noon. Uncle Chen's."

"Good. It will be fun, you'll see. I have to go now, since I must change clothes. Black slacks, I think. They'll go with the charm, and I have a pair that isn't too heavy for summer." With that, Julia Yu gave her daughter a cheerful goodbye and disconnected.

Lily's hand fell to her lap. She shook her head. "How did that just happen? How does she do that? One minute I'm trying to stop a demon from taking over the city. The next I'm agreeing to have lunch with my mother so we can talk about wedding dresses. Wedding dresses," she repeated, as if this were the most trivial thing in the known universe.

"The dress matters to most women," he said mildly. "Clearly it matters to your mother."

"It's not her wedding. It's mine, and . . ." Lily scowled. "What am I doing? I'm arguing with her now that I'm not talking to her. I hate it when I do that. And what do you mean, it matters to most women? It matters to me, too. Just not *now*."

They'd reached the complex of county buildings which included the Medical Examiner's office. Rule slowed. "You were putting off making these decisions even when there was no Chimei in the picture. You don't want to set a date. You don't care where the ceremony is held. My ring isn't even on your finger. It's under your clothes. Hidden."

"Because we haven't made the big press announcement

yet, and you wanted to keep it secret until then so you could spin things your way."

"I'm ready to make that announcement. I've been ready. You keep finding other priorities."

"Now? You want to do it now? Sure, let's hold a press conference. It won't interfere with stopping the Chimei all that much."

"You're missing the bloody point. You feel about marriage somewhat the way you did about the mate bond when it first hit. The way you do about the treaty geas. You feel it binds you, robs you of choice."

"I do not! God, where is all this coming from?"

"You need to find out why you want to marry me. I had to come to my own understanding of marriage. I know why I want this. Why I want your ring on my finger, and mine on yours."

"I agreed because I love you, you damned idiot!"

"You do, yes, but you agreed to marry me because I pushed." He'd known that at the time. He didn't regret it. But he still hit the brakes harder than necessary as he pulled into a parking space at the back of the visitors' parking lot. "You agreed because marriage is what you're expected to do. You don't have a clue why you want it for yourself."

"Thanks for the psychoanalysis. If you're through—"

"Not quite. You aren't comfortable without reasons, without knowing the what, when, and why of things. You need to figure out why you're marrying me."

"Sure. Fine. In my spare time, in between saving the city and wringing your neck, I'll figure that out and get back to you about it." She threw the door open and grabbed her laptop. "I'm getting another car, and it's more efficient for us to split up, so you don't have to hang around."

He knew when he'd been dismissed. It infuriated him. He'd meant to stay with her. She'd intended that, too. But maybe they'd best cool down separately. "Fine. I'll be at the hospital. I need to arrange for Cullen to be moved."

"Right." She slammed the door.

Rule pulled out of the parking space without screeching the

tires. He allowed himself one long glance at the front of the parking lot, where a burly, dark-skinned man in khakis leaned against a sheriff's car.

Deputy Cody Beck.

Rule did not stamp down on the accelerator when he left the parking lot. He was not a hormonally impaired adolescent.

But he wanted to.

TWENTY-TWO

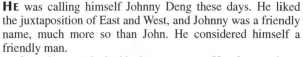

HE was calling himself Johnny Deng these days. He liked the juxtaposition of East and West, and Johnny was a friendly name, much more so than John. He considered himself a friendly man.

Over the years he had had many names. He often used one of the characters from his original name in some form, for it is good to remember one's roots. Often, but not always. His current surname spoke of those origins only in the most general way.

At times he missed China, but it wasn't the China of today he missed, so he didn't indulge in nostalgia often. No point in making himself unhappy, was there?

He'd liked Europe. They had some appreciation for the past there, and the open borders and jumbled web of law enforcement agencies had made it easy to engage in his trade. But his beloved could not be happy in Europe while her enemies lived and prospered in the U.S. When the Turning hit and the level of magic began to increase, she had needed to put her plans in motion.

He didn't begrudge moving here. There was much to appreciate about the U.S. and California and the modern world. He loved video games, especially *Grand Theft Auto*. While he might have preferred San Francisco to San Diego, there were enough people here to feed his beloved, even now when she remained attenuated. There was a large enough Asian population for him to blend in, and he could make use of the established gangs. His profession gave him an in there.

If the public transportation wasn't up to the standards of London or Paris, it was adequate to his needs today. There was a bus stop right at the hospital, though he did have to make two changes to get there.

When the bus slowed to a stop he climbed on board carrying what he needed in a white grocery sack. After some consideration, he'd chosen to play it safe. His target had already confounded him once, proving resistant to both knife and spell. He couldn't assume his other spells would work on lupi as beautifully as they worked on humans. Nor could he assume the sorcerer was too unwell to set proper wards. He ought to be—but then, he ought to be dead, too.

He purchased a day pass from the driver and took a seat. The bus was crowded, and the woman sitting beside him wanted to chat about the weather. Johnny agreed that it was very hot, then took out his phone with an apology and pretended to make some calls.

It was all very well to be friendly, but it would not do to be memorable.

Besides, the woman was too tall. He didn't like tall women. Once the city was his, he wouldn't allow any woman over five foot three in his presence. He'd considered doing the same with men above a certain height, but that wasn't practical. He accepted that some of his subordinates would be larger than he.

Johnny prided himself on his practicality. Practicality, patience, and tolerance—those were his chief virtues. He did not, after all, become angry at the woman for being tall. Poor thing, she couldn't help her height. Instead he cheerfully anticipated the day when women of her excessive inches would not be part of his daily life.

But then, he was a modest man. How could a man achieve

success if he did not understand his limits? He knew, for example, that he was not unusually bright or brave. Neither was he stupid or a coward. When he was young, he had thought one must be one or the other—bright or stupid, brave or cowardly. Now, he knew those were poles—signposts, one might say—at either end of long paths. Most people fell somewhere between those signposts, rather than at one end or the other. One might move slightly closer to one signpost or the other as life proceeded, but one would not greatly alter one's natural position.

He also understood that he was exceptional in two ways. Some quirk of ancestry had gifted him with the ability to see and use magic. Obviously, sorcery was both rare and valuable, but he took no credit for possessing this skill, just as he laid no blame upon himself for lacking great intelligence. He had not achieved the one nor failed at the other. He had simply been born as he was.

Johnny's other exceptional trait was less obvious—indeed, it was invisible to most people, and was commonly held to be twisted or perverse. A limited judgment, of course, but most people were sadly limited. They wanted good and evil painted in black and white so they knew what was what. Very few grasped the essential elasticity of those qualities. Moral behavior was contingent, always contingent, upon circumstances.

This should be obvious to historians, if not to the dreaming majority. In how many ages and cultures had it been considered acceptable, even correct, to torture one's enemies? In some cultures the eating of animal flesh was abhorred; in others, the hunter was elevated. And how many variations existed on proper sexual behavior?

Yet people clung to the idea that some acts were inherently good and performing them made one good. Other acts were inherently evil, committed only by evil persons.

And wasn't English a clever tongue in some ways? This thought had come to Johnny many times since he learned the language, and it never failed to amuse him. One committed to evil, not good; good was simply a performance. Acting as if you were good might make it so, at least in the eyes of others.

But men are always more comfortable thinking themselves like their fellows. Even now, with the fascinating things they were learning about the brain, scientists persisted in viewing abnormalities in the brain as flaws, failures, a problem to be fixed.

Johnny was naturally curious about such things, given the nature of his second exceptional trait. He had read many popularized accounts of brain research and psychology. Happily, he'd been able to conclude he was not what experts called a psychopath. Whatever might be wired differently in his brain, it didn't prevent him from making meaningful connections with others. Clearly he had a deep and loving connection with his beloved.

Psychopaths were also said to lack empathy. That was certainly not true of him. How could he take such pleasure in giving or receiving pain if he were unable to sense the feelings of others?

No doubt he would have shared the common view had he been born "normal." Johnny chuckled as he climbed down from the bus with his white grocery sack. Had he been born without his other exceptional ability, he would also be long dead. His Beautiful One would not have fallen in love with him had he been unable to appreciate the exquisite pleasures she offered.

Johnny sat on the hard bench to wait for the next bus. So many had failed his Beautiful One. This was not their fault, for they could not help it if their brains didn't make the connections his did between pleasure and pain. But it was sad, he thought, that his second gift was so rare and so unappreciated.

Not by the one who truly mattered, though. She loved and valued him as passionately as he did her. He owed her so much. She said that debt had no meaning where there was love, but she wasn't human. Johnny adored her, cherished her, and feared her, but she was not human, and she sometimes misjudged or underestimated what humans could do.

That's why he was here today without her. One of his beloved's less human traits was her manner of sleeping. While asleep, she attenuated, losing her grip on the physical—though that would change, she told him, when she fully manifested. When first they met, she had slept most of the time. Now she needed less sleep than did he, but did not know when the need for sleep might strike, or how long she would remain asleep when it did. She might sleep for a day or an hour, then remain awake for a day or a week.

She slept now. When she woke she would be angry with him, oh yes, and the thought of her anger made him tremble. But she was wrong, that was all there was to it.

The sorcerer could not be left for later. From all Johnny had learned, the man was far too good with fire.

TWENTY-THREE

LILY took some satisfaction from slamming the door—but not much. She wanted to go back and yell at Rule some more. Where did he get off, telling her what she thought, what she felt?

She couldn't believe he'd picked *now* to dump that on her. That was just wrong. *He* was wrong. What made him think she didn't know what she wanted? She wanted him, dammit. Marriage was . . .

She dragged a hand through her hair. Marriage was scary.

There. She'd admitted it. Marriage scared her, but it was the right thing to do . . . wasn't it?

She started walking.

The Medical Examiner's building was a graceless white Lego set in the midst of a sea of concrete. They were supposed to move to a new, larger facility soon—they'd long since outgrown this one, which had been built in the 1960s. But construction delays had them still working in the same old cramped quarters Lily used to visit, back when she was with Homicide.

It was stupid to feel a twinge of nostalgia for the dead house.

Cody straightened as she reached his car and fell into step beside her. "Hey, there. You're not wearing your happy face."

"Gee, I wonder why not. Big investigation, stinky corpse. What's not to put a smile on my face?"

"No, that's your just-had-a-fight face. I ought to know. I used to see it often enough."

The past ghosted across Lily's mind. It smelled like cigarettes and wet sand, burnt coffee and bourbon. She slowed without meaning to, tilting her head for a sideways look at the man beside her.

Cody's face hadn't changed much, and his body was still strong, muscular. But he didn't smell of cigarettes anymore. Or bourbon. "I was never sure how much you remembered of those fights. Toward the end, especially."

"Most of them. Most of them I remember better than I'd like. If it makes any difference, you were right."

She shot him another glance. "What, about everything? That's a dangerous thing to say."

He grinned. "I live for risk." The grin faded. "Not for booze. Not anymore."

They walked in silence for a moment, heading for the loading bay on the side of the building. "I heard," she said finally. "I heard you went to rehab."

He snorted. "Got my ass shoved into rehab, you mean. I screwed up big-time and I got caught, which was the best thing that could've happened. Course, I was too stupid to see that at the time. Not entirely stupid, because I knew it was only luck I didn't get anyone killed, but pretty damn stupid. You told me that's where I was headed. You were right."

She'd heard about it. Cody been off duty when he tried to stop a liquor store robbery. Unfortunately, he was there as a customer—and way over the legal limit already, which was why the idiot had a cab take him to the store. Typical Cody, she'd thought at the time—half asshole, half hero. He'd known he was too drunk to drive, but he'd still tried to take down an armed perp.

It could have been so much worse. Cody ended up with a slug in his thigh and the clerk got his hair parted by a stray bullet, but they both survived. The perp got clean away.

Oh, yeah, she'd heard about it. Some of CJ's friends had made sure of that. The way they saw it, if she'd stuck by him, he wouldn't have needed to drink so much. "I didn't want to be right."

He smiled. "If you're not going to take the opportunity for one helluva good I-told-you-so, I can't make you."

That smile flicked a lot of memories on the raw. She stopped, looking at him. "Did you know what Hammond and Sheffield said after we broke up?"

He shook his head. "I was too down-deep in my own miseries to pay attention to much else."

"They told everyone I'd used you. That the Armani bust should've been yours, but I used you, took the credit, then dumped you once I got some attention from the brass."

"Shit. Those assholes. I should've guessed they'd shoot off their mouths, but I didn't. I didn't think, which was typical for me back then." His voice went low and fierce. "Lily, you gotta believe me about this much. After you dumped me, I said some shit I shouldn't have. I was hurting, and I wanted like crazy for it all to be your fault so I wouldn't have to look too close at me. But I never talked you down professionally. Not to those two or anyone else."

Some of the rawness eased. Though she noted the qualifier—he hadn't talked her down *professionally*—she could let that go. After a breakup, people talked bad about the other one . . . or that's what seemed to be the norm, anyway. Lily hadn't talked about Cody at all, good or bad, but that was her norm. When she hurt, she clamped down tight.

"Okay. I believe you. Maybe we'd better let all that rest in peace now. I'm here to get a look at that body. There's a lot riding on this one." She started forward.

He fell into step beside her. "Guess I picked a bad time to drag up auld lang syne. You're smarting from whatever you were arguing about with your new man."

"You said the vic was found in a storage shed."

"I can take a hint. You don't want to talk about him, but I can't help wondering—"

"Is Magruder the pathologist on this one?'

He shook his head sadly. "Guess I might as well let it drop. You aren't talking. But you could have knocked me down with a feather when I learned you'd taken up with a lupus. Fun and games I could understand . . . well, sort of. You weren't exactly the fun-and-games type back when I knew you, but that could've changed. I hear lupi are real good at changing a woman's mind about that sort of thing. But you and he are an item, right? Been together a few months."

"I'm remembering another reason we used to fight so often. One that had nothing to do with your drinking." They'd reached the loading dock. She jabbed the buzzer next to the normal-size metal door, but the light stayed red, meaning the door was still locked.

"You fight with your lupus dude much?"

She punched the button again. "On what planet would that be any of your business?"

"Friends get to ask that sort of thing."

"We aren't friends!"

That came out too hard, too strong. The flicker of hurt in his eyes was real, judging by how quickly he hid it with a grin. "Don't think I mentioned it at the time, but that's one of the things I appreciated about you. You didn't give me that 'let's just be friends' crap."

"Cody." She dragged a hand through her hair. "You want to get together and have a heart-to-heart, fine. But later, dammit. Right now, I've got an investigation. It's not about just one guy— one lupus—who got stabbed. It's a whole, huge, scary lot more than that. That's where my focus belongs. You are not helping."

He regarded her out of eyes gone flat and unreadable, then pushed the button she'd tried twice, and held it down. "Magruder's on vacation. Davis did the autopsy. He's new, so you may not know him, but he's got a good eye."

The door opened. "You don't have to lean on the goddamn buzzer," the young man snapped. "I'm coming as fast as I— oh, hey, Cody. What's up?"

"Jamal, my man." Cody and the attendant executed an elaborate high five, then Cody intoned, "We've come to see dead people."

Jamal cracked up. Cody could do that—make the corniest line sound fresh and funny. And he knew everyone. There were one and a quarter million people in San Diego, and Cody seemed to know half of them by name. Grinning, Jamal said, "You're at the right place, then."

"Then I got one thing right today. Jamal, this is Agent Yu," Cody said as they came in.

"Sure, I know you," the attendant said, amiable now. "Lily Yu, right? But I thought you were a detective."

"Used to be. I'm with the FBI now."

"Oh, yeah, I heard about that. Want to have a seat? Dr. Davis is working on another one right now, but he'll be out to talk to you when he's done."

"I need to see the body with the wound to the heart. I can do that while I'm waiting for Dr. Davis."

"Guess that ought to be okay. He's a smelly one," Jamal warned as he started down the hall. "I'll get you a mask, but it won't help."

"Worse than a floater?"

"Four, five days in this heat—what do you think?"

The door to the second autopsy room opened and a tall, lanky man with silver-rimmed glasses, a Jay Leno chin, and dirty blond hair stepped out. He was unfastening his green surgical gown when he noticed them. He frowned. "Cody. You don't have a case here, do you?"

"Not today," Cody said cheerfully. "You called me about that one you did this morning, remember?"

"Right." His gaze flicked to Lily. "This must be the FBI agent you mentioned."

"Lily Yu," she said, moving forward and holding out her hand. "You're Dr. Davis?"

He reached out to shake automatically. His hand was large, dry, and devoid of magic. "Good to meet you, Agent Yu. You're interested in Mr. Xing, I understand."

Lily's heart kicked up a beat. Maybe she knew this vic.

"If he's the man with the wound to the heart, then yes, I am. You've ID'ed him?"

"I did that," said another voice. "It's tentative, pending the dental."

An older man sauntered down the hall from the direction of the offices. His white hair and beard gave him the look of Santa in civvies. The blue eyes twinkling behind gold-rimmed glasses heightened the effect, though Santa wasn't supposed to have . . . Well, those weren't just bags beneath his eyes. More like steamer trunks.

"T.J.," Lily said, grinning with pleasure. "You've grown fur."

He gave a nod to Cody and stopped in front of Lily, fingering his new beard. "Hides the wrinkles."

T.J. didn't just have wrinkles. He had deep, droopy crevasses. "It looks good on you, but how in the world do you get away with a beard?"

Cody's phone chimed just then. He plucked it from his pocket, glanced at it, and moved a few feet away. "Beck here."

"Doctor's orders," T.J. said.

"The doctor ordered you to grow a beard?"

"Got this dermatitis thing that's irritated by shaving."

He looked completely serious. T.J. always looked completely serious when he was winding you up, which was pretty often. The man might resemble Santa, but he had a sick and twisted sense of humor. He was also one of the best cops she knew. He'd mentored her when she got transferred to Homicide. "This your case, then?" she asked.

"It was. You going to grab it away from me?"

"I play nice, when I can."

He shook his head mournfully. "Didn't learn that from me."

Actually, she had. "You said the vic's name is Xing. Anyone I know?"

"Probably. I made him based on what's left of the tattoo on his right bicep. One of those Chinese thingies they use for writing. You'd recognize it."

The Xings had an import company. They brought in cheap pottery, souvenirs, and heroin. "Which brother was it?"

"Too short for Zhou, so it must be one of the twins. We'll need dental to be sure."

Cody put up his phone. "Lily, that was dispatch. I have to go."

There were maybe a dozen things she might say, but none seemed right. She kept it business. "I'll be in touch about what I learn here. Thanks for the tip."

Cody's dark eyes flicked between her and T.J. "T.J., good to see you—however briefly. Later." He lifted a hand in a casual farewell and headed for the door.

She didn't realize she was watching him go until the door closed behind him and T.J. drawled, "He does have a cute ass."

"That he does." Lily felt a twinge of embarrassment at being caught looking, but only a twinge. "I didn't think you were wired right to appreciate it, though. Camille know about that?"

"Camille," he said of his wife of thirty-some-odd years, "knows everything. Absodamnlutely everything. Seems like I heard you and Beck were an item a while back."

"Five years ago. It's kind of weird, running into him again." And that was enough of that subject. "I need to see the body."

"Think you mean you need to touch it."

She met T.J.'s eyes. They weren't twinkling now. The whole time she'd worked with him—with everyone in the SDPD—she'd hidden her Gift. Some had guessed, but they'd kept quiet about it. T.J. was one of those who knew and hadn't spoken. "Yeah," she said at last. "That's what I mean."

"What's this? You want to touch the body?" Dr. Davis shook his head. "That's against procedure."

"It's part of my procedure, Doctor. I'm a touch sensitive. Your DB's wounds sound like those inflicted in a near-fatal attack I'm investigating—one which involved the use of magic. If I can pick up traces of magic on the wound, I've got a solid connection."

The frown lingered. "I didn't know that sort of thing was considered evidence."

"What I learn from my Gift isn't admissible in court, but I'm allowed to use inadmissible leads in pursuance of an investigation." And tired of explaining that, but it came with the territory.

"Hmm. I suppose that makes sense."

She bit back the urge to tell him the attorney general would be glad to hear that the pathologist agreed with him. "What can you tell me about the wound?"

He was on comfortable ground again. "Entry from the rear, angled up through the fifth and sixth ribs to penetrate the left ventricle. The assailant used a very thin blade, between one quarter and three quarters of an inch in width. I can't be more precise due to the decomposition of the flesh, I'm afraid."

"That's better than I'd expected, considering the decay."

"I based my estimate on the wound to the heart itself."

Speaking of which . . . "Have you put Mr. Xing's pieces back together yet?"

"The tech is doing that now, I imagine."

"Maybe we could stop him or her. It would be handy if the heart wasn't put back yet. That's where I'd expect to find traces of magic, if any are present." That body had been rotting in the heat a few days. But she had to try.

Dr. Davis's frown seemed to be a permanent fixture. "I'm concerned about your touching any portion of the corpse without gloves. With such intensive microbial action, there's a severe risk of contamination."

Lily grimaced. "Guess I'd better scrub really well, hadn't I?"

TWENTY-FOUR

～

THERE was no magic on the corpse. Not on the entry wound or on the heart. Lily hadn't really expected to find any so long after death, but it would have made the connection between this killing and the attack on Cullen definite. As it was, she only had a "maybe."

Still, it was a strong maybe, and the detective in charge of the case was T.J. He wouldn't hold out on her. She didn't intend to hold out on him, either. The treaty might have kept her from giving Ruben information, but T.J. wasn't an agent of the federal government. He needed to know what he might be facing.

Dr. Davis personally supervised her scrubbing. He even timed her. When she was done, he allowed that she was probably safe to mingle with others and even eat.

Eating was a damn fine idea, and she knew just the spot. Rosa's was a hole-in-the-wall Mexican joint a couple blocks from the Medical Examiner's. The crowded lunchroom had frigid air-conditioning, red-hot *enchiladas verdes*, and a TV that was always tuned to a local Spanish channel. Lily agreed to treat T.J. to lunch there.

T.J. had two cases with the Medical Examiner, so while he talked to Dr. Davis about a different DB, Lily headed to Rosa's and ordered for them both. She sat where she could keep an eye on the door so she'd see him when he got there. That also gave her a view of the TV, which was showing a Mexican soap opera.

It was just like old times. T.J. had always insisted that junior detectives were obliged by code, courtesy, and common decency to pick up the check for their seniors. Now his story was that rich FBI agents could damn well afford to treat their underpaid local cousins.

While she waited for the food and for T.J., she took out her notebook. She hadn't made any notes yet about her talk with Sam. She needed to get the details down, get her thoughts moving—and to see if she *could*. Would the treaty stop her from recording information?

First, though, she made a couple phone calls. She got Rule's voice mail, which made her drum her fingers. She left him a message . . . a brief, businesslike message asking what he'd told Cynna and Cullen.

It made her stomach hurt. She didn't understand why. It hadn't been all that big a fight. Sure, she'd been mad, and who wouldn't be? He'd picked a helluva time to get all huffy about the wedding. He . . .

Was right, dammit. Anger drained out like a balloon deflating. She'd overreacted all the way around. The binding the damned treaty placed on her infuriated her, and she'd kicked out at Rule. That wasn't fair.

Rule was right about something else. She knew in her gut it was right to marry him, but . . . Well, some people might be fine going with their gut, but she needed reasons. They were bound together for life whether or not they got a license from the state, so why marry?

Instead of figuring that out, she'd pretended the question didn't matter. In some obscure way she'd felt it was disloyal to ask questions about marrying Rule.

Lily sighed. It wasn't like her to avoid asking.

She wasn't the only one in the wrong, though. Rule's anger must have been simmering awhile, but he could have brought it up earlier or left it on the back burner a little longer. Like maybe until they weren't trying to stop an undying being from wrecking the city without precipitating a wave of illegal immigration that really might destroy the fabric of civilization.

She tapped her pen on her notebook. How many Chimei were there, anyway? How did you stop them if they weren't entirely physical?

Time to get some things on paper. First she jotted down the gist of what Sam had told them about the Chimei. The treaty didn't stop her. Maybe it would keep her from showing them to anyone? She made a note to find out, then added her conversation with Li Qin, then the call from Ruben. Then sat there, tapping her pen against the table.

Some three hundred years ago, Grandmother had killed the Chimei's previous sorcerous lover. And that was weird, thinking of Grandmother being around longer than the United States . . . but the point was that killing the Chimei's lover would stop her. But it was a temporary solution, and not one Lily could use, anyway. She was a cop. She arrested people. She didn't assassinate them.

Of course, Lily could have legally killed the Chimei if the Chimei had been killable. The Chimei wasn't human. The law was in a huge muddle about nonhumans, but Congress had given Unit agents wide discretionary powers right after the Turning, when any number of creatures had been blown here by the power winds.

But she wasn't some legalized hit man, dammit. That wasn't what she did.

She also wasn't entirely human herself.

Her thoughts hitched—just this quick, mental hiccup that interrupted her as thoroughly as a siren.

She understood why it bothered her. It upset her sense of who and what she was. Until last year, she hadn't even thought of herself as Gifted. People didn't think of sensitives that way because blocking out magic seemed the antithesis of working it.

Then she'd found out that being a sensitive *was* a type of

Gift. That had unsettled her, but not for long. Once she thought about it, it made sense. This, though, was like . . . It was like finding out she was mostly female, but not entirely.

What did it mean to "partake of dragon nature"?

You have already begun to manifest one ability common to dragons, Sam had said. He'd said something about her overlooking it, too.

Mindspeech? She hadn't done that except with him, and her conversations with the black dragon were hard to overlook. How could it be possible for her to use mindspeech with non-dragons when her Gift prevented her from using magic? Did she even want to?

Automatically, Lily started to jot those questions down. She stopped with "how would."

Her notebook could be produced in court. She didn't want to be cross-examined about mindspeech or partaking of dragon nature on the witness stand.

She went back to the original question. How could she stop the Chimei?

From what Li Qin had said, the bond between the Chimei and her lover had something to do with keeping the Chimei physical, or with her ability to affect people's minds, or both. Lily needed to know more about that.

Grandmother, she wrote. And underlined it. And added Cullen's name beside it. Either the Chimei or her lover considered him a real threat. He might have some ideas about how to break that bond without resorting to murder.

Okay, assume she found the sorcerer. She knew a few things about him now, and she had a lead to follow, thanks to Dr. Davis. Assume she learned how to break his bond with the Chimei . . . big assumption there, but was that bond anything like the one she knew so much and so little about? The mate bond that tied her to Rule?

If so, did the Chimei have to be physically close to her lover?

She underlined that question. It would sure be handy if the answer was "yes." Separate the two and maybe both would be weakened or incapacitated.

Skip past the assumptions, though, and the question was: how did she arrest a sorcerer? His magic couldn't affect Lily directly, but if he started a fire, she'd burn. And if he knew how to call mage fire . . . A shiver of remembered pain turned her hands clammy.

Last year, Cullen had used mage fire to destroy an ancient staff. They weren't certain if the scar on Lily's stomach came from the mage fire itself or from the intense heat it produced. Supposedly she was immune to magical fire, but mage fire was different. Black fire, it was called. Cullen said it could burn anything.

Another difference with mage fire was that the heat was oddly contained. Localized. Cullen thought that the black fire consumed most of the very heat it produced. But the staff had been touching her when Cullen zapped it, so even highly localized heat could have burned her.

They couldn't very well test the two ideas to see which one was right. Aside from the general danger—mage fire was hard to control—Lily had no intention of letting Cullen try crisping some part of her.

Enough of that. Did this sorcerer know how to call mage fire? It was supposed to be a lost art, but Cullen had reinvented it. Someone else could have, too. She made a note to ask Cullen about that and what other tricks the sorcerer might possess.

And how did you lock up a sorcerer, anyway? Back in the days of the Purge they'd made life simpler for themselves by cutting off hands, chopping off tongues, that sort of thing. Not options the federal penal system could adopt.

Clearly she'd been shaken after hearing Sam's story. She'd missed asking several questions. If Sam couldn't or wouldn't answer them, Li Qin might be able to. Or Grandmother.

Where was she? Lily underlined *Grandmother* a second time. That was one question she might be able to answer . . . with a little help from a friend. Cynna was one hell of a Finder.

And what in God's name was Sam up to?

He was manipulating them. She was sure of it. Maybe he had to because the geas forced him to be devious. Maybe he had, like Li Qin had said, a good goal in mind. But she didn't like it.

"You so deep into your scribbling you didn't see me?" T.J. demanded. "If I'd been a bad guy, I could've popped you."

"I saw you," Lily said without looking up as she finished jotting down one more thing. "Even if I hadn't, the server's headed this way with our plates, so it stands to reason you'd be here."

He grinned and pulled out his chair. "I've got great timing. That's what Camille always tells me, and she ought to know." He waggled his eyebrows.

"Have I given you any reason to think I'd want to hear about your sex life?"

"I've seen you checking out my ass. Did you order me . . . Ah, here it is. Extra jalapeños. Thanks, sugar."

T.J. could not be brought to believe that waitresses didn't always like being called *sugar*. Lily accepted her plate with a nod of thanks, turned the page in her notebook to a blank one, and said, "Let's talk about the Xings. What have you got?"

RULE finished his account of what he and Lily had learned. There was a long pulse of silence.

He had three listeners—Cullen, Cynna, and Max. Jason was present, but sound asleep; Nettie had left to arrange for Cullen's release and transport by ambulance. Cullen would go to Sam's lair this afternoon. Various bits of medical paraphernalia would be traveling with him, as would Nettie and Jason. Nettie wouldn't stay at the lair, but Jason would.

So would Cynna, of course. Rule wondered if Sam had anticipated such a large contingent of guests when he agreed to host Cullen.

Cynna broke the silence. "So we've got two bad guys, and one's a sorcerer. Lily saw him, so we've got a physical description, but it's kind of vague and may not help much if he can make everyone except Lily think he's someone else. The other bad guy is some kind of out-realm being hundreds or thousands of years old. She's a heavy hitter magically who eats fear and can't be killed."

"Except by dragons, apparently," Rule agreed.

"Good thing I'm leaving," Cullen said. "Won't take him long to find me."

Rule looked at his friend. Cullen's skin was waxy, his breathing shallow. An oxygen mask dangled from the corner of his bed. He hated it. After some discussion, Nettie had agreed he could leave it off for brief periods. He'd interpreted that to mean whenever he was awake.

He wasn't healing. According to Nettie, Cullen wasn't any worse, but he wasn't healing. "Lily's taken every precaution she can to keep your location secret. You're here under a different name, you don't have any hospital staff caring for you who might gossip about your presence, and—"

"And the killer's a sorcerer." Cullen snorted faintly. "Think he can't find his own spell, which just happens to be in the middle of my damned chest?"

"Shit!" Cynna said explosively. "I'm a Finder. I should've thought of that. Why didn't I think of that?"

Cullen smiled faintly. "You're used to no one being able to do what you do. And maybe a little distracted."

Cynna gripped his hand and gave him a long, intent look full of the things lovers can say in silence. Rule could see worry and promises in that look. No doubt Cullen saw much more.

She spoke quietly. "No point in me trying to jazz up the room ward now. I'm not as good at that as you. By the time I had anything with a hope of deflecting a Finding spell, you'd already be lazing around the dragon's lair."

Cullen's eyelids were beginning to droop. "Where Sam's wards will do a fine job of keeping out anything he doesn't want around. Though I won't mind if he lets that bastard get close enough to be his afternoon snack."

"Sam has wards?" Rule said, surprised. "I didn't think dragons did that."

"The young ones like Micah don't. Don't think they can. Their ability to shape magic . . . seems a . . . product of age. Sam's wards . . . are elegant as hell. I'm looking forward to . . ."

"Oxygen," Cynna said firmly, grabbing the mask.

Cullen grimaced. "I don't—"

"Want to be a baby about this," she finished for him, slipping the mask on.

Rule grinned. He liked watching these two together.

Cullen took a couple slow breaths, then pulled the mask aside to say firmly, "Food."

Rule glanced at Cynna. "What arrangements has Nettie made?"

"He can eat pretty much whatever he wants," she said. "To avoid any chance of his tray being poisoned, we're supposed to go get it from the cafeteria downstairs."

"Not we," Max said. "Him." He jerked his thumb at Rule. "He's the least useful person here."

Rule's eyebrows lifted.

Max chuckled. "Don't like that, do you? Sure, you could jump someone faster than the rest of us—if you could see who needed to be jumped. You can't, I can, end of story. As for the rest of this crowd, Cynna here can tell if her wards are disrupted. Jason can deal with medical problems if needed. You're just not that necessary." He grinned evilly. "I'll have a cheeseburger and fries with the works."

Max was obnoxious, but right. Rule took down the others' requests. Jason woke up and placed an order, too, though he had to be persuaded it was okay for his Lu Nuncio to fetch his food. "You won't be able to eat all that," Rule told Cullen when he ordered three double-meat cheeseburgers plus fries. "You'll fall asleep before you finish."

"Then I'll enjoy smelling it. What did you and Lily fight about?"

"So that's what it is!" Cynna exclaimed. "I'd wondered."

Rule spoke coldly. "I have no idea what you're talking about."

"Fought about something," Cullen observed. "First, you're here without her. Second, you're pissed. At everyone. About pretty much everything. Got mad at Max for yanking at you, and you never bother to get mad at Max. What's the point? Third—"

"You are intensely annoying."

Cullen managed a grin. "See? You're pissed."

Rule decided to ignore the subject. "I think I've got everyone's requests. I'll be back with food as soon as I can. Be wary. If this sorcerer has located Cullen—"

Max snorted. "Telling your granny how to suck eggs, boy."

"Have grannies ever sucked eggs?" Cullen asked. "Seems like a peculiar thing for them to do."

"I'll go with you to help carry stuff," Cynna offered.

"That's not necessary. As Max said, you're needed here to monitor the ward."

"I'll have to reset it once you cross it, anyway. I might as well walk you to the stairs."

Perhaps, if he tied her up, he could escape without the conversation she was determined to have. Since he was unwilling to do that, he capitulated. "I'll take the elevator."

"Okay, but the cafeteria's in the basement."

"I believe I'll survive riding down five floors." Damned if he'd feed his phobia by avoiding the experience again. Doing it once was excusable. Repeating it was a step on the road to creating a habit.

Cullen spoke again as Rule reached the door. "Rule."

He paused, looking over his shoulder at his friend.

"The bastard hit me because he knows I could see him. Maybe he knows about my shields, maybe he doesn't—but he knows I'd see the magic he uses, see that he's a sorcerer. Lily can see him as he is, too."

"According to Sam, Lily should be protected from direct attack by the treaty."

"Protected from the Chimei."

That sank in one shudder at a time. They'd assumed—or Sam had led them to believe—that Lily wouldn't be attacked. Sam believed the Chimei understood and respected the possible repercussions of attacking Lily directly. But would her lover?

They didn't know. They had no damned clue, and Rule had allowed pique to keep him from standing by her. He gave Cullen a single grim nod and left to get lunch.

TWENTY-FIVE

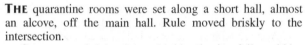

THE quarantine rooms were set along a short hall, almost an alcove, off the main hall. Rule moved briskly to the intersection.

Cynna moved right along with him, having followed him out. "Feels like crap, doesn't it? Fighting with someone you love, I mean."

"I didn't actually want to have this conversation," he said as politely as he could.

"I know. But I wanted to tell you that me and Cullen fight all the time, but we like to argue, and mostly we argue about the small stuff. With important shit we get real careful with each other, groping around in the dark wearing our kid gloves."

There was an image that almost made him smile. "Ah . . . we aren't private, you know. There are patients in most of these rooms, people at the nurses' station—"

She snorted. "The nurses' station must be half a block away. This is one long hall. As for the other patients, even the ones whose doors are open won't catch more than a word or two as we walk by."

"I'll take your word for it." Rule often had trouble figuring out what humans could hear and what they couldn't. "Did you want mustard or mayonnaise on your hamburger?"

"Sure. Either or both. Now, our style of arguing works for us, but you and Lily have a different deal going. You don't sweat the small stuff, and it's cool the way you two can negotiate instead of fighting. But now and then any couple is going to bump heads over something that matters."

They'd reached the elevator. He punched the button. He wouldn't be closed up long, he reminded himself. "This argument mattered."

"Had a feeling it did."

"And I was right." That came out a bit too strongly.

Cynna snorted.

"But I was wrong, too. Wrong to bring it up at the time and in the way I did. I hadn't realized . . ." He'd been almost as surprised as Lily at what he ended up saying. It was all true, but he hadn't meant to say it. "I didn't intend to dump all that on her now. My feelings were hurt. Once I started I couldn't seem to let it go."

"Be strange if the person who matters most in the whole world couldn't hurt your feelings, wouldn't it?"

"You just reminded me why I like you so much."

Cynna grinned. "Good for me." She stretched up—it wasn't a big stretch for her—and gave him a kiss on the cheek. "Give her a call. You'll feel better."

He didn't grin back, but he already felt better. "Go ward something."

"Will do." She gave his butt a pat. "Don't tell Lily I did that."

Now he grinned.

She fluttered her fingers in a little wave and set off back down the hall. The elevator dinged.

Two people got off. He studied them as he got on, however pointless that might be. Neither was someone he expected to see, or anyone he'd seen before. Maybe that meant they were who they appeared to be. One was an older man with dark hair and skin, in khakis and a short-sleeve shirt; the other was also male and wore a navy suit with a name tag. Both smelled human. They didn't speak to each other or make the small gestures that acknowledge a friend or acquaintance.

Just to be sure, Rule kept the elevator doors from closing until he saw which way they went—straight to the nurses' station, where the suited man was greeted as doctor somebody and the man in khakis asked about room 421.

He let the doors close and punched the button marked B.

The elevator was slow. It creaked to a stop on the third floor, where a young candy striper got on. She was blond and perky and smelled human . . . and interested. She glanced at the buttons and gave him a flirty smile. "I'm headed down for lunch, too. Want some company?"

"That would be delightful," he said as the doors closed again, "but I'm afraid I'm taking food back to some friends, so I won't be eating in the cafeteria." The elevator lurched into motion. *I'm fine*, he told himself.

The girl's smile didn't diminish. She had dimples. "Any of those friends female?"

He smiled back. He had to place a firm but gentle *no* in their exchange, but she was sweet and pretty and she smelled delightful. How could he not let her know he appreciated her? "One of them is, yes. Though she is just that—a friend—my fiancée will be—"

The lights went out. The elevator jolted to a stop. A siren sounded, and the candy striper screamed.

"We'll be all right," Rule said soothingly, even as his heart-beat jumped into panic mode. Trapped—he was trapped—

"Th-that's the fire alarm," the girl said. One small hand connected with his arm and gripped it. "There's a fire. We've got to get out. There's a fire."

She was right. Standing in the pitch blackness of the tiny box, his senses heightened by fear, Rule smelled the girl's panic—and smoke. The smoke-scent was faint. With no electricity, the fan in their hanging prison wasn't drawing in air.

There's enough air, he told himself firmly. *Plenty of air.*

"There's an escape hatch, isn't there?" she said, clutching him tightly. "I can't see. I can't reach it. There's supposed to be light, emergency lighting, but I can't see anything!"

"Shh." Rule patted the small hand clutching him and tried to ignore the wolf's panic. The man had to be in charge now. "We'll be okay. I need to think a moment."

Could the flirty candy striper be the killer? As soon as the thought occurred to him, he dismissed it. He wasn't the target. Cullen was, and no sensible killer would trap himself in an elevator away from his target. No, he'd be on the fourth floor already, or heading for it on the stairs.

But the fire . . .

He frowned. *Why* a fire?

It didn't make sense. Why would an assassin who could wander around unnoticed knock out the electronics and start a fire to get to his target? Did he plan to pick off Cullen as he evacuated?

If so, he was stupid. There were a dozen easier ways to go about it for a killer who could look like anyone. Unless the whole situation was an illusion? Was such a thing possible?

"Can you get it open?" the candy striper repeated, her voice rising. "They say to stay in the elevator if there's a power outage, but I don't want to. I don't."

He would have to proceed as if the fire, the stuck elevators, all of it was real. Otherwise he'd be frozen, more trapped than any stuck elevator could be. "We need to get out, yes." Rule managed to keep his voice calm. His forehead was damp, but she couldn't see that. "I'm going to open the doors and see where we are. I'll want both my arms for that."

"Oh. Oh, of course. The doors." Her laugh was shaky, but she let go of him. "The doors will open, right?"

Was the smell of smoke growing stronger?

"I think so." He gripped the edges of the doors and pried them open on darkness, smoke, and noise. With the doors open, he could hear people calling out—*the stairs, over here, keep calm, where's Maria, get the wheelchair, Maria!, hurry up, stairs, oh God, oh God, help me, please someone . . .*

He looked up. Not that he could see anything, but his nose told him the smoke was coming from that direction. Looking down, he saw equally little. The electricity was out everywhere, then, and the gathering smoke didn't help. He began feeling the wall exposed by the opened doors.

Yes. There were openings. He could get out.

Relief shuddered through him. His wolf calmed, willing to let the man handle this now that he knew he wasn't trapped. Rule dropped to one knee, felt for and found an opening.

Both above and below, the doors opening on those floors had sprung open, while the interior doors to their cage hadn't. In many newer systems—such as the one in Rule's apartment building—during a power outage the elevator was delivered on battery power to the first floor, where the door automatically opened. That hadn't happened, yet the doors on at least two floors had opened. And there should be emergency lighting, just as the girl had said.

In other words, the tech was fucked up. "Magic surge?" he murmured. Or something more intentional. Somehow the sorcerer had disabled the hospital tech.

And it was not illusion. Rule refused to believe any crafted simulation could be so detailed, even to the direction of the nonexistent smoke.

If all this was real, did that mean the killer was stupid, or that he was unable to disguise himself for some reason?

The attack on Cullen had been quiet, focused, perfectly executed. Not the work of a stupid man. He'd go with the idea the sorcerer's illusions weren't serving him today.

"What?"

"Nothing. We can get out," he told the girl, rising and finding his companion by guess in the dark. He gripped her arms reassuringly. "We've stopped between floors, but the door's open on the floor below, so we can get to it." First floor or second? He didn't think they'd reached the basement, but couldn't be sure.

"There's smoke. I smell smoke."

"It's coming down the elevator shaft. The fire is above us." *How far up? On the fourth floor?* "It's an awkward drop when you can't see what you're doing. I'll go first so I can direct and catch you."

"Okay. Okay. Let's get out. I need to help with the patients. They'll need help getting all the patients out."

"Good." Her sudden bravery in the midst of deep fear surprised him into kissing the top of her head. "Good for you.

You'll do fine. Sit down now. I'm going to swing down, then I'll catch you."

Without further words, he dropped to the floor, swung his legs off and out, and landed lightly.

"I'm right here," he said, taking in what he could with a quick glance. It wasn't fully dark after all. The smoke had obscured the small amount of light available from the long, narrow window above the nurses' station.

Second floor. He was on the second floor. Nurses and others bustled, called out, but in an orderly way. "I'm reaching up for you—yes, there you are," he said as he found one sneaker-clad foot. "Shove off and let me catch you."

With a little gulp, she did. He caught her easily, setting her on her feet. "You're on the second floor," he said. "Can you see? The stairs are at either end of this hall. I have to go."

"Wait," she cried as he turned, crouching to get a little spring. "You're not going back in there? You can't!"

"My friends are on the fourth floor. I need to be sure they're okay."

"But you can't!"

He did, leaping so he could seize the bottom of the elevator cage. He pulled himself up, stood, and felt for the gap he'd found earlier. The angle was awkward, but it wasn't hard to pull himself up.

Third floor. Here the smoke was thick enough that he saw little. It was hot. He didn't see fire, but in the smoke and darkness, he might not, unless it was close. The voices here were more frantic. Someone still called for Maria. He heard coughing. He hesitated, torn—he could help, he could get people out—but his wolf *had* to get to the fourth floor.

He felt for the top of the elevator. The space was narrow, but he could fit. Quickly he hoisted himself, slithering to the roof of the elevator.

Darkness and smoke. His eyes burned. But the smoke seemed a bit thinner when he stood. Quickly he pulled off his shoes and socks, then seized the cables that held the elevator. He began climbing.

He went up fast, despite the grease that made the cables

slippery. He'd climbed greased rope before. Cables were different, but not enough to slow him much.

Rule had decided on this course as soon as he knew the elevator's position. The stairs would be mobbed with people going down. He had to go up. This was the fastest way . . . or it should have been. When he reached the level of the fourth floor he realized he'd included an assumption in his plan. One that hadn't panned out.

The doors here hadn't behaved the way the others doors had. They weren't fully closed—but they weren't fully open, either, dammit. There was a dim rectangle of light maybe a foot wide. His eyes were tearing from the smoke, but he could see that pale rectangle.

Like many hospital elevators, this one was deep enough to accommodate a gurney or hospital bed. Rule hung in the center of the shaft about five feet from that dim, tantalizing opening.

He'd intended to get above the opening and launch himself out and down. That would have worked if the doors had opened all the way. As it was, he thought he could have squeezed through sideways—if there had been anywhere for him to stand on this side.

There wasn't.

He could go back down to the third floor, take the stairs up. That might make sense, but the urgency pounding through Rule kept him hanging there, staring at the opening, gripping hard with his legs to spare his arms, which were beginning to tire.

Same plan, he decided. He'd just have to twist as he fell so he could get an arm and a leg through that opening—and yank himself through. If he missed, well, falling one and a half flights wouldn't kill him. Probably. Unless he was knocked out and the fire caught him—*shut up*, he told himself, but his mouth was dry with fear.

He did not want to burn. He really, really, did not want to burn.

So get it right.

That was Benedict's voice, Benedict's words, the sort of

thing he'd said often enough when Rule trained under him. Rule found himself nodding, agreeing with that laconic inner voice.

He pulled himself higher, not thinking anymore. This was the body's job, not the brain's. The moment the arc looked right he stopped, shifted his grip to position himself—and flung himself out.

His right arm whipped out, reaching for that pale rectangle. The ball of his right foot struck the metal track with jarring force, but his knee flexed, absorbing the impact, as he shot his arm through that opening—and even as his weight tried to pull him away, his forearm slammed onto the other side of the door. He clung there, his heartbeat loud in his ears.

Damn. He'd made it.

Not done yet. Move.

He pulled his foot through first, then his body. The doors were completely inert, not sliding back as they should have, so it was a tight squeeze. By the time he emerged he'd noticed two things.

The smoke was much less here, and seemed to be coming mostly from the elevator shaft. And it was way too quiet. The hall that led to Cullen's room was dark, probably too dark for human eyes—there was enough smoke to keep light from the single window from penetrating far—but he could make out two crumpled forms on the floor.

There were voices, people calling out in fear, but they were few—and they all came from the far west end of the hall. The east side, where Cullen's room lay, was totally quiet.

"Help me," said a male voice. "Help me. She won't wake up. None of them will wake up."

The voice came from behind the nurses' station, which looked empty. When Rule moved closer, he saw over the high counter. A dark-skinned man knelt beside a woman who was sprawled on the floor. Another woman was sitting, slumped forward onto the counter.

"They're still breathing?" he asked.

The man nodded, his eyes round with fear. "But they won't

wake up. Mr. Peterson in 330, he's on a ventilator. The power's out. I don't know what to do, and they won't wake up!"

How long had it been since the lights went out? Maybe five minutes, Rule thought. It felt like much longer, but Rule had been in enough crisis and combat situations to know how time stretched. "Can you ventilate your patient by hand?"

"I change the damned sheets! I don't know how to do that other shit. I came here to get someone, but they're all asleep!" His eyes were damp. He was ready to cry, scared out of his wits—but desperate to get help for the helpless.

A good man? Or a killer bent over the woman he'd just put to sleep?

Rule took a breath. He'd decided the sorcerer wasn't using his illusions for some reason. He'd proceed on that assumption, which meant he was looking for a short Asian man, not a gangly African American. "I don't know how to do that shit, either."

"Then what do we do? What do we do, man?"

Whatever had knocked everyone out, it wasn't gas. With the air-conditioning out, gas would have still been present. Rule might throw off the effects of such a gas much faster than a human, but it would still affect him. At the least, he'd be woozy. And he wasn't.

A sleep spell, then, but not like any he'd heard of. Cullen's sleep spell was delivered through touch, not broadcast like a bomb.

Cullen. Rule had to assume that he, Cynna, and Max had been knocked out. They'd be helpless, if they weren't already dead.

Rule quivered with the need to *move.* He held himself still a moment longer. Action without information was too often disaster.

Vision was limited by darkness. Smell was hindered by smoke. He focused on hearing.

Silence. No air-conditioning, no monitors beeping, no voices from that dark hallway. He might already be too late. If—

Footsteps. Soft, barely audible—but he heard footsteps in the east hall. Someone walking, not running. Someone in athletic shoes or the rubber-soled shoes nurses often used . . . so it might be a nurse moving almost silently through the dark.

He didn't think so. He looked at the orderly, still kneeling beside the fallen nurse, and held a finger to his lips. The man's eyes widened even more. He couldn't have guessed why Rule wanted quiet, but he gulped and nodded.

Rule gave him a quick nod and set off at a run.

A few paces down the hall he leaped over the first huddled form—and nearly landed on a second one, missing more by luck than skill. Could one of them be Cynna? Had she made it back to the room before the sleep spell hit, or was she collapsed along here?

He dodged a laundry cart—and the red EXIT sign over the stairs came on. Maybe the tech was coming back. Once the level of magic decreased, it usually did.

That glow made a difference. He could see the alcove that held Cullen's room now—and the man who emerged from it. Short. Dark hair. It was too dim still to make out his features, but he wore scrubs.

The light was enough for a human, too, apparently. The man saw him and took off running.

Rule kicked it up to full speed. He reached the alcove— snarled in frustration—and skidded into a turn. He had to catch the enemy. He also had to see. Had to check on the others.

The door to Cullen's room was still closed. A white plastic grocery sack sat in front of it, ghostly in the dark. Rule slid to a stop. The sack was knotted at the top. It bulged.

The enemy had left it here. His eyes couldn't tell him what it held. Maybe his nose could. He bent. Froze. Snatched up the sack and took off like death itself was nipping at his heels.

He tried to run smoothly, keeping the impact down—but felt every footfall thud up through his frame, vibrating the package he held. Time collapsed instead of stretching. He hit the nurses' station a blink or two after grabbing the package— vaulted over the counter, ignoring the orderly, and leaped onto the cabinets lined up along the wall.

Crouched high on those cabinets, he drew back his cocked left arm and smashed his elbow through the window. A sweep of his forearm sliced his skin as it cleared out the remaining shards.

He looked out. *Parking lot. Yes. Thank you, Lady.*

Rule hurled the plastic-wrapped bundle straight out as hard as he could.

It exploded in midair.

TWENTY-SIX

❦

THE enchiladas were as spicy as ever, the air-conditioning just as frigid, but after a couple bites, Lily hardly noticed.

She tried to level with T.J., like she'd planned. She couldn't. The damned treaty had her saying something vague about a pair of bad guys she was after, both of them with magic, one of them a hit man.

T.J. knew she was holding out on him. He looked wary and disappointed. "You're not telling me much."

"I . . . can't. But your case is clearly connected to what I'm working on. We both want to find out who had it in for the Xings—or for one of them. I figure it's better if the brothers don't know we're collaborating. You going to talk to big brother today?"

"I'm planning on it. Give him a friendly ride to the morgue, see if he can ID little brother."

"Okay. When it seems like a good moment to shake him up, tell him I . . . You have to say this right. Tell him I am concerned for his health because I believe my grandmother's enemy killed his brother."

"That's it? Your grandmother's enemy?"

"He, uh, sort of knows Grandmother. Or knows about her."
Lily wasn't sure if they really had some kind of history, or if
Zhou had just heard rumors. Grandmother wouldn't say. Zhou
Xing was old-school, though. He believed things his Western-
ized younger brothers didn't. Lily suspected he had a Gift of
some sort, too, but had never managed to shake hands with
him to confirm that. "Never mind. Just tell him that and to call
me if he wants to know more."

"Should I look inscrutable?"

"You might have to settle for clueless."

He grinned around a mouthful of beans he'd raised to in-
cinerator levels with the addition of extra jalapeños. "I can do
clueless. You going to deal me in if he does call?"

"I will. As much as I can, anyway. Dammit, I want to say
more," she said, frustrated beyond words. "I *can't.*"

"Guess the muckety-mucks have you muzzled."

She grimaced. "You could say that." Though the muckety-
mucks responsible for her muzzling weren't with the FBI, as
T.J. assumed. She was afraid they were a lot bigger and badder
than that.

Who could have crafted a treaty that was literally unbreak-
able even for dragons? One that could be passed down through
blood or magical inheritance?

Old Ones. Beings who could pass for gods if they wished.
Lily's hands felt clammy. For the first time she thought maybe
she shouldn't push, shouldn't fight against bonds placed on
her without her consent. These waters were deeper and more
turbulent than she could conceive.

But she didn't know if she could stop pushing. *Like an animal chewing off its leg to escape a trap*, Rule had said. It was
a good analogy. She just wasn't sure she could do anything
different.

T.J. dragged a bite of tortilla around his plate, mopping up
the last of the sauce, ate that, and burped happily before wiping his face almost as clean as his plate. "Damn good enchiladas. Mine are better, but those were damn good."

"I know you grill, but enchiladas?" She shook her head.
"Pull the other one."

"Naw, I'm not messing with you. Camille and me have

a deal. After my time-out, I had to learn to cook. Got pretty good at it after a while."

"Your time-out?"

He grinned. "You've still got the instinct. Yeah, about ten years in she gave me a time-out for bad behavior."

"Why? What did you do?"

"You're sure nosy all of a sudden."

"I've always been nosy. Humor me, okay?"

He shrugged. "Mostly it was just stupidity, me trying to keep the job from touching her, thinking she couldn't understand, all that crap most of us pull."

"She moved out?"

"More like she handed me my hat and pointed to the door. She claims she had to get my attention. Guess she was right, but it took three months of cold suppers and a cold bed for me to stop being pissed long enough to start hearing what she said." He tilted his head. "You've got something on your mind."

"I'm just . . . well." She drummed her fingers. What was it exactly she wanted to know? "You might say I'm gathering data."

He snorted. "Pretty sure that isn't what I'd say, but you can, if you want."

"Why did you and Camille get married instead of just living together? Was it because that's what people expected?"

"Helluva question. If you want kids, you want them to have your name, don't you? Well, I guess that's a man's perspective, so you . . . shit. You're not. You are *not* pregnant."

He'd made it an order. She couldn't help grinning. "No, I'm not." On impulse, she pulled out the chain that held the *toltoi* and her engagement ring.

"Son of a bitch. You broke up with that Turner guy? You're getting married? Who to?"

"I'm still with the Turner guy. I'm going to marry him."

"Son of a bitch."

"I think you're supposed to say congratulations."

"This'll be a real marriage? The whole deal?" He waved his fork in circles, as if to indicate what a "whole deal" looked like.

"A real marriage. License, rings, vows, till-death-do-us-part."

"Son of a bitch."

"We're keeping it quiet until Rule can hold a press conference. You know what those vultures are like. I don't want to dodge idiots asking about my honeymoon plans while I'm working this case, so don't tell anyone in the department."

"That bunch of gossips. Hell, no, I won't breathe a word. I'll just let 'em know I know something I'm not telling. It'll drive them crazy." He paused to savor the prospect. "You going to go public with this soon?"

"As soon as possible." Lily wasn't sure why she'd told T.J., except that he was a friend and she was tired of not telling people. She glanced at her ring, and reluctantly slid it back inside her shirt. *Soon*, she told herself. But T.J. couldn't really help with her basic question. His generation had married automatically. You fell in love, you got married, period. Unless you were a hippie. T.J. hadn't been a hippie.

Camille had. Maybe she should talk to Camille.

Later. Right now she'd better get moving. "When you talk to Zhou," she began. And stopped, staring at the TV.

"Hey!" T.J. waved a hand in front of her face. "You daydreaming about the big wedding?"

"I've got to go." She shoved back her chair, grabbed her notebook, and jammed it in her purse. "The hospital on the news—that's Memorial, downtown. That's where Rule is. And Cullen. And Cynna." And Max and Jason and Nettie—all of them there, where black smoke billowed and sirens screamed. "I've got to go."

"You'll go with me. Shut up, Yu," he told her, though she hadn't said anything. He was on his feet, too, and pulling out his wallet. "I've got a siren. You don't. End of argument." He tossed a flutter of bills on the table. "Let's go."

She got two steps in before he grabbed her arm. "Hold up."

"What?" she snapped.

He nodded at the TV screen.

Lily caught the word *helicóptero* from the excited newscaster as the scene switched to an aerial view of an elegant black shape drifting down through the smoke like an enormous burnt leaf. Wings beat or tilted artfully as the black dragon rode the air down and down to settle on the roof of the hospital.

"Son of a bitch," Lily said.

TWENTY-SEVEN

IN addition to a siren, T.J. had a police radio in his car. They listened to that and to regular news in their mad race to Memorial. From what she could piece together, the fire had abruptly poofed out about the time Sam settled on top of the building. Firefighters were baffled.

Lily wasn't, not about the cause—but the motive had her wondering. Sam was an ethical being, but his standards didn't often overlap with human morality. Lily felt sure he hadn't suddenly decided to become a scaled firefighter.

There were reports of a bomb, garbled and unconfirmed. There was no official word on casualties, but according to someone interviewed by a reporter, the hospital's sprinklers hadn't activated and much of its tech had malfunctioned. So it could be bad.

Lily couldn't get Rule or Cynna on their cell phones. She knew Rule lived. The mate bond made that a certainty. She didn't know about any of the others.

Even with a siren, T.J. was unable to get very close. It seemed as if half the people in the downtown had fled when the dragon appeared—and the other half had left their cars or their offices to get a better look. Sidewalks and streets alike were jammed.

T.J. parked well down Frost Street. As soon as the car stopped, Lily slid out into the oven-dry heat—and jumped as a cool mental voice said, *Your mate and compatriots live.*

"Thanks," she whispered to Sam.

Memorial was big. Like many big hospitals, it had spawned a number of offspring. The campus included parking garages, buildings for outpatient care and rehab, a women's hospital, and a children's hospital. The main building, though, was shaped like a *V*. They headed toward the western tip of the *V*, weaving among stranded vehicles and gawking pedestrians.

Where had all these people come from? San Diego-ans didn't mob up outside in the summer. It was too stinking hot.

"Are any of my compatriots hurt?" Lily asked Sam. "Including Nettie. She's the clan's doctor. She's been taking care of Cullen. So was Jason. He's Nokolai."

"Uh, Lily?" T.J. glanced back at her. "You talking to me?"

"No, I'm talking to the dragon."

"Sure. Pull the other one."

Your question is imprecise. If you wish to know whether any of them sustained damage today, Cynna Weaver is coughing but essentially unharmed. The gnome is undamaged. Cullen Seabourne is in sleep. The healer with him . . . yes, I see that she is called Nettie. She is undamaged, as is the nurse with them. Rule Turner incurred cuts to one arm, but they are healing. He is under arrest.

"He's what?!"

He threw a bomb. The authorities find that suspicious.

A bomb. Lily drew a calm-me-down breath. One question at a time. "What are you doing here?"

I put out the fire and absorbed the power the sorcerer used to disable the tech in the building. Most of the tech is operational again. Some remains . . . I believe the phrase is screwed up.

"That's the phrase, all right." It explained why she'd been unable to reach Rule or Cynna on their cells. "Was that a direct answer to my question, or are there other reasons—"

"You're worrying me," T.J. said.

"I'm not the one acting weird. You bought my lunch."

He snorted.

Her hairline was already growing damp, especially at her nape. Should've put her hair up this morning. She walked faster.

They'd almost passed one of the big parking garages. She could see part of the west wing of the hospital now and some of the emergency vehicles clustered around it. There was a hydraulic truck pulled up onto the grass, its platform elevated to the third story. Wispy white trails of smoke drifted out some of the windows on that floor.

There was also a Channel 7 van straight ahead. "This way," she said, snagging T.J.'s sleeve and pulling. "Let's dodge the reporters, if we can. You know dragons use mindspeech, right? Well, Sam prefers us to answer out loud when he mindspeaks us. He says our thoughts are too muddy otherwise."

Human thoughts are muddy at all times, Sam informed her, *but worse when you don't vocalize. The officer who considers himself in charge of Rule Turner has a particularly messy mind. This caused me to misspeak, since my attention is somewhat divided. I'm monitoring several minds while watching for the sorcerer and the Chimei.*

Lily suspected "misspeak" was the dragon version of "I was wrong." "What did you misspeak about?"

The officer hasn't arrested Rule Turner. He either intends or wishes to do so. There is little distinction in him between wishes and intentions. Very muddy.

Directly ahead was a knot of people held back by a police barricade. Beyond that were streams and eddies and puddles of first responders from both the fire department and the police. From here she couldn't see where patients had been evacuated to. "Why did Rule throw a bomb?"

"He did what?" T.J. demanded.

He didn't want it to explode inside the hospital. A sensible action, but the officer disbelieves his account of events, although there is a witness to corroborate most of it.

"Where did the bomb come from?"

The sorcerer planted it outside Cullen Seabourne's room after creating the fire and attendant confusion to act as cover.

The Chimei was not with him, so he lacked her illusions. The man with you now is your friend?

"A compatriot," she said, liking the word. "And a friend."

He wonders if you are going mad. I will speak to him. He will be less useful if he distrusts your sanity.

"Okay." They'd reached the police barricade. "FBI," she told one of the uniforms at the barricade as she pulled out her ID. "MCD Unit 12, Special Agent Lily Yu. I need through."

"Omygod," T.J. said, paling. "Yes. Sure. Omygod."

"Hidden radio," Lily told the officer, who was eyeing T.J. suspiciously. "He's SDPD, but he's with me. Who's coordinating? Hennessey?" *Coordinating* was policy speak for *in charge*, and Carl Hennessey was deputy chief of operations for the Fire Department. A hospital fire was a major incident and would draw the big guns.

The officer gave her ID a good look before handing it back. "Fire's out. You'll want to talk to Captain Dreyer, ma'am. SDPD."

Lily's eyebrows rose. Policy called for a senior police officer to be on scene in cases of suspected terrorism. She could see why they might suspect terrorism. But in such a situation, policy also called for evacuating the area, not allowing civilians to mob the street and gawk at the pretty dragon.

She ducked under the makeshift barrier. "Where's Captain Dreyer? And why is no one dispersing the crowd?"

"I don't know, ma'am. I'll get the sergeant, ma'am. He can answer your—"

"Sandy!" T.J. boomed out. "Over here!"

A man with skin almost as dark as the dragon's scales looked their way. He had a sergeant's stripes on his sleeve and the build and expression of a defensive tackle about to take out the quarterback. That expression didn't lighten one whit when he yelled back, "T.J., you crazy bastard. What are you doing here?"

"Tagging along with Agent Yu." T.J. jerked his thumb at Lily. "She used to be one of mine, but she's gone over to the Feds now. Unit 12. She wants that crowd dispersed."

The sergeant's frown deepened as he took a few long

strides to join them. "Any idiot asshole would want the crowds dispersed," he said when he reached them, his voice low. "Any idiot asshole but our captain. Sorry, ma'am," he added to Lily. "Orders are for us to maintain the perimeter until reinforcements arrive."

"Reinforcements who won't be able to reach you," she said. "Emergency vehicles can't get through the mob."

The scowl tightened another notch. "Yes, ma'am, but—"

"She's Unit 12, Sandy," T.J. repeated. "She's got the fucking authority on this scene, not Dreyer."

Now the sergeant looked pained. "Magic shit?"

"Magic shit," Lily agreed, though she didn't actually know that yet. Though Sam had said the sorcerer had blanked out the hospital's tech, hadn't he? "I don't want to get you in trouble with your captain, but those people need to be moved out. Get some bullhorns. Any idea of casualties?"

"At least two. The fire was confined to the third floor."

Cynna Weaver wants you to hurry.

Lily's head jerked up. *What?*

The officer with the muddy mind has sent other officers to evacuate those in Cullen Seabourne's room. Cynna Weaver does not intend to comply. There is some logic to her position. While I do not believe the sorcerer is here, I'm unable to touch his mind directly, so there is a possibility he remains near and could finish his task. He would be a fool to linger when I am here, but we do not yet know if he is a fool.

"Plus we don't know if he has others on his string who could . . . Uh, thinking out loud," she told the sergeant, who'd looked puzzled. "Never mind. Get the bullhorns. Do what you can, and I'll have a word with your captain. Where is he?"

"The command post's in front of the arrival plaza, ma'am. The place where patients are dropped off." He hesitated, glanced at T.J.

"Don't worry about my girl, here," T.J. told him. "She can handle Dreyer."

The sergeant shook his head and muttered something. It didn't sound like he was expressing confidence in her ability to take on his captain.

Lily thanked him and took off at a fast walk, veering back

to the street to avoid the swarms of responders and their equipment. T.J. stayed beside her. She glanced at him. "I don't know Dreyer. Garcia headed Patrol back when I was in uniform. Do you know him?"

"Yeah. He's a prick. Does the job, but he's a prick. Yappy little dog type."

That was code from when he'd been mentoring her. T.J. compared people to various types of dogs. She'd often wondered what breed he thought she was, but had never dared ask. "Ankle biter?"

"You got it. He's loyal, small-minded, territorial as hell, and he thinks he's a damned Doberman, so he won't back down from a threat. You'll have to use your owner's voice."

She shot him an amused glance. "I should make him sit?"

"Damn straight. Then give him a bone he can go away and chew on."

"Sam said some officer here intends to arrest Rule. Maybe it's this Captain Dreyer."

He considers that his name.

"Okay. Uh—T.J., I'm talking to Sam now. Sam, you said the . . . damn." She could not use the word *Chimei*. It wouldn't move from her brain to her mouth. "The out-realm perp isn't here, but you can't tell if the sorcerer is or not."

I did not say that. A whiff of displeasure accompanied those words. *I said I cannot touch the sorcerer's mind directly. I can, however, infer his presence or absence in other ways. These methods do not offer complete accuracy, but they strongly suggest he has left the area.*

"The sorcerer has shields like Cullen's?"

He is shielded, obviously, but not like Cullen Seabourne. Cullen Seabourne's shields are . . . unexpected. I know of only one being who could construct layered shields of that specificity, strength, and sophistication, but he has been dead for several hundred years. I had always believed he did not share his technique with anyone, yet his shields appear to have been re-created. It is impossible that Cullen Seabourne did this himself.

In fact, he hadn't. Yet some perversity made her want to argue with Sam. "Cullen's pretty bright."

A primitive tribesman might be brilliant, but you would be astounded if he painted an exact duplicate of the Mona Lisa *without ever seeing it.*

Rule had been right. Sam was deeply curious about Cullen's shields.

I look forward to discussing them with him, true, but I would not characterize my interest as you have.

She scowled. "Quit peeping in my head."

Learn proper mindspeech and you will control which thoughts you share.

Another reference to her learning mindspeech. How unsubtle of him.

That was unusual. So was his chattiness today. She couldn't remember when he'd answered so many questions, even volunteering information she hadn't asked for. Of course, she couldn't remember a lot of her interactions with him. Most of them had happened in Dis to the other Lily, the one whose silent soul shared space with her.

Some people would say that the other Lily *was* her. Same soul, same person, right? And in an obscure, underneath-it-all sense, that was true, but it didn't feel that way. *She* didn't hold those memories. Now and then one brushed against her conscious mind, but they always evaporated quickly, like mist in the desert.

"You going to claim this for your crowd?" T.J. asked.

"I don't know. Did the sorcerer use magic?" she asked Sam. "I don't have authority here unless magic was used in the commission of a felony."

The sorcerer created the fires magically. He also used magic to disable the hospital's tech and to put a large number of people to sleep so he would not be seen or interfered with when he planted the bomb. Your laws regarding magic vary from the convoluted to the absurd, but these acts seem to fall within the purview of those laws.

T.J.'s eyes were wide.

"I guess you heard that," Lily said. "I wish I could tell when Sam's talking just to me and when he's including others in the conversation."

You could if you learned the basics of mindspeech.

"The dragon," T.J. said. "He did it again. Talked to me, I mean. In my mind."

"I know. It's disconcerting at first."

He snorted. "It's freaky damned weird, is what it is. Cool as hell, but freaky damned weird. What's this about an out-realm perp and a sorcerer?"

With a jolt, Lily realized she'd mentioned the sorcerer in T.J.'s hearing. Not the Chimei, but she'd been able to refer to the sorcerer. An hour ago, she hadn't been able to do that. "Just a sec, T.J. Sam? How come I could . . ." *talk about the sorcerer, but not the Chimei.*

I do not care to say things twice. Join your mate, dismiss the mud-brained officer, and I will explain to the extent I am able.

"Dismissing the mud-brained officer may take a while."

I will wait.

From the vantage point of the closed-off street, Lily could see the command post up ahead. The fire chief's car was there, along with two cop cars, a fire engine, and too many people. She was far enough from the building to see the roof better, too. And the dark, wedge-shaped head that peered over the edge of it, surveying the scene below him.

So did lots of others, judging by the noises some of them made. Even some of the cops.

There is no livestock here. If I am to wait, I wish to eat.

"Snack later. You're scaring people."

Fear is a reasonable response, and it may disperse the crowd which worries you.

"If they don't trample each other trying to get away."

That could be inconvenient. It is difficult to judge what level of fear is useful, given the unpredictability of those who consider themselves apex predators when confronted by a superior predator. Pack predators such as humans are particularly volatile. Shall I assure them I do not intend to eat them?

"I don't think that would have the desired effect," she said dryly.

Sweat trickled between her shoulder blades. Her heart-beat picked up. Rule was close. She knew he lived and wasn't badly hurt—some cuts to one arm, Sam had said. She knew, but she needed to see him.

To T.J. she said, "I've got two perps. One's out-realm, like I said when I was talking to Sam. The other's human and a sorcerer, the real deal. Capabilities largely unknown, though he has some kind of mental shield and, uh, sometimes he can disguise himself magically. He may be Asian. I think I saw him, and that guy was Asian, five-three or -four, weight one-forty. He's trying to take out a sorcerer who's on our side. Nearly succeeded last night, which is why our guy is at the hospital."

T.J.'s eyebrows shot up. "This sorcerer was ready to burn down a hospital to kill one man?"

"So it seems. There's an awful damned lot I don't know yet."

"Why's the dragon here? He part of this?"

"The part I can't tell you about."

"You're sounding like a Fed, Lily."

"Sorry."

The closer she got to Rule, the clearer her awareness of him became. It was distinctly sensory, this knowing, but not like any of her other senses. Touch, hearing, vision—they brought her information about everything around her: all the objects that contacted her physically, disturbed the air to create sound waves, or reflected light into shape and shadow. The mate-bond sense perceived only one thing: Rule. It told her nothing about him except where he was . . . less than thirty feet away now.

Yet if moonglow were a wind, Lily thought, it might feel like this.

Up ahead at the command post, Deputy Chief Hennessey—easy to spot in any crowd, even in his rig, because he was only a few inches shy of seven feet and skinny as a teenage boy—appeared to be arguing with a much shorter man in a wrinkled white shirt. When one of his people interrupted he listened briefly, nodded, then left with his man.

And when he and the other firefighter left, she saw Rule. He lounged against the side of a pumper truck, looking bored.

His hands were behind his back, but she could see the blood on one sleeve.

His head turned. He straightened, and their eyes met . . . and she understood why his hands were in that odd position. They were cuffed behind his back.

Anger, raw and red, poured through her. They'd *trapped* him—handcuffed him, treated him like a felon, when he was injured—when he hated being trapped, feared it, fought that fear—

No. No, she was overreacting. The cuffs probably didn't trigger his claustrophobia, since he could leave them behind simply by Changing. They were an insult and an offense, but they weren't harming him.

But she let the anger carry her forward, moving faster now. "Which one's Dreyer?" she asked T.J.

"Little guy, mostly bald, white shirt, glasses. Bear in mind that you can't kill him. And if you scare him, he'll bite."

"I've got bigger teeth."

"Lily—"

"Don't worry. I remember what you said about the bone." And as they approached the small group clustered around the command cars, she pulled out the chain around her neck. She unfastened it.

Rule's gaze was intent on her. He didn't say a word. She walked straight to him. A short man with glasses, very little hair, and a wilted white shirt with gold bars on the collar barked at her. "Who the hell are you?"

She ignored him, stuffing the chain and the *toltoi* into the pocket in her slacks. "You're all right," she told Rule.

One corner of his mouth kicked up. "I am."

She heaved a breath of relief. "Your arm—?"

"Hurts, but it isn't serious."

Deliberately she slid his ring on her finger, then turned. "Captain Dreyer," she said to the short man who was scowling at her. The eyes behind his black-framed glasses were small and close-set.

"Who the hell are you?" he repeated. "If my boys have let a damned reporter get through, I'll string someone up by the balls."

"Their genitals should be safe, then. Though you may be fascinated to learn that you have women on your squad, and women lack those particular dangly bits." She held out her shield. "I'm Unit 12 Special Agent Lily Yu. FBI. Why do you have my fiancé in handcuffs?"

TWENTY-EIGHT

~~

THE look on the captain's face was deeply satisfying. His jaw dropped. His face, already red from the heat, hit a dangerous level of crimson. "What the hell are you talking about?"

"My fiancé, Rule Turner. You've got handcuffs on him. He was injured disposing of a bomb that might have killed dozens or even hundreds of people, and you've cuffed him."

"He's a *lupus*."

She allowed her eyebrows to lift slightly. "And . . . ?"

"And he threw a goddamned bomb. And how the hell do you claim to know what he did or didn't do?"

"The dragon told me." She glanced at Rule. He wore his bland face, but something coursed behind his eyes. Humor? Incredulity? Anger that she'd chosen this of all moments to announce their engagement? "Did Sam have it right?" she asked him.

"Basically, yes. I saw the, ah, perp leave a sack outside Cullen's room."

"Outside the room? He didn't go in?"

Rule shook his head. "My nose told me what it contained. I carried it to the window behind the nurses' station, broke the window, and got rid of the bomb. An orderly saw me. I've described him to the captain. I don't know if anyone has spoken to him."

"Lieutenant James," Dreyer demanded of T.J., "who is this woman, and why did you bring her here?"

"She told you who she is, and you've got it backward. She brought me."

Rule's eyelids dipped to half-mast. He spoke too softly for the others to hear. "Your sense of timing amazes me."

It wasn't what he said. Maybe it was his voice or the look in his eyes. For whatever reason, one kind of heat flashed over into another—inappropriate as hell, wild as a grass fire, and just as hard to ignore. She took a second to settle her breath, then answered him, pitching her voice so low only he could hear. "He's pissed me off. And I get hot-mad, not cold-mad like you."

Again something flashed in his eyes—something she could almost read.

Lily turned back to the captain, placing herself between the little man and Rule. "Do you have anything—anything other than blind prejudice, that is—to discredit Rule's account of events?" She paused barely long enough for a hiccup. "I didn't think so. You need to have those cuffs removed now. You also—"

"Wait just one second. You can't tell me who to arrest or not arrest."

Her eyebrows climbed again, higher this time. "Is Rule under arrest?"

"He's a suspect. Until I—"

"Has he been disruptive? Violent? Is there any bloody damned reason for those cuffs?"

"It's simple common sense to restrain a lupus!"

"The courts do not agree with you. Have the cuffs removed. Call the officers who are trying to remove Special Agent Weaver and the others from hospital room 418."

"If anything your *fiancé* says is true, that room's a crime scene."

"The perp never entered the room. Your officers need to look for evidence in the hall. The patient in that room is under the Bureau's protection. He is a high-value consultant who has been targeted by the perp who damn near blew up this hospital. He and those guarding him will not be moved until we've completed preparations for secure and medically safe transport. In addition, you need to follow standard protocol for dispersing the crowds gathered outside the police barriers."

"Listen, I don't care who you are or what you've been sleeping with. You are not in charge here. This is a local matter, not federal, and I can have you removed if you interfere."

"Captain Dreyer." Lily advanced on him. "Magic was used in the commission of multiple felonies—attempted murder, arson, possibly conspiracy to commit an act of terrorism. So yes, I can come in here and interfere." She smiled the way a knife smiles at the prospect of parting flesh. "And that's *who* I'm sleeping with, Captain. Not what. Who."

"That is well-done," said a clear but accented female voice, "but we cannot waste time on this pig-eyed fellow."

A tiny Asian woman wearing black slacks and a thin silk shirt in purest white marched up to Lily and the captain. Her hair was silver-shot midnight, twisted on top of her head in a tight bun and pinned there by delicately jeweled hair sticks. Her posture was impeccably straight. The fine tracery of wrinkles in her face seemed an embellishment of the ivory skin, artfully spun by that great spider, Time.

"Another one?" Dreyer sputtered. "Another interfering bitch? Where did you come from? I suppose you're going to tell me you're a fucking Fed, too."

"You," Grandmother said, "will be quiet now." She stopped in front of him and looked directly into his eyes. "You will do as the federal agent told you, and you will stop making trouble."

Dreyer's face lost its rage-induced color. His eyes glazed. "Trouble?"

"You will *cooperate*." Grandmother stressed the word as if it were code. After a second her head tilted as she glanced at Rule. "Do not concern yourself with the handcuffs, however. I will see to those." She waved a hand. Her lips moved, though Lily didn't hear anything.

The cuffs clattered to the pavement.

"Thank you, Madame," Rule said politely, bringing his arms in front of him with a small wince. He rubbed one wrist. "I didn't know you could do that."

Grandmother's eyes gleamed. She was delighted with herself. "Mr. Seabourne taught me a cantrip for locks. I thought it might be useful."

Lily stared at Dreyer in dismay. He'd turned to the cop next to him—a sergeant, who looked deeply puzzled—and was issuing orders for the people in room 418 to be left alone.

Oh, shit. "Grandmother," she said, hurrying forward, "I am so very glad to see you. But you can't go around ensorcelling police captains!"

"Obviously, I can. That I do not usually choose to do so is beside the point. You were doing well, but my way was quicker." The dainty, imperial chin tipped higher. "I have been walking, and it is very hot. I believe the air-conditioning in the hospital is working once more. We will adjourn to Mr. Seabourne's room to discuss matters."

Even Madame Yu couldn't decree an immediate exodus to air-conditioning. Rule wondered if she experienced heat the way he did, or if she was closer to human norms. A hundred degrees might make him want shade, but it wasn't debilitating. Such temperatures were hard on humans, yet all around him firefighters battled disaster in spite of the heat and their heavy protective gear.

Humans did amaze him sometimes.

He waited with the other civilians while Lily and the man with her—he worked in Homicide, Rule remembered, though he couldn't recall the man's name—spoke with Dreyer and the fire department official. Lily wanted to confirm that the building was safe, to find out about casualties, and to outline the particular needs of an investigation which required evidence of the use of magic. She'd called in the FBI crime scene van, but it wasn't here yet, and much of the work of managing the scene and locating witnesses would fall to—as she put it—the locals.

Captain Dreyer was the epitome of cooperation. Rule thought he would have agreed if she'd suggested he go home and watch *Sesame Street*. It was disturbing. Pleasant, but disturbing. "How long will he be like that?" he murmured to Madame Yu.

"A day, a week." She waved her hand dismissively. "I will admit I used more power than was necessary. He has pig eyes."

In other words, she'd been pissed. Like her granddaughter. He smiled. "And did you use a similar method to get past the police barricades?"

She looked at him sternly, but her eyes were twinkling. "This is a silly question."

"Here's another one. What did you trade for with Cullen to get that unlock spell you used?" Cullen was like a dragon in one way. Dragons hoarded and occasionally bartered information; Cullen hoarded and occasionally bartered spells.

"I was very generous. I told him one way of creating a *wan chi* spell, which is a carrier spell. You do not know what that means, but he did. I also told him about an out-realm being who has lived in China."

Startled, he said, "You told him about the Chimei? When was—"

"Months ago. Hush."

The slightly scruffy older man who used to work with Lily ambled up to them. What was his . . . Oh, yes, Rule remembered now. He had what sounded like two first names— Thomas James. Lily called him by his initials. T.J.

"Ma'am," Thomas James said, "you can head inside now. But the elevators aren't working yet, and I understand the patient you're wanting to visit is on the fourth floor. Do you need—"

Madame Yu awarded his concern a single snort and started for the hospital entry.

"Guess not." James glanced at Rule. "I met her once before. Did Lily tell you?"

Rule shook his head, glanced over at Lily—who waved him on and kept talking to the fire department official—and started for the hospital entry. "What was it like?"

"Embarrassed the hell out of Lily." He fell into step beside Rule, grinning. "She'd just transferred to Homicide and I sort of took her under my wing. Habit of mine, with the young ones. I guess she said something about that to her grandmother, because a week later Lily turns up, all stiff and embarrassed, telling me her grandmother wants to have lunch with me. To check me out," he added in case Rule, not being a cop, had overlooked the obvious. "Not that Lily said so, of course. But Mrs. Yu didn't have a problem saying it."

"You must have checked out. You seem to be intact."

"That," James said after a moment, "isn't funny. She scared the shit out of me. I laughed it off—you know, made like it was the same as being interrogated by that fourth-grade teacher who terrified you as a kid. And it was, in a way. But in another way, it wasn't the same at all." His brow creased. "What did she do to Dreyer, anyway?"

Rule considered various answers, but decided to keep it simple. "Nothing permanent. The, ah, skill is one she rarely uses."

James grunted, looking thoughtful.

The ability to ensorcell with one's gaze wasn't a human talent. As far as Rule knew, dragons were the only beings who could do it. At some point, Madame Yu had been transformed into a dragon. At some point, she'd returned to her original form—but some of the dragon magic had remained. It must have become interwoven with her being so deeply that it couldn't be separated. Deeply enough that she'd passed a version of it down through the blood.

That part didn't surprise Rule. Didn't he enjoy some degree of his wolf's gifts even in this form? Didn't lupi pass their magic down through the blood, even though they mated in human form?

No, the surprising part was Madame Yu's other ability. That seemed to have little to do with dragon magic. Rule had never heard of anyone else who could turn into a—

"You think she put a whammy on me like she did with Dreyer?" James asked suddenly. "Put the fear into me magically, I mean."

"Hmm? Oh, you mean Madame Yu. No, I don't think so. She inspires a certain caution without resorting to magic. The, ah, unusual ability she used on Dreyer. . . that experience isn't one you'd mistake for anything else."

"Yeah?" His eyebrows rose in surprised curiosity. "Pulled it on you, has she?"

"Once." It had been terrifying. Infuriating. Then he'd learned why she'd done it—in a misguided attempt to draw demon poison from his system into herself. The woman lacked sense sometimes, particularly if she was protecting those she cared about. Again, like her granddaughter. "I was angry, but it was an unusual situation, and her motives were selfless."

Another grunt, this one skeptical. "You like her."

"Enormously." They reached the hospital doors. With the electricity back on, they opened automatically. The air inside was cooler, but not back to its usual air-conditioned chill.

The lobby was a mess. Firefighters and mud did seem to go together. Even here, where there had been neither fire nor hoses, there were muddy footprints everywhere. Very few people, though. A trio who looked like clerical or administrative workers were clustered behind the admissions desk, talking intently with a firefighter. There was a cop—female, young, in uniform—standing at the door to the stairwell.

No one else. Most notably, no Madame Yu. She must have headed straight upstairs.

"Just as well you and the grandmother get along, I guess, considering you're going to be family." James thrust out a hand. "Congratulations."

Rule shook his hand—and discovered it was pleasing, satisfying in a way he hadn't expected, to receive this man's well wishes. "Thank you."

"I was going to warn you to treat Lily right and all that, but I'd forgotten about the grandmother. I figure you for a man with some sense. You won't want *her* upset with you."

Rule grinned. "No, I won't."

"Good." James nodded firmly, then looked pained. "I'm going to have to go to the wedding, you know."

"Oh?"

"Camille will expect it. Camille's my wife. It's going to be a big deal, isn't it? Written up in the gossip rags, that sort of thing."

"I'm afraid so."

James shook his head mournfully. "Thought so. Tell Lily Camille will make my life hell if she doesn't get to go."

"I'll pass that on." Rule looked back at the doors. Lily was hurrying their way, her stride as quick and energetic as if she weren't wilting from the heat. "I'd like a private word with Lily before we go upstairs."

James's eyebrows rose. "Sure. I'll just head up and check out this mysterious wounded sorcerer."

Rule winced. "I'd appreciate it if you manage not to say that too loudly. Or at all."

"Heh. Don't worry about that—I'm good with secrets. Ask Lily. As for heading upstairs, I was having you on. I've got to see a man about his dead brother. Tell Lily—no, I'll tell her myself. Her stuff's in my car, and her car's back at Rosa's. I need to have a word with her to sort that out." He gave another nod and headed for the doors.

Rule watched as James stopped Lily. They spoke briefly. Lily passed him her keys. Rule did not pace or fidget. But he wanted to.

Patience was a skill he'd acquired. He was usually good at it, though he'd no more begun that way than a pup arrives prepared to wait calmly for its mother's milk. But patience had its limits. Or rather, he had his limits, and he'd reached them. He wanted to speak with his *nadia*. Now.

The moment she entered, he indicated this desire by grabbing her hand. The one with his ring on it. He traced it with one finger. "Why now?"

"It's a bone. Also an apology."

"It's a what?"

"T.J. said I should throw Dreyer a bone to distract him. So that's part of the reason—to give Dreyer a way to get back at me that wouldn't be as damned stupid as whatever else he might have come up with. He's the type who has to bite back, so I aimed him where I wanted him to go."

"You expect him to tell others? To leak it to the press?"

She shrugged. "That's the idea."

"He may not. Madame Yu told him not to make trouble."

She looked appalled all over again. "I didn't want her to do that."

"I know," he said gently. Her conscience pricked her over things that seemed to him pointless, but her discomfort was real. "It will wear off, she said."

"And when it does, he's really going to want a chunk of flesh. He won't know what happened, but he'll be scared, so he'll come after me and you and anyone else he can. Rule . . ."

He ran his thumb over her ring. "Yes?"

She sighed and looked down at her hand resting in his. "I should have asked you first. Before I started with the 'my fiancé' talk, I mean. I know it matters, all that PR stuff. It annoys me, but you're the public face for your people, so the image, the spin—they matter. We don't have time to hold a damned press conference now, so the press will probably get Dreyer's version first. That might make it harder to spin things the way you'd planned."

He studied her intently. "I'm flexible, and I'm good at spin. I'll make it work. You just wanted to distract the captain?"

"The bone was part of it," she agreed, nodding at their clasped hands as if it were them she addressed, not him. "The other part was the apology. It seemed like the best way to apologize for my foot-dragging was to wear the ring. But you get the words, too."

Now she looked up. "I'm sorry. I'm sorry I was an idiot, and I'm sorry I got mad at you for pointing out what I was doing. Or not doing. You were right. Not a hundred percent, but mostly right. I do need to know the why, but I don't have to . . . I can work on the dress and the wedding stuff while I'm figuring out the why. Because the why isn't going to change anything. I just need to know it."

Naturally, he kissed her.

Rule expected her to shove him back. They were in public. She was on duty. She grabbed his shirt in both hands and kissed him as if he were air and she'd been underwater way too long.

Rule wasn't sure which of them eased back. Probably her. He sure as hell didn't remember telling his hands to turn loose. Of course, his brain had shut right off, what with all the blood in his body being otherwise occupied, so he might have done any number of things without noticing.

"Me, too," she said hoarsely. "Oh, God, me, too. But not here. Not for hours, dammit. You could have died."

He found a little breath, enough to say, "I didn't."

"But you could have."

"A lot of people could have died today, and didn't."

"Well, you saved them, didn't you? And yourself." She shoved her hair away from her flushed face. "I need to remember that. You're good at taking care of yourself, even when you're dealing with a kill-happy sorcerer-assassin who can look like anyone."

"He can't. Look like anyone, that is. Not without the Chimei, and he was here without her today. At least that's what I concluded, and Sam confirmed it."

"Well," she said again, and nodded as if he'd handed her an important puzzle piece, "we'd better get upstairs and see what Grandmother has to say. She was hiding. Now she isn't. We'd better find out why."

TWENTY-NINE

THE stairwell was not air-conditioned. Or if it was, it was ducted very poorly. Lily gave up and took off her jacket. With all the cops around, the sight of her weapon was unlikely to upset anyone. And if it did, she didn't care.

"There were actually two fires," she said as she started up. Rule was behind her. "One on three, one on four, both near the east stairwell. He didn't want people using that one to escape, because that was his route in and out."

"I didn't think there was a fire on the fourth floor. There wasn't anywhere near as much smoke there as on the third."

"Hennessey thinks that one went out all by itself. I think our perp put it out once he'd scared people away from that set of stairs. He needed to use that hallway, and he didn't want to singe his own skin. He didn't bother to put out the one on three because it wasn't a threat to him." It was the one on three that had hurt people.

"Were many killed?" Rule asked.

"Three confirmed. One was on a ventilator when the tech went out. One was being operated on. The third breathed in too much toxic shit, they think. That's what kills most people in a fire, you know—the smoke. Inhale too much and your airways just close up. Anyway, three more are in critical condition—one is burned badly—and at least a dozen others are being treated for smoke inhalation, but aren't considered critical. They don't have a count for how many were adversely affected by the power outage."

They hadn't had to die. None of them had had to die today. The bastard was killing people on her watch. "The fire was a distraction. But why a bomb? Why didn't he just put people to sleep, go in, and kill Cullen?"

"He doesn't know us. Lupi, I mean. He doesn't know what will work on us, but a major explosion will kill pretty much anyone."

That made sense. "You said you saw the perp plant the bomb. Did you see his face?"

"I didn't actually see him plant it. I saw him emerge from the alcove. I couldn't make out his features—visibility was very poor. He's a small man, neither bulky nor tall. Dark hair. He wore scrubs."

"How did you know he was the perp?"

"At the time, it was instinct. But he was awake. He ran when he saw me."

She nodded. "Tell me what happened."

He did. When she learned Rule'd been in an elevator when the power went out, her breath hitched. That had been bad for him. He'd coped, though. He'd gotten the candy striper out, and himself—then shimmied up the elevator cable.

By the time he finished, Lily's shirt was sticking to her back. She reminded herself that her three-hundred-and-some-odd-year-old grandmother had climbed these stairs in this heat. She could, too.

That's why you didn't mind waiting, isn't it? she thought at Sam. *You knew Grandmother was coming here. You were waiting for her.*

Sam didn't answer, but she caught a whiff of response that felt a lot like the way Grandmother snorted when you said something stupidly obvious.

He didn't tell her to vocalize. Did that mean she was thinking more clearly? Or was she doing something approaching real mindspeech? How could she tell? She half expected Sam to comment on that thought—something along the lines of, "If you would learn proper mindspeech . . ."

"Sam wants me to learn mindspeech," she said abruptly.

Rule spoke from behind her. "Do you want to?"

"I don't know. It seems like I should. Mindspeech could come in handy in some situations, but what's the downside? There's always a downside. And how long would it take? I don't have a lot of free time for adult education. I guess I don't know enough about it. I'll need to ask him some questions before I decide." She grimaced at the stairs rising steeply ahead. "At least with mindspeech I wouldn't have to worry about having a conversation when I'm out of breath."

"It's only one more flight. I could carry you."

She *heard* him grinning, dammit. She didn't have to look. "With an injured arm? No, just shut up before you get me in trouble. The heat's making me grouchy."

He didn't say a word. Just moved up beside her and took her hand. And it did help. Some of her tension and grouchiness slid right out.

It was still a relief to reach the fourth floor, open the door, and step into cooler air. A burned stink lingered, but otherwise . . . "Looks pretty calm," she observed.

"More so than when I was here last," he said dryly. "About those casualties . . . do you know if any of them were named Maria?"

She looked at him curiously. "Sorry, no. I didn't get names. Do you want me to find out?"

"No, it doesn't matter."

She was sure it did, but didn't press him. She'd find out about Maria later.

"You've the look of a dozen questions ready to erupt."

"Oh, I've got questions." Many of them jotted down in her notebook, dammit, which was in T.J.'s car. "Lots of whys. Why does the sorcerer want to kill Cullen so badly? Why did Grandmother come out of hiding? Why did the Chimei show up now instead of last year or ten years ago or next year?"

"I've a guess about the last one. The Turning."

She nodded. She'd thought that herself, but it didn't really explain anything. The Turning hit last December. Why had it taken the Chimei months to show up? Had she been in China? It might take time to get her lover out of that country, even with magic helping them along. Or had she been unready in some way until now? Could they do anything to make her unready again?

Lily didn't know enough. That's why she was headed for Cullen's room instead of managing the initial investigation. Grandmother was there, and Sam was near, and they had answers.

They'd reached the alcove that led to the quarantine rooms. They'd dusted for fingerprints, Lily saw. Good. The sorcerer was probably too professional to have made that mistake, but he'd expected everything here to go boom. He might have been careless.

Max was parked in front of Cullen's door, arms crossed and glaring. "Do you have any idea how boring this is?"

Her eyebrows lifted. "Seems like you've had more than enough excitement today."

"Doesn't count if you sleep through it."

Ah, so that was it. He was mad that he'd missed the fun—or maybe he felt guilty that he'd failed. There was nothing he could have done to keep the sleep spell from working, but guilt isn't always reasonable. Lily was sure sympathy would piss him off, but had no idea what might help.

Rule shook his head. "Your power nap doesn't seem to have refreshed you much."

"If you think that I could fucking help falling asleep—"

"I don't. Do you?"

Max glowered at him. After a moment he muttered, "Smart ass," and turned and shoved the door open. "The dynamic duo is here, so we might as well go."

"Go?" Lily said.

Nettie joined Max at the door. "I'm needed to finalize the arrangements to move Cullen. Things are a mess, with so many patients needing transport to other hospitals, but Cynna persuaded the administration to make Cullen a priority. Max is going with me to be sure whoever I speak with is who he or she seems to be."

That made sense. The sorcerer was probably gone—but "probably" could sure as hell trip you up. "Good. Max, bear in mind that this guy could have confederates who lack magic but possess guns. We don't know much about him."

"We know he's powerful," Rule said. "Max is pretty resistant to magic. It took a powerhouse of a spell to knock him out."

Lily didn't smile, but she wanted to. He'd made sure Max heard that.

The scene in Cullen's hospital room was much like the one last night. Cynna stood on one side of Cullen's bed. He was awake again, but pale. Jason was on the other side, doing something to the IV drip. Of course, this time Grandmother was there, too, in the room's only chair.

Lily tossed her jacket on the spare bed, empty now, and went to Cynna. "Are you okay? Shouldn't you be sitting down?"

"So I told her," Grandmother announced. "She is cheeky. She is also pregnant, so I overlook this."

"I've *been* sitting," Cynna said. "Except when I was taking a forced nap on the floor. I'm tired of it. What is this with everyone wanting pregnant women to sit all the time?"

"Extra weight, sore feet, aching back—"

"I'm fine," Cynna said firmly. She glanced at Cullen, her worry clear.

"I'm not fine," he said crossly, "but I'm not at death's door, either. Let's get started."

"Those who are not pregnant and cheeky will sit on the floor," Grandmother informed them. "I do not wish to bend my neck."

Lily was not about to plop down at Grandmother's feet like an acolyte. "Grandmother, I need to know why you came out of hiding now. What—"

Rule put a hand on her shoulder. "Lily, I have a suggestion. This is your area of expertise, and others here are superior to me in knowledge, years, and wisdom. Yet it might be best if I take charge of our discussion. Several of you are affected by restrictions that don't include me. I don't have to mind my tongue—or have it silenced."

The treaty. He was talking about the damned treaty geas.

It is good that someone here has sense, said the familiar cool mental voice.

Grandmother gave a regal nod. Lily's nod was reluctant. It wasn't that she objected to Rule taking charge. Well, not only that. She hated the reason for it.

"Very well. Sam, can you . . . Yes, that will work. Thank you. Jason," he said, turning to the tall blond nurse, "I must ask you to leave the room for now. Sam will let you know if you're needed. He's able to monitor Cullen's condition."

Jason didn't argue. Most lupi didn't when their Lu Nuncio told them to do something. As soon as the door closed behind him, Rule turned to Lily. "Earlier I told Cynna and Cullen about the Chimei and her pet sorcerer, so everyone remaining here already knows. Perhaps this will allow you to speak freely."

"Let's find out." She looked at Grandmother, but mentally directed her comments to Sam as well. "At lunch I couldn't speak of the Chimei or the sorcerer when I talked to T.J. Then all of a sudden I could mention the sorcerer, but not the Chimei. Something changed. What?"

The sorcerer acted on his own, without his name-mate's knowledge or consent.

"Ah," Rule said. "Yes. That's what I suspected. Does this mean the treaty doesn't protect him?'

Grandmother shook her head. "The treaty is seldom so simple. The sorcerer loses protection as far as his acts today are concerned. This means Sam and I are now able to speak of him, within limits. But the treaty heeds intention. When Lily spoke to Mr. James, she did not intend the sorcerer's death. If she had, it would have held her silent."

"Wait," Lily said. "I'm confused. I don't get why the sorcerer is protected by the damned thing in the first place." She frowned at Rule. "You aren't. Why would the Chimei's lover be?"

Grandmother's gaze flicked up, as if she were consulting heaven, but more likely it was Sam. Her lips thinned. She shook her head.

"I think I can answer that," Cullen said.

Lily's head swung. "You?"

"I didn't put it together before." Cullen's voice was weaker than normal, but steady. "But when Sam said 'name-mate' the bell chimed."

"What are you talking about?"

Rule answered first. "Your grandmother traded for a spell of Cullen's. In return, she told him about the Chimei. I'm guessing," he said to Grandmother, "that your intentions were, ah, pure? You didn't intend for Cullen to go kill the Chimei or the sorcerer, so the treaty allowed you to talk about them?"

She lifted a hand and tipped it this way and that. "Intent matters. Mr. Seabourne's intentions were pure—he wished for knowledge. Mine . . . not so pure, so I could tell him only a little. The timing of things also matters. The Chimei was not in this country then, not a threat. Perhaps she had not found a lover to suit her. Perhaps she would not find one for many years, and I would be dead before any of this mattered. To the degree I believed this, I could speak."

"She didn't tell me much," Cullen said. His eyes glittered with excitement. The man could get worked up about magical matters even with a half-beating heart. "Not even a name. Not enough for me to realize the Chimei Rule described was the being she'd told me about, not until Sam used that phrase. Name-mate."

Lily found herself glancing up, as if she could see through a couple floors to the roof. Sam hadn't used that phrase before. It probably wasn't an accident he'd used it now.

Cullen had paused to get his breath. "That's the part Madame Yu told me about. We got to talking about true names. I'd run across a scrap that purported to describe a ritual for investing oneself with a true name, and wanted to know if that was possible. Some of the adepts were said to have . . . Never mind. Point is, she told me about an out-realm being who did something similar. This being was very long-lived and had a habit of taking human lovers, who she kept alive by sharing a portion of her true name. She marked them with it in some way."

Lily tapped her fingers on her thigh. "You're saying that the treaty affects this sorcerer because he's got the Chimei's name?"

"Part of her name, and I'm guessing here, but that sounds likely. A true name . . ." Cullen's voice was fading. He took another careful breath.

I will assist, Sam said. *I am unable to offer my own knowledge on the subject, but if Cullen Seabourne will think as clearly as he is able about what he knows . . . yes. Cullen Seabourne suspects there are two ways of acquiring a true name. One is to understand in the deepest ground of one's being that which will remain true of one's self in all times, in all situations. He believes this to be true of me. He suspects that adepts have such knowledge, that this may in fact be necessary to become an adept.*

Once one has such knowledge . . . his thinking grows muddy. He recognizes that words have magical significance, yet he does not see how to apply that to the possession of a true name. He is correct about his lack of perception.

He says, "Never mind that." He suspects it is possible to magically invest a living being with syllables which . . . His thinking is muddy again. He is confused about the relationship between true names and sound. He suspects there is a way to impose a name or . . . he chooses to call it an essence . . . upon a living being. An essence whose name is known. This is a way of acquiring a true name instead of learning one's own, personal name. He is aware of tales which claim that adepts did this and applies this to speculation to the treaty. He wonders if it is a named artifact which speaks to and is intertwined with the essence of those who carry it.

This is not wholly inaccurate, but it is not applicable to our current problem. He—ah, I perceive that he requires additional oxygen. I believe your tech includes a device which . . . yes, Sam said as Cynna fitted the oxygen mask over Cullen's face. *That will help. I have instructed the healer to return. Cullen Seabourne is reluctant to be put back in sleep, but will require that shortly.*

Cynna's face creased with fresh worry. "He could rest now."

I observe his physical functions, Cynna Weaver. He tires, but he does not fail.

He directs his thoughts to the Chimei once more. He believes the Chimei has surrendered a portion of her name to her lover, or somehow shares her name with him, or perhaps imposed a portion of it upon him. He remembers that Li Lei spoke of the Chimei marking her lovers. He sees differences between these variants, but believes any of them might create a bond that allows the sorcerer to use some of the Chimei's innate abilities. He thinks this must work both ways—the Chimei must need or desire the sorcerer's abilities as well. He speculates that the Chimei may be too instinctive in her use of magic to craft spells without such a bond.

He speculates on the sorcerer's desire for his death. He believes the sorcerer fears that another sorcerer might discover the name with which he and the Chimei are bonded. Cullen Seabourne considers it unlikely that anyone other than a sorcerer—or possibly, he adds, a dragon—would be able to use a true name effectively. He is wrong.

Cullen glared and dragged the oxygen mask down. "Better . . . explain." Cynna glared back at him and replaced the mask.

It wasn't Sam who explained. It was Grandmother. "He is wrong on two counts. First, it is not sorcerers who are best able to use a true name. It is those who possess one themselves."

A general silence fell. Lily frowned. "That presents a problem. I don't think any of us have a name. Except for Sam, I suppose, but he can't act against the sorcerer or the Chimei. Wait a minute. Maybe Max—"

Names function somewhat differently with gnomes, and the one you call Max is divided in his nature. Neither Cynna Weaver nor Cullen Seabourne possess their names. Li Lei does, of course. She knew her name at seventeen, but she is restricted, as am I. Lily Yu, your soul was sundered. You will not know your name until that sundering is healed. Rule Turner, however, lives with portions of two names. They are not his alone, but they are true.

Rule's nostrils flared as if he'd scented something. After a moment he nodded.

It took Lily longer to catch on. Sam was talking about the mantles—which he wasn't supposed to know about. She glanced at Rule, eyebrows lifted.

He tilted his head in a gesture that was neither a nod nor a shake. She took that to mean something along the lines of: Sam's a dragon. Who knows what he knows?

It is possible, Sam continued, *that the possession of these names will grant Rule Turner some immunity from the Chimei's mind-magic. I will speak with him privately about this.*

Lily's eyebrows rose. Rule was frowning abstractedly, maybe listening to Sam. "Good to know. Let's see if I'm following so far. If we somehow learned this secret name, which belongs to both of them, Rule could use it to . . . do what? Command one or both of them?"

I am unable to respond to your question. Cullen Seabourne speculates, but his lack of knowledge renders his speculations questionable.

There was a muffled snort from the bed. Cullen reached up to pull off the oxygen mask—and Cynna clamped a hand over it, narrowing her eyes at him. He sighed and let his hand drop.

Lily figured he must be frustrated. She sure was. The name business was important, or Sam wouldn't have spent so much time on it. But they didn't know why it mattered, how to learn a true name, or how to use it if they learned it.

Lily opened her mouth to ask another question, but Rule beat her to it. "Madame Yu, I interrupted when Lily asked why you came out of hiding. I hope you will answer that now. I also wonder why you hid in the first place. It seems out of character."

"You are perceptive." Grandmother said that much, then fell silent, her expression turning inward. Was she consulting with Sam? Checking to see what the treaty would allow her to say?

"I will answer," she said at last. "There is no longer any value to my remaining hidden. The sorcerer changed the . . .

Bah, what is the word? *Parameters*. He changed the parameters under which the cursed treaty forces us to act. With this, he placed himself in danger. He does not realize this; I think the Chimei will. She will act to protect her lover. She will act soon, and harshly."

THIRTY

GRANDMOTHER stopped there, her face grim.

"And why," Rule prompted gently, "did you hide?"

"To delay her, of course. To keep her attention on finding me. She wants me to suffer. How can she know I suffer if she cannot find me? But I can no longer delay her by hiding, so I stop hiding. I will move in with my son and daughter-in-law. Sam disagrees with this, but I will not leave them unguarded. Lily, I will instruct your sisters and brother-in-law to join me there. Once the Chimei acts, matters will be . . . less stable."

Lily tried to imagine how that would work—her mother, sisters, brother-in-law, and grandmother beneath one roof. The mind boggled. "I don't know if Susan and Beth will do that," she said dubiously. "Not without knowing what's going on, and we won't be able to tell them."

Grandmother fixed Lily with a steady gaze and answered in Chinese—a sure sign of displeasure. The gist of it was, "I have not cultivated my position as autocrat all these years to have them disobey me now. They will do as they are told."

Well, yes. If Grandmother looked at them like that, they probably would. But it was going to be lively in Lily's old home. "What kind of action do you expect the Chimei to take?"

Grandmother shrugged. "Something large and messy. Something she has done before. She has not an original mind. She has great patience, great power, but she does not change readily."

"Can you give us more of a clue?"

Grandmother's lips thinned. She shook her head.

"Okay. Back to Cullen. You said he was wrong on two counts and told us about names. What's the other way he was wrong?"

She arched her eyebrows. "Mr. Seabourne possesses more than one ability which the sorcerer fears."

"Shit!" Lily exclaimed as the obvious jumped up and bit her. "Mage fire. Of course. That's what he's afraid of. It's supposed to burn anything. Maybe it couldn't kill the Chimei, but it could damned sure hurt her."

Cullen Seabourne's thoughts contain many profanities, Sam observed. *He castigates himself for not perceiving this earlier. He speculates that mage fire might disrupt the bond between our enemies. He wishes me to share with you his belief that a sorcerer who participates to some degree in his lover's immortality might be hard to kill by normal means.*

Probably true, but killing him wasn't the goal, so that wasn't a major problem. Lily was more concerned with what to do with him once they caught him. "We'll keep it in mind, Cullen, but you're in no shape to toss around mage fire, and won't be for some time."

She glanced around at the others. "Assume we find the sorcerer. How do we incarcerate him if he can burn things down or pick locks magically or whatever? I'd rather not duplicate the techniques used in the Purge." Back then, they'd cut out tongues and lopped off hands. And that was with the people they suspected of being sorcerers, but not workers of dark magic. The ones they thought were into the bad shit they'd killed any way they could.

Rule and Grandmother exchanged a look.

"Oh, no," Lily said. "We are not going there. Murder isn't an option."

"Not for you," Grandmother said equably. "You are an agent of the law, the government. It is very bad if governments start assassinating people."

"It's not an option for anyone in this room." Lily looked at Rule when she said that. "It's also very bad if governments sanction murder by looking the other way."

He met her eyes steadily. "I'll decide for myself what my options are. But killing isn't my first choice, so we'll talk about our other options."

First they had to think of one. So far, she hadn't.

Cynna spoke suddenly. "Send him to Edge."

Lily looked at her, startled. So did everyone else.

"It makes sense," Cynna said. "We're not set up to deal with magical heavyweights. They are. Shit, they cope with elves. This sorcerer dude can't be harder to deal with than the Sidhe."

Send him to another realm. Yes. It might work. "We could sedate him," Lily said. "Catch him, keep him sedated, fly him across the country, and shove him through the gate."

"Banishment is an old punishment," Rule said, "which means there is precedent. The law appreciates precedent. In modern times there's extraordinary rendition—"

"Which is only quasi-legal," Lily said, frowning.

"*Quasi* may be as close as we can get. Given sufficient payment, the gnomes who govern Edge might agree."

"What about the Chimei?" Lily asked. "Would she be able to follow him there? Can she cross without using a gate? The gnomes might not be willing to take the sorcerer if she tags along."

"I am not sure," Grandmother said slowly. "I had not considered this before. I think she could cross, yes. I do not know if she would do so."

"Sam?" Rule said.

Chimei can travel between realms. It would be costly to her, however. I had not considered this possibility. I will do so. He was silent a moment. *I believe Cynna Weaver has changed the parameters again with her idea. I am able to tell you that this would be a temporary solution. If you are able to banish the sorcerer and if the Chimei follows her lover—which is far from certain—she will seek to free him and return here.*

"How temporary?" Rule asked.

I cannot say. Twenty years, fifty, a few hundred . . . a considerable delay by your standards, I suppose.

"It could work." Lily's mind was starting to buzz with possibilities. "I'll call Ruben. No, shit, why bother? I'd have to be able to tell him about the Chimei." She looked at Rule. "You can tell him."

"He's coming here tomorrow," Rule began.

Lily's phone interrupted with "The Star-Spangled Banner." It was clipped to her jacket pocket, so she had to retrieve that to get the phone and accept the call. "Lily Yu here."

"I'm glad you still are. I heard about the fire," Ruben said.

She winced. "I should have called. Everything's happened pretty fast, but I should have called. Cullen's okay. All of our people are, but there were casualties. The . . ." She paused, waiting to see if the damned geas would stop her.

To her surprise, it didn't. "The perp's a sorcerer. Evidence suggests he started two fires here—I'm at the hospital—using magic, plus he used some kind of broadcast spell to knock people out, so this is our case. Magic used in the commission of a felony. He wanted a distraction so he could plant a bomb in Cullen's room. Rule found the bomb and tossed it out a window."

"Mr. Turner is certainly competent."

"I think so, too. This perp's the one who tried to kill Cullen last night. He's a sorcerer, like I said, capabilities largely unknown, but he's powerful. I caught a glimpse of a man I believe was him. The man is Asian, apparent age between thirty and fifty, clean-shaven, height between five-three and five-six, weight maybe one-forty. He might be Chinese. Han Chinese, specifically. I think he is. He didn't look Mongolian or Korean or Japanese. I think he's a pro. A hitter. He likes to use a knife strike to the heart, but he can change up if he needs to. He used a bomb today."

There was a moment's silence. "That's substantially more information than you gave me this morning."

"When he started burning things, the, ah, the binding on me changed. It didn't go away, but the terms of it changed. I need to tell you about the other perp. She's the real problem. She—" Her voice shut off. Just closed up. "I can't. I can't say anything more."

"Interesting. I—"

The door opened. Lily dropped her phone and had her weapon in her hand before she even thought of it.

Nettie stepped in, with Jason behind her. "Sorry. Should have knocked first. We've got an ambulance waiting. Rule, we're short on personnel. I need you to handle one end of the gurney. Jason can tell you what to do. Cynna, you'll have to follow in a car. There isn't room in the ambulance."

Lily put up her weapon and bent to pick up the phone. It still worked. "Sorry," she told Ruben. "I, ah, dropped the phone and didn't hear that last part. Nettie and Jason are here. They're ready to move Cullen."

"I said that I'd run a check on your possible hitter."

"I looked for similars already. There's a real dearth of top-dollar Asian killers who like to use a knife to the heart, partly because most hitters prefer a gun. There's one woman who might be Asian who likes knives—descriptions for her vary from Puerto Rican to Italian to Asian—but my perp's definitely male. There's a Japanese hitter who uses a blade, but he's in top-security lockup in Kansas."

"Hmm. Did you have Ida query other nations?"

"Ah—not specifically."

"I'll look into it. I can see this isn't the time to request a report, but I need your attention for one more moment. I called in part to assure myself you were uninjured, but I also wanted to let you know that my sense of urgency increased just before I heard about the fire at the hospital. I'm flying out today instead of tomorrow. I should arrive shortly before ten your time."

"You want me to pick you up?"

"Thank you, but no. Ida has arranged all that. Take care, Lily." He disconnected.

Lily frowned as she slid the phone in her slacks pocket, clipping it to the material. "You heard that?" she said to Rule as he came up to her.

He nodded. "I'll be going with Cullen."

"I heard." Grandmother had left her chair and was saying something to Cynna, who nodded seriously. Nettie and Jason began the business of transferring Cullen to the gurney.

"After that, I need to go see Toby. Also my father and the Rhej."

Her frown deepened. That sounded like clan business—well, not the part about Toby, but the rest. She couldn't imagine what had happened that could be seen as clan business. And couldn't ask, dammit, with non-clan present.

Rule smiled and rubbed his thumb between her brows as if he could erase the frown. "I'll explain later. You'll be tied up here awhile."

"Yeah. I've got something brewing for tonight. A lead on the sorcerer, maybe."

"There are some things you need to tell me, too, it seems."

She nodded. "No time now. You're wanted."

He quirked his brows in a way that gave an annoyingly accurate double meaning to her words, then turned to help with the gurney. In a moment, they were gone.

All except Grandmother. It dawned on Lily that this might be a problem. She went to the old woman, who was two inches shorter than her. It was easy to forget that—in part because Grandmother seldom allowed others to stand around her. "Have you got transportation? You said you'd been walking. I might be able to get someone to drive you, but it could be a while."

For a moment Grandmother didn't respond. Then she smiled, oddly tender, and patted Lily's cheek. "You please me, Granddaughter. All my grandchildren please me, but it has been a special joy to watch you Becoming."

Flustered beyond words, Lily did the one thing that occurred to her. She bent ever so slightly and kissed her grandmother's cheek. The tingle of magic on her lips was dear, familiar, unique.

It didn't feel like dragon magic. It felt like Grandmother's magic.

Grandmother's smile lingered. "You are upset because I did not tell you of your heritage."

"I . . . yes. Yes, I am. Your story is your own, but that part, about my magic being from dragons—that was about me, too."

Grandmother nodded. "Our stories are never completely

our own. This is illusion. They are also the stories of our fathers and mothers, our children and ancestors, of all those we brush against for one second, or laugh with, or love, or fight, or kill. Mostly we do not see this, but it is so. This part of my story, which is also yours, belongs to Sam as well. When magic grew thin here and dragons removed to Dis, I did not go with them. With him. I needed a child, which he could not give me, so I remained.

"He returned me to this form, which was capable of children. This was a powerful working, and cost him much. He did this for love of me, knowing my need. He asked of me one thing: that if I should have a child and if that child, or that child's child, should bear anything of him, I was not to speak of it or allow the child to know. That was his to do.

"I agreed. He could have asked a great deal more. I would have agreed, for love of him."

Lily swallowed. This was a Mt. Everest of candor and revelation, and it moved her near to tears. "He expected to return."

"He knew he would. He did not know when."

"And he . . . he wanted to be the one to tell me about my heritage?"

"You wonder why. I know, as much as one may know such things about another, but I do not speak of it. That is very much his story, and a dragon story, and you are not dragon. You have an inheritance from dragons, but you are not dragon. He will tell you himself, or he won't."

"Is there . . . is there more you haven't told me? More I should know, because it's my story, too?"

Lily saw something rare on Grandmother's face then. Pure surprise. It flashed over her, melding almost instantly into a chuckle. "Oh, you are bright. Yes. There is more, and I will not speak of it today. I have reasons, which may be wrong or right, but are my best judgment. If I should die in the next few days—"

"Grandmother!"

"I do not intend it, child. But the Chimei is a formidable enemy, and she longs for my death. If I should die with these other matters untold, it will be left to Li Qin to choose the time and place of the telling."

"Li Qin? Not Sam?"

"That part of my story is a woman's story, and not for Sam to tell. Enough." Grandmother's posture changed subtly, yet unmistakably. The time for stories and candor was at an end. She glanced around. "Is there a telephone here?"

"A telephone?" Lily's mind was in too many places at once. She couldn't imagine why Grandmother—who hated telephones—suddenly wanted one.

"I require a taxicab."

"I can get you a taxi." Lily reached in her pocket for her phone. "But you hate them. You say they're all driven by incompetent apes who—"

"Bah. I have survived things you could hardly conceive. I can survive a ride in a taxicab."

Lily touched the app that gave her the Yellow Pages—and on impulse, searched for a different listing from "taxicabs." A smile tugged at her mouth. "How about a limo instead?"

"A limousine." Grandmother's eyes lit with humor and delight. "A very large one."

"Long and shiny."

"And black. I do not care for the white ones."

"Long, shiny, and black. With a uniformed driver."

Grandmother approved this with a nod. "Your mother," she announced, "will be surprised."

Oh, God, yes. Was it terrible of her to want to watch?

It took a few moments to arrange—moments she probably shouldn't have used this way. But Grandmother's childlike delight was impossible to resist. Lily prepaid with her credit card—Grandmother didn't have a purse with her, and there were no pockets for a wallet in those slacks.

Besides, this was her gift. "They'll pick you up on Vista Hill," she said after disconnecting. She grabbed her jacket, but didn't put it on. "I'm afraid the nearer roads are still closed, but maybe I can get you a lift to the pickup spot. I'll walk downstairs with you."

"You have far too much to do to escort me."

"True," Lily said, unreasonably cheerful. "But I need to do some of it with Hennessey and Dreyer, who are downstairs."

"Very well."

They left the room together. As they reached the door to the stairwell Lily said, "There's one more thing I'd like to ask."

"Yes?" Grandmother waited for Lily to open the door for her.

She did. It was still stinking hot in the stairwell, she noted glumly. "Where have you been? Where could you hide that this Chimei couldn't find you?"

"I would think you could figure that out." This was said with great satisfaction. She moved ahead of Lily to the stairs. "I have been at the zoo."

Incredulous, Lily repeated, "The zoo?"

"Of course." Grandmother started down the stairs as nimbly as if heat and age were equally unimportant. "The Chimei never knew me in my other form. I did not possess that ability until long after we defeated her in Luan, so she could not find me once I transformed. And where else may a tiger hide comfortably in San Diego?"

THIRTY-ONE

⟜

IT was hours before Lily was able to leave the hospital. When she did, it was still too damned hot.

She carried her jacket as she headed for her car. Her shirt stuck to her. Normally she didn't even notice her shoulder harness, no more than she'd notice she was wearing shoes. At the moment she was aware of every inch of it pressing against her, holding in the heat.

To the west, out over the ocean, clouds were piling up, dark mounds capped by incandescent white. She sneered at them. Twice during the current heat wave, storms had built up out at sea—and busted their guts without coming in to land, leaving the city as hot and parched as ever.

Damned teasing clouds.

She'd made sure the FBI's crime scene people played nicely with the local arson investigators. Both teams might come up with useful evidence, and even if the plan was to evict the sorcerer from their realm, they'd need to prove they had the right perp. She'd made sure Dreyer's people asked witnesses about an Asian man in scrubs. Unsurprisingly, some people had seen such a man. Lily had spoken with some of them to see if he might be her perp.

Mostly, no. There were plenty of Asian doctors on staff, and most of the reported sightings were either of a physician the person knew, or they were in the wrong place. Some were possible, though.

She really needed a picture of him. A name would be good. While she was wishing, she might as well toss in a call from Zhou Xing giving her the hitter's contact info. She . . .

Her phone played harp music. That was Cynna. She grabbed it. "This is Lily. What's up?"

"He fixed it! Sam undid the spell on Cullen's heart."

"He did? Already?"

"Well, Cullen and Sam did it together. Sam studied the spell for a couple hours. He just lay there staring at Cullen, not moving, not even a twitch. Every now and then he'd sort of hum. Finally he said he had the key to the spell, but it would be difficult to unsing because of the spell's blood-tie to Cullen. But Cullen had an idea about using this *wan chi* spell—that's way cool, by the way. He learned it from your grandmother, and it's a carrier spell, and they're usually just used as part of another spell so it will go where you want it. But this *wan chi* spell is different because you can use it on someone else's spell, which makes it good for defense. If you have it ready, you can deflect the other guy's spell. Uh—where was I?"

Lily grinned. "Sounding like Cullen." Who loved to talk about the theory and nuances of spellcraft.

"I do, don't I? Anyway, the other thing about the *wan chi* spell is it's powered by blood. So Cullen pricked his finger and Sam sang this note—he can hold a note a really long time— and Cullen used the *wan chi* spell to carry Sam's unsinging into his heart. Blood to blood, see? And the bad spell just fell apart."

"That's good. That's really, really good." Lily struggled to find words. "That's damned wonderfully, marvelously good. So Cullen's going to heal now? His body's doing its lupus thing?"

Cynna laughed. "Nettie says he doesn't need her any-more. She put him back in sleep and she's going to hang around another hour or two, just to be sure, then go home and go to sleep herself. For a day or two, she said. The damage is pretty small, really, not like when he had to regrow a whole foot and ankle. Regrowing parts takes a lot longer than clos-ing up a cut."

It wasn't just a cut. It was a cut to the heart, so some of his healing magic would be spent keeping him alive while he healed it, which meant it would heal more slowly than a cut to the leg or arm. But Lily knew what Cynna meant. "It won't be long before he's driving you crazy, trying to do stuff he shouldn't."

"Ha! I've got a dragon keeping an eye on him. Let him argue with Sam."

He probably would. Lily's grin spread even wider. "Yeah, but Li Qin is there, too. Even Cullen won't argue with her. You just can't, somehow. Have you called Rule yet?"

"I don't—yeah, wait. Nettie's signaling me that she's got him on the phone now. She called Isen already. It's a clan thing," Cynna said apologetically, as if she were responsible. "The Rho had to hear first."

"I guess." Isen had declared clan-offense, after all. Lily wasn't sure that made up for not telling Rule first, but Rule probably wouldn't agree.

She paused to look around. She'd reached the street where her car was supposed to be, according to the patrol officer T.J. had coerced into bringing it to her. Where . . . Oh, there it was.

Things were looking up. She updated Cynna briefly on the investigation while she climbed into the oven that was her front seat, wincing when she touched the steering wheel. She got the engine started—and with it, the a/c. "Um . . . could I ask you a personal question?"

"Sure." Cynna was still riding the cheerful wave.

"Why did you decide to marry Cullen? I mean, as opposed to living with him. Was it for the baby?"

"Yes and no, and I'll give you more if you tell me why you're asking."

No mistaking the curiosity in Cynna's voice. "I'm not having doubts," she said firmly. "I know that marrying Rule is right. I just don't know why."

"Uh . . . because you love him?"

"That's true whether I marry him or not." Lily grabbed her headset, touched the RECEIVE button, and slid it on so she could drive. The car wasn't anything like cool yet, but the steering wheel wouldn't burn her fingers now. Probably. She slipped the phone into its dashboard holder and said, "With the mate bond, we've already got the forever thing. So why marriage, when it's going to cause who knows how much trouble with the clans?"

"But you're not having doubts."

"It's more like I need to get everything lined up."

"Like in your closet." Cynna chuckled. "Okay. I don't know if it will help, but I married Cullen . . . well, two reasons, really. He needed the forever promise, so I wanted to give that to him. And I wanted us to be a family. An official family. We'd be the baby's family without that piece of paper, but we wouldn't be each other's family, if you see what I mean."

Lily had more family than she wanted sometimes. Cynna had no one. No family at all, save for a father she'd never known until a few months ago—a father who lived in another realm. "That makes good sense. Excellent sense."

"So did I help?"

"Yes." Not that everything had clicked into place. Lily didn't have Cynna's craving for family. She wasn't convinced families were made only with official sanction, anyway. So Cynna's reason wasn't her reason, not exactly. But it gave her a line to tug on—just like with an investigation, really. She felt that little stirring that said she was headed in the right direction. "It did. I . . ." Her phone beeped. She glanced at the display. "Ida's calling. I'd better take it."

"Okay. If you need me to Find something, though—" Cynna interrupted herself with a yawn.

Lily chuckled. "Maybe later." She accepted the call. "Lily Yu here."

Ruben's secretary was one of those people with a voice that didn't match anything else about her. She spoke crisply, which fit, but the voice itself should have belonged to a torch singer or a longtime smoker. "Interpol is sending you information on a Chinese man who is suspected of performing multiple hits over at least a decade," she said briskly. "There is no photo, but there is a composite sketch which is included as a JPEG file. Would you like me to send that to the state and local law enforcement agencies with a description, noting that he is a person of interest in this investigation?"

"Yes. Hot damn. Yes."

"Very well. He is thought to have used various names, which will be listed in the file you receive. They believe he's been using Johnny Chou most recently, though that was over a year ago. His preferred style is a single knife-thrust to the heart. Shall I contact Homeland Security to see if they have any record of him entering the country?"

"Absolutely. Though without a photo . . . will they have any way of checking records for him?"

"The facial recognition software won't work with a sketch. You are correct that it's a long shot, but they should be made aware." She paused. "I apologize for not having extended your original search to include international agencies. You are new to this work. I should have offered you more direction."

An apology from Scary Ida? Lily automatically responded with the kind of formality she might have used with Grandmother—had Grandmother ever done something as outrageous as apologize. "If you want me to accept your apology, I will, but I'm aware that the failure was mine. Thank you, Ida."

Ida cleared her throat. "I would like to ask a favor."

The mind just kept boggling. "Sure."

"Agent Weaver was kind enough to allow me to be a hostess for her shower, even though I was unable to attend. And then this—this terrible thing happened. I'm reluctant to contact her myself when she must be terribly worried, but I am anxious for her. Would you let me know when you have news about her husband?"

So Lily got to share the good news first with, of all people, Ida.

Once she ended that call, she made another. To Rule. He picked up right away. "You heard?" she said.

"I did, and God and the Lady bless Sam for it."

She laughed. "That's very ecumenical of you. Cynna said Cullen used a spell Grandmother taught him."

"Hmm. Yes, I think it was the spell Cullen traded his unlocking spell for, several months ago. This was when she told him about the Chimei."

Lily contemplated that in silence for a moment. "No," she said at last. "Grandmother is many things, but she isn't precognitive or prescient or any of that fortune-teller stuff. It has to be coincidence."

"Madame Yu may not be prescient," Rule said slowly, "but what about Sam?"

"Why does that creep me out? Ruben doesn't creep me out."

"Maybe because you know that Ruben doesn't see specific, detailed events that are months or years in the future. He doesn't manipulate the rest of us to meet those events in a specific way."

"Oh, geez, yeah, that's it. You think Sam could have known that much, that far ahead?"

"I have no idea. But the possibility creeps me out, too. I've decided not to think about it."

Probably a good approach, she decided. "How's Toby?"

"Busy. Excited. He and several others in his age group will be sleeping under the stars tonight. Supervised, of course. They left with Travis a couple hours ago."

"He's doing okay, then." Toby had been through a lot, including being kidnapped by a nutcase who thought she could put her dead son into Toby's body. He'd been in a drugged sleep during the rescue, so he hadn't seen the woman killed—which was high on Lily's list of things to be grateful for.

For a while, Toby had clung to Rule, feeling safe only when his father was near. Once they got to San Diego, though, he'd seemed to relax. "He's felt safe at Clanhome. I hate to think that's changed."

Rule thought Toby was finding his footing, although, as he said, it was impossible to know what a nine-year-old was thinking. But he considered it a good sign that Toby was so keen on the hike and campout. "Though he's annoyed that he can't go visit Cullen yet. Ah . . . he hasn't heard about the fire. You know what Clanhome's like—people don't have the news on 24/7. I . . ." Rule paused. "I feel guilty for not leveling with him."

"Parenting seems to be mostly taking your best guess and going with it. Is your best guess that Toby's better off not knowing anything about what's going on? If so, can you be sure he won't hear about it elsewhere? And when should he learn about it?"

"You ask damned uncomfortable questions sometimes." Rule was silent a moment, then sighed. "I need to tell him some of it. I wanted him to have his campout without this hanging over him, but sparing him now makes problems for him later. Did you learn anything helpful at the hospital?"

"Not really, but . . ." And she told him about Ida's call. "Interpol's sending the file electronically, so I'll be checking that as soon as I get to the apartment. What did you need to talk to Isen about, anyway?"

"You're headed for our apartment?"

"I'm headed for the shower, which happens to be at the apartment. I can't tell you how much I crave a shower. I'm sticky. Are you dodging my question about your father?"

"I spoke with him about the Chimei, of course. Also, Sam made a suggestion about my mantles that may be valuable, but he doesn't . . . It's like talking to a meteorologist who understands weather theoretically, but has never experienced snow. His insights are sound but limited. I wanted to talk to my father about Sam's suggestion."

"Which so far you haven't repeated to me."

"I lack words. If I understood Sam correctly, it has to do with . . . a way of listening. Or experiencing. I also spoke with the Rhej. The memories go back a long ways. I'd hoped there might be something in them about the Chimei, but apparently their race fought in a different corner of the Great War than we did. She couldn't locate anything relevant."

"Pity. She wouldn't have been bound by the restrictions Grandmother and Sam have. And me," she added, though it pissed her off to have to do that. "Ruben's coming in tonight. Are you going to fill him in on the Chimei?"

"I haven't decided yet. I considered asking your grandmother or Sam for advice, but on reflection decided that was likely to increase the weight on the treaty, if you see what I mean."

"Not really."

"Sam said that indirect actions have a cumulative effect on the treaty which can, potentially, break it. It seems likely that the more closely those bound by the treaty participate in an action—the more their words or acts affect or precipitate someone else's action—the greater the chance that the treaty will be broken. Asking Sam's advice would tie my decision to involve Ruben—and therefore, the government—more closely to Sam."

She drummed the steering wheel with her fingers. "I almost understood that. You know what I want."

"And that will factor in my decision."

"Um . . . I just realized that I'm one of the ones affected by the treaty, so I must affect the treaty, too, so my urging you to do it my way might add to that weight you mentioned."

"That had occurred to me."

"Shutting up now."

"You don't have to go that far."

She smiled as she turned into the parking garage beneath the apartment building. "I might as well. I'm home, or as good as. You going to head back soon? I was hoping you'd get here in time for a kiss-and-run."

"I'll head up the mountain first and talk to Toby. It won't take too long if I go four-footed. Who's running?"

"Me." Automatically she checked for anything out of place near her parking spot. Everything looked normal—no unfamiliar vehicles or odd shadows, nothing that didn't belong. "I've got a meet at seven-thirty. With luck I can shower and change and eat before I go, assuming Harry hasn't eaten all the ham."

"There was plenty left this morning. Is this the possible lead you mentioned earlier?"

"No, that hasn't panned out yet. The meet's with Cody. Deputy Beck," she added as she pulled into her spot and shut off the car.

"I remember the name. He has a lead?"

"He's got an informant who claims to know something about an Asian dude who's been doing some 'really scary shit.' I'm not optimistic. Seems like our lovebirds wouldn't leave anyone wandering loose who knew about their scary shit. But Cody says this snitch is usually on the money, so it's worth following up."

"Hmm. I'd feel better if you waited so I could go with you."

She removed the phone from its holder. "If you get here in time, fine, you can tag along. Otherwise, I'll see you when I get back. 'Bye, now."

Lily barely caught his "take care" before disconnecting. She slid the phone in her pocket, took off the headset and left it on the seat, grabbed her laptop, purse, and jacket, and got out of the car. A click locked the door. She turned—

"Miss Yu?"

The voice came from her left. She spun, grabbing her weapon.

RULE frowned at the phone in his hand.

"Problems?" his father said, strolling into the sprawling great room that comprised most of the lower level of his house.

"Horns of a dilemma," Rule murmured, putting the phone in his pocket. "I need to talk to Toby. I should have leveled with him before he left for the campout. I was wrong to put off letting him know about Cullen and the fire."

Isen nodded thoughtfully. "Did you notice that I didn't tell you that earlier, though it was painfully obvious? I cleverly waited for you to figure it out yourself."

Rule's grin was fleeting. "I did, yes."

"What's the 'but' that makes this a dilemma?"

"Lily has a meeting with an informant. It's connected to the two enemies I told you about. I'm uneasy with her going alone." Except that she wouldn't be alone. She'd be with Cody Beck.

That did nothing to ease Rule's mind. *Why should it?* he told himself. Beck might be a wonderful fellow. Rule was reserving judgment there, though he'd read the preliminary report from the detective agency. Beck was second-generation cop; his father, retired now, had been one of the first to integrate the SDPD. The man had been in rehab for alcohol, but that was several years ago, and he had apparently stayed sober since. He went to AA regularly, church not at all, and had two citations on his record since joining the sheriff's department.

All of which was beside the point. Beck was human. Rule could protect Lily better.

"You could send one of your bodyguards with her, or tagging along behind. Don't have to mention it to her."

"They could be deceived by this Chimei, if she's near."

"If your gut tells you to go, then go. I can talk to Toby for you."

Rule hesitated only a second before giving a nod. "Thank you. You'll not tell him too much—"

"Go." Isen waved a hand, shooing him out. "You think I can't choose the right things to say? Go."

Rule did.

THIRTY-TWO

~~~~~~

"WHO are you?" Lily asked, her SIG Sauer held steady in one hand. Carefully, keeping her eyes on her target, she bent to set her laptop down. Her purse and jacket had already fallen to the concrete.

The man who'd stepped out from behind one of the concrete pillars smiled. He was Chinese, probably under thirty, with a shaved head and the bulk of a bodybuilder on steroids. The suit jacket he wore was wholly inappropriate for the temperature and didn't quite hide the bulge of his weapon.

But he held his hands out from his sides. "I am no one, but I bring you a message from Xing Zhou."

"I'm listening."

"The message is written. Will you allow me to come closer so I may give it to you?"

He was young and spoke without much accent, but he'd put Zhou's surname ahead of the given name in the Chinese way. Maybe he was from Taiwan. Xing had connections there. "Please understand that I respect Mr. Xing's intelligence too much to do that. I, ah . . . I do not wish to offend with a suggestion, but I would appreciate it if you put the message on the hood of that black SUV near you, then backed away."

He nodded, smiling faintly as if he both understood and was amused by her caution. "I must reach inside my jacket to get it," he said apologetically as he moved a few paces to the side, to the SUV.

"Keep your movements slow. I'd be terribly unhappy if I shot one of Mr. Xing's people in error."

Still smiling, he did as instructed, pulling out a white envelope. He laid it on the SUV's hood, then gave her a small bow. "Mr. Xing wishes me to express his thanks for your warning. In the envelope is an additional expression of his gratitude."

"I hope Mr. Xing knows what types of expressions would be offensive to me."

"I was instructed not to open the envelope, and have not. Yet I am sure it does not contain money, if that concerns you." He turned and walked away, heading up the ramp on foot.

Lily kept her weapon out and her senses sharp as she approached the SUV and the innocent white envelope. By the time she reached it, Xing's smiling employee was out of sight.

Could be anthrax or something similar inside, she supposed, studying it. She touched it, using the back of her hand so as not to mess up any fingerprints. Xing's man hadn't worn gloves, and it might be interesting to see if his prints were on file.

No magic tingles.

Lily contemplated the envelope one more second, then decided to play it safe. She took out her phone and selected a number she hadn't used yet. "This is Lily," she said. "Code Three. I'm in the garage near my spot. I'd like an extra set of ears and eyes. Also a good nose."

She put up her phone, retrieved her laptop and jacket, and went to stand with her back to the pillar where Xing's man had waited for her—no doubt for the same reason she went there now. It was a good vantage point. Then she waited for one of Rule's bodyguards to join her.

Caution made sense when dealing with Xing. The old snake appreciated Lily because she treated him with respect, and he respected—or feared—her grandmother. He was still a snake. If he felt a need for her to die, he'd do his best to arrange it.

The elevator dinged. The doors opened and two men leaped out—José and Jacob, both Nokolai—weapons ready.

Lily frowned. "Code Three means I'm requesting an escort. That's one guard, not two, and no immediate threat."

"Yes, ma'am." José gestured for Jacob to move ahead, and Jacob—tall, dark hair and eyes, slim as a willow and just as supple—began circling the garage's echoing expanse. "But you never call us. I figured you'd probably seen a hostile, or thought one was around."

"And assumed your judgment was superior to mine?"

"Ah—"

"No, wait. Rule told you to go into emergency mode if I ever requested an escort, didn't he?"

José grimaced. "I, uh, really don't—"

"Never mind. I'll take it up with Rule later. Since you're both here, let's pretend I'm in charge. Which of you has the best nose?"

"I do," José said. "But I'd need to Change."

"Okay. Jacob, unless you've found something you need to check out, pull in close and stay alert. I had a visit just now from . . . Well, he's muscle, but muscle with brains. He works for an enemy of mine who might be acting as an ally at the moment. Or he might not. He left that for me." She nodded at the envelope, still shiny white against the black SUV. "I thought you could sniff it and make sure it's just paper."

"Okay. I can't Change back as fast as Rule does," he added. "If I smell anything suspicious, I'll growl." José gave Jacob some kind of hand signal and set down his weapon. Then he Changed.

Lily never got tired of seeing that. Or not quite seeing it, but being present as reality took on a tilt her eyes couldn't follow. The space where José stood folded both into and away from itself, and his shape tilted and folded with it—until a large black wolf stood on the collapsed pile of clothes, panting cheerfully.

Jacob joined them. He faced out, not watching José, who trotted up to the SUV, lifted up onto his hind legs, and planted his forefeet on either side of the envelope. He gave it a good sniffing, then dropped back on all fours. He wagged his tail.

"Smells kosher, huh? Okay, thanks. Let's head upstairs."

They rode up in the elevator together—a man, a woman, and a wolf. It was just as well that none of the building's other inhabitants wanted to go anywhere right that moment.

Lily didn't feel bad about calling out the troops when it turned out they hadn't been needed. If you waited until you knew for sure you were up that shit creek before hunting for the paddle, it was probably too late.

The guards on the door were Leidolf, which surprised her. It wasn't a weekend. She asked them how the weapons training was going, and got a grimace from one and a grin from the other. The grinner—his name was Mark—had won the last round at the shooting range.

Leidolf, like most lupi, had a strong distaste for firearms of all kinds. Nokolai was different because Benedict insisted that those he trained learned to handle a gun. The Leidolf guards had arrived unsure how to hold a gun, much less fire it. Rule was having his Nokolai guards train them.

So far neither side had taken a shot at the other. That had to be good. She congratulated Mark and told the two Nokolai men they could go.

José shook his head. "Me and Jacob have this watch. Mark and Steve stood in for us so we could respond to your Code Three. Guys, you can get back to your Nintendo."

Lily shrugged and went in. She supposed it was progress that Leidolf guards were working well enough with the Nokolai ones to switch off sometimes.

Harry was glad to see her. She gave him some ham and kibble, then at last sat down to open the envelope. Harry elected to join her, having gobbled the ham. He curled up beside her, purring. She stroked him as she read the handwritten note.

The enemy of my enemy is my friend.
So said our people long before these Americans existed, and so I will tell you some things about our enemy. You may know some of these things, and more I cannot guess.
He calls himself Johnny Deng, and says he is a sorcerer.

He is more than this. He has powers not seen since demons mingled with people centuries ago, and so I think he is demon or he answers to a demon.

He wishes to own the city. Not your part of the city, Lily Yu, but mine. He has taken over two small gangs already and makes an offer for my enterprises. I laugh. My brother dies. Still I would have stayed and fought for what is mine, but I receive your warning. If an enemy of your revered grandmother lives, he is a powerful man. Or more than man.

As you read this, I am no longer in San Diego.

It is good to strike the serpent's head with your enemy's hand. To help you strike this serpent, I tell you one more thing about this man. He has a small tattoo beneath his left nipple. This mark cannot be seen with ordinary vision. It is a word, but uses a character I do not know. I write it for you here.

Below that was a character written the old-fashioned way—with ink and brush. Lily scowled at it. She for damned sure didn't know the word, either. She spoke some Chinese, sure—though Grandmother said her accent was terrible—but she didn't read it at all.

I wish you success, the note ended. *Though this may surprise you, I hope you live through your battle with our common enemy. Please convey my respect to your esteemed grandmother.* It wasn't signed.

She glanced at her watch. Damn. She was tempted to call Cody and tell him she couldn't make it . . . but if this snitch of his did know anything, she needed to be there. Cody wouldn't know the right questions to ask.

If she hurried, she had time to throw together a sandwich, but there was no time for a shower. Pushing to her feet, she hurried to Rule's office—the actual office, not the dining table he usually used. She scanned the letter with its *hanzi* characters, printed it, then booted up Rule's desktop and sent the image to herself, to Ida, and to Ruben.

Seven minutes later she headed out the door—pausing to frown at the two men standing outside. "Where's José and Jacob?"

Mark grinned. "Truth is, Jacob had a hot date. Steve and I were already here, so when Jacob, uh, mentioned his scheduling conflict to José, we agreed to finish the watch so he could get there on time."

The explanation sounded reasonable, yet it bothered her. On impulse she grabbed Mark's hand.

This alarmed him. "Uh . . . ma'am?"

She shook her head and let him go. "Nothing." Just the usual furry magic, which she should have known without checking. Illusions didn't work on her. "Tell Rule I already gave Harry his ham, okay?"

"Will do."

She hurried off down the hall, purse on her shoulder, jacket once more covering her shoulder harness, with a Diet Coke in the purse and a ham sandwich in one hand. And thought about names.

Cullen had said that Grandmother had said—damn, this got convoluted—that the Chimei marked her lover in some way. Could this unknown word inscribed beneath the sorcerer's left nipple be the secret name? Could it be that simple?

Of course, there was still the business of pronouncing that word correctly, which that unknown character made tricky. Then—if it was a name, or part of one—they had to figure out what to do with it. Just saying it probably wasn't enough. Magic always needed intention. She knew that much.

But this could be a break. Plus now they had an idea about what the sorcerer wanted. Lily had a feeling the criminal empire he had in mind wasn't the Chimei's goal. Maybe she could play that, find a way to work the two against each other.

Things were looking up.

THIRTY-THREE

~~

"WHY do snitches never want to meet someplace comfortable?" Lily complained as she got out of her car.

Cody grinned. "I think someone didn't get any supper."

"I had supper." She'd eaten the sandwich in the car and downed half the soda. "What I didn't get was a shower."

They were in the parking lot of the Oceanview Mall—which completely lacked a view of the ocean, offering instead acres of concrete that had been soaking up heat all day. Having received in abundance, it was now giving back. A bit of a breeze was kicking up, though, carrying a teasing whisper of coolness. Lily glanced off to the west, where the stalled cloudbank looked like a massively bad bruise, all black and purple. Maybe the storm would move in, after all. "What now?"

"Having parked in the boonies, we now walk to section A12, where we look for a 2007 red Ford pickup, California license 3NQS750. Lowrider, orange flame on the sides." Cody glanced at her. "For some reason Javier thinks my ride's too distinctive. He didn't want me parking anywhere near him."

They started for the congested section he'd indicated. Privately, Lily admitted that, from a snitch's point of view, the setup made sense in a paranoid sort of way. Public spots were better than dark alleys or bars, and what could be more public yet anonymous than a mall parking lot? The light was fading, but not yet gone. If he was a smart snitch, he'd shown up early and would be watching to make sure they followed instructions— and that no one had followed either him or them.

"Your man always this careful?" The breeze was growing stronger, blowing her hair in her face. She shoved it back.

"Pretty much. He likes the cloak and dagger aspect of informing as much as he likes getting a little cash now and . . . Shit."

"What?" Lily stopped, her heartbeat revving. Then she realized what he was looking at. Her hand. Specifically, the ring she wore. "Oh. You mean you were, ah . . ."

"I had it in mind, yeah. I mean, a lupus—that's temporary."

Lily eyed Cody warily. "This ring says it isn't. You aren't going to do something stupid, are you?"

"Like grab you and plant one on?" Cody's teeth flashed white in a grin. "Maybe I thought about it, but, hey, I'm a cop. I can read body language, and yours is saying 'whoa, black belt here.' "

"Oh." She felt foolish. "How'd you guess? I wasn't a black belt yet when you knew me."

"You mean you are now? Shit, it's a good thing I finally did develop some sense." He wiped his forearm across his forehead, rearranging the sweat. "Guess I could take it as a compliment that your man was in a hurry to put up that big, shiny KEEP OUT sign."

A KEEP OUT sign? Like she was property? Lily opened her mouth to tell him what she thought about that attitude . . . then realized it didn't matter. It really didn't. Maybe Cody would feel better if he thought Rule had considered him a threat. "I guess you could."

He looked at her for a long moment. "He didn't, though, did he? You may not have been wearing that sparkler earlier, but you had it."

She smiled. She couldn't help it. Cody had always been at his most appealing when his good sense got the drop on his ego. "I did. We were waiting for the right moment for the big announcement, but I decided right moments can be hard to spot, so why not wear it?"

His mouth twisted in a wry smile. "Maybe you wanted to put up your own KEEP OUT sign, having just run into me again and all. You'd know that a ring was a good defense against my legendary appeal. Ah—you don't have to actually respond to that. Think I'd like it better if you didn't."

Lily grinned and started walking toward A12 again. In truth, she'd been thinking of Rule when she put on his ring, and only Rule. Well, him and giving Dreyer a black eye, if she could. "I'm not going to tell you what to think."

"There's a switch."

"I did not tell you . . . okay," she admitted. "Sometimes I did. But I was young."

"Young, but smart enough to know when to bail. Don't puff up. I mean that. You were right to hand me my walking papers. I've got a lot of regrets from my drinking years, Lily. My stupid years, I call them. I want you to know that you're the biggest one. I shouldn't have let you go."

Her eyebrows arched. "Shouldn't have *let* me?"

"Don't pick at my words, woman. If I'd gone in rehab as soon as . . . Well, once I knew you meant it, you'd have come back, and you'd have stuck by me. I knew it then, I know it now. You're the kind who sticks."

She would have. She'd hoped hard that he'd do just that— go into rehab for her sake. For both their sakes. It had been painful, giving up that hope.

They walked on in silence for a bit. They were in a busier, more crowded section now, which Lily preferred. She'd felt exposed out in the boonies.

"He's really it for you, this Turner dude?" Cody asked abruptly. "No regrets, no doubts?"

Lily had always spoken the truth to Cody. She gave him truth now. "No regrets. No doubts."

His mouth flattened into a straight line, but only for a moment. Then he slipped back into the cocky grin he wore so well. "Guess you finally found someone who worries your mother even more than I did."

"I did not get involved with you to annoy my mother."

When they first started dating, he'd thought her real goal was to shock her mother. That had been the topic of their first fight, but it grew into a shared joke eventually. "That was a side benefit."

He chuckled. "She give you grief over your fiancé?"

"He's not Chinese," she said dryly. "What do you think?" In truth, Julia Yu wasn't prejudiced in the ordinary sense. She had a keen sense of justice, donated to civil rights organizations, and voted a straight Democratic ticket. And saw no contradiction between that and her insistence that her daughters marry good Chinese boys.

They were in A12 now, passing the rear end of a dark blue panel van. A trio of teenage girls chattered their way along the center of the traffic lane, much to the frustration of a white Mustang forced to proceed at a walking pace behind them. And the Buick behind it. And the VW behind the Buick.

Four or five slots ahead was a red pickup; she couldn't see the tags from this angle. "That your man's truck?" she asked.

"Think so."

A flicker of motion in the corner of her eye was all the warning she had. In that split second—before she even knew what she'd seen—she cried out, "Duck!" and stepped to the left, pivoting.

The heavy steel chain whipped through the space where Cody's head had been. He'd dropped—and was rolling into the legs of the Hispanic tough who'd sent the chain whirling at him.

That one fell. The two behind him didn't. One had a knife, the other a baseball bat. They charged Cody, who was scuffling with the one he'd knocked down. "Police!" Lily snapped, drawing her gun. "Drop your weapons!"

The *boom-crack* of a shotgun answered her—from behind. Glass shattered as Lily dropped to a crouch, looking around frantically.

"You drop yours, bitch!" a male voice called from inside the Buick. No doubt it belonged to whoever was poking the shotgun barrel out the tinted rear window. Lily sighted quickly. She could barely make out a form behind the shotgun.

The girls screamed and scattered—one of them running

right between Lily and her shot, dammit. The Mustang, no longer blocked, floored it, and the VW rocked into reverse.

"Drop it!" the one in the car yelled. "You are so dead, bitch, if you don't put that gun down!"

Lily felt pretty attached to her weapon just then, so she replied by squeezing off a quick shot. It missed, but gave her a second's cover to turn and—oh, shit.

She'd been about to dive between the van and the Honda on the other side of it, but the space was occupied—by three more gangbangers, advancing on her single file. And grinning. One had a gun—a Glock, maybe. She couldn't see about the other two.

The black wolf seemed to come from nowhere, moving at top speed. She dropped. He leaped over her, right at the gangbangers. Two shots rang out—one from the shotgun, one from the other side of the van, and she hoped like hell that meant Cody had been able to get his weapon out.

Screaming—from the other side of the van, from behind her. She let the wolf take her back, rising to one knee to sight again on the shadowy form in the Buick. She squeezed the trigger.

Glass shattered. A choked noise, not hearty enough to call a scream. She kept her weapon steady, swinging it slightly to sight on the driver. "Don't do it. Don't think you can get away. Open the door and get out real slow."

"Get him off," someone was screaming. "Get him off, get him off!" Someone else was cursing and sobbing. And someone was growling, deep in his chest.

No, two someones. One on each side of the van.

"Cody!" she called, not taking her attention off the Buick, where the driver's door was opening slowly. "You okay?"

"Battered and bloody, but operational. Your boyfriend's got one of them pinned and I've got the others covered. One's shot, but not bad."

"On the ground. Now, dammit!" she snarled at the driver—a lanky youth, maybe nineteen, maybe less, with dirty black hair and whites showing all around his pupils. He dropped to the concrete.

"That's it," she said, standing slowly. "Arms out. Hold real still now. I'm feeling nervous. You don't want to get me excited." She advanced on the car cautiously. The driver had left the door open, and the dome light glowed brightly. The car looked empty. Was the one she'd shot dead, unconscious, or hunkered down and waiting for her to get close?

The driver was holding still like a good boy. She eased close enough to peer in the shattered window.

No, he wasn't hunkered down waiting. He was either passed out or dead—out of play for now. She took a chance by glancing over her shoulder quickly.

The black wolf was faced off against two gangbangers, snarling. They stood frozen, not even twitching. The third lay on his stomach, unmoving. In the failing light she couldn't see if he lived, but there was a lot of shiny liquid puddling around him.

A siren sounded suddenly, and fairly close. Wouldn't be long.

"Cody, can you get your perps to join us out here? And, uh, Jacob—I think that's you, right? Let your prey up now."

"All right, you heard her. Move slow and easy. Oh, look, the poor boy peed himself." Cody had an evil chuckle. "Didn't like it when the big bad wolf knocked you down, huh? Come on, you, don't whine. You're not hurt much. I used my clutch piece, and it's just a little .22."

At some point during the fight the switch had flipped from dusk to night, but the parking lot lights glowed brightly. She had no trouble seeing the three gangbangers who emerged from the far side of the van. One was limping—and yes, there was a dark spot on the front of his jeans. One held his arm, where blood was oozing from the biceps. The third looked undamaged.

Lily's heart was tripping along fast. Later, she knew, she'd get the shakes from unused adrenaline. Later she'd feel something other than relief that the one with the shotgun wasn't shooting at her or Cody or anyone else. Later she'd feel all sorts of things.

Right now she felt fine. The breeze was stronger now, definitely cool. It felt good. It felt damn good. She was alive and she felt really good about that.

Cody followed his perps with his weapon trained on them. The wolf—a gray and tan beast—brought up the rear. Cody directed his prisoners to lie down next to the driver, a suggestion the wolf reinforced with a growl.

They didn't argue. Cody spoke to Lily without looking away from the three gangbangers on the pavement. "I thought your boyfriend's name was Rule."

"It is." A pair of headlights raced toward them down the lane, coming much too fast. "That's not my boyfriend. Neither of them are."

Cody's eyes widened. "Neither of . . ."

Lily's lips twitched as she realized that Cody hadn't known there were two wolves. "Nope."

The driver behind those bright headlights braked at last, tires screeching as the Mercedes shuddered to a stop ten feet away. She nodded at the car as the door was flung open. "That is."

WITHIN fifteen minutes, an ungodly number of cops had arrived. There were a pair of rent-a-cops from the mall itself—a phrase Rule was careful not to use out loud. Lily took offense, since retired and off-duty police sometimes worked those jobs. Three patrol units and one sheriff's deputy had responded. The flashing lights from their cars added a rosy glow to the surroundings, a counterpoint to the headlights from the two ambulances. A detective, he'd been told, was on the way, as was the ME.

The man Lily had shot still lived. He was being loaded in the first ambulance now. The one José had jumped did not. José had ripped out his throat.

Rule had heard the basic outline of events when Lily reported crisply to the first officers on scene. He'd watched as she handed over her weapon—which had angered him, but she took it in stride. It was procedure, she'd said, when shots had been fired. Besides, she'd added with a sly grin, she still had her clutch piece. Cody Beck had handed over the weapon he'd fired, too, but he still had his police-issue gun.

Jacob had already Changed back and was being questioned

by one of the officers. José was still wolf. He needed more time to rest between Changes.

Rule crouched in front of José now.

The black wolf sat stiffly, not looking directly at his Lu Nuncio. The smell of blood clung to him. José was a strong and skilled fighter with excellent control as well as the three kinds of sense a warrior needs—tactical sense, common sense, and people sense. That's why Benedict had put him in charge of the bodyguards.

But this was his first human kill.

"You did right," Rule said, his voice pitched low enough that none of the humans around them would hear. "You assessed the situation and did as you'd been taught. Three attackers, all armed—you had to stop them quickly or risk my *nadia*'s life. Taking out the one with the gun frightened the others into surrendering. Lily trusted you to guard her back. You didn't fail her."

The black wolf's head lifted slightly. He looked Rule in the eye for one second, then away, his head dipping in a small nod.

Rule shifted to subvocalizing—speaking softly deep in his throat without moving his lips. "You are to say that Lily signaled you to attack. She realized you were following her, and when trouble erupted, she signaled you in the same way I would have, had I been here."

José's ears pricked up. Another nod.

Rule raised his voice to a normal level. "You're ready to Change, then? The officers would like to take your statement." He stepped back.

Rule knew Lily couldn't see what happened during the Change. He wondered if that was because she hadn't grown up seeing it, as he had. He'd read that the visual cortex of a person who'd been blind from birth was used to process the other senses, and so was not available for vision. Perhaps Lily's brain would eventually learn how to process this kind of seeing.

Or perhaps not. Rule watched as José opened the door to another reality, one where moon and earth were one, just as man and wolf were one. For those few seconds he saw both

José's forms existing in the same space at the same time. For those few seconds, what he saw made perfect sense.

Then José was a man only, the wolf gone. Rule handed him the cutoffs he'd taken from his trunk. They'd do well enough for now.

Lily had been talking to one of the patrol officers. The two of them moved closer now. Lily looked at José—at his face, that is. Lily wasn't entirely comfortable with nudity, and José was just then stepping into the cut-offs. "José, this is Officer Munoz. He needs to ask you some questions."

José looked at the young patrolman, whose face was frozen in his best Jack Webb impression: just the facts, ma'am or sir. José's nod looked much the same in this form as in his other one. "Let's get to it, then."

Lily gave a little jerk of her head, telling Rule to come with her. He did.

She stopped several feet away from the nearest officer. "You told him to say I signaled him?"

"I did. Ah—should it come up, you used the one I taught you." He made a surreptitious movement with one hand—palm held vertically, perpendicular to his body, with the fingers tight and straight. Two quick slashes. It was the standard Nokolai hand signal for *attack*. He'd already told Jacob to make the same claim.

Lily was relieved. "Good. It's not that deceitful. If I'd known they were there, I sure as hell would have signaled them."

Rule had been halfway to the city when he realized he wasn't going to make it to the apartment before Lily left for her meeting. He'd decided to follow his father's suggestion after all, and called José, telling him he didn't want Lily to know she was being guarded.

The mate sense had told Rule where to go, and the Oceanview Mall was closer to the city's edge than the apartment, so he'd managed to arrive in time to hear shots fired. By the time he leaped from his car, he'd been ready for battle—but the battle was over.

He'd raced to Lily and run his hands over her, demanding to know that she was all right. She'd allowed that. She'd even clung to him for a moment—and whispered in his ear that he needed to tell his people they'd acted on her signal.

"Will your deputy confirm this?" he asked.

"He wasn't in a position to see, so it doesn't matter."

"You think this is necessary, then? My people acted with no more force than necessary. They saved your life and probably the deputy's as well."

"I like to think I would have come up with something if they hadn't been here. There were a lot of attackers, but they were sloppy. Didn't make me for a serious threat, probably, or they'd have just shot me instead of waving their guns around and yelling. But yeah, José and Jacob saved lives today. Either mine or some of the gangbangers, because I was going to have to shoot them to stop them."

"That's reason enough for force, according to the law."

"This way, though, people will read about two lupi attacking on the signal of an FBI agent. A human FBI agent. They won't focus on how big and scary you lupi are because these wolves were under the control of a human who's allowed to use deadly force. It's like with guns. When people read about a nutcase going postal and shooting up a crowd, guns are scary. When people read about a police sniper using a rifle to take out a killer who's got hostages, they don't think, 'Wow, rifles are scary.'"

Rule smiled slowly. "That's spin. PR."

"Don't talk ugly to me."

"I've been waiting for you to ask what the hell I thought I was doing, sending the guards trailing you without letting you know."

She snorted. "It's obvious what you were doing. Why, though—that's a good question. If you'd had anything solid to worry you, you'd have called me. So was it just a hunch? Or was it because the meet was with Cody, and you weren't a hundred percent sure of me?"

"Don't talk ugly to me."

She smiled and brushed his hand quickly. "Yeah, but when I said that, there was a grain of truth in what you'd said. So . . . ?"

"Do you seriously think that if I suspected you of, ah, sneaking around, I'd send two of my people to catch you at it?"

"Put that way—no."

"Good." Yet Rule felt uncomfortable. He hadn't lied. He did trust Lily . . . but he suspected that the fact that it was Beck she was going to meet had kept his attention on that meeting. Maybe it had fed his uneasiness. How could he tell?

It didn't matter, he decided. If his feelings were murky, his actions were right. He wasn't acting like a jealous man, so—

"I guess it doesn't matter, then, that Cody said my ring was a big KEEP OFF sign."

"Good."

Lily tipped her head to one side. "Oh?"

"You're thinking I'm jealous."

One corner of her mouth tipped up. "Yeah, I am."

"I'm not—at least, it's similar to jealousy, I suppose, but I know you wouldn't act on whatever feelings you have, but—" He stopped. Ran a hand over his hair. "Dammit, Lily. He matters to you. I can hear it in your voice."

Deliberately she took his hand, her eyes steady on his. "Lots of people matter to me. I'm not in love with them. I am in love with you. Cody . . . I guess what you were hearing was unfinished business. He and I ended things badly, and that left all these messy regrets hanging around. Regrets about the way I handled things, not about us breaking up. How could I regret that? I've got you now."

A small, dark place inside Rule opened up, releasing a heaviness he didn't name. That lump of darkness met air, turned to mist, and evaporated. A smile spread over his face. The hand he held wore his ring. He ran his thumb over it. "And I have you."

"You're sounding pretty possessive there."

And she sounded pretty amused. He didn't care.

Beck chose that interesting moment to join them. He glanced at their joined hands, then spoke to Lily as if Rule wasn't there. "I've got an APB out for Javier. I can't figure this out. It isn't his style, setting us up that way."

"I imagine he got one of those 'can't refuse' type of offers." She glanced at Rule, including him. "Just before I came here I got a tip from someone who knows what he's talking about. Our perp's taken over two small gangs and wants more. According to my source, he wants to run all criminal operations in San Diego. I'm betting these clowns are from one of the gangs he's already co-opted."

"I don't know, Lily," Beck said. "These particular scum are Soldados. They're a small gang, yeah, but they're vicious, ambitious, and territorial, and their leader is Cruz Montoya. He wouldn't hand control over to some newcomer."

"If he refused, he's probably dead. We're not dealing with the usual sort of perps, Cody. If . . . Looks like the detective's here. I need to talk to—no, hell, I'd better get that." She dug out her phone.

Rule recognized the ringtone. "Wouldn't Ruben still be in the air?" He seemed to remember that Brooks's flight was to land around ten.

She nodded, touching the answer link. "Lily Yu here."

Rule heard Brooks's voice clearly. "Lily, your family is in grave and immediate danger. That's all I know, but I am completely sure of it."

THIRTY-FOUR

~

LILY commandeered a patrol car. Beck's vehicle was half a mile's hike away, Rule's was blocked by two patrol cars and an ambulance, and she wasn't waiting.

She might not have gotten away with that if the detective who'd pulled up just as Ruben called had been someone other than T.J. He told the patrol officer to quit whining and give her the damned keys.

Beck insisted on going along. It made for a crowded front seat—but since the backseat was essentially a small, mobile prison, neither Rule nor Beck was eager to ride there.

Lily hits the lights, the siren, and the accelerator. Rule tried calling everyone he had a number for—Julia and Edward Yu, Susan, Beth. Nothing got through.

Before they were halfway there, the city went crazy.

The first call on the police radio concerned Godzilla. It was quickly followed by shots fired; a brawl at Walmart; giant ants; more shots fired; people running naked and screaming along a busy street . . . all in the general vicinity of Edward and Julia Yu's home. When the first fire bloomed, opening its hungry orange petals on the roof of a home a block from their destination, they were still two miles away, but they saw the sudden glow.

Lily's knuckles were white on the steering wheel as she took the exit ramp at high speed. "Grandmother knew this would happen. She knew."

"You're right. She was expecting this, so she's prepared." Rule tensed and drew hard on the mantles. "Shit."

"Hell and damnation!" Beck leaned across Rule, grabbing for the wheel. Rule shoved him back.

"What is it?" Lily demanded.

"I just saw a demon like the one who ripped me open in Dis. I don't know what the deputy saw."

"People." Beck swallowed. "Dead people. Bodies. The car's bumping over them. I feel it. Can't you—"

"No bodies," Lily said grimly, "yet." She swerved violently, narrowly missing another car as a semi came barreling at them, straight down the middle of the road.

"You're sure."

"I'm sure." Lily braked for a turn onto a less busy, more residential street, then hit the gas again. "Close your eyes if you can't deal. Rule? Is the, uh, technique Sam mentioned doing you any good?"

This street wasn't as congested, but— "It was, but now I'm seeing people."

Lily hit the brakes. "Those are for real."

At least twenty people raced down the middle of the street straight at them. Screaming. The car fishtailed as Lily fought it. She got it stopped—but three people ran right into the stopped car. It wasn't the darkness—their vehicle was lit brightly by headlights and its strobing police light. They simply didn't see anything except whatever they believed pursued them.

Two got up and started running again. The third didn't.

"I'll get her." Cody threw the door open.

Lily's face was pale. "The Chimei's throwing out a ton of power. If it's centered on my parents' place, the effect is widespread. We're still a couple miles from the house."

"Apparently she's got a ton of power." Rule tried calling again. Nothing.

In front of the car, Cody scooped up a woman's limp body.

Two cars whizzed past, going the other way. "Knocked herself out," he called. "Open the back and I'll put her in."

Lily hit a button. "Come on," she muttered. "Hurry."

Cody slid the woman inside, slammed the door, and climbed in. Before his door was closed Lily stomped on the gas. The police radio squawked about a fire somewhere—there was a lot of static—then announced a "10-190 in progress at the Walmart at—"

It went dead.

"Magic surge?" Rule said.

"Probably. And the brawl at that Walmart we passed is now a riot."

Cody yelped.

"Whatever it is, don't believe it," Lily said.

"So you're not really sprouting horns right now, huh?"

Rule watched as a dozen gang members standing in a well-lit apartment parking lot drew guns and shot at them as they barreled past. He heard the shots even over the wail of their siren—but the sound was off. Muffled and wrong. He kept his voice steady. "I'll need to Change as soon as we stop."

"Okay," Lily said. "Why?"

"That matter I discussed with my father." She'd know he meant the mantles. "The wolf will be better able to listen in that particular way than the man."

"Is it helping any?"

"I still . . . see things. Perhaps not as many as Beck is seeing. But my other senses aren't as affected by the illusions." They slowed for the next turn, this time onto a purely residential road. A man standing in his front yard leveled a rifle at them as they approached. "Is that man—" But he heard the gun go off.

"Shit." Lily swerved. "Hit the rear of the car, I think. Oh, Christ." She swerved again—this time to avoid hitting two bodies lying, bloody and still, in the street. At least that's what Rule saw in the headlights.

Two blocks later, fire erupted directly in front of them. She didn't slow, even as the flames leaped up huge and hot. Cody yelled something profane.

He saw it, too? Or did he think they were plowing through

a swamp or a crowd of innocent people? Rule listened for the roar and crackle of fire—and didn't hear it. But every window was lit with orange flame. "I can't see anything but fire," he told Lily.

"Good thing I'm driving. We're nearly there. Shit." She skidded to a stop. "Can you see anything?"

"Just fire."

"There is a fire, but it's over a block away. I'm stopped because the street is blocked by a three-car pileup." She undid her seat belt. "I'll go the rest of the way on foot. We're close."

"I'll get out on your side, so you can guide me, if needed." He hoped like hell that after he Changed he wouldn't see fire everywhere, but if he did, he'd need help.

"Rule, if you feel the fire as well as see it—"

"Either you lead me or I follow blindly." He looked at flames. But he didn't hear them.

"I hate to say ditto," Cody said. "I really hate it. But ditto."

"All right. But if either of you feels fire as well as seeing it, get back in the damned car. And don't attack anything unless I say so." She opened her door. Rule could smell the fire, the smoky burned stink of it—but she'd said there was a real fire, hadn't she? A block away.

Rule slid across. Drew hard on his mantle. And stepped out into flame.

He felt heat—but the heat of a hot day not yet cooled from the sun's departure. Not the heat of burning. He wasn't burning. He drew a breath and concentrated on the earth beneath his feet and *listened.*

Moonsong, sweet and cool and pure. Yes. It sang to him and to the mantles, and the mantles . . . Almost he heard them, too, echoing their own notes in that song. He pulled earth up through his feet, threw himself into the moonsong—and into the Change.

His body splashed apart in ripples of agony—and reformed, the pain gone as completely as if it had never been. His vision was lower down now, the colors flatter, the perspective subtly different. His hearing had sharpened, and the world was alive with scent.

And flames still licked the air, but they were gauzy, insubstantial. He saw through them, saw Lily frowning at him as she bent to pull her clutch piece from her ankle holster. He saw real fire, too—the one Lily had spoken of, behind them and a block to the west. Those flames crackled hungrily.

He gave her a nod—*I'm well; I see you; I see truth now*—and moved aside to let the deputy out. And saw that fake-fire coated the car like a virulent ghost. Just the car, for about three feet out.

Beck's face was shiny with sweat as he hesitated by the open driver's side door. The flames were real to him. Would he burn if he believed himself burning? Surely he couldn't—

He shoved himself out—and started screaming.

Rule moved lightning-quick, grabbing the man's shirt in his jaws and dragging him several feet, away from the ghost-flames. The screaming cut off. Beck lay on his back panting, eyes huge.

"Goddammit, Cody, you weren't supposed to—are you all right?" Lily knelt beside him.

"Guess I'm alive." He pushed up on one arm, shaky. "The fire's all over the car, but it's not here. God." He held out a hand, turned it over. "I'm not crisped. It sure as hell felt like the skin was melting right off me." He looked at Rule. "Thanks."

"You're both seeing fire," Lily said flatly. "The same illusion. And it's just on the car?" Rule nodded. "That's not good. That's focused on us, and it's . . . shaped, intentional. It's not just your fears being pulled from your head. She gave you fire on purpose."

Rule growled and took a step forward.

"You're right. Let's go. Cody, can you—okay, guess you can," she said as the deputy climbed to his feet. "Let's move."

Lily set off at a lope. Rule ran easily beside her—and the deputy kept up with both of them.

Despite Rule's current form, the man remained very present. And thinking hard.

Cody Beck had real courage. Rule hadn't expected the man to be a coward—Lily wouldn't have cared about him if he were craven or stupid—but he hadn't expected that degree of bravery.

Cody Beck was also about half crazy. His courage was real, but foolhardy. Had the ghost-fire extended well beyond the car, Rule might not have been able to get him out of it in time. He could have died, the injuries so real to his brain and senses that his heart stopped. Or he could have been thrown into shock, forcing them to deal with him instead of the threat to Lily's family.

Rule-wolf snorted at all the words the man dragged through his head. Cody Beck was strong and admirable, yes. And flawed, but who was not? And he was not right for Lily . . . which was clear to the wolf without all that thinking.

Lily's parents lived in a lovely middle-class section of the La Jolla area. There were streetlights on every corner, porch lights, and landscape lighting in many cases. Yards were small, but beautifully tended. Some were xeriscaped or graveled; some stubbornly retained their grass lawns. There was a lot of stucco, of course, in a mix of colors and styles. It was a pricey neighborhood, but Edward and Julia Yu had bought their home many years ago, when there were still a few bargains to be found.

Tonight smoke and ash from the fire drifted over the yuccas and the palms, the pale driveways, and the red-tile roofs. And the dogs howled.

In the yards, they howled. In the houses, they howled. Little dogs, big dogs—every dog for blocks around was howling. Whatever fell magic the Chimei used, it spoke to dogs, too.

Rule could almost feel that magic pressing on him, and understood the animals' need to howl. As he ran—an easy pace, much slower than his top speed—he leaned heavily into *listening*. He listened as he would for the moon's song, but it was those separate notes he leaned into, the notes the mantles had echoed when he Changed. The notes that named them, perhaps. Could a snatch of moonsong be a name?

Yes—clearly, yes. Sam possessed his name, and what else would a dragon be named by but dragonsong?

He didn't see monsters looming in the darkness. He saw

a woman sitting in her driveway, deep scratches on both bare arms, rocking herself and sobbing. He saw another auto accident—two cars, their front ends smashed and permanently mated. No drivers or passengers, though he smelled blood. He heard Cody Beck's harsh breathing and smelled his fear, but the man ran steadily. Rule wondered what he saw.

Then he saw smoke billowing from a second fire, dark enough to show against the smear of stars. It was farther away, but perhaps larger than the first fire. He didn't hear the bustle and shouts of firefighters. He did hear sirens, but they weren't close.

Where were all the people? Aside from that lone woman, he saw no one, heard no one, smelled no one. It was night. They should be home from work, busy with dinner and family. Were they cowering in their houses, frozen by fear? Killing one another? Running in packs down other streets, maddened by visions too terrible to face?

Then, as they passed one house, he heard screams inside. Several voices, not just one. Lily stopped. He shoved at her. *Keep going. Our enemies aren't here. To stop this, we have to stop our enemies.*

Beck pulled his weapon from its holster. "I'm going in."

She slapped his arm—the one with the gun. "Put it up. Put it up, or you're going to shoot what you think is a rapist and it turns out to be a ten-year-old. You go in, what will they see when you try to save them? A monster come to eat them? And you won't know if what you see is real, or which parts are real. How can you help if you don't know?"

"Then, dammit, if you can tell—"

Lily didn't answer. She just started running again. Faster.

Rule ran beside her. So, too, did Beck—with his weapon back in its holster.

They were nearly to the Yus' street. That was it, less than a block away now. The Yus' house would be to the left, the third house on the left. And at last he heard people. Voices talking—one was Madame Yu. She told someone, "Leave or die. Your choice." And laughter. Ugly laughter.

Then a shot. Two shots, close together.

He glanced up at Lily, torn. He doubted she could have

heard her grandmother from this far away, but the shot—that, she'd heard. She waved him ahead. "Go. Go. I'll be right behind you. Go."

Rule kicked into his top speed. In seconds, the other two were well behind. He rounded the corner.

There it was, the Yus' home—a pale, pretty stucco split-level with a double-wide driveway that swallowed most of the front yard. In a flash, with the air streaming past, he took in the scene. Lights were on—inside and on the porch, plus muted solar lights lining the drive.

And in that driveway, a crowd of young men, maybe a dozen of them. Another gang? The wind brought him their scents—sweat and cigarettes, beer, weed. And gunpowder. He couldn't see from this distance and in the dark how many had guns, but he smelled the gunpowder.

They weren't firing, though. They were staring at the porch—where a vortex of shadow and color swirled.

Madame Yu didn't Change the way he did. It took her a bit longer.

Rule barreled into the nearest one from behind before the rest even saw him. He simply knocked that one flat and sprang onto the next, slashing an upraised arm with his teeth. He spun, ducking and going low, aiming for the hamstrings of one swinging a baseball bat at the spot where he'd been one or two slow seconds ago.

A shattering roar rent the air. A streak of orange, black, and white launched into the midst of the gang members. A Siberian tiger—about ten feet, nose to tip of tail, of snarling fury—was among them.

Now they screamed.

Madame Yu was not a dainty fighter. She slapped out with claws that could take down a black bear. Blood flew. Within seconds, the fight was over. Rule trembled with the need to pursue as those still able to move ran off, but the man restrained the wolf.

Madame Yu may have felt a similar frustration. She roared again.

A wolf knows better than to approach an angry tiger, however friendly and respectful they might be toward each other in their other forms. Rule yipped to get her attention, then pointed with his nose at the house, ears pricked. Her tail lashed. She nodded, going so far as to wave one huge paw, as if urging him to go in.

She'd left the front door ajar. He ran toward it. She didn't, heading instead around toward the back of the house.

Good. Those in front could have been a diversion for others coming in the back way.

Inside, he followed his nose—and found an amazing sight. In the dining room—a small room, with only one window— the dining table was gone. Instead the floor held a pair of mattresses. On them lay Madame Yu's family—son, daughter-in-law, two granddaughters, and grandson-in-law. Peacefully, deeply asleep, all of them. Susan was snoring slightly.

He stopped, staring. Then shook his head and wished this form could laugh. She'd drugged them, one and all. How she'd persuaded or tricked them into it he couldn't guess, but she'd made sure the madness wouldn't reach them.

After a second's grinning appreciation, he went back into the tidy living room. Not so tidy now, with shards of glass littering the floor. At least one of the shots he'd heard had shattered the large picture window.

He nudged the door open wider and trotted onto the porch. Madame Yu flowed around the corner of the house, sleek and supple. She looked up at him and shook her head once.

Clear of intruders around back, then. He yipped and wagged his tail to tell her everything was fine inside, then went to look at the bodies. There were fewer than he'd thought. Oh, yes— the scent and blood trail told him the one he'd tried to hamstring had managed to stand and wobble away.

Still, five were dead, and one was badly injured. Of those five, four were Madame's kills—not surprising, since Rule had avoided killing as much as possible. Not from any squeamishness, but practicality. Dead humans created complications. Rule didn't object to taking responsibility for all the deaths, but tiger kills did not look like wolf kills.

Either he or Madame Yu should Change back and do something about the bodies, then. And about the injured man. Lily wouldn't be happy with the body count, but . . .

Lily. His head jerked up and he looked toward the corner. Where was she? She was slower than he, but she'd been running. She should be here by now. So should Beck.

He took off running—knowing, even as he denied it, that he was too late. The mate sense told him that.

Rule found Cody Beck crumpled on the sidewalk just around the corner. He was unconscious, his head bloodied in back, but breathing normally.

Lily was gone.

THIRTY-FIVE

LILY woke slowly, with a twist of nausea and a pounding head. But she was not disoriented. She knew exactly what happened to land her . . . wherever the hell she was.

Her thigh stung. That's where the dart had gone in. She remembered what felt like a wasp sting, dizziness, the panicked certainty that she'd been drugged. She didn't remember falling, but no doubt she had.

She lay on something softer than a floor, but not much. A cot, maybe. Above her was gray concrete. Same to her right side, a featureless cement block wall. Moving her gaze, she saw a single dangling light in the ceiling . . . a corner where wall met ceiling, the top of a door . . .

The door got her attention. She sat up slowly—and everything spun, then went dim. She damn near fell off whatever she was sitting on.

"Don't worry. The worst of it will wear off soon." The voice was male, cheerful, with an English accent.

The pounding in Lily's head didn't ease, but after a couple swallows she was fairly sure she wasn't going to throw up, and her vision cleared.

She was in a room perhaps twelve feet by twenty. Concrete block walls, standard eight feet high. Light courtesy of two lightbulbs hanging from the ceiling, one at each end. No windows. A vent high in one wall—air-conditioning, she guessed, since the temperature was on the chilly side. Two doors. One was in the wall across from her. It was ajar, but not enough for her to see what lay beyond. The other was at the far end of the room, and closed. That door and a small, old-fashioned refrigerator flanked a short counter that held a hot plate. There was a cabinet above that. Three large packing boxes partly blocked her view of the refrigerator.

Clearly that was the kitchen end. A Formica-topped table and four chairs separated it from Lily's end, which was the bed/living room. She sat on a thin bunk fastened to the wall. There was one just like hers on the opposite wall.

The man sitting on the bunk across from hers was *him*. The sorcerer.

He looked so happy and innocuous—a short, middle-aged man with thinning hair and a hint of a potbelly, wearing khaki shorts and a bright pink shirt. She didn't see any weapons, but he wore a diamond ring on one finger and a small medallion hung from a chain around his neck. Magic shit, probably.

"Hello, Johnny."

He beamed. "So you've learned one of my names? Good for you!"

She was fully dressed except for her shoes. They'd taken her shoulder harness and ankle holster, she discovered with a quick touch, as well as her weapons, her phone, and her watch. But she wasn't tied up. Why wasn't she tied up? "I thought you liked knives. What did you shoot me with?"

"Oh, a little cocktail of my own. A professional can't always indulge his preferences, you know, and I'm not allowed to hurt you. Just as you can't hurt me."

"You might be wrong about that." She was too wobbly still to jump him, but that would pass, and whatever spells he had handy wouldn't work on her. "Johnny Deng, you are under arrest for the use of magic in commission of multiple felonies."

That made him laugh out loud. He slapped his knee. "I am going to enjoy you, for however long you are with us. My beloved thinks that won't be long, however. She's usually right." He looked to the right, at the door that was ajar.

Something pale poured through that door. It was translucent, almost transparent in spots, but it wasn't mist or fog. Its boundaries were too clearly defined for anything airborne, and it flowed like a thick liquid, flowed right up beside Johnny Deng sitting on the bunk. Gradually it coalesced into a shape. Between one blink and the next, that shape became a woman.

More or less a woman.

She breathed, Lily noted, fascinated. Her breasts rose and fell almost imperceptibly, but she was breathing. Her limbs were long and thin; her shoulders and chest disproportionately wide. Like a crane, Lily thought—long, thin limbs, broad through the chest and shoulders to support the wings she didn't have.

She had the feathers, though, a fluffy cap of down on her head, but her features weren't birdlike. Neither was her skin. It was white, and it gleamed. The shine was subtle, like the luminescence of a pearl.

She sure looked solid. Real. And physical. She sat there barely but perceptibly breathing and looked at Lily with eyes the color of storm clouds. And didn't speak.

"I don't have a name for you," Lily said, "other than Chimei, and that's a race. What do I call you?"

"Enemy, I think." The voice was soft and high and lovely. The accent, like Johnny's, was British.

"If you won't give me a name to use, I'll have to make up my own," Lily said. "Kun Nu." *Kun* meant a large, mythical bird, like a roc. *Nu* meant woman, wife, or daughter.

"S'n Mtzo has told you of me."

She pronounced Sam's Chinese name differently than Grandmother did, somehow removing vowels without losing the syllabic rhythm. "He told me your people and his fought each other in the Great War, and after it."

"Did he speak of the treaty? There's a silly word." She gestured gracefully with one hand. The fingers were very long, very thin. "Your English word suggests so little of the reality. Did he tell you he wishes to save your world from me and my people?"

"Something like that." The nausea was gone, and the dizziness. Her head still ached, but it no longer pounded.

"He lies. It is a habit with dragons, the lies designed to prod their little people this way or that. I have no people. He manipulates you, human. He uses you. His true wish is to kill me. This has always been his goal. It always will be."

"And what is your goal?"

Her lips curved in a smile, a touch smug, that made Lily think of Dirty Harry after he'd stolen a bit of ham. "To live, of course. That is my purpose. That is the very soul of my creation. To live."

"You've got a few other goals, though. You like fear."

Her tongue touched her lips just once, delicately. "Living is primary, but to live well, that is important, too. Fear . . . Humans relate to fear so oddly. You crave it, creating stories and images—movies, television, books—which allow you to taste fear, yet leave your body undamaged. I understand the disinclination to sustain damage, but why then do you deny your love for and fascination with fear? You, too, enjoy it, if not as purely and keenly as I am able to. Yet you condemn me for my taste." She shrugged. "Humans are mostly silly."

"Not all of us, beloved." Johnny smiled, stroking her thigh.

She in turn gave him a smile as tender as a mother with a new babe. "You are a precious exception, my love."

Lily launched herself across the room. One step, two, pivot, body bending, foot angled to strike with the side, not the toes—

A wall slammed against the side of her head, knocking her to the floor in a sudden, awkward heap.

Now her head was really pounding. And her jaw. She moved it carefully, then felt it with her fingertips. Probably not broken.

"Did you forget? Or did S'n not tell you? We are allowed to protect ourselves, Johnny and I." The voice was light, amused. "Just as you may try to protect yourself."

Lily blinked swimming eyes. The Chimei stood over her, smiling. Johnny-boy still sat on the bunk, his hands on his

knees, leaning forward as if watching the ninth-inning-with-
two-men-out ball game.

He looked delighted. But then, his team was winning at
the moment, wasn't it? "She packs a punch, doesn't she?" he
asked cheerily.

"Yeah." Lily had been aiming for the sorcerer, thinking he
was the Chimei's weakness. She'd caught a glimpse of white
in the corner of her eye as she went into the kick, but she
hadn't really seen anything.

And that was a clue. She eased herself into sitting up, rubbing her jaw. "Good trick. You went fuzzy so you could move
faster, didn't you? Must be handy. But it cost you something,
I'm guessing."

The Chimei was amused. "There is a cost, but not so much
of one as you are paying. You cannot sustain many of my
blows, human, while I can offer them for hours and hours, if
I wish. I . . . What is the phrase? I pulled my punch so as not
to injure you permanently." She gestured at the bunk. "Return
to your place, unless you wish me to put you there. I assure
you I am strong enough to do so easily, without allowing you
to damage me."

Lily did not like doing anything Kun Nu wanted, but she
didn't want to be handled, either. She rose to her feet slowly,
trying not to jar her head—and had to stop and swallow back
the bile. She managed not to stagger to get to the bunk. "You
may not have achieved that aim. I'm pretty sure I'm injured."

"Not seriously." The Chimei returned to her place beside
her lover. She tipped her head to one side. "You are afraid a
little, but not as much as I expected. Why not?"

"You aren't allowed to hurt me."

"I'm not allowed to harm your body, save in self-defense.
Do you believe the only harm is that which damages you
physically?" She gave a little trill of a chuckle. "Oh, there.
Now you fear. Do you enjoy it?"

"No." Lily licked her lip and tasted blood. It was puffing
up, too. "So your only goal is fear?"

"I have other goals. The happiness of my beloved . . ." She
stroked Johnny's arm fondly. "That is precious to me. And the

suffering of your grandmother. That is necessary. I will eat her power, and you will help me."

"I could have sworn that wasn't allowed—you harming her, I mean, and eating her power would surely harm her. I notice you didn't mention children. Offspring. Or becoming, uh, wholly physical."

"Children." The voice was still light and pure. But something vast and powerful moved behind those human-seeming eyes, darkening them. They changed even as Lily watched, turning alien and black. Wholly black, with no whites at all. "You touch on what you should not, human."

Lily's heartbeat kicked up. Saliva pooled in her mouth, forcing her to swallow. "I'm a pushy bitch. Sue me."

Abruptly the black faded back to gray. She laughed. "I think not, but I will either eat you or make you wish you had died. Perhaps I can do both. As for becoming wholly physical . . . you choose one word correctly, no doubt by accident, for you grope after that which you cannot understand. I am, as you see, physical now, but this form is costly to maintain without my Becoming. I am very close now. Your grandmother will provide the last of my needs so I may Become." She folded her long-fingered hands in her lap. "It is just that she do so."

"You want revenge. She killed someone you cared about."

"I lost him." That was grief, surely, wild and unsated, in the stormy pools of her eyes. "She stole him from me, and caused me to unBecome. She must atone."

"What about all the people who lose someone because of you? Do they get a shot at making you atone?"

Her eyes were clear gray now, and breathtakingly indifferent. "Humans die. It is your nature, as it is mine to live. Why fling your anger at me? I did not cause you to be as you are."

Lily's jaw clenched—which hurt like hell, so she made herself relax those muscles. "I saw bodies tonight. Bodies of people who didn't have to die *now*—people who died in pain and terror because you wanted their fear. You stole their lives from them. You stole them from those who love them. Your grief isn't pure and holy just because it's yours. It's all the same—the grief you cause, the grief you feel."

"You are wrong, but you lack the scope to know this." She rose to her feet. "I speak to you of these things both to poke at you and because you may have a choice to make. Did you know there is a technique to drain the magic from another?"

"You alluded to that."

"There are two ways to do this. One requires the permission of the person being drained. One does not. Both are painful. I cannot force your power from you, for that would be against the treaty. I can, however, take what is offered." She smiled. "By you or your grandmother. I believe you will offer to allow me to sip at your power."

"You have some strange beliefs."

She just stood there, smiling. Johnny stood up. "Don't like that idea, do you? Can't say I blame you, but you'll do it." He nodded in a friendly way, turned, and opened the door that had been ajar, revealing stairs. He jogged up with little taps of his feet.

Were they in a basement? No windows, cement block walls, stairs going up. What the hell—why not ask? "Is this a basement?"

"We are belowground. It is called a bomb shelter. I believe humans in this country expected to all die in nuclear war some years back, so some built these shelters."

"Cozy."

"S'n Mtzo will not be able to sense you here—earth blocks him. Did you know that? In addition, my love and I have crafted other layers of protection. This will prevent any humans from finding you. Oh, and I should warn you." Clearly she was enjoying doing so. "One of the wards will be triggered if you try to escape. This will cause this shelter to collapse, burying you."

"Isn't that a lot like killing me?"

"I have warned you, so you are able to avoid dying."

"Stretching the treaty pretty far, though, aren't you?"

The Chimei tipped her head. "Has S'n Mtzo deceived you about the treaty? It is quite literal in its binding. I cannot kill you, but I can keep you as long as it pleases me to do so. You will have food and water and air, and your wastes will be disposed of. You won't be harmed, save for what you offer willingly, so I abide by the treaty. But you will not leave this room until I am ready for you to do so."

Breathe, Lily told herself. *Nice and slow*. Fear was a largely physical reaction. She'd do what she could to keep from giving Bird Woman any little tastes. "Us puny little humans have a saying. It goes something like this: fuck you."

"You try to control your fear. That increases its savor." She smiled, hands clasped in front of her, almost as if she were praying.

On the stairs, two sets of feet sounded. One was Johnny—tap-tap-tap. The other sounded less certain. "And here comes the reason you will allow me to sip at your power. The same reason, as you will see, that the other sorcerer will not trouble us."

Lily didn't recognize the feet that she saw first, but she knew the ankles. The calves. Surely no other ankles and calves were decorated with those particular arabesques.

Cynna's belly moved into view, her blue T-shirt straining against the mound of baby beneath. She moved awkwardly. The stairs were steep, and her hands were fastened behind her back. Johnny was right behind her, and he wasn't fooling with a no-weapons look now. He pressed the barrel of a submachine gun to Cynna's back. "Here she is, Beloved," he said. "Unhappy, but undamaged."

Cynna met Lily's eyes, and sighed. "Hey, there."

"This one is not covered by the treaty," said the Chimei. "I can do anything at all to her. I can give her pain or fear, abort her offspring, kill her outright. Whatever I wish. But I give you the power to stop me. Only offer a sip of your magic, and I will leave her alone. For a time."

Fury turned Lily's vision red. Her hands clenched at her sides.

"More anger than fear? Your friend is afraid." The Chimei smiled and smiled. "Consider your power, little human. Your decision. I will return when it suits me and you will tell me what, if anything, you offer. Whatever your decision then, you will remain here as long as I wish. Will that be a week or a year? Five years, or a decade? I have not decided, but at some point I will allow your grandmother to trade herself for you.

You will be free then, and she will be fed and tended, and have nothing taken from her that she does not willingly offer."

"You're backing the wrong horse, Kun Nu. Grandmother won't agree."

"She already has." Her smile grew radiant. "I will keep her for a long, long time. And while she suffers, so, too, will S'n Mtzo."

THIRTY-SIX

"BROOKS here."

Rule held his phone with one hand and drove with the other. "This is Rule Turner. Lily has been taken."

"Taken?" The jolt of surprise was clear in Brooks's voice. "My Gift can be damnably capricious. It didn't warn me. When I wasn't able to reach her on her phone, I hoped the problem was technical. During the riots, much cell coverage was disrupted."

Riots? Was that what they were calling it? "Much of everything was disrupted," Rule said grimly. "They've also snatched Cynna. They're using her to threaten Cullen, to keep him from looking for them. They say they'll trade Lily for her grandmother—but not yet."

"They've already sent their terms to you?"

"They made contact with Sam. They plan to hurt Lily." Rule's throat tightened too much for speech. He swallowed and forced himself to go on. "Madame Yu believes one of them will drain Lily of her Gift. It's a slow process, and that's why the delay in making an exchange. I intend to get Lily away from them. If you're willing, you can help. I'll tell you who has her, everything I've held back—but you have to come to me at Clanhome. I'm on my way there now."

"Without Lily to affirm your words, I'm unsure if this is, indeed, Rule Turner I'm speaking with."

"You're allergic to iron and steel. You learned this in Edge."

A moment's silence, then Ruben said, "That is persuasive, if not . . . Yes? Just a moment," he told Rule. And put him on hold.

The woman in the passenger seat spoke. "I am not persuaded this is wise," Madame Yu said. "Bringing Brooks in changes the balance."

"The Chimei already changed it. You said as much."

She was silent a moment. Her hands gripped each other tightly in her lap. "I did not think she could do a new thing. I was wrong. This taking of hostages is new."

Brooks came back on the line. "I just spoke with the officers I sent to look for Lily. They found the patrol car she borrowed. In the backseat was a young woman, a civilian, dazed and incoherent. In the front seat was a sheriff's deputy, unconscious. There was a note saying he'd been enspelled, but paramedics suspect a concussion. He's being taken to emergency now."

"That won't hurt him, but he's unconscious due to a spell, not a head wound." As Rule had said in the note he'd left with Beck.

Brooks absorbed that in a brief silence. "What did Lily send me from your computer this afternoon?"

Rule's eyebrows shot up. "I don't know. I haven't been to the apartment since she was taken, and before that . . . First she was attacked by a gang. Then we raced into the madness, hoping to save her family."

"Are they hurt?" His question came quick, urgent.

"They're unhurt, but asleep. I've had them moved to Clanhome until they wake up." Rule glanced at Lily's grandmother. "Most of them are asleep, that is. Madame Yu is with me."

"I will speak with her."

Rule passed her the phone. He'd never been able to figure

out how much of the tiger she retained when she was two-legged. Had she heard Ruben's side of the conversation?

"Mr. Brooks," she said, "what did my granddaughter send you?"

Apparently she had.

"A copy of a handwritten note, which includes a word or phrase in Chinese. I'm having it translated, but there is a problem. My translator doesn't recognize one of the characters. Madame, are you confident that the person with you is, indeed, Rule Turner, and that he is not being coerced or affected in some way?"

"I am completely certain of it. Who was the note from?"

"A man believed to operate a criminal gang with ties to the Taiwanese underworld."

"Zhou Xing?" It was as much demand as question. "His name is Zhou Xing?"

"It is."

"Ahh." That was almost a purr. For the first time since learning her granddaughter had been taken, some of the tension eased from those slender shoulders. "Excellent. Bring it with you when you come."

"I haven't said I will come."

"Consult your Gift," she snapped. "You are supposed to be able to follow a hunch. Attempt to do so."

Another silence, longer this time. "I will come," Brooks said simply.

"**TOILET** paper. Boxes of it," Cynna muttered. "That's not much help, but lightbulbs? Plastic knives? What were they thinking?"

The two of them sat on the floor of their temporary prison, surrounded by what they'd plundered that might prove useful. The door their captors had left through—the one leading to the stairs—was locked by both magic and a dead bolt. The other door led to a tiny bathroom with a chemical toilet, a tiny sink, and five five-gallon bottles of water.

"This is probably where they've been holed up themselves.

They didn't expect to use it as a jail." The lightbulbs were an especially odd find because there wasn't actually any electricity in their little cell, as a bit of investigation had shown. The bulbs plugged into the ceiling glowed anyway.

"I bet some of this stuff was already here when they made this their hideout. Most of the stuff here is pretty old, like someone stockpiled it years ago."

"Could be." Among their finds were five extra lightbulbs. Unlike those in the ceiling, they didn't glow. Lily had broken one and was wiggling the longest shard of glass loose from the socket. "Their schedule got pushed up when Johnny went after Cullen on his own, putting him in danger. I'm betting they've got something else in mind for us, long-term. It isn't ready yet."

"Makes sense. That ready?" She held out her hand.

"As ready as I can make it." Lily gave her the long glass sliver.

Cynna took it and closed her eyes. She sat cross-legged, her lips moving, though Lily didn't hear anything.

The sorcerer had taken Cynna before he and the Chimei rained madness on a square mile of the city. She'd been stopped at a traffic light, on her way back to Sam's lair after dropping Nettie off at Clanhome; he'd hit her with a sleep spell. That was all she knew until she woke up, hands cuffed behind her, in the back of an old panel van.

There'd been two young toughs watching her. Members of the Padres, Lily thought, judging by what Cynna reported about their clothing and tattoos.

Abruptly Cynna stopped her silent chant and slashed her arm with the glass. Blood welled up in the shallow cut. Quickly she dragged a small plastic knife through it.

"It looks the same," Lily said dubiously. Except that the plastic was still white and pristine, without a drop of blood on it. Weird.

"Let's see what it does." Cynna ripped a page out of a magazine and drew the knife down the paper—which split as if the serrated plastic were a razor blade. She grinned. "Damn, I'm good."

"You are, but did I mention that you're sounding more like Cullen all the time?"

"I think you did. Got another one for me?"

They had three plastic knives. Now that they knew Cynna's spell worked, they needed two more glass shards, but they had to be at least two inches long. "The rest of the pieces aren't long enough. I'll break another lightbulb."

The next bulb shattered into way too many tiny pieces. Lily's lips thinned. Her hand felt shaky as she reached for another one. *Easy does it,* she told herself. She hadn't wrecked their chances by wrecking one lightbulb.

The next lightbulb broke perfectly, leaving three long, lovely pieces. Lily handed her one. "I should sweep up the broken glass first." They had a broom, an actual broom. They planned to make it nice and pointy at one end, using the newly sharp plastic knives.

"Wait till I'm finished. This takes a whopping lot of concentration." Cynna closed her eyes again.

They were being careful about what they said out loud. Lily hadn't found a camera or a bug, but there might be something she'd missed. And Cynna thought their captors might be able to eavesdrop magically. "They couldn't listen every minute," she'd said, "because they have other things to do, and they'd have to concentrate to listen in that way. But we'd better assume they can hear us."

Lily had asked if that kind of listening was mind-magic, or another kind. Mind-magic wouldn't work on her, but a spell that picked up sounds would pick up her voice as well as anyone else's.

"It's not mind-magic," Cynna had said, "but I don't have a clue how it's done. We know it's possible, but I don't think anyone in this realm knows how."

"Anyone but Johnny, you mean?"

"It seems possible. He knew a lot about Cullen, didn't he? I've been thinking about that. If this Chimei's been around a few centuries, she could know a lot of spells that are lost to the rest of us. That's probably why her pet sorcerer could do that sleep-spell bomb. It's something she taught him."

So Cynna chanted silently as she turned a plastic knife into a potentially deadly weapon. And Lily didn't refer to their plans for the broom, once she'd swept up the broken glass they didn't use.

Their weapons might be taken from them. The Chimei was powerful. So was the sorcerer. But Lily had realized something, and managed to convey it to Cynna by speaking elliptically.

When Rule had said the Rhej had no knowledge of the Chimei in the clan's memories, Lily had been disappointed. But there was an upside, a very large upside. It meant that the Chimei knew little about lupi.

The Chimei didn't know how deeply lupi treasured their babies. She'd made a bad mistake when she kidnapped and threatened a woman who carried a lupus babe.

More important, the Chimei clearly didn't know who Cynna was. They knew she was Lily's friend and Cullen's wife, so thought they had a hostage with double value.

They did. But Cynna was also the Rhej's apprentice. And Lily was pretty sure the Chimei didn't even know the Rhejes existed, much less what they meant to their clans. She certainly didn't know about the memories they carried . . . memories Cynna had so recently begun acquiring.

The spell Cynna used now was from one of the earliest memories, from the time of the Great War. That's why she had to chant it rather than use what was inscribed on her skin.

One other thing the Chimei didn't know about: the mate bond.

Bird Woman and Johnny had gone to a great deal of trouble to hide Lily and Cynna where neither dragon senses nor human Gifts could find them. They'd done a good job of it, according to Cynna. Cynna's Finding sense was so muffled by the wards she claimed she couldn't Find the sky from their prison.

But the earth and wards had no effect on the mate bond. They had no effect on the mate sense, which told Lily as clearly as ever in what direction Rule was, and how far away.

He'd be coming for her, and for Cynna. He wouldn't be alone. They'd do their best to be ready.

*   *   *

THE sky was dark, overcast, the moon and stars hidden behind clouds that refused to drop their burden of water. Beneath that heavy sky, Clanhome's meeting field was as full as it had been two nights ago. But this time, there were no children running madly around the field. No women laughed and danced. Only lupi were on the field tonight.

Nokolai was going to war.

At one end of the field, Rule hugged his son. "I'll see you again soon."

Toby squirmed away. "*Maybe* you will. You can't promise, or Grandpa wouldn't have shifted the heir's portion."

"The Rho did that," Rule corrected firmly. It had been necessary, the removal of his heir's portion. But the ache of loss was keen.

Toby repeated Rule's correction, but his face was pure stubbornness. "The Rho did it because you could both get killed."

Rule nodded. "You're right. We can't know what will happen in battle, and we can't risk losing the mantle entirely. But I am a very good fighter—and your grandfather is undefeated."

Toby frowned hard. "That's 'cause he doesn't fight Uncle Benedict."

"True." Rule's throat closed.

Toby looked at Benedict, standing tall and grim on Rule's left. "It's temporary, though. Giving Uncle Benedict the heir's portion of the mantle is temporary."

Benedict spoke gravely. "That, as always, is the Rho's decision. But I do not want it. And the mantle does not want me. It wants my brother."

That startled Rule. "You can tell—"

"Hush," Isen said. "Toby, you must go to the Center with the other children now."

Toby nodded, but spoke, low and fierce, to his father. "I don't want to be here. I don't want to be safe when everybody else isn't!"

"No more than I would want to be safe if you weren't. But it eases me to know you're safe, and it's for me to go and you to stay. You've the harder duty tonight. As does Benedict, and the others who don't go to battle with us. It is very hard to wait."

"I—I want you to go. I want you to get Lily back, and Cynna. You have to." Toby's voice didn't quiver, but it was a near thing. "But I don't see why you and Grandpa both have to go."

Rule glanced at his father, standing to his right. Isen spoke. "You understand what happens tonight? You understand why this is not just a rescue of two clan members?"

Toby nodded. "It's not just about them. It's about the clan, too, because of the memories, and the Lady."

"Yes. You must also know that a Rho doesn't call war and sit back from battle. In this battle I must be close, for without the mantle, the charms the Rhej made won't work. And without your father, of course, we could not find Lily and Cynna." He clapped Rule on the back. "Not that I'd be able to hold him back, anyway, with Lily in danger. But we need him."

Toby sniffed, nodded, and stood as straight as a nine-year-old body could. "Okay. I'll see you later, too, Grandpa." That was said defiantly.

Isen laid his hand on Toby's head. "You will. And whether you believe such promises or not, I promise it. Go with Sybil now."

The child tender led Toby away. He would wait with her at the Center, with other children whose fathers went to battle tonight.

That was a small number. Only those with charms to guard them from mind-magic would fight, and even going without sleep, the Rhej had been able to make only ten of those in the twenty-six hours since Lily and Cynna were taken. She'd used a spell from the memories to make those charms . . . a spell lost to the rest of the world since before the founding of Rome. A spell that been used in the Great War, and not since.

Those charms should protect against the Chimei—but they didn't know how much. Lupi had never fought against Chimei. They wouldn't know how well the charms worked against this particular enemy until they faced her.

But though only a dozen would fight tonight, in a few moments, all of Nokolai would be at war. If neither Rule nor his father came back from tonight's battle, Benedict would be Nokolai's Rho—and he would continue the war.

This, for lupi, was the meaning of war: it didn't end until the enemy was defeated. There might be lulls, but there were no truces.

All lupi had been at war with one enemy—their Lady's enemy—for more than three thousand years. That *she* had been far from their realm and untouchable for most of that time changed nothing. They remained at war with the Great Bitch, and would until *she* was dead or forever defeated.

Isen gathered his two living sons with a glance. The three of them strode into the waiting throng.

The crowd of lupi fell silent. Waiting.

When the three men reached the center of the field, they halted. Rule and Benedict stationed themselves to either side of their Rho and a couple paces back.

Isen raised his arms and his voice. "Nokolai! You have heard of our enemies. You know what they have done. Twice they attacked one of ours—at a baby party, and at the hospital. Twice they failed. And now they have stolen our Chosen, touched by the Lady—"

Growls erupted from more than three hundred throats not designed for growling.

"They have stolen her, and our Rhej's apprentice. You know Cynna. You know she is with child, carrying a clan babe, a lupus babe. They threaten her. They threaten the baby."

The growls were louder this time. A few of the younger men lost control and Changed.

"But Cynna is more than a mother, precious as that is. They have stolen she who will carry the clan's memories! She who will bring the Lady among us! Lady-touched, both of them— Chosen and Rhej-to-be, both taken!"

Now they howled—human and lupine throats alike.

"Our enemies are powerful. Make no doubt of that. One— the Chimei—is ancient and canny, and cannot be killed. She can control the perceptions of hundreds at a time. She feeds on fear. I am told that if she is allowed to fully manifest herself, she will be more powerful than any who have walked this earth since the Great War. Her sorcerer has power, too, and spells we can't guess at, and he shares some of her immunity to damage, so he will be hard to kill. And together they have allies, human gangs. This is no small thing we do, going against such foes."

The answering growls were low, and to Rule's ears said clearly, "Who cares?"

"But we have a sorcerer, too. And allies of our own—some here, some elsewhere." Isen waved—and a huge black shape descended from the sky to land at the far end of the field. He had riders, two human shapes who bestrode his shoulders near the base of the neck. One was female, and old. One was male and recovering from a heart wound—and very good with fire.

"Nokolai." Now Isen's voice dropped to a normal level. Every man and wolf on the field fell silent, straining to hear. "Our Rhej has spoken to me—because the Lady has spoken to her."

Utter silence. There was no shifted foot, no slightest rustle of clothing, no quickly indrawn breath.

"The Lady gave our Rhej one word." His voice was quiet now, conversational. Only lupus hearing enabled those at the edges of the crowd to hear. "One word." He waited, then boomed, "Nokolai—I cry war!"

THIRTY-SEVEN

THE glowing lightbulbs didn't turn off. It was hard to tell time in a windowless room where the light didn't change. Had they been there two days? It was more than one day, Lily thought, but she didn't know how much more.

"Gin," Cynna said, spreading her cards.

"You're going to clean me out of my imaginary millions."

"I'm up by three hundred big ones, by my count. You're not paying attention."

No, she was too busy worrying.

Rule had found her already. She'd felt him draw close, then linger in one spot perhaps a hundred yards away. And then he'd left. He'd left a very long time ago.

He needed to plan, she told herself. Whatever he planned might take time to pull together. That made sense. The long delay did not mean something had happened to him. He was alive; she knew that much.

But wouldn't Kun Nu enjoy having a second hostage to use against Lily? Wouldn't she relish the shock as she dumped Rule's unconscious body in the little prison with Lily and Cynna?

Lily pushed to her feet. "I'm not good at waiting. I'm not good at not *doing* something. I'm going to do some stretches."

"That's part of Bird Woman's plan, making us wait. Making you wait, I should say," Cynna said matter-of-factly as she gathered the cards again. "She doesn't care if I get antsy and jumpy, but she's hoping you do."

"I know. I still need to move."

There was one small open space of floor between the bunks and the cot. Lily lay down there, trying to focus on her body and breath. She stretched her arms over her head.

The earth groaned. And twitched.

It was a quiet sound, almost a grumbling, as if the rocks around them had a minor complaint—one they threw off with a little shudder Lily felt all along her body.

She looked at Cynna and saw the fear in her friend's eyes, a fear that matched her own. Then, determinedly, she began her yoga stretches.

This was the third time they'd heard the noise. The third time the earth had trembled. The first time it happened, Lily had been hit by the irrational hope that the little shudder might somehow mean help was coming, even though she knew Rule wasn't near.

Cynna's guess was more likely. "Is it her?" she'd whispered. "Is she pulling a shake, rattle, and roll on us?" Lily had had no trouble figuring out what she meant. The Chimei might well be causing mini-quakes to scare them.

If so, she'd hit on a great technique. There was a crack in one wall now, up near the ceiling. Dust sifted down from that crack as Lily brought her knees to her chest.

It was also possible that the little tremors had nothing to do with them or the Chimei. This was California. Quakes happened.

LIKE any war, this one involved a good deal of waiting.

It was after midnight. Rule lay flat on his stomach in the dirt, taking advantage of the cover offered by scrubby growth at the edge of a small woods—sage and bindweed and some kind of sedge, their scents mingling with that of the tiny white flowers on a struggling toyon bush.

Also with the scent of the hamburgers the gang members had grilled earlier, and that of the other lupi hiding, as he was, in the weeds and grasses around a dilapidated house just outside the city. One of them lay very near Rule—one who must be finding this wait extremely difficult. Cullen often said he was not a patient man.

The clouds had moved off, the moon was three-quarters full, and Rule could see his targets clearly. From Rule's vantage point he could see the side of the house, some of the front yard, and most of the back—if you could call bare dirt a yard. The house they watched had probably been abandoned for years before its current occupants moved in. If not, someone had liked living rough. The roof had fallen in on one side. There was a porch light out front and two floodlights in back— the floodlights apparently so the gang members could see to play cards and drink beer.

Sixteen were in view now. There were thirty-six altogether. Four of the others were patrolling the area immediately around the house, though with their limited senses it didn't do them much good. The rest were sleeping in the more intact part of the house.

Thirty-six armed gangbangers against a dozen lupi warriors and one sorcerer. Good odds, especially since the lupi wearing charms were Benedict's best. The obvious move was to kill the sentries silently, then shoot the ones drinking and playing cards outside from a safe distance, then go in and clean up the sleepers. Nasty, but obvious.

Also disastrous. The place was warded to hell and gone. One of those wards, the outer one, was made to repel small objects like mosquitoes or bullets.

Fortunately, getting in the house wasn't the goal, unless things went wrong. Lily wasn't there.

Rule's mate sense wasn't as strong as Lily's, or maybe he wasn't as good at reading it as she was. But from this close, it was crystal clear. He knew exactly where she was . . . roughly twenty feet behind the house, and at least that far underground.

He took some comfort from her nearness, even as he swore silently at the wait. He hoped she took comfort in knowing he was near, too—though she might well be cursing him for doing nothing for such a long time.

But this part wasn't his to do. Only, dammit, if they didn't hurry, the Chimei and her lover would be back, and then—

Cullen poked his side. He looked at his friend, who was still pale. He wasn't healed, wasn't ready for this, but they needed him. Which was just as well. Needed or not, he would have come.

Cullen tipped his chin to their right.

A small, gray-skinned head poked up out of the dirt ten feet away. It was hairless and too round, but had the appropriate number of eyes with a single nose placed between them and the mouth. But the nose was somewhere between pug and snout, the chin was missing, and the eyes were too large altogether.

The gnome looked around, blinking, until he saw Rule, then heaved himself up out of the ground. Only after he left it could Rule see that there was, indeed, a hole there.

He trotted over to them. He was wearing fuchsia shorts with yellow suspenders. "Is having troubles," he whispered. "Granite upcropping. Hard to work with, is. Stubborn."

Rule spoke in a voice too soft too carry—not truly subvocalizing, though, because gnomes' hearing was as limited as humans'. "You told me about the granite an hour ago."

"Is stubborn, granite," he repeated, his big eyes blinking. Gnomes in this realm lived underground, and this youngster seemed to be one who was adapted for darkness. "Is also problem of ward. Very good ward someone is building. Max is saying to telling of you, thirty minutes maybe. Maybe less, maybe more. Is having go slow. Reshaping too much, too fast, and ward is triggering, rock collapsing."

That was almost exactly what he'd said the last time he popped up to give them a progress report. Rule held on to what remained of his patience. The little gnome was someone's nephew—one of the elders, he thought. The elders who were currently repaying a debt by tunneling through stone to reach the bomb shelter behind the house.

The gnomish elders could move rock magically—and they could do it without triggering the ward. "Thank you. If you would give the Rho that information, I'm sure he'd appreciate it."

Blink, blink. "Where is he being?"

"The same place he was the last time you brought us a report. Over by the large boulder you admired."

The little fellow gave a single nod and trotted off.

Rule settled down to wait.

Tonight's mission was to get Lily and Cynna out. Get them to safety. Ideally, they would do that without a fight, for the Chimei and the sorcerer weren't here. Sam had claimed he could lure them away, and he'd been right. When Rule led Max and Cullen to this house, the Chimei and her lover had been gone.

That was early in the afternoon, around one. More than eleven hours ago. Max had brought the elders, and they'd been working ever since. Tunneling toward the bomb shelter. Slowly.

Faster than anyone else could *do it*, Rule reminded himself. Certainly no one else could do it as secretly as the gnomes. And as hard as the waiting was, every hour the Chimei and sorcerer didn't come was another hour closer to getting Lily and Cynna out. Another hour, too, for Cullen to heal. At this point, every hour of healing helped.

Rescuing the women would not end the war. That would end only with their enemies' deaths or complete defeat. If Rule lived through this night and their enemies were undefeated, he would travel to Leidolf Clanhome and call Leidolf to war. If Isen lived, he would call up Nokolai's subject clans, who must answer a call to war.

And if neither of them lived, Benedict would become Rho. And he would call up Nokolai's subject clans, and continue the war.

The Lady had granted the Rhej one word. That word was *war*.

From well behind him, a mourning dove called. Rule stiffened. That was the signal from the lookout near the road. Someone was coming. If the lookout could see who it was, and that he was short and Asian, he'd . . .

The dove called again, twice.

That was it, then. The sorcerer was coming. They were out of time.

Isen had never been very good at birdcalls. The rapid-fire *coo-coo-coo-coo* of a black-billed cuckoo—which didn't actually live in California—was the only one he could do well. "Plan B," Rule whispered.

Cullen gripped Rule's arm, then pointed at the sky and whispered, "That's her."

What? Rule didn't . . . No, wait—something pale and misty, almost invisible, flowed along a route he thought followed the dirt road that led here, as if following a car on that road. He switched to subvocalizing. "What do you see?"

Cullen answered the same way. "Power. Lots and lots of it."

"Do you think she's finished the transformation Sam spoke of?"

"I don't know. The power is . . . It's different than anything I've seen before. It oscillates, or flickers, or . . . maybe it isn't fully in our realm. Maybe she can't hold it here consistently until she's here consistently."

"That would be good." He glanced to his left, at the tall boulder where he'd sent the gnome. His father wasn't visible, of course. He forced himself to relax. And waited some more.

"Dammit," Cullen muttered very low, "they're supposed to have been tracking the patrollers. How long does it take to—"

The cuckoo sang again—four quick notes. The gang members patrolling near the house had been dealt with.

Rule *pulled* viciously hard and fast—exploded out of the bushes on four feet. A moment later, so did four others—four wolves wearing collars. Collars with a small charm fixed to them. They raced at top speed for the yard where the men were taking heed of them—taking heed slowly, to Rule's eyes. Too slowly to keep them alive.

A dozen lupus warriors against thirty-six gangbangers was good odds. Five against thirty-six would be harder. But the rest had the harder job—they had to keep the Chimei and the sorcerer busy long enough for the gnomes to finish.

No one could be left alive at their backs.

Rule raced past the point he'd been told marked the first ward. Nothing happened. He raced past the place the second ward was supposed to be. Nothing.

The sorcerer or the Chimei set very good wards, more sophisticated than anything Cullen could do—one to keep out small objects like bullets. Another that would repel humans.

Didn't do a damned thing to slow down a wolf. Rule heard a shot as he leaped for his first target. His teeth slashed through the man's jugular. Blood sprayed everywhere, including down his throat, hot and sweet.

Then the other four wolves were amid the men.

A HUNDRED yards away, an erect old woman stepped out into the middle of the dirt road, just where it met the yard, and began drawing a circle in the dirt.

She wasn't alone. On her left side stood a beautiful young man, a trifle pale, wearing a diamond in one ear and another around his neck. On her other side an older man planted his feet. He was grizzled and bearded and looked like some minor forest god.

A white panel van trundled down the road toward them. The driver must have seen them. He hit the gas.

"Chimei!" the older man boomed as the van raced toward them. "Sorcerer! You have offended my Lady, and we are at war!"

The niceties had been observed. From either side of the road, the six two-legged Nokolai warriors opened up—with machine guns.

The van was riddled. It veered hard right—a tire blew out, and it skidded into the ditch.

The shriek of some vast bird of prey split the air.

TWENTY feet belowground, rock groaned. Dust sifted from the cracked ceiling. Lily gripped her makeshift spear tightly and looked at Cynna.

Rule was here. Almost here, anyway—close, so close. He'd been close for hours. She'd woken up to feel him near and had let Cynna know—or hoped she had—by setting her makeshift spear close at hand and handing Cynna one of the magically enhanced knives.

Since then, she'd lost another five hundred thousand at gin. It would have been more, but Cynna was distracted, too.

Moments ago he'd rushed closer. She'd sprung to her feet, spear ready. For what, she didn't know—but God, she was so ready for *something*.

The earth grumbled louder. And trembled.

Cynna bit her lip. "Maybe we should get under one of the b—yikes!"

A big chunk of the cement block wall closest to her had turned to dust. Peering out of that dusty hole was a small gray man.

No, a gnome. Three feet tall, weird little snoutlike nose, no chin. Baggy fuchsia shorts with yellow suspenders. A gnome.

"Bad thing is coming!" The gnome beckoned urgently. "Hurries you!"

The hole—the tunnel—was sized for a gnome, not for adult human women. "You heard the gnome," Lily said. "Hurry."

Cynna didn't argue. They'd long since settled that protecting the baby came first—and the baby wouldn't get out on his own. She got down on her hands and knees and started crawling.

Lily got down on her hands and knees, too, while the little gnome fairly hopped with fearful urgency. "Hurries, hurries!"

The lights winked out. The damned glowing bulbs they'd been unable to shut off went out on their own, leaving her in absolute darkness, blacker than any night.

The little gnome shrieked—and shoved Lily hard, toppling her on her side. He pounced on her, curving his little body over her as if those fragile bones could shield them both—as earth and rock shrieked along with him. And everything overhead collapsed.

THIRTY-EIGHT

THE agony and bliss of the Change whirled through Rule.
When it ended he stood two-legged and naked in mud sticky
with blood. He grabbed one of the weapons on the ground—an
assault rifle, the reason he'd picked this spot for the Change.
The model was unfamiliar, but it was similar enough to what
he'd used. He fired a quick round.

The man at the window who'd been firing at them fell
back. "Carl!" Rule snapped at a wolf streaking for the window, clearly intending to leap in. "Wrong way! Go get the
damned package!"

Carl skidded, whirled, and raced the other direction.

Rule hit the dirt as someone else began firing from the
house, rolling until he was behind the picnic table that still
held playing cards and beer cans. It wasn't much cover.
"Remy, Jones—take cover and Change. We need weapons to
keep them busy until Carl gets back."

He didn't call Mike. Mike lay still and unmoving in the
bloody dirt. One of the gangbangers had gotten lucky—briefly.
Very briefly.

Rule sprayed another round, providing cover for the others

as they Changed. Remy was almost as fast he was, but Jones took a little longer.

Seconds later, a naked man with pale Irish skin stood in full view—for less than a second. Then he was rolling. He ended with a SIG Sauer much like Lily's in one hand, and snapped off two shots quickly. Around the corner of the house, Jones finished his Change and dived for the nearest weapon—a sub-machine gun clutched in a dead man's hand.

And a large tawny wolf raced up beside Rule and dropped a small, Bubble-Wrapped bundle from his jaws.

"Good." Rule ripped at the Bubble Wrap to reveal a pair of grenades. They'd been stashed just the other side of the first ward, ready to be retrieved. He raised his voice. "You in the house! You have ten seconds to surrender! Throw your weapons out!"

On the other side of the house, fire bloomed. And vanished. Something white and almost transparent flowed overhead.

The earth shook and screamed. It shimmied against Rule's belly where he lay prone. He raised his head to look over his shoulder—and a rectangular section of ground twenty feet away gave way, collapsing into itself like a sinkhole.

"Remy! Take over!" And he was on his feet, running bent low. That was training, not conscious thought. So was the zigzag he used. He barely noticed the bullets kicking up dirt around him.

At the edge of the cavity he once again hit the ground. *She's alive, she's alive. I can feel her . . .* but so fragile, so human, beneath that load of earth and crumbled masonry.

He climbed down carefully—not thinking of his own safety, but desperate not to send anything shifting. He knew where she was, exactly where she was. Should he Change again? A wolf digs well through dirt but lacks hands to move any large stones.

Hands first, and quickly. He went to hands and knees— would have gone flat so as to spread his weight out better, but the spot over her was too uneven. He began digging, scooping dirt and small rocks away with his hands.

When the ground beneath him shifted he cried out in rage.

A hole appeared right where he'd been digging. A small

gray head poked out, looked around—blinked when he saw
Rule—then popped back down.

"Wait!" Rule cried. "Wait! Is Lily—"

Then a very human hand gripped the edge of the neat, circular hole. Another hand. Rule leaned forward, grasped those
hands—and stood, lifting.

"Ow! Shit! Pull!" Lily exclaimed as he pulled. Her head
appeared, dusty and brown, her eyes blinking. He let go of
one hand to quickly slide an arm around her shoulders as they
emerged. She wriggled—and came out of the ground.

The two of them ended up lying in a tangle on the crumbled
earth. "That was tight," Lily said. "That was way too tight. He
only knows one size for tunnels, and that's his size. He saved
my life."

"You're all right." Rule ran his hands over her frantically.
"You're not hurt."

"Scraped and bruised, that's all." She stopped to cough.

Sudden dread made him freeze. "Cynna?"

"In the tunnel. She was in the tunnel when the ward pulled
everything down. Mel says she's fine. He says gnome tunnels
do not collapse. No," she corrected herself with a faint grin,
"he sniffed, very superior, and said, 'Our tunnels is never collapsing. Real earthquakes is not collapsing. This bitty shake is
not collapsing.'"

Now Rule was the one blinking. "Mel?"

She grimaced. "I can't say his whole name. The little elder
who saved me."

"I thought he was . . . Never mind." Rule heaved to his feet,
but stayed bent over so he wouldn't provide a target. He gave
Lily a tug to get her on her feet. The cavity was deep enough
that she could stand straight.

Carl poked his nose over the edge. He yipped happily when
he saw Lily.

Behind him, an explosion made the ground shake again,
followed quickly by a second blast.

Rule looked at his friend. "The ones in the house didn't
surrender."

Carl shook his head.

Rule had a quick flash of the kind of devastation the grenades must have wreaked. He shut it away. No time for that now. "Okay. Go back to Remy. He's in charge of your group. I'm heading around front."

"What's happening?" Lily asked.

"My father, your grandmother, Cullen, and six clan are fighting the sorcerer and the Chimei." He gave the steep side of the cavity an appraising look, found a likely handhold, and started up. Dirt crumbled and he shifted, got close enough to get an arm over the edge, and heaved. "Five of us tackled the gang members in and near the house," he continued, reaching down to pull Lily up. "They're either dead now or very close to it."

She helped as much as she could, scrambling with her feet. Once again they ended up tangled together in the dirt. "All of them?" She was slightly winded. "How many is all of them?"

"Thirty-six."

She looked at him for a moment, then gave a quick shake of her head. Like him, she'd deal with that later. "What's the plan?"

"As soon as Remy makes sure there aren't any left to pursue, he and Carl will take you to the cars. They're a couple miles away—we couldn't risk being spotted. The gnomes know the spot. They'll take Cynna there."

"Did you take a blow to the head? I'm not going to the damned cars."

"You're unarmed. You're a potential hostage. The Chimei—"

"You're not just unarmed, you're unclothed. And the Chimei is a lot more likely to kill you than me."

"Lily, the whole point of tonight's mission is to get you and Cynna safely away. No one can leave until you do."

"And you think Johnny—"

"Johnny?"

"The sorcerer. He goes by Johnny Deng. You think he and the Chimei are going to say, 'Okay, you can all go home now,' once I'm not around?"

He scowled, furious. And unsurprised. "Come on," he said roughly.

*   *   *

BUT Rule didn't lead her to the front of the ramshackle house. He took her first to the place he'd left his weapons. As they ran, he briefed her in a low voice about who was here and why.

Charms made by the Rhej using an ancient spell. The Lady speaking. Nokolai at war. "How can you win such a war?" she asked, her voice quiet.

"We've made plans," he said vaguely as he handed her a nice little semiautomatic Glock. It wasn't her SIG, but it would do. "There's a chance the Chimei can hear us, if she tries, so I won't go into detail now."

She stuck the plastic knife she'd held on to all this time in her pocket. "Sam somehow lured the bad guys away, you said. How?"

Rule stepped into his jeans. "He made it seem his lair was unguarded. He thought the Chimei wouldn't be able to resist trying to get at Li Qin. Apparently he was right."

Lily shivered. If the Chimei hadn't been so eager to collect another hostage with which to torment Grandmother, she might have tried to force Lily's "freely made offer" already. "But Li Qin—is she all right?"

"Madame Yu assured me Li Qin would be safe. If she believes it, I'm inclined to." He shouldered an assault rifle.

"Where *is* Sam?"

"He RSVP'd his regrets."

"What?"

He grabbed her hand. "Come on. We'll come at them through the woods."

The ground was rough and it was dark among the trees. Lily couldn't go fast without tripping over something. She was making noise and slowing him down. "You could go ahead."

"No."

"Did Sam say the treaty wouldn't let him help?"

"Something like that. Shh."

The Chimei had claimed Sam was lying to her, using her. Lily figured that was partly true—the black dragon was manipulating all of them. But the Chimei had even less reason than Sam to speak truth to Lily. She had wanted Lily cowed and fearful, and persuading her she couldn't trust the dragon would help that along.

Only . . . Sam should be here, dammit. The sense of betrayal was strong. Treaty or no treaty, he should have found a way to be here. If nothing else, he could soak up extra magic, leaving less for the Chimei and Johnny to grab and use.

Rule stumbled. She stopped. Alarm made it hard to keep her voice soft. "What is it? Are you okay?"

"I take it that means everything didn't suddenly go dark for you."

"No. Aren't the mantles working?"

"Only one mantle, and I grew careless." He shook his head as if to clear it. "I wasn't relying on it as I should. I hadn't needed to until now. The Chimei was focused on the others, I suppose."

"What do you mean, only one mantle?"

"Later."

Lily took the lead for the next part. Rule said his vision was clearing as he got used to leaning on the mantle, as he put it, but her sight was unaffected.

The woods ended abruptly—more so than they probably had an hour ago. Where there must have been brush and grass there was now burned stubble.

Lily stopped. Rule stopped beside her, one hand on her shoulder.

Perhaps twenty yards down the road, a white van lay tilted in the ditch. Lily didn't see anyone there. Not Isen, not the other lupi.

Closer, three people stood where a dirt road dead-ended in a baked earth yard. Two were together—Grandmother, as erect as always. Cullen, not so erect. He was on his knees, and looked like he was fighting to keep from hitting the ground with his face.

Ten paces away from those two, the Chimei paced. Or one version of her did. Kun Nu, Lily had called her. Bird woman. Now she was all bird.

She wasn't the size of a dragon. Not even close. But as

birds went, she was huge—at least the height of an ostrich, but shaped something like a crane or stork, with a raptor's strong beak and a long, forked tail. She was white still, pristine white and glistening in the moon-drenched darkness.

LI Lei stood with her hand on Cullen's shoulder, turning to keep Kun Nu in view as the enormous bird circled them. He had fought hard, the lovely Cullen, fought well and valiantly. No blame to him that he was not as strong as a being who had been gathering power for three centuries. "You cannot break my circle," she said in Chinese.

The great bird's beak melted, along with the rest of the face, so that a woman's face looked at Li Lei from atop that bird body. A familiar face, though Li Lei had not seen it outside her nightmares in so very long. "I can," she said in her high, pure voice, using a dialect Li Lei also heard in her dreams at times. "I will, eventually. I have time."

She spoke truly. Given enough time, she would undoubtedly figure out how to break the circle, though it was set specifically against her. That was a warding so old Li Lei should have forgotten it. Perhaps she would have, if she hadn't practiced it faithfully every decade for all these years.

Or perhaps not. Some things one doesn't forget. The past flowed around Li Lei now like thick cream. It was sweet, in its way, for all that the memories that swam in the air were of her own dying. Sweet because she'd succeeded—and terrible, for she also remembered the flames and the screams.

There had been no way to spare the others, those who worked for that first sorcerer. At the time she'd told herself it did not matter, that they deserved their fate for consorting with him. She'd been very young then.

There had been no way to spare herself, either. She, too, had burned and screamed.

Then Sam had come, a great black shadow plummeting out of the darkness and smoke to land beside her dying body. *You are not dead yet,* he had said, fierce and complete as only a dragon could be. *I wish you to live. Be dragon with me.*

She had chosen life, life and wings and Sam, and he had

sung over her, sung one of the Great Songs, one which had gone unheard since the Great War.

Dragon bodies heal much, much better than human bodies.

"I think your little sorcerer is dying," the Chimei said, smiling.

"You have thought that before and been wrong." Though he was spent, badly spent. When the lupi opened up with their guns on the van driven by this new sorcerer lover, they'd immediately faded back into the bushes, as they'd been told to do.

It was wise. The sorcerer had lived, as she'd expected. He'd had to draw heavily on his lover for the power to heal those wounds, but she'd shared her power generously.

He'd lived, and sent fire after the two-legged wolves who'd tried to kill him. Cullen, in turn, had banished those blazes, one after another.

"Did he use himself up like you did when he attempted to throw mage fire?" She smiled sweetly. "He lacks your strength, my enemy. I was too high for him to reach with his little black flame. He missed."

"I didn't."

"No." She stopped her endless circling now. Her eyes glowed with hatred. "You did not miss. You stole him from me."

Li Lei knew whom the pronoun referred to. "You swim in the past, too," she observed. "But I think for you it is an ocean, and you never find shore."

"If I found a shore, I would turn away. I am loyal to my loves. I do not leave them. I do not forget vengeance. Break your silly circle, my enemy. Break it and honor your word now, and I will allow the little sorcerer to live."

"Ah, you refer to my agreement to exchange myself for Lily." Li Lei smiled. "I lied."

The shriek sounded like the bird, not the woman. "Filthy, treacherous, evil—you lied? You dare stand there and tell me so? I will drink your granddaughter's blood along with her power!"

"I think not." Li Lei slid her hand in her pocket. She didn't let herself look away from the great bird, though blast her, the

Chimei had stopped in the wrong place. She couldn't see the van. She had to settle for listening.

"Are you going to throw a spell at me?" the Chimei asked. "Do you have some little charm in your pocket like those your wolf demons used?"

"Those little charms worked. You do not know what pot you've stirred."

"By all means, try your spell or charm. It will break your circle and will not hurt me at all."

Delay. She must delay, keep the enemy talking. Li Lei pulled her hand out of her pocket. She held a piece of paper. Ruben Brooks had not seen the point of her having a physical token, but he knew little of such things. "This grants me the authority of an agent of the United States government to place you and your lover under arrest."

The Chimei erupted in peals of laughter. "Oh, your granddaughter did this same thing! She told my Johnny he was under arrest. She was helpless, our captive, yet she tells him this."

Li Lei wished fiercely that Lily were here now to share the joke.

"But I regret that you are already insane," the Chimei said, her laughter fading. "I had so looked forward to achieving that myself. Will it be as much fun to torment you when you are already insane, I wonder? Or is this mere senility?"

"The treaty recognizes the right of official agents to establish order in their realms. Order which you have disrupted." The piece of paper Li Lei held made her an official agent of those responsible for Earth's order. It made many things possible which had not been possible before . . . such as pronouncing certain syllables.

Or teaching someone else how to say them.

"Do you think that means it will allow you to harm me? To kill my lovely Johnny?" She was scornful. "You understand very little."

"Perhaps," Li Lei murmured—as at last, at last, her ears caught a sound from over by the van. Dirt scuffed by a foot, or—

"Li A'wan Ni Amo!" Isen thundered.

The Chimei froze. For one moment—that moment of hearing part of her true name, the name Lily had found, the name

Li Lei had tried to make sure Lily would find—shouted by one who possessed a true name, she was helpless.

As was her lover.

Isen Turner—his skin blackened with burns in places, his beard singed half off, his clothes missing entirely—wrestled the sorcerer out from behind the van. He dragged him along quickly, out into the large, open space of the road.

The Chimei shrieked. And blurred.

And Sam was *there*. With a suddenness that made Li Lei's heart skip in spite of everything, the black dragon popped into being overhead—so close! And plummeting toward Earth like a hawk, talons outstretched.

This was the plan. When Sam went unseen, he was out of phase with the world—a trick he had learned from demons while he sojourned in Dis, so not one the Chimei knew or understood. He had waited overhead, out of phase, invisible even to the Chimei's nonphysical senses. Waited for the moment he could act.

It happened fast, almost too fast for her eyes to track. Sam seemed certain to crash into the ground—but those vast wings beat once, twice, slowing him just enough. Isen threw himself to one side and rolled. The sorcerer tried to scramble away also, but he was too slow. Much too slow.

The talons closed around him. With another buffeting of wind that sent dirt flying, the wings beat, and beat again—and Sam rose, the little sorcerer held tight in his grip.

"No!" the Chimei screamed, halfway between forms, between solid and otherness.

Kun Nu, my granddaughter-by-magic has named you, Sam said as he rose higher. *Kun Nu I will call you now. I give you this chance, this last chance, to choose.*

"You cannot harm him! You do not dare!"

I will not harm him. I will take him to a portal on the other coast, where agents of the human government wait, prepared to hand him over to the authorities in what they call Edge. You know that realm as Vei Mo Han. *They know how to lock up a sorcerer there, Kun Nu.*

"You break treaty!"

You took a hostage. I may take a hostage now, too. The

treaty strives for balance. Had you forgotten? Sun's form was so high now Li Lei couldn't see him, save as darkness against the stars. She thought he circled, though. *But I will not take him from you if you agree to go home to your realm, to your people. You will be allowed—*

"Pah!" She drew herself up, becoming for the moment more physical than not, more human than bird. "I have no people."

Thousands of Chimei still live.

"The Surrendered. I spit on them. They are not my people. My people are dead, all dead—and my children. Dead because of you and yours. I am the only one left. Do not think you fool me, S'n Mtzo. You hunger for my death so you will be free of the treaty."

I hunger for your death, Sun agreed. *My people died, too. Too many of them died. In spite of this, I will forgo your death and live with the binding if you return to your realm. Go there and take your lover with you. You do love him?*

"I do. He is all that I have." Tears—real, human tears—glistened in eyes gone pale with grief. "Johnny, my Johnny!" she cried. "I will come for you!"

Do you love him more than you love vengeance?

"I will have both!" Her eyes turned black as suddenly as a light can be switched on. Or off. "I will have both! You will not stop me!"

I already have. Swear on the treaty that you will return to your realm, and you may—

But she'd made her decision, it seemed. Quick as a wind springing up from nowhere, she faded to mist—and shot off toward Isen Turner, just now rising stiffly to his feet.

THIRTY-NINE

LILY stood planted to the earth, numbed by too many revelations, too many events, coming too fast. She didn't recognize the threat to Isen until Rule took off running.

Then her feet got the message and she sprinted full-out.

What did the stupid man think he could do to the Chimei? He couldn't hit her, stab her, bite her, bind her—actually, Lily couldn't do those things, either. But at least she wasn't subject to Bird Woman's magic.

Though how she could use that immunity to help Isen, she didn't know.

Rule got there first, of course. He skidded to a stop, dropping to his knees. It took Lily a few more moments to get close enough to see clearly what was happening.

Isen lay flat on the ground, his eyes open and staring. White mist, peculiarly defined at the edges, covered his face like a glistening, translucent shroud. His chest didn't move. He wasn't breathing.

Rule was shoving at that otherness, but his hands slid off every time, as if Kun Nu were ice, not mist. "I can't move her. I can't move her."

Lily dropped to her knees and tried the same useless pushing. She felt the surface of the thing, utterly slick, slightly cooler than her own skin. Utterly immobile, as if it had the weight of a huge boulder, not a bird. "Shit, shit, shit. Get off of him. Get off."

"He's not breathing," Rule said. "She's gone down his throat. She's in his lungs, goddamn her. Sam—do something. Stop her."

There is only one way to stop her, Sam replied. *And I cannot do it.*

The Chimei couldn't do this, couldn't be allowed to do this. Rage rose, choking Lily as if she were the one with another being stuffed down her throat—and memory, dim and unclear, rose with it. Once before she'd tried to stop someone from using magic to destroy. But she couldn't remember, dammit, couldn't think of what she'd done.

"Hell," she panted. "If I'm related to dragons . . ." Dragons soak up magic.

My granddaughter-in-magic, Sam had said.

There are two ways to take another's power, the Chimei had said. One is voluntary. One is not.

Lily put her palms flat on the cool, white otherness. And *pulled.*

But this was no Earth-Gifted human witch willfully, insanely burning herself out in an effort to destroy.

This was Power.

Lily's hands sank inside that whiteness. And power roared up her arms, a crawling horror of it, hot and icy and everything at once—every kind of sensation at once, every kind of magic, stretching into dimensions so alien Lily couldn't grasp what she touched, what she held . . .

What held her. For the white mass came flowing up out of Isen, flowing up over Lily's arms. It hung there in front of Lily, trapping her—and it formed a mouth.

That mouth, obscenely female, hissed, "Did you think you could absorb my power, little human? Oh, you surprised me with your trick, but you are no dragon, and the male human who betrayed my Johnny is dead. His heart stopped before you startled me with your trick. Now I will stop your heart, and your lover's. I will kill you all slowly and eat your fear as you die."

"You c-can't. The treaty—"

"Poor, stupid little not-dragon. You broke the treaty. When you tried to take my power without my consent, *you broke it*." And she swarmed up Lily's arms, her shoulders—Lily dragged in a breath and held it as cool white otherness covered her face.

Overhead, Sam began to sing.

Dragonsong is not like any other sound. Rule once compared it to a didgeridoo, a hollow instrument played by Australian aborigines. Lily had listened to recordings of didgeridoos, and it did sound a little like dragonsong . . . and nothing at all like it.

At the same time that something cool and repellently solid flowed into Lily's nose, flowed down inside her, dragonsong flowed into her, too. In through her ears, and in through some channel that had nothing to do with her ears.

In that song, she heard what she knew. What she was.

How did you know? she asked, even as the world grew gray and hazy to her vision and her lungs filled with unbreathable otherness. *How did you know?*

Child, he said, and his voice was tender as she had never heard it, gentle and large and intimate, *I held you as you died. How could I not know your Name?*

And then he gave her another word. This one was cold, colder than any word could be, and it cut into her, cut all the way to the core of her.

Remember.

SHE leaped from the cliff—leaped willingly, but not peacefully, her heart in a riot of love and grief for all she surrendered, her mind blanked by terror of what she did.

THE Chimei shuddered inside Lily. And began to withdraw. Slowly, then more quickly.

*   *   *

LILY fell and fell—as she had in dreams, but this was no dream; this was what had happened, was happening, the air whistling past so fast, burning her eyes. Her body tumbled helplessly.

THE whiteness left her lungs, her throat. Her nose. She dragged in a breath, her chest heaving. *No*, she said to the Chimei without using any of the precious air—but she said it gently, for she knew. She knew what to do.

Lily—all of Lily, for her soul was no longer sundered, nor any of her memories hidden—wrapped her arms around the whiteness, not letting it escape as she fell to the rocky beach below. Held her, held on to her with the Gift that was hers, the dragon's gift. She held the Chimei as she died.

"LILY? God, Lily, I can feel you, but if you don't wake up and answer me, I'll—I'll—"

Lily opened her eyes on Rule's frantic face. "I'm here," she whispered. She was lying on her back, she noted dimly. On the ground.

Rule's eyes closed. He shuddered. "Thank God. Oh, God, I thought I'd lost you. Are you hurt?"

"Dizzy," she murmured. "Help me sit up, okay? Oh, shit— your father—"

"CPR works on lupi as well as humans," Isen said gruffly. "Once you pulled that creature out of me, Remy got my heart started up."

Lily turned her head and saw Isen sitting nearby. A tall young man she vaguely recognized kneeled beside him. Remy, she assumed.

"I want to sit up," she repeated. Rule helped, moving so that his body braced her. That was good. Wonderful. "Was I out long?"

"No, it just seemed like forever. Are you sure you're all

right?" he asked. "The Chimei's gone," he added hastily, as if she might not know this. "All at once, she vanished."

Not vanished, Sam said. *She is dead.*

"What?" Rule looked up.

Sam was coming in for a landing again—this one much slower than the last. He still held Johnny, but the sorcerer was limp—unconscious, maybe? Or had losing his lover killed him? *It is the only way to kill a Chimei. Created to not-know death, they cannot die until someone shares a death with them.*

"Shares a death?" Rule repeated blankly.

Dragons are the only ones who can do this—or we were, until tonight. In Dis, Lily died. That she also lived does not make her death less real. She shared that death with the Chimei.

"I broke the treaty," Lily said dully.

No. Small actions accumulate. As an agent of order, you tried to stop the Chimei without killing her. She thought your attempt to drain her power broke the treaty, but her thinking was badly warped, or she would have sensed it still in place—strained, stretched, yet still intact. When she tried to kill you—that broke the treaty.

Rule looked at her, questions in his eyes.

"If you're trying to ask how I did all that, well . . . I lack words." That's what he'd said to her often enough. "Rule, I remembered. Because of Sam, I remembered everything. The part of me that was with you in Dis—she's here now, all the way here. I mean I'm here now. I'm not . . . I'm all of me."

He wrapped his arms around her and held her gently, pressing a kiss to her hair. She smiled and let her eyes close again. *I love you.*

He jolted. "Lily?"

"What?"

"You didn't say that out loud."

That startled her eyes open. "Shit."

Grandmother arrived at the same time as half a dozen lupi—some clothed and two-legged, some naked and two-legged, a couple still on four feet. She was propping up a wobbly Cullen. Cullen's face was strained, his eyes frantic. "Cynna?" he said hoarsely.

"She's all right," Lily said quickly. "She's fine, and so is the baby. The gnomes got her out."

His eyes closed. "Okay," he said simply—and slid to the ground.

After a few frantic seconds, they confirmed that he'd passed out, not died. His heart still beat.

He is well enough, Sam said, sending dust flying as he settled to the ground several dozen feet away. He set the sorcerer's body aside. *This one is not.*

Lily looked at Grandmother, standing unnaturally quiet in the midst of the lupi, her face tender and sad and happy all at once. "You arrested her. The Chimei."

"You heard." Delight rang through Grandmother's voice. "I did. It is important to follow the forms of such things."

"I have a few questions," Lily began—and broke off, frowning.

For some reason everyone—well, everyone but Cullen, who was unconscious—seemed to find that terribly funny.

FORTY

ON August eleventh at shortly after one in the morning, Pacific Daylight Time, in cities around the world—in Seattle, Chicago, Washington, D.C., Tokyo, and Beijing, and twenty more—dragons flew. As they flew, they sang. In every city in the world that had a dragon, people for the first time heard dragonsong.

Not everyone heard it, of course. Those who did stopped their cars or their feet, stopped whatever they were doing, and listened. Just listened. Many of them wept, but later couldn't say why.

No one recorded it. No one who heard it even thought of trying. They didn't know the why of that, either.

In the U.S. the TV talking heads speculated madly about the reason for this unprecedented behavior—of dragons and people both. Oprah had three of those who'd heard it on her show. In China and Canada, the governments politely inquired of their dragons what was up. In Hollywood, agents tried frantically to contact the dragons to offer contracts.

The dragons didn't care to discuss it. Neither did those few humans—and lupi—who knew why the dragons sang.

The most innately sovereign species in existence was free of a binding that had been passed down, through blood and magic, for more than three thousand years. The last of the un-surrendered Chimei was dead. The treaty was no more.

August 13th at 10:09 P.M.

RULE knelt in front of his Rho and shuddered with relief.

Nokolai's mantle—the heir's portion—rested in him once more. He looked at his brother, kneeling beside him. "Benedict," he began . . . and ran out of words.

Benedict's mouth kicked up at one corner. "Still can't quite believe I'm happier without it, can you?"

Rule looked at him helplessly. "It's not that I doubt your word."

Benedict regarded him a moment. "When you were seven or so, you found a puppy. Brought it home. Cute little thing, about half grown. A basset, wasn't it?"

"Yes." Rule's smile started as he saw where this was going.

"You didn't know about collars and tags. You thought you could keep it, so you were sad for a full week after Dad found the owners and they took him home. If you'd known about collars and tags, you wouldn't have counted on keeping that little dog. You'd have had a good time with it while it was there, and been fine when it left."

Now Rule's smile was easy. "You understand about tags and collars."

Benedict nodded. "I do. The mantle itself—yeah, that felt good. But I don't want the stuff that goes with it, so while we had a good time together, I'm glad to let it go back to its owner."

He rose, gave their father a nod and a smile, then said to Rule, "I'm still not talking to you."

With that, he left.

Rule stood, too, watching his big brother leave. "Some-times I don't understand him at all."

"Just because he loves you doesn't mean he wants to talk to you."

Isen's eyes were twinkling in his uncannily naked face. With his beard burned half off, he'd had to shave the other half—and complained about that way more than he had the burns on his arms and chest. But then, the burned skin would heal a lot faster than he could regrow his beard. Hair growth wasn't affected by healing.

Rule thought he knew what his father meant. Benedict did love him, hadn't wanted Rule to worry about him, and hadn't gotten over his anger at Rule's decision to marry. But he sighed. "Sometimes I get tired of my family's 'don't ask, don't tell' policy."

Isen's eyebrows climbed. "Now I'm mystified."

"We don't say things straight out." Or ask things straight out, and why not? Why not just ask? "What are you planning to do about my marriage?"

"Ah." Isen started to rub his beard, found bare face, and scowled. "All right. Straight out, then. You remember what I told you to do when you're Rho and you've got a messy situation and you don't have a clue what to do about it?"

Everything clicked in place. "Look mysterious and knowing and stall until I figure something out."

"That's right. I'll tell you that I personally think it's a mistake, you marrying. Any of us marrying. But you've said you think the Lady wants change." He shrugged. "I don't know. She hasn't whispered in my ear—that's for damned sure. But it's possible. So I'm waiting to see how things shake out."

Rule was suddenly awash with emotion. For a little while, he'd thought his father was dead. Isen's heart had stopped for so long . . . but it had started again. "I'd like to take my father to dinner," he said. "But he hardly ever leaves his place."

Isen's eyes twinkled. "Bit of a stick-in-the mud, is he? Maybe an agora—what's that word? Agoraphobic."

Rule nodded solemnly. "Something like that. If you should happen to see him—"

Isen hooted with laughter and grabbed Rule, hugging hard.

Rule hugged back, his eyes damp. "I love you, Dad."

"Love you back." And Isen slapped him on the back to prove it.

*   *   *

LILY'S mother had graciously granted a two-day reprieve on their lunch, but Wednesday rolled around—as it has a habit of doing—right on schedule. Resigned, Lily sat at a red-draped table in her uncle Chen's restaurant with a menu, a glass of water, and—to the waiter's clear disapproval—a cup of coffee.

It was five minutes after noon. Her mother was late. Her mother was never late. The atomic clock could be set by Julia Yu's punctuality. Lily couldn't decide whether to be worried or annoyed.

Maybe she'd had trouble finding parking. The place was packed. If . . . Oh, my.

A slim, upright figure escorted by a deferential hostess was making her way through the crowded tables toward Lily. She wore pristine white silk trousers and a tunic with a Mandarin collar. The tunic was the color-soaked red a 1940s movie star might have worn on her lips and nails. "I am joining you," Grandmother announced as the hostess held the chair for her. "Your mother is delayed. She will be here soon."

A dozen impulses and questions whirled through Lily. Did her mother even know Grandmother was joining them? Or was her mother late because Grandmother told her to be? Or had Grandmother persuaded her the actual time was twelve thirty, or . . . .

In the end, Lily smiled helplessly. "It's good to see you, Grandmother. You look fantastic."

"Red is a good color for me." Grandmother waved the hostess away. "We will not order yet. You may bring me some tea. You are drinking coffee," she informed Lily.

"Yes, I am."

"Hmph. Li Qin sends her love. She is very glad to be home again. She wonders why you have not yet been to see her."

Lily's eyebrows rose. "*She* wonders that, Grandmother?"

"I assume she does. I do not wonder. I know. You feel shy with me."

Lily's mouth opened to deny that—and closed again. Because suddenly, unaccountably, she did feel shy, or something very like that.

Grandmother patted her hand and spoke softly. "You have just woken to your name. You do not understand it, but you know it. I am the only one you might ask, but you do not know what to ask."

Wordless, Lily nodded.

The server set a small china pot on the table. Grandmother inspected it, sniffing the steam. "You have prepared it correctly, I think. Loose tea, no bags? Yes. Thank you. I will let it steep."

Grandmother folded her hands on the table as the slightly flustered server departed. "I will tell you the secret of true names. We know them when we understand the secret about death—which is, of course, the secret about life. Which is not a secret at all."

"But I—I don't understand death. I remember it happening. I don't understand it."

"You mean you do not understand what comes after death. No more do I. This does not matter. A baby reaching for her mother's breast does not know what comes after not-baby. She sees not-baby around her, but she does not truly see until she becomes not-baby herself."

"You mean that death is a transition."

"Silly word, *transition*. All words are silly when we speak of this, so mostly we do not, or we let silly people do the speaking. I like the Buddhists, who do not mind being silly. They speak of the fallacy of duality, the confusion of either-or thinking. These words are as close as any to what you and I know."

Lily shook her head. "They aren't my words. They don't . . . they don't touch what I know."

"Lily. You know now that having been, you can never not-be. Just as I, having been dragon, can never not-be dragon. And while I was wholly dragon, I was also human, for I could not undo having been human. Living does not undo life. Death does not, either. Life and death are not either-or."

Words that would have been gibberish to her last week unlocked everything now. "You mean it's all real. It's all true.

Cullen said a true name comes from the part of us that doesn't change, but he was wrong. Mostly wrong, anyway, because it's all change, and it's all true."

"Yes. Now, stop carving up what you know with words. The pieces left from that carving do not make sense." She took a moment to pour her tea. She inhaled, frowned faintly, and sipped anyway. "Sandra learns, but she does not yet have the art."

Lily grinned suddenly, thinking of a limousine. Black, not white, because Grandmother disliked the white ones. "And having been a child, we can't not-be a child."

Grandmother's eyes twinkled. "I do not know what you mean." She took a sip of tea, shook her head, and set the cup down.

Love and amusement mingled in Lily, making her next words softer than she wanted, more tentative. "I have some questions about things that *can* be chopped up into words."

Grandmother snorted. "You wish to know about myself and Sam. Very well. You may ask. It is good for children to acquaint themselves with their ancestors."

And that was the kernel, wasn't it? "Most people don't have an ancestor around to ask! I mean . . ." Lily gestured vaguely. "Over three hundred years, Grandmother! That's . . . How is that possible?"

"I have been dragon. I cannot not-be dragon. Dragons live much longer than humans." She shrugged. "I do not share in their longevity fully. My life will be longer than most, but not as long as a dragon's. More than that I do not know."

Lily's heart beat faster. "Will my father live longer than most, too?"

"Ah." Sadness clouded the old woman's eyes. "I do not know, but . . . the magic did not go to him, did it? There is a property of my lineage, passed to me by my mother from her mother and back for many generations: our magic wakes only in the females of our line. It can be passed along through a son, but the son cannot touch it. The magic I passed down was not my original magic, of course, yet it still wakes only in the female, not the male."

Lily grappled with a jostling crowd of questions, trying to order them. "What do you mean, it wasn't your original magic?"

"When I was young, my magic took the shape of fire, but I burned out that Gift. When Sam transformed me, he breathed into me the magic of dragons. This is the magic I have passed on to you, though it takes a different shape in you than it has in me."

"Did Sam turn you into a dragon to reward you for stopping the sorcerer?"

"Oh, no. He did it to save my life. Dragons possess great healing, but they cannot heal humans, and Sam did not wish me to die." Her expression softened as her gaze focused on a memory only she could see. "Later, he said he had known my death was very likely, but he did not accept this. Dragons wish always to have their way." She chuckled. "As do we all, but dragons wish this with great intricacy."

"Is Sam precongitive?"

"This is a human word, a modern word. I do not use it. Sam knows certain things. Back in China, he knew the Chimei would come, and he prepared me without telling me what use he would make of me. The treaty restrained him from that, but he could warn his apprentice, and he did. He told me that one day a Chimei would come, and I was to persuade my family to leave their home. He said he would release me to flee, too, if I wished. Though he did not intend that I leave," she added pragmatically. "That is the way of dragons. They do not constrain, but they manipulate. But Sam did not know the Chimei's lover would murder my family. His planning did not include that."

She sighed once, softly. "In the end, the choices were mine. Vengeance is the choice of a dark heart, and my heart was very dark. I had to be close to kill the sorcerer, so I became a servant in his palace. I guessed that I would have to use what the lovely Cullen calls mage fire."

"You didn't know?"

"Many things Sam did not speak of until I was dragon and entitled to such knowledge. But he had instructed me in the use of black fire—an oddly dangerous teaching for a new apprentice! When the sorcerer came, I understood why."

"You did use mage fire, then? Cullen says that only a sorcerer can call it safely."

Grandmother snorted again. "In this, Cullen Seabourne is right. I had a great deal of power. I was good with fire. But I did not see power, so when I called black fire down on my enemy, I could not see what I wrought. I killed the sorcerer." No matter what she'd said about vengeance and a dark heart, after three centuries her voice still rang with satisfaction when she said that. "But I could not control the fire. It burned . . . too much. I called it back to me, but I knew . . . The black fire feeds on what it burns, you see, and so more power returned to me than I had spent. I burned. I was neither alive nor dead when Sam came to me, but with a foot in both. He sang . . ." Her voice drifted off into memory and wonder.

Softly Lily said, "Dragonsong. I remember it so well."

"Yes. And you have heard Sam sing one of the Great Songs, I think, when he returned you and his people from Dis. You understand when I say it is worth dying to hear such song." Her grin flashed, as sudden and unexpected as a rainbow. "Even better if one does not die."

Lily surprised herself by laughing. "It is, isn't it?"

"And now, if you have exhausted your curiosity—"

"Not quite. Grandmother . . ." It was harder than she'd expected to speak of this. "The Chimei said she was the last of her kind. Sam said there were other Chimei who might descend on Earth if the treaty were broken and overwhelm us." Someone had lied. Lily wanted it to be the Chimei, but she couldn't quite convince herself of it.

Grandmother said nothing for a long moment, then repeated what she'd said before. "Dragons do not constrain, but they manipulate."

"In other words, he lied."

"No. Sam did not know if other Chimei still lived outside their realm. It was possible she was the last, but until her death freed all dragons, he did not know."

"And the Chimei who live in their home realm? The Surrendered, she called them."

"When Chimei return to their realm, they are altered. They surrender immortality and no longer feed on the fear of others."

"There was never much chance of a horde of Chimei turning our world into their feeding ground, was there?"

Grandmother shrugged. "The greater threat was that she would breed, but there was a chance of other Chimei coming here. It was not great, but with such consequences, do you wait until the odds are bad to throw the dice?"

Lily drummed her fingers on the table. "I am not a pair of dice, and I don't like being treated like one."

"Who would?" Grandmother's voice held sympathy, but no apology. "And now, if you are out of questions—"

"Not quite. I still don't know when you gained the trick of turning tiger. And about that lineage you spoke of—"

"Do not interrupt," Grandmother said sternly. "I will not speak of that today. Do you wish for some advice?"

"Not particularly."

Sternness melted into a chuckle. "Who would?" she said again. "Unsought advice is useless. Indulge me anyway. Living is very serious, very real. It is also always a game. If we are wise, it is very real, very terrible, and very lovely, and a good deal of fun." She patted Lily's hand once more—and rose. "I have changed my mind. I am not staying for lunch."

Automatically Lily stood, too. "But . . ."

"I am not so fond of shopping, and you and your mother need time with only the two of you. You do not argue, but you wish to," she observed. "Be kind to your mother, Lily. She does not know what we know, and her life is not always easy." Humor lit those bright, dark eyes. "I am a remarkable person, but I am a very bad mother-in-law."

Lily sat, dazed and vastly amused, as her grandmother made her exit. After a few moments, curious, she sipped from Grandmother's tea. It was cold, but otherwise tasted fine.

"You are drinking both coffee and tea?" her mother asked from right beside her.

Lily jumped. "You startled me. I was, uh, thinking. The tea was Grandmother's, but she had to leave. She wanted me to offer her apologies." She hadn't exactly said so, but her actions were an apology of sorts. Maybe.

Julia Yu sighed. She was a tall, slender, beautifully dressed woman with lovely eyes and a receding chin. On her, the lack of chin was somehow a feminine touch. "Your grandmother is a very odd woman sometimes. Don't tell her I said that," she added, seating herself.

"Of course not."

"We have a great deal to discuss," her mother said with satisfaction. "I brought a notebook so we will not lose track of our ideas. Have you ordered?"

"I was waiting for you. Mother . . ."

"Here." Julia pulled a full-size spiral notebook out of her very large purse and slid it across to Lily, along with a pen. "You take notes. I've lost my reading glasses again, I'm afraid."

They were probably right there in her purse, but her mother hated being seen wearing them. "Okay. Mother, I want to thank you. I've been difficult, I know, but I . . . You didn't approve of my relationship with Rule at first, but you changed your mind. You're throwing yourself into arranging our wedding. I want to thank you for that."

"I still do not approve of you and Rule Turner. He is a good man, I suppose, but a poor choice for you. He isn't even Chinese."

Lily jerked as if she'd been slapped. "But—"

"Lily." Her mother looked fond, but impatient. Pretty much the expression she'd worn when Lily was five and spilled her milk twice in a row. "I don't have to agree with your choices to support you."

"Oh. Then the wedding . . . You're doing that to support me, even if you don't agree with my choice of husband?"

"Really, Lily, what do you think a wedding is for?"

Since that was the question she'd been asking herself—and a few others—she was briefly speechless. "Tell me what you think marriage is for. No, really. I want to know." Her parents had a good marriage. Lily didn't understand it, but they truly did. "For raising children?" she hazarded.

"That's important, of course, but women have raised children without marriage for thousands of years. Marriage," she said firmly, "and especially the ceremony which announces it, the wedding . . . That is how we say to the world, 'These two are now a family, and with this joining our families are joined, too. And you had damned well better respect that.'"

"You . . . That . . . You never say *damn*." Warmth flowed over Lily. *Yes*. Yes, that was exactly why she was marrying Rule. All of the other reasons were true, too, but *this* was why the mate bond and living together weren't the same as marriage. "Thank you, Mother," she said, reaching across to squeeze her mother's hand. "That makes perfect sense."

Julia Yu looked surprised and gratified. "You haven't said that to me often," she observed dryly. "Now, in your situa- tion . . . Ah, Sandra." Julia Yu looked up at the server who'd just arrived, smiling. "Lily will have the orange chicken. I be- lieve I want the moo shoo pork today."

Lily opened her mouth to tell her mother not to order for her . . . and closed it again. Why fuss? She really did like the orange chicken.

"In your case," Julia went on after the server departed, "with your marriage being so—so potentially controversial, it is extremely important that we put a good face on the cer- emony. Everyone must see that your family is behind you completely in this marriage."

Even if they weren't, not completely. But for the first time, Lily saw that this mattered to her mother. What it meant to her.

Love. It was all about Julia Yu's love and concern for her daughter—maybe not arriving in the form Lily kept looking for. And maybe it arrived with some overly controlling strings attached, too. But love just the same.

"Okay," she said meekly. And as they talked, she made notes.

They'd finished their meals by the time they reached the big decision: the Dress. Her mother was talking about various designers, some bridal magazine article she'd read, and where they might go to look at various styles.

An idea flashed into Lily's head. It felt right. "Mother, I've been thinking," she said, though she hadn't, not until this mo- ment. "Oh—sorry, I interrupted. But I think I'd like Chinese style, not a—a princess gown or a ball gown or any of that."

Her mother stopped talking. She tipped her head to one side, her eyes narrowing. Slowly she nodded. "Yes, that might work. Some of your generation are doing this, you know, using Chinese touches in their weddings. You are not an ordinary American bride, are you? You are Chinese American. And you are not marrying an ordinary American man. But nothing off the rack," she added in quick warning. "Nothing cheap."

"Of course not. Though with my budget, it can't be too—"

"Lily!" Julia was horrified. "You are not going to deny me and your father the chance to buy your wedding dress!"

Oh. "Thank you, then."

"Now, how Chinese do you want this dress to be? Do you want a *chi pao*?"

"I don't know. I guess I'll have to look at some dresses, but . . . yes, a *chi pao* sounds right. In silk, maybe white or ivory, with embroidery in matching thread. Something subtle."

"Embroidery? What kind?"

"A dragon." Lily smiled. That felt perfectly, absolutely right. "I'd like a beautiful Chinese dragon on my wedding dress."

Look for the next lupi novel by Eileen Wilks

BLOOD CHALLENGE

Coming soon from Berkley Sensation!
For an excerpt, visit the author's website at
www.eileenwilks.com.

Eileen Wilks

USA Today **Bestselling Author of**
Mortal Danger **and** ***Blood Lines***

NIGHT SEASON

Pregnancy has turned FBI Agent Cynna Weaver's whole life upside down. Lupus sorcerer Cullen Seabourne is thrilled to be the father, but what does Cynna know about kids? Her mother was a drunk. Her father abandoned them. Or so she's always believed.

As Cynna is trying to wrap her head around this problem, a new one pops up, in the form of a delegation from another realm. They want to take Cynna and Cullen back with them—to meet her long-lost father and find a mysterious medallion. But when these two born cynics land in a world where magic is commonplace and night never ends, their only way home lies in tracking down the missing medallion—one also sought by powerful beings who will do anything to claim it...

penguin.com

M110T0907

Enter the tantalizing world of paranormal romance

MaryJanice Davidson

Laurell K. Hamilton

Christine Feehan

Emma Holly

Angela Knight

Rebecca York

Eileen Wilks

Berkley authors
take you to a whole new realm

penguin.com

M4G0907

Enter the rich world of historical romance with Berkley Books.

Lynn Kurland

Patricia Potter

Betina Krahn

Jodi Thomas

Anne Gracie

Love is timeless.
penguin.com

M9G0907

Discover Romance

berkleyjoveauthors.com

See what's coming up next from your favorite romance authors and explore all the latest Berkley, Jove, and Sensation selections.

Fall in love

- See what's new
- Find author appearances
- Win fantastic prizes
- Get reading recommendations
- Chat with authors and other fans
- Read interviews with authors you love

berkleyjoveauthors.com

M1G0907

Penguin Group (USA) Online

What will you be reading tomorrow?

Tom Clancy, Patricia Cornwell, W.E.B. Griffin,
Nora Roberts, William Gibson, Robin Cook,
Brian Jacques, Catherine Coulter, Stephen King,
Dean Koontz, Ken Follett, Clive Cussler,
Eric Jerome Dickey, John Sandford,
Terry McMillan, Sue Monk Kidd, Amy Tan,
John Berendt…

You'll find them all at
penguin.com

Read excerpts and newsletters,
find tour schedules and reading group guides,
and enter contests.

Subscribe to Penguin Group (USA) newsletters
and get an exclusive inside look
at exciting new titles and the authors you love
long before everyone else does.

PENGUIN GROUP (USA)
us.penguingroup.com

M224G1107

Photo courtesy of the author

Eil—— **lling**
aut ————— **alist,**
and ———— **ment**
Av ———— **ebsite**
at

Eileen Wilks's novels of the lupi are a "must-read for anyone who enjoys werewolves with their romance."* Now the
USA Today bestselling author returns with an incendiary
tale of dark magic that threatens everything Lily and Rule
hold dear...

As they plan their wedding, Lily Yu and Rule Turner, a prince of
the lupi, are facing a great deal of tension from both their families. Not everyone can accept their mixed marriage: she's Chinese;
he's a werewolf. Even Lily's grandmother is acting strangely distant, though Lily and Rule are about to discover that her behavior
has nothing to do with their upcoming nuptials.

A powerful, undying nemesis has come to San Diego to exact vengeance on Lily's family—and turn the city into a feeding ground. It's
up to Lily and Rule to stop her, in spite of ancient treaties and an
inheritance passed down through the blood. Otherwise San Diego
could go up in flames, and they won't live to make it to the altar...

Praise for the Lupi Novels of Eileen Wilks

"Fast-paced and nail-biting reading."—*Fresh Fiction*

"Intense...Intricately crafted, loving, lavish."—Lynn Viehl, *USA
Today* bestselling author of the Darkyn series

*#1 *New York Times* bestselling author Patricia Briggs

ISBN 978-0-425-23305-4

5 0 7 9 9

9 780425 233054

EAN
S

$7.99 U.S.
$8.99 CAN